W9-AAV-607

STAR TREK® VOYAGER™
MOSAIC

STAR TREK® VOYAGER™

MOSAIC

A Novel

Jeri Taylor

POCKET BOOKS
New York   London   Toronto   Sydney   Tokyo   Singapore

This book is a work of fiction. Names, characters, places and incidents are products of the author's imagination or are used fictitiously. Any resemblance to actual events or locales or persons, living or dead, is entirely coincidental.

POCKET BOOKS, a division of Simon & Schuster Inc. 1230 Avenue of the Americas, New York, NY 10020

STAR TREK is a Registered Trademark of Paramount Pictures.

A VIACOM COMPANY

This book is published by Pocket Books, a division of Simon & Schuster Inc., under exclusive license from Paramount Pictures.

ISBN: 0-671-56311-4

First Pocket Books hardcover printing October 1996

10 9 8 7 6 5 4 3 2 1

POCKET and colophon are registered trademarks of Simon & Schuster Inc.

Printed in the U.S.A.

For Alex

ACKNOWLEDGMENTS

A list of those who properly deserve my thanks would probably extend far beyond the reader's toleration threshold, so I will try to delimit this account:

—John Ordover has been an unflagging source of support and enthusiasm, always when I needed it most.

—Brannon Braga, Ken Biller, Lisa Klink, and Joe Menosky are the writing staff who provide constant inspiration; Rene Echevarria defected briefly from *DS9* to add his welcome voice.

—Andre Bormanis provided the ultimate in technical sustenance: science that was clear, concise, and simple.

—Rick Berman and Michael Piller made me a part of the *Star Trek* universe in the first place, thereby changing my life.

—My mother and father each shaped the person I have become, and are contained within these pages.

—My husband, who is my heart, makes my every day a time to be treasured.

CHAPTER

1

FOR A FEW, MAGICAL MOMENTS, KATHRYN JANEWAY FELT AS IF she were back home in Indiana. The air was warm and slightly humid; there was a scent of something that was almost like newly mown grass; and a gentle insect hum lulled the senses. She could almost forget that she was on an unknown, unnamed planet in the Delta Quadrant and pretend that she was hiking in the rolling hills of her home state.

Her eye fell on a bank of billowing white bushes—a fluffy mass of fronds that looked almost like pillows. It was tempting to lie down for a few moments, savoring the warm afternoon. She reached out and lightly touched one of the thick fronds; it yielded gently, promising a soft cushion.

Janeway glanced around at the rest of her away team, busy scanning for edible foodstuffs: Chakotay, the darkly handsome first officer, led a group of young ensigns who were clearly enjoying their first time on land in over a month; the sound of their laughter rang through the lush valley they were exploring. Chakotay, she knew, was wise enough to let them have some fun. A field trip on a verdant planet was just the thing to raise youthful spirits after a month of isolation on a starship.

Half a kilometer away, near the mouth of the valley, her Vulcan security officer, Tuvok, led the second contingent, which had been assigned the task of collecting foodstuffs deemed safe. That determination would be made by Neelix, their Talaxian guide, cook, self-proclaimed morale officer, and all-around handyman. Janeway smiled, imagining the interplay between the two. It had become Neelix' obsession to bring joy to Tuvok's life—an effort which the staid Vulcan greeted with a noticeable lack of enthusiasm. But Neelix was undeterred, determined to dispel what he insisted was the cloud of gloom that surrounded Tuvok.

Janeway inhaled deeply. It was so much like home—the faint scent of moist soil, a hint of floral fragrance on a gentle breeze—that she decided to yield to temptation. She fell back onto the mound of soft, pillowlike plants and closed her eyes, as if she were lying on a mound of hay. Back home.

The warmth of the planet's yellow star warmed her face. Insects droned ceaselessly; it would have been easy to drift off to sleep. But she wanted these few moments to be hers—to daydream, to pretend for this short time that she wasn't sixty-eight thousand light-years from Earth, that she wasn't carrying the extraordinary responsibility of getting her crew home safely, that she wasn't struggling to keep alive everyone's hopes that the journey could somehow be foreshortened. For just these few minutes, she would lie here and imagine that she was back on Earth, had managed to get *Voyager* home, had seen her crew welcomed as heroes and returned to the loving arms of their families and friends. Then she had transported home to visit her own family—and Mark.

She had finally managed to resolve her feelings for Mark. It had taken over a year before he wasn't forever creeping into her thoughts, before she stopped hearing his voice, his laughter, in her mind. She had put away his pictures because they only helped to keep the wound open; she decided (although she sometimes doubted it) that after more than a year, he would have written her off as dead and moved on with his life. And that she must do the same.

Recently she had realized that she didn't quite remember what he looked like.

So this daydream would not be about Mark. It was only about home, about the part of her life spent in one of the most beautiful parts of the country, the agricultural paradise of Indiana. She thought of her mother, and imagined their post-homecoming conversation.

"There were times when I didn't think we'd make it," said Janeway. "You can't imagine how hard it was to keep my spirits up—but I had to, because I couldn't risk the crew losing heart because their captain did." She was sitting in the sunny breakfast room of the home she'd grown up in, mellow with pine paneling, sunlight filtering through an ancient sycamore tree that grew outside the window, its graceful branches swaying in a gentle breeze.

Her mother, wise and warm, smiled at her. "Heaven forbid you ever show the slightest weakness. Is that what being a captain means? That you're not allowed to have the feelings everyone else has?"

"That's how it seemed to me. I had to set the standard. I had to be confident. And it worked—I *did* get us home."

Gretchen Janeway reached out a hand and caressed her daughter's cheek. "And I'm so proud of you."

"Proud enough to bake me some of your caramel brownies?"

Gretchen laughed, started for the kitchen. "I already have. I knew that's the first thing you'd ask for."

Lying on the soft, billowing plants, Janeway smiled to herself. She'd tried to replicate her mother's brownies—the effort cost her four days' rations—but the result was so disappointing that she couldn't bear to eat them. She'd run into Jerron, the young Bajoran, and given him the plate of treats; his incredulous delight was more rewarding than eating the brownies could ever have been. Jerron's pain in the early days of their journey had been palpable; gradually, he had been losing his anger and was becoming more comfortable, starting to feel himself a member of the crew. Janeway made it a point to make him feel cared for, and the young man was responding.

She wasn't sure how long she'd been lying there, drifting and dreaming, when she sensed that something was wrong. The smell had changed: the fragrant, grassy aroma had altered somehow—it had an *edge* to it, a—what? A metallic quality?

Janeway opened her eyes and sat up, saw that both teams were aware of something, were scanning with an increased urgency, pointing, calling to each other. She jumped to her feet, and in the same instant identified the odor: ozone. An electrical burning.

And that was the only warning they got.

Suddenly, there was a sizzling *snap!* A green arcing light pierced the air, and the ozone smell became acrid. Janeway twitched involuntarily, as though she'd suffered an electrical shock. The air itself had become charged by the bolt of—what? Plasma? She scanned quickly and detected a hot, electrically energized field unknown to the Federation database.

A hot wind began to stir, intensifying the burning smell; Janeway's nostrils began to sting. Out of the corner of her eye, she noticed the cottony white bushes begin to ripple in the sultry wind, but her mind quickly focused on her crew.

Chakotay and his young group were already on the move, heading toward her, when three or four more bolts of green sliced through the sky, crackling and smoking. This time Janeway heard herself cry out as pain slashed through her body. Were they under attack? Or were they simply caught in an unexpected natural phenomenon? It hardly mattered—whatever these strange flashes were, they were clearly dangerous. She had to get her people out of there.

She hit her commbadge, noting that Chakotay was doing the same, as undoubtedly Tuvok was also. "Janeway to Voyager . . . We need emergency transport." She repeated the message several times before accepting what she had already suspected: that the electrical disturbance was interfering with the communications system, and it was doubtful the transporters would function through the interference.

Then the air crackled with energy bolts, sizzling and sparking. She heard a scream and saw someone fall to the ground. The hot wind began to gust violently, and the hissing sound of the arcing flashes became deafening. Janeway called out to Chakotay, but her voice was swallowed in the noise and the wind. She waved her arm at him, gesturing him to the mouth of the valley. Ahead of her, she saw Tuvok and his group already on the run. She began sprinting toward them.

But her body wouldn't behave as it should. Her legs were shaky, uncoordinated, like a newborn lamb's. She stumbled and then shuddered as another series of green flashes ripped through the air. Now it felt as though oxygen had been depleted from the atmosphere, and her lungs rasped as she drew stinging air into them. Reflexively, she began scanning again, and discovered a possible shelter: in the mountains that ringed the valley were a series of caves; if they could find an opening they might be able to escape this brutal attack.

Chakotay and his group came stumbling toward her, gasping, struggling against the wind. One of the ensigns collapsed to the ground; two others immediately pulled him up. All of them looked frightened but not panicky. Janeway pointed toward the mountains. "Caves," she yelled, but she barely heard her own voice over the roar of the wind.

Chakotay nodded; he understood. He turned and began herding his young charges to follow Janeway, who was moving toward the nearest outcropping of the mountains, scanning for a possible opening as she went.

Suddenly the tricorder disappeared from view. Janeway registered that fact, then realized everything had disappeared; she saw only a field of black punctuated by jagged green slashes. She barely had time to realize that there had been another series of energy bolts when the pain hit her.

She felt as though she were on fire, muscle and tissue seared, bodily fluids boiling. With an involuntary cry, she fell to her knees, stunned and shuddering. For a moment she was blind, desperate for oxygen, and in agony. But she forced her mind to take control. She stilled herself, locating the pain, isolating it, containing it until it began to subside. Gradually, the green slashes in her vision began to fade, the blackness receded, and she lifted her head.

The young officers were scattered on the ground like deadwood, writhing and moaning. Chakotay had already begun rising shakily to his feet, assessing their condition. One by one they began to get up, faces pale with shock, staggering, but on their feet.

We won't survive another round, Janeway thought, and she lifted her tricorder to scan for the nearest opening in the mountains. Then, ahead of her, she saw Tuvok's group crowding toward a dark slash in the cliff side. She realized they had found the mouth of a cave and she whirled to motion to Chakotay; but he'd already seen and was yelling at the group, gesturing toward the mountain, urging them forward.

The ragged group tried to run, fear of another bombardment of energy bolts propelling them against the fierce wind. Janeway's legs felt like gelatin, but she forced them to drive forward. The roar of the wind thundered in her ears; her lungs burned and streaks of green still obscured her vision. The side of the mountain seemed kilometers away, but she knew it wasn't—it couldn't be more than forty meters now. Tuvok's group had disappeared into the cave, but her Vulcan friend remained outside, moving toward them, prepared to help.

Thirty meters . . . The wind whipped dirt from the ground, making it even harder to breathe. Janeway glanced behind her to make sure the others were with her; they were, heads down, doggedly forcing their shaking legs to move. Chakotay brought up the rear, ready to help stragglers.

The ozone smell began to build again, and Janeway realized it was the harbinger of another attack; she picked up the pace, yelling at those behind her to hurry. Ahead of her the mouth of the cave yawned like a gaping maw; the figure of Tuvok swam before her, mouth moving, calling to them soundlessly as his words were swallowed in the wind.

And then she was there, Tuvok's arm steadying her, his firm grip infusing her with strength. She turned and waited as the young people lurched toward the cave opening and tumbled in. Only when they had all entered did Janeway, Tuvok, and Chakotay turn to follow them. The crackle of an energy buildup pulsed through the air; the eruption of a massive charge of bolts created a percussive wave that pushed them through the entrance, and they fell headlong into the cool darkness of the cave.

As soon as they were inside, the roar of the wind receded; the cave was a muffled haven, the air was clean and cool, and the dreadful energy of the plasma bolts, which they could hear outside, didn't penetrate the heavy rock. Janeway looked up, squinting in the darkness. As her eyes adjusted, she saw the entire away team huddled in the cave, drawing soothing moist air into burning lungs. Neelix was moving among them, comforting them, checking for injury. She turned toward Tuvok and Chakotay, who were already counting their people, making sure everyone had made it to safety.

"All accounted for, Captain," said Tuvok. She nodded and looked at Chakotay, who seemed to be counting a second time. She noted a worried furrow on his forehead, slightly distorting the distinctive tattoo he wore on his temple.

"What is it?" She moved toward him, fearing the worst. He turned to her, and his eyes told her she was right. "Who isn't with us?"

"Jerron," he answered, and they both hurried to the mouth of the cave. She spotted the young Bajoran almost immediately, a crumpled blue form in the distance, where they had all taken the first blast that had driven them to the ground. He must have been separated from the others and left behind when they were temporarily blinded.

Janeway immediately started forward, only to feel Chakotay's strong grip on her arm, pulling her back. "I'll get him," he said, but Janeway jerked her arm loose. "Commander, you're to stay with your team. Tuvok, too. That's an order."

Chakotay held her glance for a moment, not responding, but Janeway didn't wait for his acquiescence. Taking one last gulp of good air, she hurled herself out the cave opening and into the raging plasma storm.

It had mounted in intensity even in the few minutes they had been in the cave. Instantly, Janeway's lungs were burning; the air was bitter and caustic; she began to cough uncontrollably. Her eyes watered in the swirling dust. Her legs, which had regained some strength in the cave, turned mushy again, and she felt herself stagger. If she could reach him, get him back before the next round of plasma bursts, she'd make it. But she wasn't sure either of them would survive another attack.

She felt her body begin to go slack, reluctant to go farther, and she steeled herself again. Jerron was only ten meters ahead; she could reach him. One step, then another, fighting the brutal, swirling wind, dizzied by the deafening noise, each breath like breathing flames, she pushed ahead.

Jerron wasn't unconscious. He was staring at her with dull eyes, as though he were looking at something unreal, something his mind couldn't reconcile. His uniform was scorched, and Janeway realized he had taken a direct hit by a plasma bolt. How had he survived?

As she reached him, he pushed himself upright, reaching out an arm. She grabbed it, and he tried to stand, but his legs wobbled and he swayed against her. She struggled to stay on her feet until Jerron steadied himself. Then, bracing each other, they started toward the mouth of the cave.

Janeway smelled the unmistakable odor of an ozone surge. The plasma bolts would hit before they could get to the safety of the cave. She picked up her pace, urging Jerron on, hoping they could somehow outdistance the gathering plasma swell. The cave opening yawned ahead, not fifteen meters away; they could do it.

But Jerron stumbled, and they both went crashing to the

ground. Without conscious thought, Janeway threw her body on top of the young Bajoran's, to shield him from the worst of the blasts.

It was the most ferocious attack yet, filling the air with snapping, arcing green bolts that clutched at the ground like the tentacles of some hideous beast. Janeway squeezed her eyes shut, but even so ragged streaks of green irradiated her lids. The fiery pain seemed to sear her from the inside out; she couldn't even hear her own scream. Her body thrashed as though in the throes of a violent convulsion, bucking and leaping uncontrollably, and the ragged gulps of air she drew between screams produced even greater agony.

And then her father lifted her up.

She felt his strong arms grip her, pulling her across the ground, his handsome, sturdy face calm and unworried, smiling down at her in reassurance. Janeway smiled back and relaxed into the journey, gliding across the terrain, feeling as though she were skimming on a cushion of air like a hovercraft. The air had cleared, and was sweet and cool; the pain was dissipating. She looked up again, wanting to see her father, wanting to look into his clear gray eyes just once more. . . .

Chakotay was staring at her, his face just inches from hers. Her eyes fluttered slightly and she tried to sit upright.

"She's all right," she heard Chakotay say, and she looked around her. She was in the cave again, Jerron at her side, Tuvok and Chakotay leaning over them, still coughing from their exposure to the plasma-infused atmosphere. They had rescued her, and Jerron; Chakotay's strong arms had saved her, not her father's.

She looked at Jerron, whose color was returning. "He has suffered no permanent damage, Captain," intoned Tuvok, "and neither have you." Janeway nodded. She took a deep breath and leaned back against the wall of the cave.

Death had been cheated once more. Everyone was safe.

"I can't really call them nightmares. But they make me feel . . . anxious. Sometimes I wake up and my heart is pounding as though I'd just run five miles."

Janeway sat in the doctor's office, telling him of the strange dreams she'd been having in the weeks following their experience with the plasma storm—dreams she had had before in her life, though they hadn't recurred since she had journeyed to the Delta Quadrant. The holographic doctor sat patiently, listening, brow furrowed, as though puzzled by what she was saying.

"And they're all so similar. I'm always in a house of some kind . . . a house that has many rooms, and I have to get into a certain room, because it's dirty and has to be cleaned—but there's a closed door blocking my way."

The doctor regarded her curiously. "Houses . . . with many rooms?"

"Yes. Once I dreamed I discovered an entire deck on *Voyager* that I hadn't realized was there. It had dozens of rooms, and I knew it was important that I make sure they were all clean. But I couldn't even get out of the first room because the door to the next one was closed and locked."

"And—are these dreams frightening to you?"

"No . . . not frightening. But they're—unsettling. I don't understand them."

The doctor crossed his arms and fixed his eyes on her. "I'm not certain what you want from me, Captain. The dreams don't sound particularly harrowing, and apparently they don't interfere with your sleep. In that I'm not a practicing psychiatrist, how can I help you?"

Janeway regarded him fondly. The holographic doctor had become one of her favorite people. His acerbic nature had not lessened in the course of a year and a half, but everyone had learned to tolerate it—even appreciate it. The parameters of his programming allowed for almost no bedside manner; but in spite of his brusque gruffness, he had an endearing quality.

"I'm honestly not sure, Doctor. I just thought I should mention it. As part of my general medical file."

"I suspect it's a temporary phenomenon, and unless you find these dreams debilitating, I wouldn't worry about it."

"They're not debilitating. Just—bothersome."

The doctor didn't respond, and turned away from her, busying himself with a padd. Janeway studied him for a moment and realized he was taking far more time with the padd than was necessary. The doctor, she was sure, had something on his mind.

"Is there some way I can help *you,* Doctor?" His head snapped back at her; he was always surprised at a demonstration of instinct. He seemed to ponder her question briefly, then, in his matter-of-fact way, blurted it out.

"It's been a full ten months since Lieutenant Torres and Ensign Kim began working on a mechanism by which I can leave sickbay. I can't believe they are incapable of solving the technical problems after that amount of time, so I must conclude that they're not putting their full efforts into the matter. Probably because I'm nothing but a computer program."

Janeway rose, put a comforting hand on the doctor's shoulder. "Please don't jump to that conclusion. You are valued and respected, and we couldn't get along without you. Everyone on the ship cares about you. Especially me."

Although he would never admit it, the doctor was a sensitive and vulnerable man. His feelings could be hurt easily. And he never failed to respond to an expression of empathy. None of this was forthcoming at the moment, of course; he sniffed slightly, and his mobile face underwent a few ripples of expression, but when he spoke, he was as terse as ever.

"If you say so. But I'll find that easier to accept once there are *results*. The proof, I believe the saying goes, is in the pudding."

She smiled. Colloquialisms always sounded a little strange coming from the doctor, but before she could reply, an ominous hail from the bridge interrupted them.

"Chakotay to the captain."

"Janeway here."

"You're needed on the bridge, Captain. We may have a problem."

"On my way."

When she entered the bridge from the turbolift, the faces of the bridge crew looked grim. Janeway moved immediately to Chakotay.

"We've been hailed by a Kazon ship," he reported. "He was none too friendly, and insisted we wait for them to intercept us. He didn't make an outright threat, but it was certainly implied."

Janeway felt a twinge of foreboding. Any encounter with the Kazon was potentially dangerous, although it had been some time since they had run into any of them; she had hoped that *Voyager* might possibly have moved outside the bitterly disputed turf of the various warlike sects.

"Did he state his purpose, Commander? Or identify his faction?"

"He said he was Maje Dut of the Vistik, but didn't give any clue as to what he wanted."

They had never interacted with the Vistik, but Janeway had heard of them. They were a group smaller than the Ogla and the Nistrim, which seemed to be the most powerful of the groups, but they had figured in a disastrous alliance that had threatened to coalesce the Kazon into a unified force—a catastrophic prospect for *Voyager,* which could deal with individual factions but couldn't hope to survive a massive and cooperative Kazon armada.

Options: they could make the diplomatic choice and wait for the Vistik ship, hoping there was a reasonably benign reason for the meeting. And, after all, one Kazon ship didn't pose a particular threat. What's more, they had detected a planetary nebula nearby that might warrant some investigation. These nebulae, formed when older stars began to shed their outer atmosphere, were magnificent and fascinating. Janeway had studied the Alpha Quadrant's Helix Nebula and welcomed the opportunity to investigate another of these massive phenomena. It could occupy the time while they waited for the Kazon.

But she found herself rejecting that option even before it was a fully formed thought. The Kazon had proven time after time that they couldn't be trusted. They were warlike and volatile, and any encounter could prove hazardous. She knew that they had once been horribly oppressed themselves, but freedom from their tormentors had not resulted in growth or enlightenment; it had led only to an endless series of battles among each other, battles that frequently harmed innocent bystanders. Like *Voyager.*

She wasn't going to jump to the whip of some unknown Kazon Maje; she wasn't willing to delay their journey by even a day to accommodate someone who more than likely would pose an unreasonable demand or a vindictive threat. She turned to Tom Paris, the young, sandy-haired lieutenant who was, as he had promised on their first meeting, the "best damn pilot" she could find.

"Mr. Paris, we're not waiting around for a Kazon that won't even do us the courtesy of telling us what he wants to discuss. Continue your course for the Alpha Quadrant, warp six."

"Yes, *ma'am.*" Paris was obviously pleased with the

decision. He was still—would probably always be—a bit of a daredevil, someone who struggled at times against the yoke of Starfleet protocols, but whose skill and intelligence were such that he could get away with risk-taking that might undermine others.

Janeway knew, however, that she would hear something different from Tuvok, and before that thought was even completed, she heard his voice from the security station: "Captain, it is my duty to point out that the Kazon Maje will be highly insulted by this decision; we risk his enmity by ignoring his request."

"Noted, Mr. Tuvok. But I have yet to hear what might be termed a 'request' from a Kazon. They tend to make demands, and I don't feel like yielding to a demand."

"As you wish, Captain." Tuvok was imperturbable as ever, but Janeway imagined she could sense approval from him. No one liked being pushed around by the Kazon. In fact, Janeway thought she felt a general uplifting of spirits on the bridge; on an expedition where they frequently found themselves at the mercy of their circumstances, it was bracing to take a stand, to thumb their noses at the dark forces of the Delta Quadrant.

News of Janeway's decision hadn't yet filtered down to the mess hall; if it had, Neelix' mood of well-being might have dissipated. He frequently failed to share the intrepid—what he would call reckless—convictions of the Starfleet crew. Neelix had survived in a dangerous quadrant for many years through guile, cunning, and an instinctive sense of self-preservation, and he didn't fully understand the adventurous nature of Janeway and her people. They were daring, certainly, and to be lauded for their courage, but Neelix had learned through a lifetime of struggle that a small step backward could often save one's life. Plunging into the unknown might be exciting, but he had quite frankly had enough excitement to last him for a long time.

At the moment, he was concentrating fiercely on decorating a large cake. It was triangular in shape—particularly difficult to achieve, especially in the jury-rigged kitchen he had cobbled together from odds and ends he had scrounged around the ship—and made from Grissibian *nocha.* The closest equivalent in the Alpha Quadrant was a substance known as chocolate, but Neelix found it a pallid imitation. *Nocha* was denser, richer, creamier, and of all the *nocha* he'd tasted, none compared with the Grissibian variety.

He had been saving this *nocha* since a chance encounter with a trader who had been willing to part with it in return for a quart of Vulcan ale. Neelix didn't know what Vulcan ale was; the recipe was in the replicators and many of the crew prized it above any other refreshment. He had found it a valuable commodity in trade: usually one sample of the brew and the bargain was sealed.

Grissibian *nocha* was a delicacy that couldn't be described, only experienced. He remembered his first taste, when he was a boy on Rinax, before the disastrous war that had claimed the lives of all his family. His father had managed to procure some of the rare treat and brought it home to his family. He had handed Neelix a square of a mild-looking substance, slightly oily and a pale beige in color. But when Neelix bit into it, his senses were overwhelmed; the *nocha* was an intense, dusky explosion in his mouth, the creaminess of it moistening every part of his tongue, his throat, his stomach. The sweetness was powerful but not cloying, and seemed to travel directly to his brain, creating an almost narcotic sensation of deeply felt pleasure. His father had laughed to see his son's expression of utter delight.

It was an experience he had never forgotten. In fact, the night his family had died in the horrendous explosion caused by the weapon known as the Metreon Cascade, the thought of that brief moment of bliss was one of the memories that flashed through his mind.

The cake he had made was for two people: Kes, simply because he adored her more than life itself; and Tuvok, because he was determined to bring a smile to the Vulcan's lips. Somewhere inside, that man had the capacity for joy, Neelix was sure of it. He had made numerous attempts to unleash it, but Tuvok had stoically resisted every one of them. Now, with the Grissibian *nocha* cake, Neelix was sure he had a winner. No one could resist this *nocha,* he was certain, not even Tuvok.

He was taking pains to present a cake that not only had an exquisite flavor but was delectable to the eye, as well. He was squeezing colored icing from a modified hypospray (he had borrowed it from sickbay; he was sure the doctor wouldn't mind) into an intricate design on the cake's surface, a delicate, looping scroll that complemented the smooth surface of the *nocha.*

It had required all his willpower not to sample the *nocha,* or the cake, before it was presented to his two recipients. He felt somehow that the occasion would be undermined if he partook of the cake's savory delights before they did, that its potency would somehow be lessened. Now, as he bent over it, eyes squinting to make the decoration perfect, the chocolaty aroma wafted over him, through him, permeating his senses with an overpowering urgency. It seemed to beg him to taste, to sample just the tiniest crumb, one that no one would ever notice was gone.

But he resisted the siren call. He was nothing if not disciplined; that was another quality he had developed in

17

his peripatetic life. He'd learned that giving in to every indulgence was a quick way to lose one's edge; denial had a tendency to fend off complacency and keep one sharp.

He was so engrossed in his task that he didn't hear the soft footfall behind him, wasn't aware of anyone's presence until Kes' soft voice was almost in his ear. "That looks delicious. What is it?"

He whirled in dismay. "Kes—what are you doing here?" Her beautiful elfin face, framed by its cap of feathered blond hair, stared back at him in surprise.

"I just stopped by to say hello. Shouldn't I have?"

Her consternation undid him, as always. He hastened to reassure her. "Of course you should, sweeting, I'm always delighted to see you. It's just . . ." He trailed off, wondering if he could still preserve the surprise.

"Just what?"

Neelix' mind raced, but he could think of no plausible explanation that wouldn't give away his plan. He opted for honesty. "It was supposed to be a surprise. For you and Tuvok."

Kes' beautiful face erupted in a smile, and she gave Neelix a gentle kiss. "You're so thoughtful. But—why me and Tuvok?"

"You, my love, because I want to share an amazing taste sensation with you. And Tuvok because . . . because I'm certain this exquisite cake will make him smile."

Kes regarded him fondly. "You just don't understand, Neelix. Tuvok is Vulcan. He isn't *supposed* to smile."

"I do understand. I understand that the poor man experiences none of the delight that comes from pleasure. What a wretched way to live! If he can control his emotions so well, why not just suppress the negative ones and allow the positive ones to rise to the surface?"

"Don't you remember what happened when he mind-melded with Lon Suder? Anything other than total control could allow very violent, ugly emotions to overwhelm him. It's hard to imagine that tasting a cake would be enough to break through his reserve."

"This isn't just a cake. It's an *experience.* As you'll discover this evening, my dearest."

Kes' smile was sweet as she departed for sickbay. Neelix returned to his ministrations on the cake, gleefully anticipating Tuvok's response to it, never imagining that the evening would be occupied by activities far more dire than eating Grissibian *nocha* cake.

They detected the planet at nine hundred hours, and Captain Janeway was pleased. It was a particularly fortunate discovery, for they hadn't collected any supplies after the electrical storm on the last planet—which Chakotay had wryly named "Sizzle." Food stores were dwindling and they had to resupply as quickly as possible.

The heart of the system was a K7-class yellow dwarf star, rich in helium and perhaps ten billion years old—a bit of a senior citizen. The fourth planet had an oxygen-nitrogen atmosphere and according to sensors was abundant with flora. The possibility of food was temptingly high. There was no indication of a population, although Janeway noted that some formations had a curious symmetry that might warrant investigation.

Cautious after their experience on Sizzle, she ordered an exhaustive series of sensor sweeps, looking for any aberration on the planet or in the atmosphere, anything that might produce an unexpected phenomenon. Only after she was satisfied that they wouldn't be blindsided again did she order the away teams to the transporter room. Tuvok was to take one group only and make an on-site inspection before calling for additional crew. He named Harry Kim to the team. She remained on the bridge as they took their leave, and she chalked up the small chill she felt as they left to a draft from the turbolift.

Tuvok's team consisted of himself, Kim, Neelix, Kes (at Neelix' request), and twenty Maquis and Starfleet crew. Kim's presence wasn't strictly necessary, but Tuvok believed that away missions were good for the young man. They gave him the experience he needed in disciplining his emotional responses to dangerous and startling situations. Harry always seemed to appreciate the opportunities, though Tuvok suspected it was more to get out into the open air and release some of the natural energy of youth than to practice controlling his emotions.

Tuvok's first order of business was to investigate those suspiciously symmetrical formations; he wanted to make certain there wasn't a population on this planet that had gone undetected for some reason. They had beamed down within a kilometer southeast of the formations, and would proceed cautiously toward them, all the while scanning continuously. The landscape of the planet was not so Earth-like as the prior planet had been (he would not call it by the ridiculous sobriquet Chakotay had chosen for it); the terrain was shot with volcanic rock and the soil was slimy, with a greenish cast to it. The flora was completely unfamiliar.

It was Harry who first speculated: "Lieutenant, those formations are constructed. I'd bet on it."

"A wager would have no effect on the outcome of your observation, Ensign. Either they are constructed or they're not." He could never understand the human belief that betting enhanced one's argument.

A ridge separated them from their group and the location of the formations, now only forty meters away.

Quietly, cautiously, the team climbed the ridge and crouched on its rim before raising their heads to peer over it. Tuvok gestured to the others to stay down, and he slowly crept forward, lifting his head to peer through thick underbrush at the formation before him.

Even then, he wasn't sure what he was seeing.

A tangle of undergrowth wove in erratic designs over a mound of stone rubble that stretched for nearly half a kilometer in either direction, and that might or might not have once represented a structure. There was a vague order to the rubble, but it was so clumped with weeds and bushes that it was difficult to discern a pattern. One feature, however, identified the mass of stone and brush as having at some time been subject to intelligent hands: a brilliant, cobalt blue spire rose from the center of the mound, gleaming in the sunlight which reflected off its glossy planes.

Nothing—not mound, rubble, or spire—gave off any suspicious readings. There was no sign of life. Whatever this mound had once been, whatever the purpose of the radiant blue spire, they functioned no longer. Tuvok motioned for the team to move forward; if the mound was the remnants of a dead civilization, that knowledge should be included in Starfleet's cartographic database.

The team spread out around the mound, tricorders aimed and busily recording data. Kim, in particular, seemed fascinated by this possible archaeological find, and he eagerly took the point of one wing of the team. And it was his cry of discovery Tuvok heard first after he disappeared around a large boulder.

When the others caught up to him, they gasped at the sight: an arrangement of delicate skeletons, which at first glance appeared to be of winged humanoids, was spread in a deep circular indentation in the ground. The skulls were strong, elongated ovals, with large eye holes. The rib cages were humanoid in shape, while long, hollow-boned arms ended in hands of six digits, including an opposable thumb. The leg bones were short and somewhat stubby.

But Tuvok realized it was the wing bones that had caused the collective gasp. Now they were tucked in close to the body, but clearly when extended they would have stretched two meters or more. These beings would have had the capacity to soar high into the air above the surface of this planet, dipping and sailing on the breezes, then coming to land on their short, squat legs, which would have afforded them locomotion of a much more limited sort. Did they spend most of their time in the air, these winged beings?

And just how, Tuvok wondered, should this species be categorized: as humanoid or avian? It possessed qualities of each in a way no one had ever seen before. Kim, speaking excitedly, ran down the possibilities. "In Earth's development, modern birds began to branch off from reptiles shortly after the first mammals appeared. It's certainly possible on some planets there could have been a branch of avian mammals that eventually evolved into winged humanoids."

Tuvok looked at the faces of his group, all of which reflected a reverence for this burial place. It was, he felt, quite appropriate. He scanned one of the skeletons.

"The cranium of this being suggests a large brain; in all likelihood they were intelligent. I would suggest this burial grouping was arranged by similar beings, and that these creatures do not represent intelligent animals cared for, and buried, by a higher order."

"The grouping indicates a death ritual, doesn't it?" Kim's brow was furrowed in concentration. He seemed to have been particularly affected by the discovery.

"Indeed. There are a number of inferences to be drawn from what we see here: this may be a family group; it might represent a being of some social power and his or her subordinates; or it may represent the victims of a particular disaster—plague, perhaps, or disease. Without further information it would be impossible to make a clear determination."

"There don't seem to be any artifacts buried with them." This was from Kes, who as always was curious about everything.

"Quite right. And again, there are inferences one can make, but little way to delimit them without more evidence."

"Look at that, Mr. Vulcan." Tuvok lifted his head to see Neelix pointing at something a hundred meters distant. It was another spire, deep blue like the first. It had not been visible from their original position; in fact, it would only be visible from where they were standing—near the foot of the first spire.

"It is common in many species to link burial sites with visual markers," suggested Tuvok. "We may be able to follow a trail of such markers until we arrive at a sacred site."

"If we find that's the case, it would be the first documented evidence of such behavior in the Delta Quadrant," said Ensign Greta Kale, a young woman with blond hair, dark brown eyes, and a sprinkling of the spots humans called "freckles" across her nose. "What does that kind of commonalty say about the origin of all species?"

It was an insightful question, but Tuvok didn't look forward to answering it. There was a great deal of controversy about that very matter. Why were there more similarities than differences among most species? It argued for some original link, a commonalty of origin among the galaxy's species that had never been satisfactorily addressed. Many believed that an alien group from another galaxy had "seeded" the primordial soup of all the planets at the point when the building blocks that would produce life first began to develop. Others believed that a powerful, unseen supreme being had created life, full blown, in an instant. Tuvok himself preferred a more scientific explanation: basic matter—the elements and their various molecular combinations—from which the galaxy was formed was common. These building blocks would have been distributed throughout the galaxy as stars and planets were formed. Why would it not follow, then, that the stuff from which life developed had many common qualities, and that the development of humanoids along similar lines was to be expected, rather than questioned?

"I will let you make your own judgment about that, Ensign, based on your individual beliefs." Kale smiled at him; apparently it was the answer she had expected.

"Can we do it, Lieutenant? Follow the marker, see if there's a trail?" Kim looked at him with what could only be described as eagerness. The young man was clearly caught up in this mystery and wanted to pursue it.

"I see no reason not to," answered Tuvok evenly. But Neelix jumped in. "I must remind you that our primary mission is to gather food supplies. This paleontological stuff is very interesting, of course—I myself am an amateur archaeologist of some experience—but let us not lose sight of our priorities."

"Quite right, Mr. Neelix. I suggest you detail a group of ten and scout the area for foodstuffs. I will take the others on a scientific investigation."

"Fine. Kes, you're with me—"

"Oh, no. I'm going with Tuvok." Tuvok, like Neelix, noted her tone of voice and knew she was determined. Neelix nodded and quickly counted out the ten who would be with him. Tuvok was aware that they all seemed disappointed, but unlike Kes, they were too steeped in Starfleet discipline to refuse. Neelix led his small band away from the mound and began scanning for edible plant forms.

Harry Kim led the others, eagerly marching toward the second spire, eyes scanning upward as though he might suddenly spot one of the soaring creatures who had once sailed these skies. Tuvok continued to check his tricorder frequently.

There was no inkling of the real danger that would come from those skies.

It could not have been more sudden or unexpected. One minute Janeway was in her ready room, relaxing with vegetable bouillon while reviewing personnel reports. Strictly speaking, that wasn't her responsibility; the first officer's review was all that was officially required. But Janeway enjoyed the process, finding that it drew her closer to her crew. If a junior officer in quantum mechanics was having a rough week, she wanted to know about it. Lunch with the captain, or a private chat over afternoon tea, could work wonders in reviving flagging confidence or dispelling a touch of homesickness.

A dull ache had burrowed its way just behind her eyes. She hadn't slept well last night, having revisited the house with many rooms and finding, inevitably, the closed door. After that, she had tossed restlessly, trying to find the position that would induce sleep. When that failed, she had risen early and now, several hours later, was feeling the consequences of the fretful night.

Then there was Tom Paris' startled voice over the comm—"Bridge to Captain, we have a rapidly approaching"—and then a horrendous explosion. Sparks flew from her monitor. The lights went out entirely and then were replaced with low-level emergency lighting. Janeway made her way to the door even as the ship shuddered and jolted, threatening to throw her off balance.

The doors flew open at her approach and she stumbled onto the bridge. "Report," she barked, noting as she did that smoke was filling the space; one officer was unconscious on the ground.

"A Kazon vessel, Captain. It stayed in high warp until the last second, then dropped out and attacked. We were sitting ducks." She knew Chakotay was already handling the situation, rerouting power, activating defensive systems, and assigning damage control.

"Taking evasive action, Captain." Tom Paris' hands flew over his controls as he skilfully maneuvered the ship. "But we've taken damage to the impulse engines."

"Shields at fifty-seven percent, hull breaches on decks four and fifteen. There are reports of casualties on all decks," Lieutenant Rollins said crisply; he was filling in for Tuvok at Tactical.

"Prepare to return fire. Ready forward phaser banks." Janeway swung into action, her mind automatically moving into combat mode. "Fire at will, Mr. Rollins."

"Aye, Captain, firing forward—"

A sudden volley of explosions overwhelmed the rest of what he said. She couldn't even be sure he had fired the phasers. In spite of Paris' manuevers at the conn, the Kazon ship was still with them. Two consoles exploded and several more went dead. Smoke battled the filtering system and won.

"Shields at thirty-four percent. Hull breaches on decks three through fifteen. Weapons arrays off-line."

"Captain, we can't hold out. We'd better try to get out of here." Chakotay's voice was implacable as he suggested retreat.

"Agreed, Captain," chimed in Paris. "At least we've got warp drive now; who knows how much longer before we're dead in the water?"

Janeway hesitated briefly. The away team was still on the planet. She didn't want to abandon them, but if they stayed where they were they could be destroyed, and certainly of no help to the crew on the ground if that happened.

"Janeway to Tuvok," she intoned, but there was no reply. "The long-range comm system is down, Captain," said Rollins. Another bone-shuddering jolt rattled them, and Janeway wasted no more time. "Set a course for that planetary nebula we passed, Lieutenant. Then put us into rapid high warp—let's see if we can't catch them napping."

"Yes, ma'am." Janeway noted that Paris smiled slightly; she knew there was nothing he enjoyed more than outfoxing an enemy with his piloting skills. And she also realized he knew she wasn't abandoning Harry and the others— she wouldn't quit until she had them back. Now they had to lick their wounds and make repairs, and taking cover in the nebula was the only prudent course.

The sudden leap to warp did indeed catch the Kazon by surprise; *Voyager* had several minutes' advantage and was able to enter the planetary nebula, which, with its clumps of star matter millions of kilometers across, offered a perfect hiding place. They entered the massive, stately plumes of gas and were safely concealed deep within the dark dust lanes of the nebula before the Kazon ships realized what had happened. Janeway made sure repair teams were in action, checked with the doctor as to the number of wounded and the severity of their injuries, then met with the bridge officers. Her plan was straightforward enough: make repairs and regain strength, then get back to the planet as soon as possible, hoping to outmaneuver the Kazon and beam up their away team.

She was amused when Chakotay "ordered" her to her quarters; it was imperative for all of them to rest while they could—they'd need to be at their sharpest when they headed back to the planet—but she felt slightly like a child being told to take a nap.

And again, she couldn't sleep. She tried going through all the exercises and procedures she had developed over the years for bouts of insomnia: a cool, darkened room, breathing patterns, relaxation exercises, meditation—and when all else failed, a glass of warm milk. But in spite of her efforts to quiet her mind, one thought came crowding back. Her crew was stranded. She had to get them back. It was the second time in as many months that she had faced this problem and the fiftieth since they'd been flung to the Delta Quadrant. Her life since then had been a series of challenges and crises, and most of her energies had gone into coping with them. She'd been tested time and again, pushed to limits she wasn't sure she could withstand, and then pushed further. Would it ever let up? Would there ever be a day that she wasn't called upon to solve some insoluble problem, to overcome some life-threatening obstacle? The thought of throwing up her hands, acknowledging that she was too tired and weak and simply didn't have anything left to give—that thought became tempting. She was tired of challenges. There was a time when they energized her, but now they threatened to overwhelm. She wanted to feel safe again, secure and protected, knowing someone else was watching out for things. . . .

CHAPTER

2

CROUCHED WITHIN THE KNEEHOLE OF HER FATHER'S DESK, four-year-old Kathryn listened to the sound of the tock-tock-tock of the grandfather clock in his office.

She was careful not to make a sound, for she knew her father needed to concentrate, and a small child fidgeting at his feet would have distracted him. He was working—he was always working—on a starship design, and the various clicks and beeps of his padd punctuated the silence in the room, offering odd counterpoint to the sonorous clock. Kathryn loved hearing the sounds of the padd; they were oddly soothing, a reminder that he was there, a connection to him. Sometimes she pretended the sounds were in fact a private code they shared, that he was sending her messages that no one else could interpret.

"Daddy to Goldenbird . . . my ETA is fifteen minutes . . . rendezvous with me in my study at sixteen hundred hours . . . this is top secret . . . Daddy out."

Kathryn smiled as she snuggled in the kneehole. Maybe

it would be only fifteen minutes more, maybe it would be longer. But the reward for her patience and stillness would be worth it: she and Daddy would do their games. She would have him to herself for a time. And for that, Kathryn would gladly have sat quietly under the desk for hours.

She'd been spending a lot of time in Daddy's study lately, ever since Your Sister had come to their house. Your Sister didn't seem to be much more than a wriggling movement inside a soft blanket, but her arrival had had a profound effect on the household. Mama was hardly ever in evidence now, except when she walked with the small bundle in the blanket over her shoulder, patting its back and singing softly to it. So far, Kathryn had not heard Mama singing *her* song to Your Sister, but knew that was because Mama and Daddy had not yet decided on a name for this new presence. Kathryn had her own thoughts about that, but so far no one had asked her.

Her father's leg shifted slightly next to her and she sat up quickly. Did this mean he was almost done? Was he closing up his padd and getting ready for the games? She held her breath, afraid of causing distraction, but she continued to hear the sounds of the padd. Daddy wasn't ready yet.

She settled back again, mind running over the games, practicing, readying herself so she would be perfect. She intended to surprise Daddy by knowing every single thing today—and even more—so he would ruffle her hair and say, "That's my Goldenbird . . . what a clever girl you are!" The prospect of hearing those words made her heart quicken.

She sat like that, contained and quiet, for another half hour. She could tell because the grandfather clock chimed every fifteen minutes, and there were four fifteen minutes in each hour. Two of them was half an hour. She had figured that out when she was three.

She heard a familiar click and realized that Daddy had snapped shut his padd. She held her breath for a moment, for sometimes he would open another, but she saw his legs withdrawing from the desk. He was done, and she knew exactly what would happen next.

Now she heard him pacing the room, as though looking for something. "No, not there," he intoned, and she smiled. A few seconds later, he said, with a hint of exasperation, "Not there either. Hmmmmm."

Her smile grew as she listened to this careful ritual. "I could swear I heard a little bird in this room . . . but I can't find her. Where could she be? Is she hiding in the replicator?"

Now Kathryn had to cover her mouth with her hands— in the replicator! How silly, how could she do that? She felt a giggle building.

"Oh-oh . . . maybe she got into the fish tank . . . she's after my African lionfish . . . you naughty bird, you'd better not bother my lionfish!"

Now the giggle was starting to tickle her throat; she tried to push it down and instead it came out through her nose as a little snort.

"What's that? What did I just hear?" His mock-stern voice moved closer to her. She scrunched into the tiniest ball she could become and covered her face with her hands. Then she heard his voice right next to her. "Why . . . it's a bird all right. It's a Goldenbird, and she's hiding *under my desk!*"

Now Kathryn looked up as she felt his hands on her, pulling her out. She shrieked with glee as he picked her up effortlessly and swung her around the room. "Goldenbird is flying . . . all around the room . . . up . . . and down . . . and down . . . and up . . ." Kathryn's laughter pealed as

31

her father swung her in delicious circles and dips and then finally lowered her to the floor.

"More, Daddy, more," she pleaded, but he knelt down close to her.

"I'm sorry, but we don't give free rides around here. What do you have to do for a ride?"

"Earn it."

"And how do you do that?"

"Win the games."

"Are you ready?"

"Yes, Daddy, all ready."

His wonderful face looked down at her. Gray eyes twinkled, sandy brown hair fell over his forehead. Daddy's face always looked happy, she thought.

"Very well. Did you work on the sevens?"

Kathryn took a breath, plunged into the scary unknown. "I worked on the sevens . . . and the eights. And the nines."

His look of amazement was reward enough for all the work she'd done. She giggled again, delighted that she'd surprised him. She knew he'd never have expected her to learn so much.

"Eights and nines, eh? Those are very big numbers for a little girl. Are you sure you want to take this chance? You'll win your ride if you just get the sevens."

"I'm ready. I can do it."

"But if you make a mistake on the eights or nines . . . no ride."

"I know."

He smiled, and his look of genuine pride made her shiver. "Well, then. Nine times eight?"

"Seventy-two."

"Eight times seven?"

"Fifty-six."

"Seven times four."

"Twenty-eight."

"Eight times eight."

"Sixty-four."

"Nine times . . . eleven."

She paled. They'd never gone past the tens. She had memorized everything up to a multiple of ten, but eleven represented an area of computation she'd never considered.

"That's not fair, Daddy. We've never done elevens."

"You've proven you can memorize very well. But it's important you learn how to *think* about numbers. I'm expecting you to move to the next level of mathematics."

Her mind threatened to panic. She couldn't do this, he was betraying her. How could she answer something she'd never even thought of? She would have to admit to him that she couldn't do it.

This last thought ripped through her mind, searing it like a jagged lightning strike, and she felt the beginning of tears sting her eyes.

Daddy was looking at her, patient but unyielding. She knew he would not back down, would not simply take pity on her. He would expect her to come up with the answer. That realization was somehow calming to her, and she sank to the floor, sitting with her legs crossed and her hands folded in her lap, eyes closed. She forced her mind to close out the room, the grandfather's clock, and Daddy's presence looming above her. She concentrated on the numbers, trying to see them in front of her.

Nine tens was easy. She learned weeks ago that for ten times anything you just added a zero. So nine tens was ninety. She tried to see them in her mind, lined up in ordered rows: nine lionfish in one row, nine lionfish in a second row, nine lionfish in a third row. She proceeded this way until she could see all ninety fish, whiskered and malevolent, spread out in her mind's eye. If those were ten rows, she needed only add one more row. Eleven rows of fish . . . eleven nines. Ten of them are ninety, and if she *added* nine more—

"Ninety-nine." She opened her eyes and looked up at him. He was regarding her with a strange expression that she did not come to understand for a long time. He swooped down and lifted her up, holding her close to his chest. For a long time he didn't say anything, and she was terrified she had made a mistake.

"Is that right, Daddy?" Her voice was a whisper.

"Exactly right." He sat her down and tousled her hair. "What a clever Goldenbird you are. How did you do that?"

The smile erupted on her face. "I could see the numbers. I just added another row."

He gazed at her fondly. "You know what? You not only get another ride—but you and I are going to the cornfields together."

This was the ultimate reward. Kathryn's favorite place on Earth was the cornfields of the agricultural park in which they lived, row upon row of stately tasseled figures, marching in unison, bending and swaying in the summer breeze, dancing on the wind. Sometimes when they went there, she and Daddy invented little stories they acted out—the cornstalks were Starfleet cadets, marching on the parade ground, or they were a corps de ballet, with beautifully gowned ballerinas dancing in unison—and sometimes they played hide-and-seek. Last year, when she'd watched the harvest, she cried for the loss of her companions.

She put her hand in Daddy's, and they walked out through the wide doors onto the patio. Her heart was thudding with happiness, and she wished she could preserve that moment forever.

CHAPTER

3

JANEWAY'S HEAD SHOT UP AND HER EYES FLEW OPEN AND FOR A moment she didn't know where she was. Childhood memories, recollections, and feelings hung about her, vaporous and fleeting. She tried to cling to them but they receded like shadows in the rising sun. Then the present came snapping back at her: she was on *Voyager* and they were in danger. The Kazon lurked outside the nebula and part of her crew was stranded on an alien planet.

A check of the time showed that she had slept for over an hour, though she would have sworn her eyes hadn't closed.

"Janeway to bridge."

"Rollins here, Captain.

"Can you give me an update?"

"Repairs are continuing. Engineering reports that we should be under way again in about four hours."

"Thank you, Lieutenant."

Now was the time to rest, to recharge her batteries in preparation for the ordeal that lay ahead. She lay down again, and tried to recapture the comforting feelings of home and family she'd been experiencing before she woke. She must've been dreaming . . . but what about? She couldn't retrieve it . . . every time she thought she'd snagged something with a corner of her mind, it slipped away again. . . .

CHAPTER

4

"RACQUET BACK . . . TURN YOUR SHOULDERS . . . NOW—
uncoil!"

The commands were endless. They became a ceaseless
drone in her mind, a part of her unconscious. "Sleeve to
the mouth . . . lengthen your follow-through . . . racquet
face steady . . . level your backswing . . ." Her tennis
coach's voice rolled over the net from the opposite end of
the court as smoothly as the balls she hit. Coach Cameron
made it look so easy. But most of Kathryn's balls went into
the net or out of bounds, no matter how hard she tried. She
was getting frustrated.

Kathryn was on one of the tennis courts of a small
athletic complex near her home. It was the locus of what
were known as "traditional" games—tennis, golf, and
swimming. Another complex nearby housed contempo-
rary activities, which included hoverball, Parrises Squares,
hurdleleap, and loft circles. That's where Kathryn would

much rather have been. She was *good* at most of those games.

The Indiana spring was in fulsome bloom, with forsythia and dogwood emerging in an ecstasy of color. The air was fragrant and warm; two months later baking heat would join with oppressive humidity to create a veritable steam bath, but now the May morning was pleasant.

Kathryn, however, had no appreciation of either the landscaping or the weather. She jabbed ineffectually at a stray lock of hair that kept falling in her eyes, trying to hook it around her ear. It would only fall forward again. There seemed to be nothing she could do to her thin, fine hair that would keep it out of her eyes when she exercised.

"Kathryn, come up to the net." Coach Cameron was walking to her side of the net, racquet in hand. She was a short, muscular woman with thick blond curls and a smiling face. Kathryn wanted to look just like her when she was grown up, but even at nine years of age she realized that her hair would never look like Coach Cameron's. And neither would her tennis strokes.

"I want to check your grip." Kathryn put her hand in the forehand grip and Coach Cameron inspected it carefully. "That might be the problem," she said. "Your grip is rotated too far to the right, so the racquet face is coming through at an angle. See?"

She swung Kathryn's arm through an exaggerated stroke. "You're hitting the ball up, and that's why so many of them are going out. Turn your hand back this way just a little." Coach Cameron rotated Kathryn's hand slightly to the left. "That should level out the stroke."

It felt *awful.* How could she hit the ball at all? Her hand clutched the racquet like a claw, foreign and unnatural. She practiced a stroke and felt as though her arm were some new appendage she'd never used before.

"I can't do it this way," she protested, but Coach

Cameron wasn't about to accept that. "It feels strange because you got used to the other way. It'll take a while before this grip feels natural."

Kathryn didn't reply, but marched stoically back to the baseline. As she did, she saw something that made her mood even blacker: Hobbes Johnson, arriving early for the lesson he took right after hers. That's all she needed, jerky Hobbes Johnson to see her make a fool of herself. He was a year or two older than she, thinner than the scarecrows that stood in the cornfields, upper teeth protruding slightly, dark hair unruly under his tennis cap. *Nobody* wore a tennis cap, it was the dumbest thing in the world, but it was just what you'd expect from him.

"Hi, Kath!" he called out, waving at her. She didn't answer. She hated being called Kath. No one called her that except this toad. And he was too ignorant to realize she was ignoring him, and smiled broadly at her.

She turned and waited for Coach Cameron to start hitting balls to her, trying to get the feel of the new and uncomfortable grip change. The first ball she hit into the net. The second hit the ground in front of the net. She could feel Hobbes's eyes burrowing into her from behind. She was humiliated.

"Try squeezing the handle of the racquet as you make impact," called out Coach Cameron. Kathryn did, and hit the ball wildly to the left. She tried again and missed it entirely.

"I can't *do* this!" she wailed, and threw down her racquet. She'd have done anything to be allowed to stop right there. But Coach Cameron wasn't about to let her off the hook. "You have five minutes left in your lesson, Kathryn. And we're going to use them. Now—keep your eye *on the ball.*"

In the next five minutes, she managed to hit maybe ten balls over the net. The others went wildly astray. By the time Coach Cameron called an end to it, Kathryn's eyes were beginning to sting with tears of frustration. She couldn't look at Hobbes. She walked toward her tennis bag, eyes on the ground.

"Hobbes," said Coach Cameron, "I have to go inside for a few minutes. Maybe you could warm up with Kathryn?"

"Sure," Hobbes said agreeably, and Coach Cameron walked away from them and toward the office of the tennis facility. Kathryn kept her face down and opened her racquet cover, sticking the racquet inside. Perspiration dripped from her; she was hot and angry. She thought of the cold juice waiting for her at home.

"Don't you want to hit some?" asked Hobbes, the disappointment in his voice not hidden.

"I *hate* this game," said Kathryn emphatically. "I don't know why my parents want me to play it. It's a waste of time. I'd rather be playing Parrises Squares."

"Your parents are traditionalists, like mine. That's why we live in the agricultural community. That's why we go to the school we do."

Only Hobbes would use a word like "traditionalist," Kathryn thought. He was such a vulk that he didn't realize his grownup vocabulary sounded ridiculous. She began stuffing her things into her tennis bag.

"I don't see why that means I have to learn to play tennis. It's a ridiculous game."

"I think it's fun."

"You can hit the ball across the net."

"I couldn't two years ago."

She looked up at him. Hobbes played so well she'd assumed it came naturally to him, like mathematics did to her. "Really?"

"My first coach told me I should forget tennis and take up hoverball."

"Why didn't you?"

"I guess because he made me mad."

This was surprising to her. Hobbes was such a quiet, meek boy that the thought that he could get mad would never have occurred to her.

"Coach Cameron makes me mad, too. But she makes me feel like quitting."

"Quitting is easy. I didn't want to give old Epkowicz the satisfaction."

"I'm telling my mother this was it. I'm not going through this anymore."

He regarded her solemnly. She felt uncomfortable under his scrutiny, as though he were judging her: she was taking the easy way out. Well, so what? If she never had to experience the disgrace she had felt today, she'd gladly take Hobbes Johnson's censure instead. She batted an errant lock of hair out of her eyes.

"Well, so long, Hobbes. Have a good lesson."

"If you'd ever like to hit some, let me know."

"Sure."

"Sometimes playing with kids your own age is better than working with the coach."

"You're probably right."

"How about tomorrow?"

The thought of being seen playing tennis with Hobbes Johnson was enough to make her toes curl under.

"I have piano tomorrow. And I have to help my mother with something."

His earnest eyes gazed at her. She realized that Hobbes was accustomed to being rejected by his peers, and for a brief moment she considered accepting his offer. But then the vision of facing Emma North or Mary O'Connell and admitting she'd spent time with him overwhelmed her. "Sorry," she mumbled, and picked up her bag and slung it over her shoulder.

"Maybe another time," he said mildly, and she nodded

and walked away. What a terrible day this was turning into.

It didn't get better when she announced to her mother that she was quitting tennis. Her mother was a tall, gracious woman with curly brown hair—why did *everybody* have better hair than she did?—rich blue eyes, and a beautiful smile. When she was very young she used to do whatever she could to make her mother smile, because her face looked so happy when she did.

Her mother wasn't smiling now. She sat in the breakfast room, listening quietly as Kathryn poured out her woeful tale. "I'm no good at it, and I hate it, and I'm never going to get better. I'm *not* doing it any more. It was embarrassing! Vulky Hobbes Johnson was there and I couldn't even hit the ball."

"Please don't call your friends vulky," murmured her mother.

"He's not my friend. And it was horrible to have him see me be humiliated." She felt tears begin to sting her eyes again as she relived the awful experience. "I want to play Parrises Squares. I could be on the fourth-grade team, Mrs. Matsumoto said so. But even if I don't get on the team, I'm not going back to Coach Cameron, I don't care what you say!" The tears began spilling out of her eyes, and the pent-up emotion of the day erupted, and she shuddered with great sobs.

Her dog, Bramble, a little wire-haired mutt, had been sitting quietly nearby, and now he became alarmed and came up to her, tail wagging, sticking his wet nose against her leg.

Her mother regarded her pensively, then held out her arms. "Come here, my angel."

Kathryn fled into her arms. There lay refuge; there lay comfort. She had been rocked in her mother's arms since she was born, and though she knew she was too old now, she still loved the feeling of haven. There, on her mother's lap, she was safe from the world; tears were dried, feelings were soothed, anxieties calmed. She was sure this would be the end of tennis lessons. Bramble, too, seemed to feel the crisis was over, and sat at the foot of the rocking chair, gazing up at the two with big dark eyes.

Her mother rocked her, and stroked her hair, and wiped her eyes, and murmured "There, there," the way she always did. But when Kathryn was calm again, her mother began talking.

"I know it's hard to struggle with learning a new skill. And no one likes to feel frustrated or humiliated. Anyone would be upset by feelings like that." Kathryn nodded. "But not everything in life comes easily. Some things require struggle. And if we don't learn how to make that kind of effort, we won't be prepared to learn the difficult lessons of life."

With a sinking heart, Kathryn realized what her mother was saying. "You're not making me go back! I won't do it! I don't care!"

But her mother kept talking, calmly and soothingly. "So many things come easily to you, Kathryn. If we let you quit everything that was difficult, you wouldn't learn to work for what you earn. You'd expect everything to be easy. And life isn't that way. What you must work to earn, you value more. So it's important that you not quit tennis. If you have to work harder to learn to play—then you have to work harder. It may not seem that way now, but you'll be very glad later on that we didn't let you quit."

Kathryn felt like crying all over again—it wasn't fair!—but suddenly the whoop and clatter of her sister Phoebe rang through the house. She was coming home from her play group; she carried artwork and crumbling cookies and, as usual, exuded the energy of a hurricane.

"Mommy, Mommy, Mommy, we baked cookies and I did fingerpaints and clay and—" Phoebe came skidding to a halt when she saw Kathryn on her mother's lap. "I want lap, too," she announced firmly, and began crawling onto Gretchen Janeway's already crowded legs.

It isn't *fair,* thought Kathryn. Phoebe wasn't upset, Phoebe wasn't being forced to do something she hated, Phoebe didn't need comforting. Phoebe even had curly hair! Why did she have to share? Kathryn felt misery begin to envelop her completely, and she slid off onto the floor.

"I'm going to my room," she announced, and marched away with Bramble toddling after her, hoping her mother would be really, really sorry she'd driven her away.

She shut the door of her room firmly—no one could accuse her of slamming it, but it felt good to hear the louder-than-usual snap as it closed—and threw herself on the bed. Bramble immediately jumped up and snuggled next to her, and Kathryn wrapped her arm around his warm, woolly body. Tears continued to roll out of her eyes as she indulged in her miserable feelings, and soon she felt Bramble's silky tongue licking the salty droplets. This was almost as good as her mother's lap. Bramble had been lapping up her tears ever since he was a puppy, and Kathryn was convinced he did it because he *knew* it made her feel better (and not, as Daddy had suggested, because he was attracted to the salty taste).

Daddy. Would he let her quit tennis? Kathryn pondered that one for a minute, then dismissed it. She couldn't remember when Mommy and Daddy didn't agree on issues like these. Was that part of being traditionalists, too?

She looked around her room, which didn't look like the room of any of her friends. They had spare, minimally furnished rooms with no evidence of clutter; Kathryn's was decorated in a style she knew was ancient: a white

44

four-poster bed with a ruffled flounce, lace curtains at the window, shelves lined with stuffed animals. Her mother had shown her pictures of rooms like that from centuries ago; their whole house looked like an ancient heirloom from the twenty-second century. She supposed that was how "traditionalists" decorated their houses.

The chime of her desk console interrupted her thoughts, and she rolled over to see that it was an incoming message from her friend Mary O'Connell. Kathryn wiped at her eyes and ran her fingers through her hair; Mary was always immaculate, and she didn't want to appear mussed by comparison. She pushed the control on the console, and Mary's cheerful face appeared on the screen.

"Kathryn, guess what?" bubbled Mary. She was a vivacious girl with huge brown eyes and satiny hair so blond it was almost white. She looked as though she were about to burst with some wonderful news, and indeed, without waiting for Kathryn to make a guess, she barreled ahead. "I'm captain of the fourth-grade Parrises Squares team!"

This announcement hit Kathryn like a slap, and that must have been apparent to Mary, because she looked puzzled. "What's the matter?"

Kathryn wasn't going to tell her that she was better at Parrises Squares than anyone in the fourth grade, including the boys, and that if anyone should be captain it should be Kathryn Janeway. Instead, her voice rising once more into a wail, she poured out her lament to her friend: "My parents won't *let* me be on the team. I have to learn stupid *tennis* instead! It's not fair—we could be on the team together!"

Mary was instantly sympathetic. "I don't understand. What do they have against Parrises Squares?"

"You won't believe this—they think it's too easy for me."

"That doesn't make any sense."

"And I have to keep taking tennis lessons because it's *hard* for me."

Mary's grave face stared out from the screen. "Your parents do have some funny ideas sometimes."

"Well, I'm going to show them. They can make me keep taking tennis, but I don't have to like it. And I'm never going to be any good at it. Sooner or later, they'll see it's a waste of time."

And having made that decision, Kathryn began to feel a lot better. She reached down and scratched Bramble on the tummy, his favorite place, and he rolled over on his back in ecstasy.

But then Daddy came home with his amazing news, and she forgot all about tennis.

She was going to take her first trip into space. Her first ride on a shuttle. Her first visit to Mars Colony.

"I have to go next week," Daddy explained to all of them—her, Phoebe, and Mommy—as they sat around the dinner table. Kathryn was only picking at her food, partly from excitement and partly because she preferred replicated food over the meals that her mother cooked with real food. *Why* couldn't they do things like other people?

"Starfleet's sending a group to examine the colony's defense systems. It will take a couple of days and I thought maybe it was time for Goldenbird to get a taste of spaceflight."

Kathryn's heart hammered in her chest. A trip with Daddy—and not just a trip but a visit to another planet! She'd been dreaming of this since she'd been old enough to realize that people could travel through the stars to other worlds.

"I want to go, too!" yelped Phoebe. Kathryn's head whipped toward her instantly.

"You can't. You're too little."

"Kathryn . . ." murmured her mother.

"Daddy, can I? Can I go, too?" Phoebe's impish face looked imploringly at her father, blue eyes wide and intense. She looked so pathetic that for a brief moment Kathryn thought Daddy might actually say yes.

"I'm sorry, Phoebe, but Starfleet has rules. You're a little young."

Phoebe's eyes welled up with tears, and even Kathryn felt sorry for her.

"Phoebe, you can use my padds while I'm gone. As long as you're careful."

Now the blue eyes turned toward her, tears instantly retreating. "I *can?*" Phoebe constantly badgered Kathryn to use her padds, with their myriad games, stories, and songs.

"That's very thoughtful, Kathryn," said her mother.

And it was. Ordinarily she wouldn't let Phoebe within ten meters of her things. But she could afford to be generous tonight. She was going to Mars!

The transport to San Francisco was no different from any other: a brief moment of disorientation as one's vision obscured, then a tingling sensation as different surroundings sparkled into clarity.

Kathryn and her father materialized on one of the transporter pads of Starfleet Headquarters; waiting for them was a small retinue, including an admiral, two captains, and a lieutenant who stood deferentially behind the others.

"Well, Edward," said the admiral to her father, "whom do we have here? A stowaway?" He was a tall, florid man with Irish red hair that didn't quite look under control. His smile was lopsided and cheerful.

"A future cadet, I hope. Admiral Finnegan, may I present my daughter, Kathryn."

Kathryn knew how to behave in situations like this. She approached the man, offered her hand, and said, "How do you do?"

The older man smiled down at her. "I do very well, beautiful lady. How about you?"

She blushed at his compliment. "Fine, thank you, sir." She was wearing a brand-new turquoise jumpsuit that her mother had replicated for the occasion, and she imagined that it resembled the uniforms worn by her father and the others. She felt crisp and military.

"Captains Laurel and Dobrynin, Lieutenant Kashut, Kathryn Janeway." Kathryn shook hands with each of them, solemnly and politely.

"Shall we?" Admiral Finnegan gestured again toward the transporter pad. "Our shuttle is ready and we have a pilot standing by."

And once more they dematerialized, only to find themselves, seconds later, in the spacedock which orbited Earth's northern hemisphere.

Kathryn had never seen anything so astonishing.

It was huge, with cavernous hangars and dozens of docking piers, cargo bays, and corridors. Windows to space were everywhere, affording incredible views. Earth swam below them, blue and cloud-shrouded, a stately orb that soared majestically in the starry heavens.

Kathryn had seen pictures, of course, but nothing had prepared her for the sight of her planet from space. She stood at one of the huge windows, staring at the jeweled sphere, trying to figure out where Indiana was.

"Amazing, isn't it?" She looked up to see her father standing next to her. "I remember the first time I saw Earth like that. I was about your age."

"Is that when you decided to join Starfleet?"

He smiled at her, gray eyes crinkling at the edges. "I think I decided that before I was born."

"Did you mean it when you told them I'd be a cadet someday?"

"Only if that's what you want."

"It is, Daddy. More than anything."

He put a hand on her shoulder and looked down at her for a moment. He did that from time to time, and Kathryn never knew what he was thinking.

"We're ready to go now," he said, and she took his hand as they entered the shuttlebay.

Standing at stiff attention next to a Starfleet shuttle was a cadet wearing the uniform of Starfleet Academy. He looked very odd to Kathryn. His skin was a light golden color, and his eyes were pale. She tried not to stare at him. Admiral Finnegan nodded to the cadet as they entered the shuttle.

"We have a very important young guest today, Mr. Data, so make this flight nice and smooth."

"Yes, sir," replied the cadet. He had a gentle, soothing voice. Kathryn looked up at him as she passed by, and this time he didn't look so strange. He had an air of imperturbability that was appealing.

The group took their seats in the shuttle, and the cadet boarded last. He began working the controls, and Kathryn was reminded of her piano teacher, whose fingers roamed so effortlessly and precisely over the keys.

"Shuttle *Curie* to docking control. Ready for pre-launch sequencing." The cadet's voice was as confident and poised as his demeanor.

"Control to *Curie*. Prelaunch sequencing under way. You may proceed."

The cadet continued his manipulation of the controls.

The hatch closed, the shuttlebay decompressed, and the small craft lifted smoothly off the deck, heading for the giant doors which even now were gliding open.

"Shuttle *Curie* to docking control. Approaching portals. Ready for egress."

"Go ahead, *Curie*. Smooth sailing."

Kathryn held her breath. It was a regal moment, endowed with wonder and mystery. Gracefully, silently, the vessel passed through the massive portals and into the inky void of space.

Only the faint hum of the impulse engines broke a silence that seemed almost holy. Kathryn sat with nose pressed against a window, staring back as the spacedock receded from view, growing smaller and smaller until she could no longer see it. Earth was diminishing, too; soon it was a small blue dot and finally only a circle of light.

Three hours later, Mars became a visible disk. Kathryn stared as it grew larger and larger; the first discernible feature she spotted on it was a whitish spot, almost like a tiny star, twinkling at one edge of the disk.

"That's the southern polar cap," said Daddy, as though reading her mind. "It's always the first thing you notice on Mars. Even though the planet's been terraformed, the southern polar cap is still frozen—but it's mostly carbon dioxide that's frozen, not water."

Kathryn searched her memory for her history lessons, and wished she had given them as much time and attention as she had science and mathematics. She vaguely remembered reading about the colonization of Mars, but it had struck her at the time as somewhat unremarkable. After all, space travelers now flew to other systems, other sectors; what was so amazing about a colony in one's own planetary system?

But as multi-hued Mars loomed in front of her, it seemed extraordinary indeed. Patches of red were still visible on the planet—oxidized dust, which had given it the nickname "the red planet" several centuries ago. But now there were vast areas of blue and green, and wisps of white water-vapor clouds hanging in the atmosphere. It didn't look like Earth, but it looked like a fertile, living planet.

The transformation had been a massive undertaking, made possible with help from the Vulcans, the first off-world species to make contact with humans. That memorable meeting had taken place in 2063, the year Zefram Cochrane had launched the first warp flight and alerted the spacefaring Vulcans that Earth was ready to take its place in the interplanetary community.

Kathryn had studied all that in her history class. How Cochrane's revolutionary discovery had lifted Earth from the chaos it had endured in the early part of the twenty-first century, how the arrival of the Vulcans had forged an alliance that carried Earth into a technological renaissance that eventually resulted in the creation of such now-familiar conveniences as replicators and transporters.

But the first great project was the colonization of Mars, and she was not clear on the details. However, she was not about to admit that to her father, and so she affected a nonchalant attitude and informed him, "I know all about that, Daddy. We studied it in school."

And so there was no more discussion of Mars, even though Kathryn would love to have heard the details.

Soon they docked at Utopia Planitia, the huge orbiting space station that also served as a shipbuilding facility for Starfleet, and then were transported into an operations center on the surface. It was a large room full of equipment—consoles, monitors, what seemed like thousands of blinking colored lights—and people busy manning that equipment. Kathryn was fascinated. She wanted to stay in that room and try to figure out exactly what everyone was doing, what function all those blinking lights served. But that was not to be.

"Mr. Data, would you please give our young guest a tour of the colony? You're familiar with the place, aren't you?" Kathryn noted that Admiral Finnegan's Adam's apple bobbed up and down as he spoke.

"Indeed, sir. I completed an engineering honorarium here a year ago. I am thoroughly familiar with the colony and its environs." The cadet turned to Kathryn. "I would be pleased to act as your guide, Miss Janeway."

Kathryn smiled inwardly at the man's formality, but she would never show her amusement—that would be impolite. Solemnly she looked at him and said, "Thank you, sir."

Kathryn looked at Daddy, who was already moving off with the others, heads together, in deep conversation. She felt a momentary twinge of something she couldn't identify as she saw him walking off. She was alone here, on another planet, and Daddy was leaving her. She felt her heart start to beat more quickly, and there was a funny sensation in her stomach.

Then she heard the cadet's quiet, placating voice. "Strictly speaking, Miss Janeway, it is not necessary for you to address me as 'sir.' I do not outrank you, for you have no Starfleet rank at all."

"Then what should I call you?"

"Data would be satisfactory."

"Data?" Kathryn tried to find a polite way to phrase her next question. "Is that a common name among your species?"

"I have no species. I am an artificial intelligence, and so far as I know, the only one of my kind."

Kathryn stared at him. She knew she was being rude, but she could hardly believe her ears. "Are you saying . . . you're not real?"

52

"I assure you I am quite real. However, I lack any true biological component. I was constructed and then programmed." And, to demonstrate, he snapped open a portion of his wrist.

Kathryn almost jumped. Revealed under his skin—skin?—was a mass of circuitry, a complex web of optical fibers and blinking lights. She looked up at him, amazed, and dozens of questions began flooding her mind.

"Who made you? And programmed you? Where did it happen? How did you get into Starfleet Academy—" Suddenly she stopped and covered her mouth. "I'm sorry. I'm being too curious. Mommy says I have to be careful or I might hurt people's feelings."

"I have no emotions which might be wounded, so you may feel free to ask me any question you like. I shall be happy to respond."

And as they toured Mars Colony, Data began to tell her about his unique origins. Within minutes, Kathryn had lost her anxieties, and found that she was in fact comfortable asking him anything and everything, for he seemed to know more than anyone she'd ever met, even Daddy.

"Terraforming Mars was a viable concept by the end of the twentieth century," he told her. "But all the theorizing was done envisioning only the technology that existed at the time. No one ever imagined making contact with the Vulcans, or what a technological breakthrough they would help us establish."

They were walking outside in a Martian atmosphere that no longer required spacesuits or even O_2 concentrators to breathe. Before them swept a vast plain studded with oak trees—genetically engineered, to be sure, but recognizable just the same—that grew to towering heights because of the low Martian gravitational pull. Beyond that lay the deceptively gentle slope that led to the top of Olympus Mons, the highest point on Mars (and three times as high as Mount Everest, the highest point on Earth); it, too, was covered with trees, though pines predominated at the upper elevations.

"Warming the planet was accomplished in a fraction of the time twenty-first-century scientists had predicted. Water and oxygen were liberated from the subterranean permafrost and genetically engineered bacteria were introduced into the terrain. This began the terraforming process. There were colonists living on Mars as early as 2103, but they needed atmospheric suits in order to breathe outside a biosphere. Not quite one hundred years after that, Mars possessed a breathable atmosphere."

They had approached a huge, man-made quarry that, Kathryn noted, contained water. "These are quarries left by the first mining projects on Mars," explained Data. "The earliest colonists utilized local resources, mining the elements to build habitable structures."

Some of Kathryn's history lesson came back to her. "They mined something that helped them make concrete. . . ."

"This is correct. Basaltic regolith exists in large quantities on this planet. Refined and mixed with water, it forms a crude concrete. This process was far more efficient than trying to bring building materials from Earth."

"Why is there water in the quarry now?"

"When the quarries were abandoned, they filled with water from the underlying cave systems. Mars had quite a wet beginning, you see; rivers, streams, and lava flows carved caves just as they did on Earth."

The pale being stared down into the clear water of the quarries. "In summer these quarries are quite popular as swimming sites." He glanced down at his small charge. "Although I am told that adults frown on children utilizing them in that way, since they are not serviced by lifeguards."

Kathryn smiled to herself. This fascinating person said things that were funny, yet she was sure he didn't intend them that way, or even realize that's how they came out.

But her mind had filed away an interesting piece of information: children weren't supposed to swim in the quarries. Why that seemed interesting, she wasn't sure, but it did.

CHAPTER

5

HARRY KIM WAS FASCINATED. FOR THE PAST TWO HOURS, THE trail of burial markers had led the group from one site to another, each one larger and more elaborate than the one before. The arrangements of the flying creatures' delicate skeletons became more complex as they went, curves and loops and spirals composed of the bleached white bones of the beings who had once inhabited this place.

"What do you think it means, Lieutenant?" he asked Tuvok. "It seems as though we're being led somewhere—somewhere important."

Tuvok, he knew, was more concerned with reestablishing contact with *Voyager* than with conjecturing about an archaeological site. But Harry also knew that it wasn't unusual for an away team to lose temporary contact with the ship, as there were many kinds of interference that would cause trouble with the long-range comm system. And he was too caught up in the present mystery to worry unduly about what was probably a routine mishap. He waited until he had Tuvok's attention.

"It may be," the Vulcan mused, "that the eventual goal will be what the inhabitants considered the most important site—the grave of a leader or great dignitary, or possibly the location of sacrificial offerings."

Harry stared at the intricate grouping of skeletons that lay before them, dozens of them laid out in a series of concentric circles. Was it possible these magnificent creatures had been sacrificed to some deity, living or imagined? The thought gave him a chill, even though he knew through his studies that many species—including his own—had at one time performed such rituals.

Unbidden, the moment of sacrifice flashed through his mind: a priestly knife held high, plunging, gouts of blood spraying a feathered spasm, then stillness, great wings forever closed. He shook his head to clear it of such disturbing thoughts and began to search for the next blue spire, the marker for the next site.

He couldn't find it.

Perplexed, he turned toward Tuvok, who was also scanning with both eyes and tricorder, his dark forehead furrowed. "I don't get it, sir," said Harry. "It doesn't seem like this should be the end of the line—there's nothing particularly special about this site."

"Agreed, Ensign. It may be that the location of the final site is hidden, protected in some way in order to provide a defense against defiling or looting."

Harry looked around. No clues presented themselves. The green slime of the ground was unmarked; the flora dense and solid. It was as though the trail simply ended. And yet he knew there must be more. The trail had been so clear, so explicit.

And then the thought struck him, like a spoken voice in his mind: *"For anyone on the ground."*

The trail could be followed by anyone on the ground. But these were beings capable of flight. The markers of the final location might be visible only from the air.

"I've got it, sir," he said excitedly. "There must be a pattern that can be seen from the air, not the ground."

Tuvok understood immediately. "That would be logical, Ensign. Proceed with that hypothesis."

"I'm going to enter the coordinates of every marker we've encountered. The tricorder will able to extrapolate an aerial view."

Excited now, he plunged into the overgrown thatch of the vegetation that surrounded them.

Jal Sittik emerged from the Kazon shuttle and moved eagerly into the hot sunlight.

Today would be the day he would achieve greatness.

He took a deep breath, drawing warm air into his lungs, feeling them expand and imagining they were drawing power into his body—power that would, on this day, cause him to achieve a great triumph: victory over the puny Federations.

Jal Sittik put his hands on his hips and faced into the sun, filling his lungs with strength, summoning his virility so that his men could look on him and derive strength from him, and bless their good fortune in being part of his great destiny.

He knew that he struck a fine figure for his men to witness. The adornments in his hair were impressive: for each of his kills, he had woven a Behrni stone into a lock of hair. By now, his head was crowned with a mass of the veined green stones. After today, there would be more.

He thought of the glory that would soon be his as his eyes scanned the strange, alien landscape. His Maje would reward him handsomely. He would sit at the right side of his leader, whispering into his ear, counseling him on matters of battle and intrigue. Other men would envy him, jealous of his strength and courage, and would urge their sons to emulate him.

And, finally, he would erase the humiliating—and completely unwarranted—stigma that had attached itself to him following an ugly little encounter with the Nistrim. Memory of the incident still burned within him, like a burning coal that retains heat, able to sear flesh for hours.

How could he be faulted because a young man took foolish risks in order to earn a name? He was a warrior, not a nursemaid. And if young Hekkar chose to make what amounted to a suicide run on a Nistrim encampment, how could Jal Sittik be held responsible?

Maje Dut, however, saw the incident differently. Sittik had been severely treated, held in chains for two weeks; the wounds to his wrists and ankles were just healing, and he would carry the scars forever. Proudly, of course.

He was certain some members of his squad had given the Maje a flawed report of the incident. Miskk, for one, could be counted on to color the story so that Sittik would emerge in the worst possible light. Miskk was a sycophant, shamelessly willing to exploit the fact that young Hekkar was the Maje's nephew and that his death would understandably leave the irascible Dut in a vengeful fury. Miskk would learn that betraying Jal Sittik was a grievous mistake.

For today he would erase the memory of that prior mishap and replace it with triumph. Maje Dut would embrace him once more. Women would ache for his recognition. They would parade before him, dressed in provocative gowns, oiling and scenting themselves in their efforts to arouse him, desperate to be chosen by Jal Sittik.

But he would take his time. He would drive them into a frenzy of display by not responding to them. He would toy with them, pretending disdain, until they went to greater and greater lengths to capture his attention.

By the time he made his selection, there would be nothing the chosen woman would not do for him.

Sittik surveyed his men. They were edgy and keen for battle; he had whipped them to a furor of blood lust, and they were eager to enjoin the enemy. Several were young men who had not yet earned their names; they were particularly eager to distinguish themselves, preferably through killing their adversaries with their bare hands.

Power rippled through his veins; he could feel it, a palpable energy that was both mastery and desire. Erotic stirrings coalesced with the anticipation of combat, a potent narcotic that made him heady with anticipation.

"Today!" he shouted to his men, a promise of victory, and was rewarded with their resounding war cry. Was there anything more glorious, he wondered, than the comradeship of fellow warriors at the moment of battle?

Then he struck out across the overgrown terrain, confident and eager.

Neelix had been successful in discovering any number of edible plants—tubers, fruits, and vegetables—that could be harvested and that showed no toxicity after tricorder scans. There was an entire grove of a spicy red fruit that was shaped like a sphere, had a pleasant, crunchy texture, and appeared abundant in nutritional elements. The grove was deep and thick, the gnarled trunks and thick leafy canopy shutting out almost all light. Nate LeFevre stood next to him, peering into the gloom.

"The fruit might not be good in there," the rangy, redheaded crewman said. "No light's getting in. I doubt the fruit would ripen."

"No matter," replied Neelix. "We'll harvest what we can

from the periphery, then move into the interior. If the fruit's no good, we don't have to pick it."

"I'd like to get as much as we can," proffered LeFevre. "That's the best food I've eaten in a long time."

Neelix sniffed. He couldn't understand the culinary preferences of humans. Leola root, prized *everywhere* as a rare delicacy, went unappreciated by *Voyager*'s crew. And this new fruit, while perfectly acceptable, seemed ordinary to Neelix. There was no accounting for taste.

The group of ten had seemingly gotten over their initial disappointment in not going with the archaeological group, and were collecting the foodstuffs earnestly, talking and laughing with irrepressible good spirits. Greta Kale was energetic and good-humored; she set a standard for the others, and Neelix was grateful for her presence.

He was scanning the fruit grove aimlessly, wondering if there was any purpose in moving into its dark depths, when he noticed something disconcerting. On the tricorder there were ever-so-faint but unmistakable life signs emanating from within the grove—an animal species, from first indications. They might be harmless, but it was one more argument against venturing into the dark and foreboding forest.

He turned to tell the others to start collecting the fruit when he detected yet another life-sign reading—this one far more disturbing. He hit his commbadge.

"Neelix to Tuvok."

"I'm here, Neelix."

"I'm reading humanoids on the planet. A sizable group, no more than two kilometers from here, and moving toward us."

"I read them, also."

"Perhaps we should return to *Voyager* to be on the safe side."

"That would be the prudent course. But we have lost communication with the ship."

This was disquieting. Was there damage to the comm system? Or did the humanoid presence on the planet indicate that *Voyager* was under attack? Neelix hoped Tuvok had been thinking of the problem and already had a plan in mind. He was not disappointed.

"Mr. Neelix, do you have a fix on our location? I believe we should unite our groups."

"I have your coordinates, but we'll be taking an indirect route. A direct line to you would take us through a thick grove of trees I'd prefer not to wade through."

"Understood. Bring your group around it."

And that's what Neelix intended to do. But almost as soon as the group had been collected and given their orders, that possibility was snatched from them. Ensign Kale moved toward him, freckles standing out on her pale face.

"Mr. Neelix, my readings show that if we move in an easterly direction around the trees, we'll run into a deep ravine. It'd be pretty tough to get across—maybe impossible. If we go in a westerly direction we'd be moving directly into the path of the humanoids."

Hesitating before making a decision, Neelix scanned in the direction of the humanoids once more, didn't like what he saw, and checked his readings again. Now the life signs could be read clearly: they were Kazon, and they were moving quickly. Neelix stared into the tenebrous depths of the copse of trees, ominous and foreboding. He pointed. "This way," he said, and instantly trotted into the murky, tangled corridor of trees before he could think better of it.

CHAPTER

6

KATHRYN RACED THROUGH THE HERB FIELDS, HEART POUNDING and lungs burning. How could she have lost track of the time? One minute the morning had been fresh and cool, sun low in the sky and dew still clinging to the herb gardens. What seemed like minutes later the sun was overhead and beating mercilessly down; hours had gone by and now she had only minutes to get ready and meet the team at the transport site.

She clutched the padd in her hand as she ran. That's what had betrayed her, of course. She'd gone out to her favorite study spot, a hilly knoll between herb fields, with a willow tree that cast delicate shadows on the ground below. Kathryn had climbed the tree several years ago, when she was nine, and discovered a comfortable "chair" of tree limbs, against which she could sprawl comfortably and read, study, or just daydream.

She loved the tree. If she was troubled, she came to it. If she was faced with a problem, an hour in the tree frequently provided the solution. If she faced a difficult test in school, the leafy bough of the tree provided a tranquillity that cleared the mind and made study efficiently easy.

She'd come there early this morning because she was determined to understand the derivation of the distance formula. She was convinced that if she did, Daddy would be so proud of her that he'd spend more time at home, more time with her, the way he used to when she was little.

She didn't know what had happened lately, why Daddy had to be away from home so much. It used to be that he would transport to Starfleet Headquarters once or twice a week, staying at home the rest of the time to work. But something was going on; she had sensed it about a year ago, when Daddy began to transport to San Francisco almost every day. Occasionally she heard him talking with Mommy, and she had heard him mention a species called Cardassians. And when he talked about them, he seemed very worried.

He began staying in San Francisco for days at a time, then weeks at a time. It had been a month since she'd seen him, but he was going to be back tonight. She desperately wanted to show him she could derive the distance formula, and watch his face light up as he realized what she'd been able to do.

Finding the numerical value of the distance between two points was simple, of course: just plug the Cartesian coordinates of the two points into the padd and it would give you the distance.

The hard part was to find the formula that would apply to any pair of coordinates. That was the kind of thinking Daddy expected of her. But in spite of hours of working the problem, coming at it from every angle she could think of, the solution remained elusive. And then she looked up and realized how late it was.

She burst onto the patio of her house, right by a startled

Mom and Phoebe, and past Bramble, who rose immediately to run after her, through the door and into the breakfast room, down the hall to her room. She slammed the door open and began stripping off her clothes, reaching at the same time for the uniform on her bed. Haste made her hands clumsy, and she stamped her feet in frustration; under her breath she said one of the words that weren't supposed to be said except at times of great distress. Pants were on, then shirt and jacket, shoes. She glanced in the mirror and saw that she looked frazzled and unkempt. There was no time to do anything with her hair, so she ran her fingers through the fine, reddish brown locks and watched them lie limp on her head, damp from perspiration.

Habit made her reach for the cylinder of sun protector; she tapped the lever that opened the dispenser at the top of the cylinder—

—and screamed as something leapt out of the cylinder, something long and serpentine, springing up and at her in an explosion of energy. Her heart raced in shock and her stomach knotted as she stumbled backward, tumbling back and catching herself awkwardly on one wrist.

And then she heard Phoebe giggling.

She looked and saw her eight-year-old sister standing in the doorway, hands cupped over her mouth, unable to choke back the giggles that erupted from her. Kathryn stared at her, then looked over to see the thing that had erupted from the cylinder. It was a long coil of polymer that had been jammed down into the container of sun protector—the one thing Phoebe knew she would never leave for a game without using. She stared at her sister, trying to understand this cruel betrayal.

"It isn't funny!" she yelled. But that only made Phoebe laugh harder.

Kathryn turned and grabbed her bag, brushed past her

sister at the door, and ran outside toward her hovercycle. She had only minutes to get to the school transport site; she was frantic, unprepared, and furious. And in that state she would have to function as captain of her tennis team.

Kathryn and her team materialized on the transport pad of the Academy Institute's athletic department. Like all the Institute's facilities, the transporter site was sleek and pristine, a cool, blue-gray room, spare and unadorned. An Institute cadet manned the console, and like all the others, she was (it seemed to Kathryn) faintly condescending.

Kathryn had wanted to attend the Institute. Each state had such a school geared for a pre-Starfleet Academy curriculum, and created to channel the best and the brightest right to San Francisco. Kathryn could easily have qualified, but her parents had instead chosen The Meadows for her and Phoebe. They believed the Institute provided too narrow a curriculum for young people, and preferred the more liberal, wide-ranging philosophy of The Meadows, which emphasized creative experiences and physical conditioning along with academics. Its goal was to produced well-rounded young people, rather than superstars of select disciplines.

Kathryn would have been much happier at the Institute. She wouldn't have had to take such pointless, traditional studies as piano, ballet, and cooking. *Cooking,* for heaven's sake! Who would ever need to know how to cook? She could have concentrated on mathematics instead.

She and her six teammates stepped off the pad; the uniformed, female cadet barely inclined her head toward them. Students from The Meadows were considered somewhat odd, generally undisciplined, and most definitely inferior. Kathryn made an inner decision to return to the transport site victorious, and make sure the condescending cadet knew it.

The seven team members carried their tennis bags toward the Institute's beautifully landscaped courts. The school was an immaculately groomed facility, with rich green lawns and precisely planted shrubbery surrounding low, sleek classrooms. Kathryn always felt ambivalent about being on the grounds; on the one hand she loved the ordered neatness of the place and felt comfortable there— as though she *belonged*—but this was offset by resentment that she wasn't a permanent student there, and had to endure the cluttered atmosphere of The Meadows, whose sprawling grounds lacked both symmetry and organization.

Heat waves rose from the ground, and billowing white clouds hung heavily in the sky. The air was damp and close; it would rain before nightfall. These weren't optimum conditions for playing a grueling tennis match, and Kathryn had no doubt that today's would be grueling.

She had played her rival before. Her name was Shalarik, a Vulcan exchange student whose imperturbable demeanor on the court was unsettling. But she was attackable, and if she was broken early, her tightly controlled emotions became an obstacle, because she was unable to use her feelings to generate momentum.

Kathryn's advantages lay in her head. She could analyze an opponent's game with mathematical precision, then devise countermeasures to thwart and frustrate the adversary on the other side of the net. That tactical capacity was what had made tennis tolerable, and gradually turned it into a challenge that she had determined to conquer. Her backhand was the first stroke to solidify, and it became a formidable weapon. She loved the feel of it, the coiling of her body, knees bent deeply, the drive forward as she uncoiled and whacked the stuffing out of the ball. It gave her an intoxicating sense of power. Two years later, she was captain of the team.

Strategy was key today. If she could keep pressure on Shalarik, hitting deep to the baseline, punishing her with the powerful backhand, trying to force a short ball so she could come to the net, she could win. And at least she would greet Daddy tonight with a victory to report.

Four hours later she was crawling through a muddy field, sobbing uncontrollably, soaked to the skin from a pounding thunderstorm. Wind whipped at her, driving stinging rain into her face, and her throat ached from the harsh sobs that racked her.

It had been humiliating.

From the beginning of her match, nothing had gone right. She was unfocused and erratic. Her stamina was low (probably as a result of her two-mile run through the herb fields) and she tired early. Shalarik's controlled, precise shots were unerring; she kept Kathryn off balance all afternoon. No strategy Kathryn tried was successful, and the Vulcan broke her serve immediately and then just kept winning.

Kathryn won only one game in the entire match, which ended 6–1, 6–0. Her loss allowed the Institute team to win the match and the season. She had let everybody down.

Her teammates had tried to console her, but she was beyond solace. She refused to go to the transport site— walk by that snotty cadet?—and instead struck out, walking, determined to hike the entire twenty miles back to school, punishing herself for this intolerable defeat.

The storm burst only minutes after she started out. There had been a quickening of the breeze, a sudden drop in temperature, and then the first crack of thunder followed only seconds later by lightning. So close so quickly! The noise was unnerving, and she stepped up her pace.

But only minutes later the clouds burst open and deposited their abundant load into the wind-whipped atmosphere, and almost immediately Kathryn was drenched and the ground beneath her had turned to soup.

She slogged on, legs covered in mud, mud sucking at her shoes and creeping in to coat her feet. The rain lashed at her even harder, and the wind almost hammered her off her feet. She had to lean into the wind, head down, driving forward with all her strength.

Tears began to sting her eyes, and then they poured freely, mixing with cold rain; great sobs began to rack her. Never in her life had she been more miserable. And yet the very misery was soothing; she *deserved* to be miserable after today.

Somewhere in the distance, she saw the faint lights of a hovercraft. It shouldn't be out in this storm, she knew; hovercraft were at risk in storms. Whoever it was was probably looking for cover.

Then she realized how dark it had become. The wind had died down a little, and the thunder seemed to be moving on, but there was still a steady downpour. And it was night. Kathryn reached automatically for her bicorder, which would give her bearings, then remembered that she was in her tennis uniform. She stopped, turning around in the rainy darkness, and realized she had lost her sense of direction. No stars were visible, no distinctive landmarks stood out. She could make out fields, and rolling hills, and a wooded area, but which way was home?

Her tears dried up as her mind went into gear. What should she do? Stay put, that's what. She'd always been told that if she was lost she shouldn't wander. Sit down and stay there.

The rain was diminishing. She put her tennis bag on the mucky ground, sat down next to it, and then laid her head on the bag, an impromptu pillow. She could sleep right here, and tomorrow when the sun came up she would find her way home. She realized she was exhausted. She closed her eyes, and her mind drifted to analytic geometry and the distance formula. She felt drained of energy and emotion, and her mind became still and calm. And as soon as she stopped trying so hard to get it, the solution immediately became apparent to her.

It lay in antiquity. Nearly three thousand years ago, a visionary mathematician named Pythagoras had developed a theorem that related the sides of a right triangle to the length of the hypotenuse—the distance between two end points. With sudden, vivid insight, Kathryn realized that this was the solution to the derivation of the distance formula.

And then her father lifted her up.

She felt his strong arms grip her, pulling her to him, his handsome, sturdy face etched with concern and relief. Kathryn smiled at him and relaxed into the journey, safe in his arms until he had put her into the hovercraft and wrapped her in a blanket.

"I saw lights," she murmured, still drowsy. "Was that you? You shouldn't be out in a storm."

"You were out here, Kathryn. I had to find you."

"I'm sorry, Daddy."

"What were you thinking?"

"I lost my match. I didn't deserve to come home with the others." She felt his eyes turn to her, and he was quiet for a moment. "But guess what?" she went on. "I figured out how to derive the distance formula. It's the Pythagorean theorem, isn't it?"

She heard him chuckle. "You're a funny little bird, you know." He eyed her mud-splattered body. "Tonight you're a blackbird." There was a silence, and then he looked over at her. "Kathryn, I want you to promise me you'll never do anything like this again. We were all worried sick about you."

"I promise, Daddy." She waited for him to praise her for

figuring out the distance formula, but he didn't talk about anything except how frightened they'd been. When they got home, her mother put her in the sonic shower and then tucked her into bed with hot soup, but Daddy had gone to his office and didn't even come out to say good night.

Under the warm covers, sipping hot soup, Kathryn was nonetheless ice cold. Her heart felt like stone. Daddy didn't even *care* that she had derived the formula. She was more miserable than she had been lying in the cold mud with the rain pouring down on her.

CHAPTER

7

THE CAPTIVE LAY ON THE TABLE, EYES GRADUALLY LOSING A struggle to stay open as the narcotic had its inevitable effect on his system. It had proven necessary to keep the prisoner under almost constant sedation, a situation Trakis, the Trabe physician, regretted because he was uncertain as to the ultimate effect of such high levels of drugs on this alien being.

However, unless he was narcotized, the captive had demonstrated an alarming unwillingness to cooperate with Trakis' examinations. Perhaps all members of this species were similarly truculent, or perhaps this one was particularly fierce, but Trakis had no intention of coming to bodily harm in order to aid the Kazon-Vistik in their vain quest for control of the sector.

A noise startled him as the door to the ship's laboratory opened, and Nimmet entered, swaggering slightly, as always, adopting an air of lofty condescension intended to make Trakis feel insignificant.

Would it matter, wondered Trakis, if Nimmet knew that his posturing had quite the opposite effect: made Trakis feel decidedly superior to this preening toady Kazon, who rendered himself ridiculous with his mannered arrogance?

Nimmet was his Control. He had been assigned to Trakis soon after the physician had been abducted from the Trabe outpost on Slngsnd and brought to the Kazon ship. Trakis was not the only Trabe on board, but he was the only physician. The smug but foolish Vistik hadn't even bothered to abduct a physician until they had a specific purpose—as though they had no need of regular medical examinations themselves. Pride would be their undoing, Trakis reflected.

"Well?" Nimmet all but barked the question. Trakis turned to look disdainfully at him.

"You have eyes. You can see. I've done nothing more."

Nimmet's eyes flared. Trakis knew he became furious when treated with such disrespect, but he also knew Nimmet couldn't retaliate: Trakis was necessary to their mission and couldn't be harmed until it was completed.

Afterward, of course, was a different story, but Trakis was already laying his plans for escape before he became expendable.

Nimmet advanced toward him, narrowing his eyes to slits and adopting his most menacing growl. "Why not? Maje Dut is waiting for your report."

"The Maje will have to wait. I cannot do these procedures any faster than they can be done."

"Do you know what the Maje would say if I told him that?"

"He would explode in a tirade of fury, threaten to cut off my fingers, and then realize he has no choice but to let me proceed as best I can."

Nimmet then tried to squeeze his eyes into even narrower slits as though that would intimidate Trakis, but the physician knew how to respond to this posturing. He turned his back and approached the captive, now unconscious on the table.

"I can perform the examination now," said the physician matter-of-factly. He was busily keying controls at a large console, quickly scrolling through blocks of data. "Although with this outmoded equipment I can't guarantee the accuracy."

"That is equipment the Trabe constructed," Nimmet reminded him, still trying to get the upper hand in the relationship.

"Over a quarter of a century ago. The Kazon have simply driven our technology into the ground—no upgrades, no innovations, no advances whatsoever. It's a wonder these ships still fly."

"Our engineers have maintained them expertly. As they have the medical equipment. Do not try to excuse your own ineptness by blaming the technology."

Trakis turned slowly to face him. His voice was calm, almost pleasant, as he said, "Perhaps you would prefer one of your own physicians to attend to this matter."

Nimmet flushed. The Kazon had no healers, at least none that didn't do more harm than good. He gestured toward the captive. "Hurry up and do what you must before he wakes up again."

Trakis turned back to his console and began reciting in a near-monotone: "The specimen is approximately one half meter in length and possesses the familiar tripartite construction of parasectoid species: there is a head, birax, and abdomen; the exoskeleton is hard-shelled. There are two sets of wings—durable forewings that resemble the alytron of similar species, and more delicate hind wings folded underneath. Two antennae and four mandibles are present. The head presents an elongated snout with biting jaws.

There are three compound eyes. The underbelly is soft and is green mottled with black.

"The respiratory system is unique; it is clearly constructed for air-breathing but there are adaptations which permit it to exist in various environments. There is an unusual fluid circulating throughout the creature's body, similar in some respects to lymphatic fluid, but possessing superconducting electrical and magnetic properties."

As he spoke, he was aware that Nimmet barely listened. The Kazon didn't understand this medical jargon, didn't care about it, didn't want to be trapped in the bowels of the ship serving as Control to a physician. And it was this indifference that Trakis intended to exploit when the time came.

Neelix and his group had moved quickly into the gloomy grove of trees, but they were soon forced to slow down. The undergrowth was thick and tangled, ripping at faces, hands, uniforms, and hair. It was so dark they had to turn on their wrist beacons, and even then the beams of light seemed to get swallowed in the fetid darkness.

The odor was cloying, a rancid dampness with the telltale sweetness that bespoke rotting flesh. Neelix' mind went briefly to the reading of life-forms he had detected earlier, but he thrust those thoughts out of his mind. They had to get through this dense thicket and unite with Tuvok before the Kazon found them. What followed them was far more threatening than what might lie ahead.

They moved deeper into the copse, the undergrowth thicker all the time, the putrid stench more intense. Neelix turned around to check on the group.

"Everybody present and accounted for?" he queried cheerfully.

"We're here, Mr. Neelix." Ensign Kale's voice drifted from the back of the group.

Neelix turned around again to see what seemed to be an impenetrable obstacle—a solid wall of brush and thicket. Neelix played his beacon around it, looking for a gap, at first finding nothing. Then, at the very bottom, he discovered what looked like a small burrow, a hole that showed evidence of broken branches and so was probably a route that had been used before, probably by some kind of animal. Neelix knelt down and shined his beacon into the hole; it seemed to tunnel through the underbrush for quite a distance. It might take them all the way to the other side.

But that would require a squirming journey on one's belly, inching through the moist, decaying carpet of the forest, into a thick darkness that could conceal—anything. He turned back to the group.

"This looks like the only way through."

The young faces looked at the uninviting tunnel without enthusiasm. No one was eager to crawl into that gamy, sour-smelling burrow, and they all seemed to be trying to come up with another option. But LeFevre wiped out that line of thinking. "Kazon . . . they've reached the clearing."

That meant they'd be moving into the thicket in minutes. Neelix and his group had no choice. They had to try the tunnel.

Neelix took a breath and tried to sound confident. "I think this will take us right through," he said, smiling optimistically, then dropped to his knees and plunged into the jagged opening that might or might not lead them to safety.

Immediately, he began to regret it. They could have taken a stand and fought the Kazon, instead of crawling like insects through this fetid passageway. Brambles snagged at his hair, and he couldn't see a foot ahead. It was moist and hot in there; a dank steam rose from the decaying sludge and the stench was worse than ever. He forced himself to think of Kes, her delicate beauty and her gentle touch, and it helped him to stave off the queasiness he was feeling from being trapped in this hot, smelly enclosure.

He put his hand down in a pile of slime that seemed to be a mixture of fur, bone, and runny gelatin. He didn't want to think what it might once have been. He concentrated on moving steadily forward, inch by reeking inch, hearing behind him the crew, gamely following his lead.

He heard a soft, chafing sound, as though heavy rope were being pulled along the ground, and he turned quickly, shining his beacon into the impenetrable undergrowth. He had a brief impression of slitted eyes that disappeared as the light hit them. Even though he was sweating in the hot, foul air, he was suddenly chilled to the bone. He stepped up his pace.

Eventually, the narrow confines of the tunnel seemed to widen, and soon he was able to crawl without nasty thistles ripping his face and hands. The air seemed slightly cooler. Then he was able to lift his head up, and finally to get to his hands and knees and eventually to stand upright. The tunnel had given way to a wide, canopied passageway, even more spacious than the one they had first entered. Neelix felt like breathing deeply for the first time since they had penetrated this uninviting forest; he turned as the others began emerging from the tunnel, grateful and gasping.

When the last one had crawled free, Neelix lifted his phaser. "Kale, LeFevre, Hutchinson, train your phasers on that thicket. We can make it a little tougher for the Kazon to follow us." Phaser fire collapsed the tunnel, and Neelix smiled to think of the Kazon trying to find their way out of the rancid tunnel.

Ahead less than half a kilometer they could see a small flash of sunlight—the end of the trek through the dense copse of trees and overgrowth. Tuvok's group was beyond, just minutes away now. Neelix waved the group forward and, with a lighter step, they made their way toward the glint of light.

Then something began dropping from the trees.

Neelix sensed, rather than felt, a heavy weight plummet through the air behind him, barely brushing the back of his head and then thudding onto the ground. Puzzled, he turned around in time to see a dark coil enclosing LeFevre's shoulders, heard LeFevre's sudden gasp and then a strangled cry of distress. Neelix had time to register only a dark, serpentine shape before he realized more of them were dropping from the trees, directly onto the hapless crew, hissing fiercely, an awful, caustic sound that heightened the terror of the sudden attack.

And the smell was dreadful. These creatures were the source of the putrefying odor they'd been smelling since they entered the forest, and the viscous fluid that they extruded from long, tubular snouts was a miasma of death and decay. Neelix felt his gorge rise, and he fought a wave of nausea.

He saw LeFevre struggling against tightening coils, hands groping desperately to find the long head that darted just out of his reach. Neelix lifted his phaser, afraid he'd hit LeFevre if he used it. The young man made a strangled cry of pain, and Neelix realized the reptile had encircled him and was crushing his ribs.

The tubelike head of the creature swung into Neelix' vision; ancient, glittering eyes caught his briefly, before Neelix pointed the phaser and blasted directly into those unblinking bronze slits.

There was a thrashing as the serpent's head was flung backward, and then it went limp, coils relaxing and falling away from LeFevre, who gasped for air, drawing in great sucking lungfuls as he pulled the now-flaccid body of the huge reptile from his torso.

Neelix looked up to see the others in similar struggles; a desperate, feral dance was being performed in the dark passageway as the crew wrestled with their hissing attackers. Those who weren't entwined tried to rescue their comrades by phasering the heads of the serpents, but the beasts were deft and agile and getting a target was difficult.

Neelix spotted Greta Kale sagging in the crushing embrace of mottled coils. He started to sprint toward her, then suddenly felt a pressure on his ankle; looking down, he saw a snaky coil wrapped around his leg and a foot-long snout moving toward his head. He fired blindly, missed, saw the coil envelop his leg and begin to tighten, felt his leg go numb immediately, looked for the elongated head, which was bobbing and weaving, fired again and hit the mark, saw the tubed head drop heavily to the ground, and felt his leg regain feeling.

He turned to Greta, who was already turning blue, eyes popped wide. He couldn't isolate the serpent's head; in desperation he put the phaser tip directly against the reptilian body and fired.

The serpent exploded.

A stream of matter and fluid sprayed Neelix, who threw up his hands to ward off gouts of tissue and cartilage. Bits of bone stuck to his face and hair, but Ensign Kale was released, and he could hear her ragged, shallow breathing once more. She moaned, and Neelix guessed she had broken ribs.

Glancing around, he saw that the situation seemed under control: serpents lay dazed or writhing on the ground, and all the crew were standing, some bent over, drawing grateful breaths of air, others warily eyeing the huge coiled reptiles on the ground and scanning the trees for more of the vicious animals.

They weren't, strictly speaking, snakes. On their dark, mottled bodies were a series of small leglike appendages,

JERI TAYLOR

which would serve to give them traction on the ground and a better grip on their victims. Their long snouts could spread wide to ingest prey far larger than they. All in all, they were perfectly hideous creatures.

Neelix shuddered slightly, grateful for Starfleet's powerful phasers. He wasn't sure his would have had the same effect.

He motioned for someone to help him with Greta; they hoisted her between them and hurried toward the light that beckoned to them from the end of the passageway with a comforting golden glow. It seemed to promise safety.

Tuvok scanned once again: Neelix and his group were nearing his location; the Kazon were behind them and moving steadily. It was imperative they find cover.

He turned to eye the members of his squad, who were investigating the terrain for some kind of protection against the Kazon. It did not look promising. There was no high ground to hold, no cover except the woods through which Neelix was now proceeding. Tuvok disliked the prospect of a ground battle with the Kazon without some tactical advantage, but at the moment he saw none.

He turned to see Ensign Kim scanning the ground intently. The young man had been trying to discern a pattern of some kind that could be seen from the air and that might mark the location of a protected tomb or tombs; before they had realized the Kazon were on the planet Kim believed he had identified such a pattern. But that search had stopped as soon as the dangerous intruders had been identified. Now everyone was scanning for caves, which might provide protection.

"Lieutenant Tuvok!" Kim's voice rang through the air. "I've found something!"

Tuvok turned to see Harry standing about fifty meters

away, waving at him. Then the young man abruptly disappeared.

Tuvok was on the run instantly, plunging through the brushy weedbed. As he neared the spot where Kim had disappeared, he could hear the young ensign calling to him.

"This is it, Lieutenant—this is it!"

As Tuvok approached, he realized that a circle of earth had collapsed, not haphazardly, but symmetrically, as though triangular quarters of the circle had given way from the center. A series of gentle ramps was formed, which Tuvok now descended carefully to join Kim, who was standing at the conflux of the triangles, which had deposited him in the center of a huge and cavernous underground vault.

"This must be the tomb. We can use it to take cover."

"Quite right, Mr. Kim. I'll get the others."

Tuvok climbed to the surface once more and hit his commbadge. "Tuvok to all hands. Regroup immediately."

At that moment, he saw Neelix and his group emerging from the forest. He could tell they had wounded among them, and Kes was already on her way to give aid. They were a motley-looking group, hair full of twigs and leaves, uniforms covered with mud and slime, faces bloody. A few were limping; Ensign Kale was carried by Neelix and LeFevre; all bore the signs of trauma. What had they endured?

"This way, Mr. Neelix. We've found cover." The Talaxian gave him a wan smile and herded his group toward Tuvok. Kes was scanning Ensign Kale, assessing her condition.

"We've had quite an adventure, Mr. Vulcan," Neelix began. "I'm sure you'll want to hear all about it—as soon as we've taken cover, of course."

"Of course." Tuvok did not look forward to another of Neelix' endless discourses. The Talaxian had somehow gotten the impression that Tuvok looked forward to hearing him describe his many adventures, in tedious and incessant detail. Even Tuvok's great store of patience was tested by the Talaxian's congenial wordiness.

Tuvok insured that everyone made it safely into the underground cavern, then approached Kim, who was scanning the carved rock wall of the chamber.

"There must be a control apparatus down here to close this thing up. There's one on the surface, pressure-activated. It was disguised in the stonework, but its gravimetric signature was different from the surrounding matter." He moved his tricorder systematically over the wall, looking for any anomalous readings or energy signatures.

"Funny," he mused as he scanned, "I can't figure out what these walls are constructed of. It looks like some kind of stone, but I'm getting strong organic readings from it as well."

"The Delta Quadrant possesses many materials which are unknown to Federation science," offered Tuvok.

"I just hope, whatever it is, it's strong. Strong enough to keep the Kazon out."

"Let us also hope they cannot activate it as we did."

Most of the others had begun to fan out, scanning and exploring. Neelix' group simply sat down, clearly exhausted. Kes moved among them, tending to the injured.

"Ah," said Kim with obvious satisfaction. "Stand back, everybody, I think I've got it." He put his palm on a particular panel in the wall, and with a whoosh of air the ramps began to lift quietly, fitting perfectly together to form a ceiling piece, inexorably shutting out the sunlight.

It was pitch black. Wrist beacons began to snap on, and Tuvok spied magnesite, which he infused with phaser energy for light and heat. Others did the same. A warm glow began to illuminate their new surroundings, erasing ominous shadows and creating an environment that Tuvok hoped would soothe his team. For the moment, they were safe, even if safety lay in the mysterious underground vault of an unknown alien species on a planet sixty-eight thousand light-years from home.

In that way, they waited for the Kazon.

CHAPTER

8

THE GROUND WAS ROUGH AND ROCKY; A JAGGED STONE BIT into Kathryn's leg as she lay, facedown, at the top of the stone quarry, peering at the swimmers below. The sun was high overhead, but unlike the muggy summers at home it was never hot on Mars.

She turned her head toward Emma North, lying next to her; Mary O'Connell was just beyond. All were in swimmers and shirts, and carried bags jammed with music and games, snacks, sun protector, and other items designed for an afternoon of swimming.

"If they see us, they'll tell our folks," Mary said in a hoarse whisper. "I can't believe I let you talk me into this."

Swimming at the quarries on Mars Colony was dangerous and strictly forbidden by their parents. The water was deep and cold, access was difficult, and jagged rock wasn't kind to bare skin. The girls knew, though, that *everyone* did it at some time or another; it had become a rite of passage.

Kathryn had wanted for years to swim the quarries. Starfleet had extensive officers' facilities on Mars Colony, and her family had visited there on a number of summer vacations, but her parents had always kept a close eye on her. Now that she was fourteen, they had relaxed their guard somewhat.

"What are you worried about? People have been swimming here for years. Decades."

"We're still not supposed to be here."

"No one will ever know."

"They will if those people down there see us."

"They won't," said Kathryn confidently. "We're not going there."

Now Emmy look vaguely concerned. "But . . . that's the quarry everybody goes to."

"Not us. I know where there's a smaller one. There are lots of them, actually, a whole network of them that stretch for kilometers through these hills."

"How do you know?"

Kathryn smiled, remembering the day five years before that still was etched indelibly in her memory. "Someone I used to know showed me. He took me all around the colony. Did you know if you use a breathing gill and swim underwater in some of these quarries you can access the cave system under Olympus Mons? There's a whole honeycomb of caves and underwater lakes. To get through them, you have to stay underwater for as much as a kilometer at a time until you reach the next cave. Someday I'm going to do that."

Both girls looked at her as though she'd sprouted warts. "That sounds *awful*," said Mary, and Emma nodded in vigorous agreement. "And dangerous."

"I think it sounds exciting. I know others have done it."

"Have they all come out alive?"

Kathryn hesitated. Data had in fact mentioned a fatality

85

that had occurred during the Olympus Mons cave trek, but that had only intrigued Kathryn, made her more determined to take the challenge someday. She knew, however, that Emma and Mary wouldn't share that response.

"As long as you're an experienced diver it's not dangerous," she said firmly.

"Are you experienced?"

"I have my certification now. I need more practice. That's why I want to go to the quarries."

"I thought we were just going to swim and have fun." This from Emma, who was looking more dubious all the time.

Kathryn sighed. It was getting harder and harder to enjoy Emma and Mary's company. They'd been her best friends since they were little, but it seemed lately they'd become fearful and nervous about every activity she suggested. She was glad she wouldn't be going to school with them any longer.

At long last, she would be attending the Academy Institute. She had battled her parents for years over this issue, and they finally relented when she won the prestigious state mathematics award. She would spend her final four years of preparatory school at the place she knew she should have been attending long ago.

There, at the Institute, she would find new friends, friends more like her who were curious about things, and liked adventure and new experiences. No more tennis, no more piano and ballet. She was finally going to be allowed to enter the twenty-fourth century, and she couldn't wait.

"How far away are these quarries?" Mary sounded uneasy, and Kathryn knew she and Mary were both getting nervous about being so far from the colony.

"Not much farther. Just beyond that next rise."

"We're pretty far away from anyone. What if something happens?"

"Like what?"

"An accident."

Kathryn shot her a look of disdain. "There are three of us. Someone can always go for help." But she knew from the guarded glance the other girls exchanged that they weren't comforted. Kathryn stopped abruptly and faced them.

"Do you want to go back? If so, go ahead. I'll swim by myself."

"Kathryn, that's dangerous. You should never swim alone."

"I'd rather do that than spend time with people who are going to be moping around waiting for dire things to happen." She stood rock still, eyeing Mary and Emma sternly. As she expected, they couldn't hold the look; their eyes danced away nervously and scanned the Martian hills. "Well?" Kathryn shot at them, and Mary looked back at her first.

"We said we'd come and we did. Let's not argue about it."

Kathryn nodded and turned back in the direction of the quarry, heard the other two follow her, and breathed a sigh of resignation. They seemed so *young* to her. How could they all possibly be the same age?

They were climbing a rise that was studded with huge boulders and rocky outcroppings; they had to weave their way through narrow passageways that twisted and wound like a maze. Then they emerged into the open, and found themselves standing on an upward-sloping expanse of flat rock beyond which they could see nothing except sky; a sheer drop-off awaited them. As they neared the edge Emma and Mary hung back, approaching slowly. Kathryn went to all fours and then stretched herself out, inching toward the drop-off.

The abandoned quarry was arrayed before her: steep,

chiseled stone walls that still bore the marks of ultrasonic drills, plummeting down fifty meters to the surface of a clear lake some five hundred meters in diameter. It was a foreboding sight, stark and mysterious, and Kathryn felt her blood tingle with a mixture of apprehension and excitement.

"How are we supposed to get down there?" whispered Emma. Kathryn turned to her.

"Why are you whispering?"

Emma turned to her, dark eyes wide, face pale. "I don't know. It just seems weird here."

"It's strange and beautiful—kind of wild. I like it." Kathryn's eyes were scanning the terrain as she spoke, looking for a route to the water below.

The quarry walls weren't smooth, but craggy, with plenty of handholds. They could make it down.

"We climb. With rough rock like that, it'll be easy."

"I'm not doing that." Mary stood up, looking down at them with total resolve. "That's just asking for trouble."

Kathryn started to retort, but suddenly they all heard the unmistakable sound of footsteps—someone was climbing the rise behind them, moving through the maze of rocks. Mary dropped back to her knees, and guiltily, they all tried to press themselves behind outcroppings. Was it one of their parents? Had someone seen them leave the colony and strike out across the Tharsis plain?

The footsteps came nearer, scuffling on the gravelly ground. A few steps more and the person would emerge from the rocks and out into the open. Kathryn held her breath; she was sure it would be her father, furious with her for having broken an explicit rule.

A figure emerged from the passageway, backlit by the sun and unidentifiable, but it was a man, and he was tall and slender—and Kathryn's stomach turned queasy. It had to be her father.

"Hello, ladies. Going swimming?" The voice was familiar but was definitely not her father's. Kathryn rose and as the figure moved closer, he turned and his face was illuminated.

Hobbes Johnson.

Relief and dismay struggled for supremacy inside Kathryn: that it wasn't her father was a vast comfort, but the sight of Hobbes Johnson, lanky and dull, was about the final dismal touch in a day that had been rapidly going downhill.

"Hobbes, what are you doing here?"

"I could ask you the same thing. Aren't the quarries off-limits to you?"

"At least there are three of us. You came by yourself. That's foolish."

"No, it wasn't. I saw you leaving. I figured you were going to the quarries."

Kathryn felt a rush of annoyance, which, on top of her frustrations with Emma and Mary, pushed her from irritation to anger. "Don't you think if we'd wanted your company, we'd have asked you?"

Hobbes paled at the attack, and Kathryn was immediately sorry. She didn't mean to hurt his feelings, she was just irked. But she saw Mary and Emma looking at her in shocked surprise, and realized she'd gone too far.

"I'm sorry, Hobbes. I didn't mean it . . . it's just been a frustrating day. I really want to go swimming, and I can't seem to get any enthusiasm from these two."

Mary's dander was still up. "I *was* enthusiastic—until I realized how reckless and dangerous this is. Kathryn wants to *climb* down the face of the quarry. That's ridiculous."

"Only way to get there," said Hobbes mildly.

"Well, I'm not doing it. I'm going back."

"Me, too," chimed in Emma, and both rose to their feet.

Kathryn stared at them. Were they abandoning her? Leaving her here with *Hobbes Johnson?* She glared in disbelief.

"Fine," she heard herself saying. "Go on back. If you're not brave enough to do it, I don't want you around." Again, she immediately regretted her words. It was as though her mouth were an organism unto itself, acting without her permission. She saw Mary draw herself up, hurt and angry.

"If you have any sense at all, you'll come back with us. Face it, Kathryn—this was a terrible idea."

"If I decide to do something, I'm not going to back out just because it gets a little difficult. But you do whatever you want." Kathryn's face felt hot, and she realized she was just being stubborn, but the more the conversation went on, the more she felt herself dig in.

"Come on, Mary. Let's go." Emma looked eager to leave the quarry and the unpleasantness. Mary gave Kathryn one more somber look. "Kathryn?"

Kathryn merely shook her head, obstinate. The two other girls shrugged, lifted their bags, and headed for the maze of rocks that would lead them away from the quarry and back toward the colony. Kathryn watched them leave, suddenly feeling alone and friendless.

And worst of all, now she was stuck with Hobbes Johnson. She gave him an awkward glance. He was watching the retreating girls, face impassive. What should she do? Wait a decent interval and then follow them? She couldn't imagine spending another two minutes with Hobbes.

She looked down at the water below, remembering her determination to make it down there, to swim in the clear waters of the quarry, to practice her diving techniques. She felt Hobbes' eyes on her and looked up at him.

He wasn't quite as vulky-looking as he used to be, but no

one would ever call him attractive. He no longer wore braces, but a few red pimples dotted his face; apparently even dermal-regeneration treatments didn't work on his acne. Kathryn thought it looked disgusting.

And he was as thin as ever, a long, reedy boy with a skinny neck and hair that tufted in unruly patches on his head. And there they were, alone together at the top of the quarry. Now what?

"Want to give it a try?" Hobbes' voice was as neutral as ever. It was as though he were suggesting they take a walk through the cornfields.

Kathryn hesitated, options warring within her. She really, really wanted to swim in that quarry. She really, really didn't want to do it with Hobbes Johnson. She glanced down again, saw the clear water below, beckoning to her.

She shrugged, feigning tedium. "Might as well." She hefted her bag, rearranged the straps to carry it on her back, and edged toward the cliff wall to search for the best starting place.

"It's over here," said Hobbes, walking to a small crevasse a few meters away. He stepped easily into it, swinging his body around and deftly grasping handholds. He began climbing confidently down the quarry face, hands and feet finding their way with ease and efficiency.

Kathryn was impressed. She'd done her share of rock climbing—credit The Meadows with that, for including this ancient sport in their physical curriculum—and had always enjoyed the challenge, but she lacked ease and style. She moved to the crevasse, immediately saw the places where Hobbes had found purchase, and began to follow him down the steep wall of the quarry.

Ten minutes later, they stood on a stone shelf that protruded over the water, a natural diving platform.

Hobbes had already opened his bag and was removing his breathing gill and thermal tripolymer suit. Kathryn looked at him in surprise.

"You're going to dive?"

He glanced up at her as he calibrated his breathing gill. "That's why I come here. I'm looking for an opening into the Olympus Mons cave system."

She thought maybe she hadn't heard him correctly. "You? You're looking for the Olympus system?"

His gray eyes sought hers. "Why? Do you know about it?"

She nodded. "Some day I'm going to explore the caves. I'd like to map the system."

"How did you know about the caves?"

"Someone from Starfleet once told me. How did you?"

"I read about them. Some obscure story I found in a historical database at the library."

It figured. Hobbes always had his nose in a padd—and never one anyone else would be caught dead reading.

"So," he continued, "my dad and I have been diving the quarries since last year, looking for an entrance. We've covered about seven of them. We were here a few days ago but my gill started malfunctioning and we had to leave."

"You dad lets you dive the quarries?"

"Sure."

No wonder Hobbes was so strange—he came from a strange family. *No one* let their children go to the quarries. What could his father have been thinking?

"Well, I hope you have enough sense not to dive alone."

"Of course not. Usually I'm with dad. Today I have you."

Something about the placid ease of his presumption rankled Kathryn. She almost said she didn't want to dive, just to punish him for jumping to the conclusion that she'd dive with him, but in time she remembered that it was exactly what she wanted to do, and there was no point in spoiling her day. For once, she managed to squelch herself before she said something she regretted.

Quickly, she pulled on her thermal suit, an intricate web of nichrome filaments that would keep her body comfortably warm even in near-freezing water. They both had equipment they'd used in school, where diving had been taught along with rock climbing, tennis, and swimming. Lightweight tripolymer body suits, vented fins, and the breathing gills, which constantly extracted breathable oxygen from the surrounding water, much like the gills of a fish. Long ago, humans had used bulky oxygen tanks, and then rebreathers, which processed exhaled air, removing the carbon dioxide by mixing it with alkaline hydroxide, and then injecting the resultant oxygen with helium. These tanks would allow divers to stay underwater for up to twenty-four hours at a time.

Now, of course, they could be under for as long as they wanted, just like fish.

They checked each other's buddy lights, readjusted their gills, and then lowered themselves off the platform and into the water.

The first thing she noticed was the cold. The suits they wore were light as cotton, but chemically treated to keep them warm at temperatures as low as two degrees C. Even so, Kathryn felt cool immediately.

The second thing to strike her was the pristine clarity of the water. She felt she could see for a hundred meters—if there had been anything to see. No flora graced this chilly lake, no fauna inhabited its depths. There was nothing except rock and water.

The silence soothed her, as it always did when she was underwater. A sense of tranquillity enveloped her, and she swam effortlessly through the clear water, keeping her eye on the two green buddy lights on Hobbes' back, signaling that he was doing fine.

He was stroking steadily downward, moving toward the periphery of the quarry, searching for an opening in the wall—a crack, a dark spot—something that might indicate the presence of a cave system beyond.

They swam like that for some forty minutes, methodically searching the quarry walls, but finding nothing except impenetrable stone. They had circumnavigated the quarry twice, the second time at a significantly lower depth. Then Hobbes signaled her to surface, and gradually they floated their way to the top.

Kathryn was grateful. She was unpleasantly cold, and thirsty; she wanted to get out for a while, warm up, and have a piece of fruit. But Hobbes had other ideas.

"I think I saw something."

"Where?" Kathryn had been looking as carefully as he had, she was sure, and had detected nothing that resembled an opening in the stone walls.

"It's quite a bit lower than we were. I'd like to go back one more time, leave you at about twenty-five meters while I go check it out."

"That's pretty deep."

"But not past our safety limits. Remember, with Mars's lower gravity, water pressure isn't as intense as on Earth." He eyed her as they trod chilly water. She really wanted to get out and dry off, but she wasn't about to admit that to Hobbes Johnson, of all people. So she nodded and refit her breathing gill. He did the same, and they sank underwater once more.

She followed him down to twenty-five meters, then saw his hand signal for her to hold there. She watched as he stroked deeper into dark waters; she could barely see the flutter of his fins as he moved steadily down into the gloomy depths where sunlight could not penetrate.

Then he disappeared completely.

Kathryn felt a coldness in her stomach which was icier than the quarry water. How would she know if anything happened to him? How deep did he plan to go? How long would it take?

She forced her mind to quiet, breathing steadily, focusing on the sight of her hands floating in front of her, pale and ghostly. Gradually the panic faded, and she peered once more down into the depths of the dark water. She hadn't brought an aquadyne torch, never figuring to be this deep, never thinking she'd have a reason to go where there was no light.

She saw nothing.

Ten minutes passed, and she knew it was time to act. Gradually, she moved herself deeper, breathing regularly, pulling herself down through the water.

As far as she could see below her, there was only darkness. She scanned the wall of the quarry, hoping to discover whatever aberration it was that had drawn Hobbes to these deep waters.

And then she saw it—another five meters below her.

A dark gash in the side of the wall, barely visible in the gloom, no more than a faint shadow. Was that what had caught Hobbes' eye? As she got closer, she could see that the shadow was in fact an opening—a black trench in the rock face some ten meters wide and five meters tall. She pulled steadily toward it.

And then she realized *it* was pulling *her.*

A current was flowing into the opening. She realized that meant it was the ingress to an underground river, perhaps even a network of subterranean caves extending deep into the planet's crust.

She let the current pull her toward the mouth that was now yawning just below her.

And realized, too late, that as soon as she was on a level with the opening, the current became immeasurably stronger, and then she was sucked into the dark hole, out of control.

Desperately, she struggled against the pull, quickly realized it was too strong for her, and lunged for the wall of the cave mouth.

Incredibly, her hands found purchase. An upward-thrusting shard of rock allowed her to grip it firmly, stopping her inexorable drag back into—into what?

Fear paralyzed her for a moment. She thought of her father, how she had been so afraid it was his footsteps they'd heard climbing toward the quarry, wishing now that it had been him and that she were safely back in the colony with him—chastised, to be sure, even restricted. But alive.

Where was Hobbes? Had he been sucked into this channel as well? Clenching the rock with all her might, she gradually turned her head and looked behind her.

She saw the two green buddy lights another five meters in, glowing dully through the pitch black water, not moving, but flickering in and out of her view as the currents of the water struck them. Hobbes must have found something to grab on to, also. For the first time, she realized she could see absolutely nothing; no light penetrated here, and only the flittering green lights interrupted the terrifying darkness.

She'd have to inch her way back to him. She carefully let go with one hand, the other scrabbling along the wall, feeling for a handhold.

She found one. Releasing her other hand, she clutched at the new hold, body pressed as close to the wall of the channel as she could get it. The sucking current was less pronounced there.

Then she repeated the process, minute after agonizing minute, creeping backward centimeters at a time through the darkness and the relentless tug of the icy water. Why, she wondered, wasn't Hobbes doing the same? Pulling himself forward, little by little?

By the time she reached the two lights, she realized why. He wasn't on the cave wall, but out toward the center of the channel. He must have found an obstruction to hold to, but he couldn't reach the wall. He was stranded.

How was she going to reach him? Did he even know she was there? He must—if she could see his buddy lights, he could see hers. Clamping her hands around a small rock outcropping, she gradually extended her legs into the center of the channel, guiding them toward the buddy lights.

And felt them touch a body. Then rubbed them on that body, trying to communicate, trying to get him to realize that he had to grab her legs.

It didn't take long. She felt a hand around her ankle, then another, and suddenly the pressure on her was twice as strong, as Hobbes' body weight was pulling against her. Would this work? Could she possibly pull both of them out of this underwater tomb?

She had to get him toward the wall, where he could grab hold and help pull. She let the force of the current help her sweep her legs toward the wall, felt his body pulling on her legs, pulling so hard she wasn't sure she could hang on, felt one hand begin to slip—

And then the pressure on her legs was released. She turned around and saw the buddy lights behind her, against the wall. He had managed to find a hold.

And then the real struggle began. Pulling even herself against the flow of water was almost impossible. Her fingers were cold, nearly numb; they slipped against the wet rock. Desperately she scrabbled the wall to find a grip.

Slowly, impossibly, she pulled herself toward the mouth of the channel, imagining that it was slightly lighter there, that the water was gray, not black, and that the opening was only a few meters away and soon she'd be out of this hellhole, looking toward sunlight filtering down into the water, moving toward the surface and warmth.

But before she ever reached the gray, her hands found a corner. An edge.

She was at the mouth. If she could turn the corner, she was out.

She reached her right hand around the edge of the cave, pawing for a grip. She found nothing but sheer rockface.

She felt panic rise, felt her heart begin to pound, forced the feelings down. There had to be a way. She felt Hobbes behind her, bumping her feet, and knew they were very close to making it.

Holding her grip with her right hand, she twisted her body in the water so that she was pressed face-first against the wall. This way, she could extend her left arm higher than she'd been able to reach with her right, though it was in a more awkward position.

But with her left hand, she felt a blessed indentation, not much, but enough to dig her fingers into. Would it give her enough leverage to swing her body around and outside the cave?

She paused for a few breaths before trying it. Gripping the indentation as hard as she could, she knifed forward in the water and pushed her body so it twisted out of the opening, staying flat against the wall on the outside. The current was weak there, and she could actually swim along the wall, away from the opening. She turned to see if Hobbes would follow.

What seemed like minutes passed. She was numb from cold, and still faced a slow rise to the surface. *Come on, Hobbes,* she thought intensely, *I did it, you can do it.* She peered toward the dark gash from which she had safely emanated, willing him to appear.

And he did, rolling around the corner in much the same fashion she had, flattening himself against the wall until he had risen high enough to where the current was no longer a danger to them. They eyed each other in the murky gloom, making gestures of joy and victory, rising only as quickly as they could safely ascend.

In ten minutes, they were on the surface, then onto the platform, toweling vigorously to restore warmth to their bodies, eating and drinking and laughing with a giddiness that belied the trauma they were processing.

When they had rested, warm and full, they climbed the quarry face again, giggling at how easy it seemed compared to what they'd been through. On the top, they looked back down at the water that had so recently tried to destroy them both.

Hobbes eyes sought her face. "You saved my life, Kath," he said simply. "I'll never forget that."

She shrugged, embarrassed. "You'd do the same for me."

"Yes, I would," he said, and there was something in his voice that made her look sharply at him, but she saw nothing in his face.

"Well, we better get back," she said, feeling suddenly awkward.

"I'd say that's a very good idea," said a voice from behind them, cold and potent.

They whirled, and Kathryn saw her father standing there. "What were you two thinking? You know the quarries are off-limits."

"It's my fault, sir," Hobbes said instantly. "I've been here with my father, and I asked Kathryn to come swimming with me."

Her father's eyes shifted to her. "Kathryn?" he said

simply, and while every part of her wanted to let Hobbes' gallant statement stand, she knew she couldn't lie to her father.

"Hobbes is being a gentleman, Dad. I was here with Emma and Mary. I talked them into it. Hobbes came later." She glanced at Hobbes. "Thanks anyway."

Vice-Admiral Janeway tapped his commbadge and then took each of them by an arm. "Janeway to Ops Center. Three to beam in."

And in an instant they were standing inside Ops, where curious officers looked at them, smiling at the incongruity of two young people in swim gear standing in the pristine room.

Kathryn's father ushered them into an adjacent corridor. "Is there anything else you have to say about this little escapade?"

"It just seemed like fun. We swam and we dived some." Kathryn held her father's gaze firmly. She wouldn't lie to him, but choosing to omit some of the details seemed perfectly justifiable. There was no way she was going to tell him about their near-miss in the cave opening.

"But you knew you weren't supposed to be there?"

"Yes, Dad."

"You're grounded for the next week, Kathryn. And no holodeck privileges, either. Hobbes, I expect you to tell your parents about this. What they decide to do is up to them."

"Yes, sir."

"Dad . . . " Kathryn was trying to keep the despair out of her voice. "We're only going to *be* here another week. I made plans, and there's a party next Saturday—"

"You should have thought of that before you headed for the quarries. Now go back to quarters and be prepared to spend the week there."

She felt tears begin to form, and quickly blinked them

back. There was no way she was going to cry in front of him, no way she'd let him know this unfair punishment meant anything to her. She lifted her chin and looked him right in the eye.

"Yes, *sir,*" she snapped, and turned on her heel and stalked out. As she left, she heard Hobbes talking softly with her father, apologizing, trying to take more responsibility for the incident, hoping to spare Kathryn. She hated him for it.

Indignation mounted in her. How could her father treat her like this? He was never around anymore, always off conferring with Starfleet officials—what right did he have descending on her just to mete out punishment? The unjustness of it enveloped her like a noxious fog.

But those thoughts didn't suppress the one that had tickled her mind ever since they had climbed up the rockface from the quarry: some day, she would go back there. She would be prepared. She would dive into the quarry, enter the cave opening, and explore the Olympus Mons system. No matter what her father had to say about it.

CHAPTER

9

"REPORT." CAPTAIN JANEWAY STRODE ONTO THE BRIDGE WITH renewed determination. She had managed to sleep for another hour, and now felt focused and clearheaded.

"Repairs still under way, Captain. Warp engines are still down, but impulse could be on-line shortly. The weapons array is partially restored; we have one phaser bank operative."

"Any sign of the Kazon?"

"As far as we can tell, they're still in orbit of the planet. This nebula fogs up the sensor readings a bit, so we can't track them as accurately as I'd like."

Janeway sat at her chair. "Bridge to Engineering."

"Torres here, Captain," a voice answered. Janeway had no doubt that B'Elanna Torres, the half-Klingon chief of Engineering, had been hard at it since the attack.

"What's your closest estimate on impulse capability?"

"Within the hour."

"And warp drive?"

There was a silence. Then, somewhat carefully, "I'm not sure. We're having some problems."

Janeway thought it through. They couldn't show their face to the Kazon without warp capability and with only one phaser bank. They would be completely vulnerable. Better to take a little more time and get every system working.

"Keep me posted, Lieutenant," she said, and signed off. She had just turned to Chakotay when Tom Paris interrupted, urgency in his voice.

"Captain, we've got activity in the nebula. It's a ship."

"Kazon?"

"I think so. In this soup it's hard to tell for sure."

Janeway's mind raced. Without weapons, without warp, with sensors inaccurate, it was folly to try to engage the enemy. They were going to have to be the fox in this hunt.

"Go to minimum energy signature. Shipwide. Set shields to scatter active scans." As soon as she'd spoken, lights began to blink out and there was a decline in the ambient hum that always accompanied life on *Voyager*. Consoles flickered to darkness; only a few dim emergency lights near the deck provided illumination. It was a ghostly atmosphere. But with all systems off-line except life-support and passive sensors, they would be almost impossible to detect. Now, they simply had to wait and hope the Kazon would tire of the hunt and go away.

Jal Sittik stood in the midst of an overgrown copse, trying not to let his men know how perplexed he was. The Federations were proving remarkably elusive. First they had vanished into the depths of a thick grove of trees and brush that Sittik, following, had found impenetrable; then they reappeared on the other side of the copse, almost within view, registering clearly on his sensing indicator.

His squad should have overtaken them easily. But they

were nowhere to be seen, and had all but disappeared from the indicators.

Sittik put his hands on his hips again, a pose of confidence that he felt would satisfy his men while he tried to decide what to do now. But to his irritation Jal Miskk approached.

Miskk's headdress was only slightly less elaborate than his own, another fact that irritated Sittik. He believed Miskk cheated with his markers, claiming kills that were not personally his, but those of the entire ship. Sittik would personally never stoop to such deception, and it annoyed him that others might think that Miskk could claim anywhere near the number of kills that he had.

Miskk now looked at him with a gaze that was unmistakably insolent. "Well," he sneered, "where are they?"

Sittik glared at him, swelling his chest as much as possible in order to intimidate Miskk. "Are you saying you don't know?" he sneered right back.

Miskk's eyes narrowed and the two men stared at each other, the challenge charging the air between them. Sittik enjoyed these moments, for he had a stare that could wither even the most arrogant of his comrades.

And, after a moment, Miskk looked away. Sittik crowed inwardly, a silent cry of victory. He loved conquest. The moment caused him to envision briefly the barely clad bodies of the women who would be awaiting his triumphant return to their colony.

He swept his sensing indicator along the horizon, arm extended fully—a gesture of power. His men would see his strength, his confidence, and realize this momentary setback was just that, a minor obstacle to their eventual victory.

He pointed toward the thick grove of fruit trees that lay less than half a kilometer away. "They've taken cover again," he announced. "Your group will flush them out."

"If they're so close, why are there no readings on our sensing indicators?"

"I see life signs in the grove," retorted Sittik. "Do as I say."

"I don't believe the life signs are those of the Federations—"

"Miskk, I am in charge of this mission. Obey my command or it is you who will spend two weeks in chains."

Sittik was gratified to see Miskk flush with color, start to speak, and then swallow his reply. With a curt nod, he gestured to his men and they moved toward the dense grove of trees.

Then Sittik resumed his scanning, desperately trying to figure out where the Federations really were.

Harry Kim was getting frustrated. But it was better than sitting around, wondering if the Kazon would find them.

He and Kes had begun to explore the underground structure as soon as Tuvok had organized the group into teams. It was proving to be vast, and so far was producing more mystery than enlightenment. There were kilometers of mazelike corridors that would have taken days, if not weeks, to chart.

But that was all. Corridors, all constructed of that strange material which possessed organic qualities. No chambers that he could detect, in spite of the most sensitive of tricorder readings. No bodies, no skeletons, no drawings, no artifacts. Nothing that might be expected in a tomb of what had seemed to be such a ritualized society. After he and Kes had been searching for half an hour, he turned to her in frustration.

"I don't understand it. They went to great lengths to hide this structure; it must have been of value to them— but there's nothing here."

"There must be something here. We just haven't found it yet."

"Tricorders aren't showing anything that would give us a clue." He turned in a circle, tricorder extended. "Just stone . . . stone . . . and more stone. Or whatever one calls this stuff. It looks like an inert mineral, but it definitely has an organometallic component."

Then suddenly his eyes widened as he spotted something besides stone on his readout. "Kes—are you getting a reading? Up above ground?"

Kes lifted her arm to point in the same direction he was, and he saw her brow furrow slightly. She looked over at him. "Kazon," she said grimly.

Unmistakable Kazon life signs flickered on their tricorders. The Kazon were above them, tramping through the sod that served as the ceiling for the underground tunnels. They couldn't hear anything—the ceiling piece was half a meter thick and well insulated with sod—and they assumed the Kazon couldn't hear them. Yet they found themselves whispering.

"Kim to Tuvok."

"I'm here, Ensign."

"I'm picking up Kazon life signs above us."

"Acknowledged. We have the same readings. All teams should be at the ready. But stay where you are. I'd rather have us spread out in order to make it more difficult for them to detect us."

"Yes, sir." He turned to Kes, who continued to study her tricorder intently.

"If we read their life signs, you'd think they could read ours."

"Maybe they can. But figuring how to get down here is a different story. I found the mechanism because I realized what the pattern on the ground represented. But I'm betting the Kazon were just tracking us. They haven't gone through the thought processes I did. As far as they're concerned, we were on the surface, and now we're not. I don't think they'll figure out how we got here."

"I hope you're right."

"Let's keep going. I'd like to find out what this underground maze is all about."

She nodded and they moved off down the corridor, scanning continuously, wrist beacons bravely knifing through a darkness that seemed to have been undisturbed for—how long? There were nothing but questions here.

For another fifteen minutes they wound their way through corridors, carefully charting their course on the tricorders; without that map, they'd never find their way back to the others.

They searched the walls, the ceilings, the floors—everything, for a sign, no matter how tiny, of something besides the strange building material.

And came up empty.

"I'm stumped," Harry admitted. "There just doesn't seem to be any reason for all these passageways. Can you imagine how long it must have taken to build them?"

"Whoever did had a lot of patience. Maybe that's something you could use a little more of."

He looked sidelong at her and grinned. Kes was soft-spoken and unassuming, but underneath her dainty exterior was a will of iron and an insight into others that was extraordinary. Of course, she had unique mental abilities—even she wasn't quite sure what they entailed—but even so, she had a way of getting right to the point of things.

"Noted. But the unbelievable amount of time they spent on this layout only supports my argument: it was extremely important to them. Something's here, something they wanted protected above all else."

"A leader's body? Treasure? A map?"

"Any of the above. Or none of them."

"Whatever it is, I can't imagine that it could be of much use to us. Maybe we should think about getting back to the others."

Kim had already begun thinking the same thing, but he didn't want to admit it. "I'm not curious because we might find something useful. I'm curious because it's so mysterious. All those skeletons, and now this underground maze—I just want answers."

Suddenly he heard her emit a little gasp, and he stopped immediately, shining his wrist beacon toward her. In the glare of the light, her eyes looked like those of a cat's in the moonlight, wide and wary.

"What is it?"

"I don't know. Something . . ."

Harry studied her carefully. She was partially telepathic. Was she sensing something there in the soundless, lightless corridors?

Slowly, she turned in place, eyes closed now, as though trying to locate the source of some vague, faint melody. Her mouth was slightly parted, and he could hear the delicate sound of her breathing. Then she shuddered slightly. He waited, not wanting to interrupt whatever it was she was experiencing.

Finally, she turned back to him, eyes open once more. "I seemed to hear something . . . something far away . . . and then it faded."

"What did it sound like?"

"It's hard to describe. Maybe—like water, dripping onto wood."

"Could you tell where it was coming from?"

She shook her head. Clearly the moment had passed. "Didn't you hear it at all?"

"Nope. Not a thing."

She took a breath, then looked at him a bit sheepishly. "It's gone. I can't get it back."

"Then let's keep walking."

They proceeded down the corridor, scanning carefully, until they reached a bend that forced them to turn right.

When they did, they saw three armed Kazon warriors straight ahead of them.

The first strike of the Kazon ship arrived with only seconds of warning, snapped by Tom Paris from the conn position. "Kazon weapons powering, Captain."

A scant heartbeat later *Voyager* was rocked with the unmistakable *thooop* of percussive plasma flares.

"They're trawling," said Chakotay softly. "Just sending out flares and hoping they hit something."

Even so, it was unnerving. Janeway hated the feeling of powerlessness, just sitting, waiting, hoping, depending on luck that the plasma flares wouldn't hit them, or if they did, that the damage would be minimal. She preferred to be on the move, active, taking charge and doing things her way. But sometimes that wasn't an option. She'd learned that over the years, the way she'd learned most of the lessons of her life: painfully.

So she hunkered down in her chair, trying to quiet her mind, listening to the muffled explosions of the Kazon flares, and trying not to think about those she'd left behind.

CHAPTER 10

CHEB PACKER PUT HIS HAND ON HER ARM TO HELP GUIDE HER through the darkness, and Kathryn felt a thrill ripple through her, ending in her fingertips, which tingled intensely. She still felt that sensation every time he touched her, every time he looked at her, every time he smiled his funny crooked smile at her.

She loved everything about him. She loved his dark hair with the one funny lock that kept falling over his forehead. She loved his eyes, which were the deepest shade of blue she'd ever seen. She loved his broad shoulders and strong arms. She loved his intellect, which was as formidable as any she'd ever encountered in someone her age.

She still couldn't believe that of all the young women at the Academy Institute—all of them the best of the best— Cheb was attracted to her. She was not the most beautiful; she frankly thought she looked like a tomboy with her angular features and her whippet-thin body. She was not the most brilliant; though she always ranked near the top

MOSAIC

in her classes there were always those who surpassed her. She was not the most talented or the most athletic. And yet, in this, their senior year, Cheb had pursued her.

Until she'd begun dating Cheb, she never thought of herself in comparison to other girls. But now she found herself thinking of them in a competitive way: Bess Terman had a much better figure; Allie Keagle had better skin; Nath Malone had a better sense of humor. Everybody had better hair.

What did he see in her?

Ahead, in the cold dark woods of southern Ohio, Anna Mears giggled, and immediately Cheb hissed a "Shhhhhh" at her. Why he felt the need to be quiet, she wasn't sure. The chance of anyone's being out in these particular woods at this time of year was remote. It was frigid, and the ground was covered with icy snow that crunched under the footsteps of the four young people who walked, single-file, along a barely visible path among the trees. Only the moon, radiant in a starry sky, illuminated their way.

They had made the transport—completely unauthorized, of course—from school. Cheb claimed to know how to cover evidence of their maneuver so no one would realize they had commandeered a transporter for a purely personal, nonschool function. He had set it to bring them back in two hours from their beam-in site.

That had been less than a kilometer from their ultimate destination: the Magruder Mansion, an abandoned structure deep in the woods of a southern Ohio farm. Cheb had told them about it, how he had once gone with his older brother and his pals to see it, how intriguing and spooky it was, and how easy it would be for them to use the school's transporter to get there. He had made all the arrangements for this clandestine visit.

It seemed as if they'd been walking forever; the air was cold enough to burn her nostrils, and her feet were numb.

But Kathryn felt warmed by the touch of Cheb's hand on her arm. She gazed upward, looking for familiar stars, and saw leafless branches arching upward toward the sky, stark and desolate. Orion dominated the sky, and Sirius shone brilliantly above the southern horizon. Castor and Pollux, the Gemini twins, hung close to the zenith.

"There it is," she heard Cheb whisper, and the group drew up behind him, peering through the darkness toward the huge dark shadow that loomed ahead of them.

"It was built in the twenty-first century," breathed Cheb. "But it was modeled after castles in Ireland and England over a hundred years before that."

Kathryn had seen pictures of such castles, but seeing one in person was a different matter. It was set on a knoll, and loomed above them, four stories towering into the night sky. Crenellated gables, turrets, and pinnacles jutted from different levels, gradually building up to a massive central tower. She was awed by its power and majesty.

"Let's go." Cheb started toward the mansion.

"How do we get in?" asked Blake Thomas, a thin, serious boy who was Captain of the Parrises Squares team, and one of the academic standouts of the senior class. His acceptance into Starfleet Academy was a foregone conclusion.

"Through the basement," said Cheb, leading the small band of adventurers through drifts of crackling snow to the back of the house, where he disabled motion sensors and opened a ground-level window, then helped them climb down into the basement.

Now, they could use their lights. Cheb and Blake turned on palm beacons and played them around a cavernous room that was elegantly appointed, with wood paneling and vaulted ceilings. Running the length of the room were two wooden alleys, separated by deep grooves.

"What are they?" she asked Cheb, and he smiled at her. "Bowling alleys," he answered, but that told her nothing.

"It's a game that was popular until about a hundred years ago. You rolled a heavy ball down this wooden alley and tried to knock over an arrangement of ten pins."

Kathryn shook her head. It sounded ludicrous. But people had played some very strange games in the past.

"Whose mansion was this, Cheb? And why was it abandoned? Does anyone own it now?"

"It was built early in the twenty-first century by a wealthy man who was an amateur historian. He wanted an authentic Irish castle for the woman he loved, who came from Ireland. So he spent a fortune having it built here, in Ohio. But she was never happy here—too isolated, too far from home. She wanted to leave him, but he begged her, pleaded with her, even threatened her. One day, she vanished, leaving a note that she was going home. He was so distraught he packed up, moved out, closed the house, and never came back. The castle has been empty for three hundred years. It's kept up through a provision in his will, but it's never to be occupied again."

They all reflected silently on the strangeness of this tale. It was grand and romantic, and perfectly suited the ambience of the imposing structure. It seemed neither improbable nor far-fetched.

"Of course," continued Cheb, "there were rumors that he killed her. Buried her somewhere here, in the house. Maybe in this basement."

Kathryn shot him a glance. "Are you trying to scare us with ghost stories, Cheb?"

He shrugged. "Just telling you what I know."

"Let's see the rest." Anna had found the stairway up and was heading toward it; the others followed, climbing upward in the darkness. Cheb and Kathryn were last, and she felt him pull her back, holding her behind for a moment. Then he moved close and kissed her.

Kathryn was amazed that her knees suddenly felt wobbly and jelly-like. You really could get weak in the knees! That was the effect Cheb Packer had on her, and she liked the sensation, enjoyed the stirring of such powerful feelings. Her fingertips were an explosion of sensation; tiny, intense firecrackers danced within them.

They followed the others upstairs, and discovered them in a huge, paneled dining room, whose table and chairs were covered with sheets, lending a ghostly presence to the room. It was a once-elegant room, boasting of a huge marble fireplace at one end and a ceiling that was stenciled in a faded design of shamrocks and thistle.

The young people removed the sheets from the furniture, opened the duffels they'd been carrying, and began to set up the picnic dinner they'd brought. That had been their plan—to hold a feast in an Irish castle. They'd brought soup and sandwiches and Kathryn's mother's caramel brownies. Blake lit candles and they sat in the flickering light around a carved wooden table with bear claw legs.

"You realize," said Cheb, "that probably every one of us is going to end up at Starfleet Academy next fall. I propose we repeat this dinner—next February in San Francisco." Cheb searched in his duffel and extracted a bottle of wine. "A toast to the occasion."

"Is that real?" asked Anna. "It's synthehol, isn't it?"

"This is an authentic Pinot Noir from northern California," said Cheb, pouring some into a cup and sniffing it with the elan of a wine steward.

Kathryn wasn't sure how she felt about real alcohol. She'd never actually tasted it; she had experimented with synthehol because it was a substance over which one had control. Alcohol was not, and she'd always considered it somewhat subversive because of that.

Cheb tasted it, pronounced it satisfactory, and then moved around the room, pouring for each of them. Kathryn watched to see if anyone else would refuse, but no one did. When he reached her, she found that she couldn't be the only one in the group to say she didn't want it. She watched as Cheb poured her some of the dark red liquid. Well, one cup couldn't hurt—and it did seem in keeping with the romantic atmosphere they were creating.

Cheb raised his cup, held it high, said solemnly, "Next year in San Francisco," and they all took a sip of the wine. It tasted like liquid velvet to Kathryn, dark and pungent.

They munched sandwiches and sipped hot, fragrant soup, talking softly as they gazed around the shadowy room. Ancient damask wallpaper was threadbare, peeling in places, lending to the air of faded grandeur. The house was like an aging doyenne, trying to present the elegant façade of youth, but showing instead its wrinkles and gray roots.

One bottle of wine split among four of them gave each a little less than two cups apiece. Kathryn found herself wishing there were more; a rosy warmth had permeated her body, a pleasurable sensation that enhanced the glow she always felt when she was with Cheb.

"All right," he announced, "time to explore the rest of the house. Wait till you see the bed on the third floor. It's a huge four-poster with this incredible brocade canopy."

Cheb led them into a huge entrance hall, around which wrapped an ornate carved staircase that climbed four stories to a central skylight high above. It was intimidating and foreboding, but utterly inviting at the same time. The young people moved toward the stairs, ran their hands over a burnished wood banister that, strangely, was polished and dust-free. Kathryn inspected her fingers.

"You'd think it would be covered with dust. It's almost as if someone has polished it." She sniffed at her fingers and caught a faint scent of pine oil. "And not long ago."

Cheb shrugged. "Magruder's will provided for the house to be kept up. There may have been a cleaning crew in here recently."

But now Kathryn detected another vague scent, a woody, smoky trace that was there one moment, then gone. "Do you smell that?" she asked. "It's like . . . like a fireplace that's been left to smolder."

The others stared at her. She realized that she was the only one of the group who would have had any experience with a fireplace. There was one in her house, and her parents lit a fire frequently. But that was because they were traditionalists; most families whose children attended the Institute would not have such an archaic feature in their homes.

They had climbed to a landing which held a huge, elaborately carved armoire. It, too, had been recently polished, and gleamed in the reflected light of their palm beacons. Again, Kathryn couldn't resist running her fingers over the lustrous wood, as though by doing so she could make a connection to the former inhabitants. But Cheb pulled her on.

As they climbed upward, their lights created strange, ghostly shadows, elongated patterns, distorted and eerie. Kathryn found herself feeling apprehensive. She was not a fearful person, and gave absolutely no credence to ghost stories—and yet she found herself remembering what Cheb had said about the former mistress of this castle. Had she met her death here, at the hands of a willful, possessive husband? Did her bones lie silently within the walls of this edifice? Had it become not only her monument but her tomb?

She tried to shake off the feeling. She was now a little

light-headed, a sensation she owed to the wine, and it wasn't pleasant. She didn't like not feeling completely in charge of her faculties; it made her vulnerable. She vowed not to drink real alcohol again.

"There—there it is again," she said. "Don't you smell it?" This time the others had to acknowledge they did. Noses wrinkled against the odor of burned wood, rank and sour. Kathryn looked upward, eyes straining in the murky darkness, looking for signs of an answer to this mystery. Long shadows played on the walls, which were painted in murals of the Greek classical style: nymphs and satyrs romped on Elysian fields, presenting a bizarre vision of an idyllic era which had existed only in the imagination. It looked malevolent, somehow, in the flickering darkness; the figures were grotesque and distorted, and smiles took on a sardonic quality. She shivered, and followed the others.

"Look at this," Cheb announced. It seemed to Kathryn that his voice had become amplified, slicing through the still house like a plasma torch. The loudness made her uneasy.

He was pointing at a segment of the mural; on it, an idealized rendering of the very castellated mansion they were standing in stood atop a knoll, surrounded by heather fields.

"That's this castle, as Mr. Magruder imagined it in Ireland. And this couple—is Magruder and his bonny bride, the fair Mary Joanna Dugan."

Kathryn stared at the couple who stood in front of the castle, radiantly happy. The man's arm was around the woman's shoulder, protectively; she gazed up at him with adoration shining from her eyes. Her hair was auburn, long and flowing, tied off her face with a blue ribbon that matched the azure of her Grecian gown.

He was sturdy and rock-jawed, eyes glinting with determination, mouth set in a smile that seemed to bespeak not joy, but success. "My world," she imagined him saying, "under my control."

"Kathryn, come on." She looked up to see Cheb waiting for her; the others had already mounted the landing to the third floor. She shook off a chill and pulled herself away from the images of the couple and their dream-castle. And then she smelled the acrid wood smoke again, stronger than ever.

She looked up at Cheb, seeking comfort in his grave blue eyes. Because she was suddenly very, very frightened. "Someone's here," she whispered to him, and was relieved when he smiled and ruffled her hair. "Yeah," he said, "it's the ghost of Mary Dugan."

His jesting made her feel better. She was being silly, of course. They were alone in this isolated mansion, and she was letting her imagination play tricks on her. Ghost stories, indeed. She grinned back at him and they climbed to the third-floor hallway.

Where they found the others, pale and quiet, staring down the hall.

Kathryn turned to follow their gaze, and saw what they saw: a flickering light was emanating from the crack under a closed door. She took an involuntary breath and clutched at Cheb's sleeve. A coldness began seeping through her.

To her horror, he began moving down the hall toward the light. She pulled on his arm, hissing at him. "What are you doing?"

"No one's supposed to be here. We should find out who it is."

"*We're* not supposed to be here. Who are we to police anybody else?"

"I'm with her," said Blake. "Let's get out of here."

"Are you *afraid?*" said Cheb, and the challenge in his voice was unmistakable.

"Yes," replied Blake easily, thereby dissolving Cheb's confrontation. "This has stopped being fun."

"Is that how you'd be if we were exploring an alien planet? Turning tail and running if you didn't think it was *fun?*"

"Sorry, Cheb, I'm not rising to the bait. I'm leaving. Anybody else with me?"

There was a charged moment and Kathryn suddenly felt things were completely out of control. She wanted to go, but now if she said so, it would be insulting to Cheb. Why had he turned this whole thing into a confrontation? Why had he made this a competition about bravery?

But she was spared the need to make a decision. As the four young people stood in the dark hallway, caught in indecision, the door they had been staring at suddenly flung open, and a wraith with flowing auburn hair and a blue gown came screaming at them, brandishing a lit candelabrum.

Anna screamed and bolted down the stairs, followed by Kathryn and Blake. Cheb hesitated briefly on the landing, but the woman's crazed wails were menacing, and even he finally turned and started down.

Above them, the woman stood shrieking epithets in a shrill, high tone that made it hard to distinguish just what she was saying. They could see now that she was old, her hair a ratted tangle of gray, her body thin and frail. Kathryn caught snippets of words—"out of my shame," and "never"—but not enough to make sense of.

And then the woman threw the candelabrum at them.

Kathryn felt it whiz past her head, a heavy presence displacing air, a rank smell of burning tallow, and then it thumped onto the stairway, candles still burning. Cheb, slightly behind them, sidestepped it; Kathryn slowed to wait for him, and as she turned to look up the stairs, she saw the draperies burst into flame.

119

They knew the mansion had been built before fire-suppression technology had become mandatory; they knew the old, dry drapes and furnishings would be like tinder. Already the flames had climbed the drape and it was smoking profusely. Kathryn glanced up and saw the woman, fist at her mouth, staring at the fire and retreating down the hallway.

"We have to put this out, Cheb," she said quietly. The panic she had felt earlier was beginning to wane as a sense of purpose and duty overtook her. "She'll be trapped up there and die."

Blake and Anna had stopped running and were climbing the stairs back toward them. The fire had now engulfed most of one drapery. "Let's do it," said Cheb, and they all ran back up toward the flames.

"Pull down all the drapes—we can use them to beat the fire out." Blake and Anna began to do that, while Kathryn and Cheb turned to the burning drape and, grabbing hold of still-hot chunks of the cloth, tried to tug it from its moorings. Soot and charcoal smeared their hands, and thick smoke made it hard to breathe; they both coughed desperately and their eyes watered.

Suddenly the burning material ripped loose and came tumbling down toward them. Cheb shoved Kathryn hard and she stumbled down the stairs as he jumped after her to avoid being trapped under the flaming drape. An edge of it caught him on the head, however, and Kathryn saw with horror that his hair had begun to burn.

She leaped toward him, spreading her hands on his head, blotting out the fire. There was a moment's registration of pain, but she shut it away, refusing to focus on it.

"Let us through!" Blake and Anna were hauling one of the drapes they had managed to pull off its tracks, and they flung it on top of the one that was burning; then they jumped on top of it, jumping and stomping on it to smother the fire underneath. Within minutes, a pall of bitter smoke hung in the air, but the fire was extinguished.

Sooty and adrenaline-fed from the ordeal, the young people sat on the stairs, drawing ragged breaths. Then Kathryn looked up toward the landing and saw the pale face of the old woman as she stood silently, watching them. Kathryn's eye caught the woman's, and she saw terror and vulnerability. Then the woman drifted backward, out of sight.

The fire, the danger, the success of their efforts—all these had vanquished the earlier anxieties she had felt, and now she rose, staring after the woman.

"What are you doing?" Cheb's voice was challenging, authoritative.

"I'm going to find out who she is and what she's doing here."

"We've got to get out of here."

"You were the one who wanted to go see who was in that room." Kathryn was beginning to feel annoyed with Cheb; he wanted to be in charge of everything.

"We have to be at our beam-out site in fifteen minutes. That doesn't leave any extra time."

"Go ahead without me. You can come back for me later."

"No, I can't. Not without someone knowing about an unauthorized transport."

"Then maybe someone will have to know. I can't leave that old woman here, after the fire, without knowing who she is and if she's all right."

She held Cheb's look for a hard moment, realizing as she did that she had never confronted him about anything, had always deferred to what she felt was his superior decision-making capacity. For a moment, she doubted herself. Was he right? Was it foolish to stay here when the safety of home was only minutes away? When they could be out of this place without anyone knowing they'd ever been here?

But the memory of the fear in the old woman's eyes was too urgent to be ignored. She couldn't leave now. She forced herself to hold Cheb's gaze.

And finally he looked away.

"Be at the beam-out site in an hour. I'll arrange another transport." There was no bitterness in his voice; it was completely neutral, as though they were discussing the weather.

"Fine." She saw the others start down the stairs, and she went the other way, onto the landing, and down the corridor where the mysterious door stood open, spilling flickering light onto the threadbare carpet. She moved toward it soundlessly, without apprehension, pulled along as though by an unseen thread.

CHAPTER
11

HARRY AND KES HAD PULLED THEIR PHASERS INSTANTLY, flung themselves against the side walls of the stone corridor, and trained their weapons on the Kazon.

Strangely, the Kazon seemed unaware of them, and instead turned in place, looking around them, speaking softly to each other.

Speaking *silently* to each other, in fact. Harry realized they were talking and gesturing with some energy—why couldn't he and Kes hear them?

He saw Kes looking upward and realized she, too, was aware of something strange. He glanced back at the Kazon and now saw that they were standing against a background of foliage. Of course there was no foliage down here—but there was above ground. The figures of the Kazon moved off; he uttered a short laugh and holstered his phaser.

"What is it? Where are they?" asked Kes.

"It's an ancient device. On Earth they called it a camera obscura. There's a lens up above, positioned so it reflects an image onto this surface." Harry examined the smooth wall against which they had seen the Kazon, and saw that it was a finely ground surface. Images projected onto it would be seen in a well-detailed and undistorted reflection. That was why the Kazon had seemed so real.

"It's odd," he mused, studying the wall. "A camera obscura is primitive technology, but this surface is very sophisticated, composed of several hard polymer agents."

Kes looked around them, playing her wrist beacon in all directions. "I wonder if the fact that it's here means there's some significance to this location."

He shot her a glance. "I think you're right. The fact that someone could be warned of activity on the surface from here would suggest this is someplace they wanted to protect."

They looked around to realize they had reached a T-intersection in the corridors, with the "screen" forming the back wall and two branches of tunnels extending right and left from it. They began searching all the walls carefully, running their hands over the surface, looking for any detail, any design that might provide a clue to the importance of this intersection.

Ten minutes later, they were still searching, when suddenly Kes' head snapped around and she froze like a bird anticipating a predator.

"What?" Harry said, but she shushed him, straining as though to hear something far away. Then she began moving down the corridor to the left, walking with a sureness that belied the inky blackness of their surroundings.

Harry followed. Kes seemed in touch with something, and he had learned to trust her instincts. He kept her in the beam of his wrist beacon, and she seemed to float before him, a dainty, weightless creature gliding in the blackness.

Suddenly she stopped, and lifted her hand to stop him, too. Then, slowly, she turned to him, and he saw an expression of wonder and anticipation on her face.

"Somewhere close . . . I know it's here. . . ."

"What is?"

But she kept turning in place, as though trying to tune in to whatever extrasensory perception she was experiencing. "I'm not sure. I hear that sound again . . . it's . . . it's a clicking noise."

"Like a code?"

"I don't know."

Harry scanned everything and was about to give up when the tiniest blip registered on his tricorder. What was it? He moved in the direction he had picked up the reading, and approached what seemed to be a dead end to the tunnel. They'd run into these over and over again, and never did they show any distinguishing mark. Nor did this one, he determined after a thorough search.

He was ready to turn back, when his eye flickered to something high on the wall perpendicular to the dead end. It's a wonder he spotted it; it called no attention to itself and appeared only as a slight crack in the stone. But it was the shape that caught Harry's eye: it was exactly like the cobalt blue spires he had followed on the surface, which pointed the way from grave site to grave site.

"Kes, look at this." She moved to him and stared upward.

"It's like the spires we saw up above."

He stretched out his arm and extended his hand so his finger could reach the small etched design. He touched it, applying only slight pressure.

There was a sense of movement, and then a rush of chill air filled the corridor. They turned, shining their beacons, to discover that a panel had opened in the side wall. A set of stone stairs led downward into darkness, and a cool, moist breeze wafted upward. Curiously, Harry felt no apprehension. The dark stairway seemed inviting. He turned to Kes and saw that she was smiling, and then they began, without a word or a question, to descend.

CHAPTER

12

THEY HAD BEEN SWIMMING UNDERWATER FOR THREE QUARTERS of an hour, and things were getting worse all the time. In spite of the fact that he knew kicking up silt would greatly hinder their vision, Cheb seemed to keep bumping into outcroppings, or dropping a foot to the floor of the channel. A cloud of silt erupted from each of these intrusions, blocking Kathryn's vision and threatening to clog her breathing gill.

One small dark part of her mind wondered if he was doing it on purpose. Cheb had definitely not recovered from the devastating news that his admission to Starfleet Academy had been rejected. She had been accepted, along with their friends Blake and Anna, and a number of others from the Institute. But Cheb, although winning acceptance at any number of prestigious colleges and universities, didn't make the cut at the Academy.

He had been stunned, then angry, then frighteningly

withdrawn. Kathryn had tried to comfort him, but he was disconsolate, and frequently lashed out at whoever was in range.

"It's because I got a disciplinary reprimand after we went to that castle last winter. It never would've happened if you'd left with the rest of us."

"Cheb, we were both reprimanded for that incident. Not just you."

"But you became some kind of heroine because you found that old woman."

"She was sick and confused. She needed help. I helped her. That's all."

"So you came out of it a saint, and I took all the blame."

Kathryn had stopped talking at that point. There was no point in reasoning with him when he was so upset; he could color anything with his revisionist view of the past. It was true Mrs. Klamer's family had been deeply grateful to her for finding their aged grandmother. The old woman, failing mentally and fascinated for years by tales of the Magruder Mansion, had somehow managed to leave her family home in Kentucky, travel hundreds of miles to southern Ohio, and take up a brief residence in the ancient castle, fantasizing that she was Mary Dugan Magruder.

Kathryn's intervention prevented a possible tragedy, and the Klamer family was copious in its praise of her. But it was true the Institute had disciplined her, along with Cheb, for the unauthorized use of the transporter.

She didn't think the incident had anything to do with his rejection from the Academy; privately, she suspected he had been too arrogant in his interview, but she didn't feel like saying that to him.

Now, she had begun to wonder if their cave-diving trip was a good idea. They'd had it planned for months—Kathryn had been working on it since she was fourteen—

and it didn't seem right to cancel it just because Cheb was disappointed. In fact, she hoped the adventure would take the edge off his frustration and leave him more hopeful about his future.

But it didn't seem to be working that way. Cheb had been terse and short-tempered ever since they left Earth on the shuttle for Mars. Her father had arranged the trip as a graduation present; they would stay in Starfleet quarters and enjoy the privileges of the Officer's Club.

Of course, her father didn't know about their plans to go cave-diving. And there was no need for him to. She and Cheb would explore the quarry caves for a few days, camping underground, and return to Earth within the allotted time.

But the trek she had looked forward to for so long, with such anticipation, was being soured by Cheb's depression. Like kicking up silt: she knew he could be more careful, but he wasn't, he was making it less pleasant for her so she wouldn't enjoy the experience any more than he.

They had been swimming through a long, tubular chamber filled with stalactites and stalagmites that jutted from above and below and threatened to snag them as they were pulled along by their hydromagnetic drives. Cheb was unspooling the guideline as he went, and she periodically fastened it to an outcropping. They would need this line to direct them back when they returned.

When the water stayed clear, Kathryn could see the formations in the light of her aquadyne torch, a mysterious and elegant arrangement of spires, like an underwater city of towers and turrets. It was a mesmerizing sight, and she imagined the millennia it had taken to form those spires, millimeter by millimeter, as dissolved calcium was slowly released by evaporating water, forming deposits that hardened and grew to astonishing proportions.

She realized they might be the first living creatures to have seen these formations.

This was what she had come for—for the ineffable thrill of seeing what hadn't been seen, of knowing what hadn't been known. She was inexorably drawn to the unexplored, fascinated by the unfamiliar. She wanted to savor the excitement of discovery, to revel in the anticipation of turning the next corner and finding something marvelous and unique.

She didn't particularly want to nursemaid Cheb Packer's hurt feelings.

Ahead of her, the water cleared, Cheb rose abruptly, and she realized he was surfacing. After nearly an hour, they had found an air pocket.

And what an air pocket it was. As her head broke the surface of the water, Kathryn's light shone into a massive, cavernous room as big as several soccer fields. The ceiling rose fifty meters over their heads, and dripped with stalactites in wondrous, majestic patterns. It was like surfacing into the interior of a massive cathedral.

Cheb had swum to a rocky "beach" and crawled ashore; she followed him, removing her gill breather. "This is incredible," she said, and her voice echoed strangely in the hollow stillness.

"We can set up a camp here. There's enough level ground."

Kathryn unstrapped the waterproof pack from her back and dropped it to the ground. In it were concentrated food packs, dry clothing, and thermal blankets. Immediately, she began to roam, examining the stalactites that hung from the ceiling, still forming, still dripping with water, each drop leaving a minute quantity of calcium which would harden and lithify, gradually growing the inverted steeple of mineral deposits longer and longer.

129

"Isn't it amazing, Cheb? They're still forming. We're seeing a process that's been going on for millions of years."

He shrugged. "It happens the same way on Earth."

"But we're not on Earth. We're on Mars. And we may be the first people ever to see these caves, to see these stalactites form."

"Who has the oatmeal? Is that in your pack or mine?"

She stared at him. Was he going to be like this the whole time? She took a deep breath, determined not to let him ruin the trip. "I think it's in yours."

He grunted and bent over his pack, searching through it, tossing items this way and that. Sloppy, she thought. He'll be sorry when he has to repack.

She wandered around the huge chamber, studying the formations, ruminating on the natural processes that had been interrupted on Mars by its long freeze, and which now were proceeding once more, the millennia-long hiatus nothing more than a tiny blip in the evolution of the planet.

She heard Cheb continue to paw through the pack, grumbling and muttering under his breath, and she smiled to herself. He was going to make himself as miserable as possible. He would make sure he—

The speck of white almost went unnoticed. Her head lamp swept by it and her brain must have registered it unconsciously because she wasn't aware of having seen anything. And yet something made her turn back and inspect the stratified wall again.

And there it was: less than two centimeters long, an oval-shaped, striped ribbon, bisected by a dark line that ran lengthwise. The fossilized remains of an animal, embedded in this cave wall for eons.

"Cheb! Come here!" Her voice rang with excitement but was dampened in the heavy cave air.

"What?" He had stopped rummaging through his pack, but made no move to join her.

"Look what I've found!" She couldn't believe his stubbornness. If he'd gotten this excited about something, she'd have been there in a second. But he stared at her, looked around, looked back, and finally began shuffling in her direction. The dark lock of hair fell over his forehead—the same tendril she had once found so endearing—and she thought it gave him a scruffy look, unkempt and messy.

She located the fossil with her headlamp and pointed to it. "See? The fossil?"

He peered at it. "So?"

"That line there, the one that runs the length of it . . . I think that's a spinal rod. I think this is a chordate."

He looked skeptical. "How could a chordate have developed on Mars?"

"I don't know. But there it is."

"You're guessing it's a chordate. You don't know for sure."

"I did a senior honors thesis on vertebrate anatomy. I studied chordates then. This looks just like some of the oldest ancestors of the vertebrate branch of animals on Earth. The ancestors of man."

"Could you help me find the oatmeal now?"

Fury welled in her. He had to be doing this on purpose. Finding evidence of chordates on Mars was completely unexpected, a remarkable discovery. It would require a reexamination of all the planet's evolutionary history. This was possibly a major scientific breakthrough and all Cheb could think of was his stomach.

"No, I could not help you find the oatmeal. If you packed it, it's there. If you didn't, it isn't. I'm going to look for more fossils."

He took on an aggrieved, wounded look, instantly the victim. "What's gotten into you? I don't deserve to be barked at like that."

"Yes, you do. You've been in a sour mood for weeks. Isn't it time you at least made an effort to get over it?"

His eyes narrowed at her retort. "Thanks for your terrific compassion. For such exquisite sensitivity to my feelings. It's really great to realize your best friend doesn't give a damn about you."

She felt as though she'd been impaled by a spear. Of course he was still hurt and disappointed. She shouldn't have snapped at him like that; there were better ways to handle the situation. When would she ever learn to control her tongue?

"I'm sorry, Cheb. I just didn't understand why you wouldn't be excited by my finding that fossil."

He turned and moved back toward their packs. "Is this what the week's going to be like? You jumping all over me like some Circassian hellcat every time I open my mouth?"

"That's not fair, I didn't—"

"I can't think of anything worse . . . being trapped underground with someone who delights in pointing out all one's defects."

"Cheb, what are you saying? I haven't done that—"

"Do you think I haven't noticed the past few weeks? How cold you've been? How withdrawn?"

"Me . . . ?"

"Are you saying you aren't aware of how you've been?"

Kathryn felt a familiar confusion returning. They had been through this before. Cheb had the maddening ability to turn things around one hundred and eighty degrees, to twist anything she said, drawing on just enough truth to make her begin doubting herself. She wasn't going to let it happen this time.

"I don't think *I've* been different at all. You're the one

who's changed—ever since you got rejected by Starfleet Academy."

"Thank you. I need to be reminded of that."

"But you said . . . just a few minutes ago . . . you said you were feeling bad. You accused me of not being sensitive to you."

"I don't remember saying it had anything to do with Starfleet. You're the one who's been making me miserable."

She felt blood roaring in her ears. The whole thing was taking on a surreal air—the pit-darkness, illuminated only by their headlamps, the fantastical underground cathedral room, the damp chill of the trapped air—and she began to feel disoriented. Was Cheb making sense? Was her perception of the last weeks flawed? Had it all been her fault?

"What . . . are you saying?"

"The way you've treated me. Like hitting a guy when he's down. I think I could've handled the whole Starfleet thing a lot better if I'd had any support from you."

"But I thought I did, I was . . . I've tried to help . . ." She felt inarticulate and clumsy. He was staring at her, disappointment etched on his face.

"If that was your idea of helping, that scares me. I think you're the one that needs help, Kathryn."

Her head reeled. She couldn't believe she was hearing this. She tried to calm herself and took several deep breaths, but before she could say anything, Cheb knelt down and began reassembling the things he'd taken from his pack.

"What are you doing?"

"Packing up. I'm not spending a week in these conditions with you."

"But—we've planned this for a year. And I really want to look for more fossils—"

He stood up and his dark blue eyes flashed in the glare of

133

her lamp. "That's so like you, Kathryn. 'I really want to look for more fossils.' You're a true scientist, I guess, if fossils mean more to you than what's happening to us."

"To us? What's happening to us? Cheb, why are you being like this—"

He knelt down once more and began stuffing his pack. "I'm going back. You can come or you can stay here."

"I can't stay here alone, that's ridiculous."

"Then let's get ready to go."

She stared at him for a moment, mind still unable to accept that he was serious. But as he finished repacking, she saw that he meant it. He was leaving. And if he did, she would have to.

Briefly her mind danced over the idea of staying, just to prevent him from being able to manipulate her; but one quick look around this caverous room and the prospect of staying there alone was overwhelming.

She picked up her pack and strapped it on, adjusted her aquadyne torch lamp, and fit her breathing gill into her mouth. Cheb did the same, and without another word they both walked into the water for the long swim back.

CHAPTER

13

THE KAZON HAD BEEN TRAWLING FOR OVER AN HOUR, PEPPER-
ing the nebula with percussive plasma flares. Sometimes
they seemed close; sometimes they were only a distant
vibration. At one time Janeway thought they had given up
and gone away, as they hadn't felt any jolts for almost
thirty minutes. But then, in the distance, their sensors
registered the distinctive *thoop* of the bombs growing
closer once more.

Chakotay studied his console. "They're on a direct
course, Captain. Heading one-four-nine mark seven."

This was ominous. Until now, the Kazon ship had
clearly been trawling, sending out flares in a random
pattern, hoping for a hit. Now it was bearing down on
Voyager, seemingly having detected the ship and homing in
on it.

"Shields," said Janeway quietly. They had dropped
shields in order to prevent the energy signature from being

detected, but now it seemed wiser to protect themselves from a possible attack.

The percussive devices grew louder, and *Voyager* began to tremble, then shake, from the shock wave of each detonation.

"Bridge to Engineering. Status."

Torres' voice was brisk and calm. "I've almost got warp engines back, Captain. I've been concentrating on that—still only one phaser bank on-line."

"Acknowledged. Let me know the minute you've got warp capability."

"Aye, Captain."

Chakotay was still studying his console, his forehead knotted in concentration. "There's no doubt about it. They're heading right for us."

And as if in violent confirmation, a weapons blast hit *Voyager*'s shields, jolting the bridge and everyone on it. "Those weren't plasma flares," said Paris loudly. "They've shifted to their primary disruptor weapons."

"Shields at eighty-four percent."

"Return fire." Janeway didn't like revealing their weakened weapons systems, but they couldn't continue to sit here without retaliating now that the Kazon had definitely located them.

Phaser fire arced through the nebula, illuminating the dark gases in eerie patterns, and then lancing through the Kazon ship's shields.

"Direct hit," said Chakotay with satisfaction. "They felt that one." But no sooner had he spoken than *Voyager* took three more hits in rapid succession. Smoke from an explosion somewhere in one of the conduits began to seep onto the bridge.

"Shields at seventy-one percent."

"Return fire. Bridge to Engineering. What's happening with warp drive?"

"Almost there, Captain," came Torres' reply.

"I need it now, Lieutenant."

"Understood." In Engineering, Torres was working frantically, beads of perspiration forming on her ridged Klingon brow. She had been realigning the dilithium-crystal articulation frame, desperately trying to restore warp power, and she was almost there. Only the antimatter injectors remained to be reinitialized. Lieutenant Carey was at her side, calculating parameters for the warp core ignition sequence, and with luck, they'd have warp capability in seconds.

"Engineering?" Janeway's voice displayed no emotion, but the quick repetition of her request indicated their desperate plight. A huge jolt rocked the ship, and Carey went flying across the room.

"I'm okay," he called quickly, "don't stop working."

Torres hit the final commands for reinitialization, and was rewarded with the familiar sound of the warp core humming to life.

"Torres to bridge. We're on-line."

"Understood, Engineering. Good work."

On the bridge, Janeway looked toward Paris. "I want to go to warp from within this nebula, Lieutenant. What's your assessment of the repercussions?"

Tom Paris hesitated only a second. "It's always dicey to go to warp from a full stop, but I'll increase power to the inertial dampeners; we might get bounced around, but I think we can do it."

"And the effect on the nebula's gases?"

"That's another matter. There are volatile elements in here, and the sudden energy charge of our warp engines could ignite them. I'd say it's unpredictable."

Janeway hesitated only briefly. "We have to try. Let's do it."

"Yes, ma'am." Paris deftly fingered controls and *Voyager*

shot into warp; inertial dampeners held but the crew was bounced around like rag dolls for nearly twenty seconds. Then things smoothed out.

"Damage report." Janeway felt like she'd just gotten off a bucking horse, and there was a ringing in her ears. Chakotay was already studying his console.

"No damage to the ship . . . minor casualties on deck four. Nothing serious."

"Should I set a course, Captain?" Paris was ready, hands poised over controls.

"Fly a random evasive pattern. Let's try to buy some time until we see if that ship intends to pursue."

"Aye, Captain." And once more a troubled quiet fell on the bridge as Janeway risked the game she enjoyed least: playing for time.

Trakis the physician was aware of two sets of eyes: Nimmet's, impatient and glowering, and the captive's, which were just beginning to flutter open. It was regaining consciousness.

The last time that had happened the captive had responded by ejecting a blast of dark fluid from a proboscis on its underbelly; Trakis had just avoided being sprayed by the noxious stuff, and, as he quickly realized, a lucky thing for him. As expected, the secretion was highly corrosive, and began to etch patterns into whatever it touched. It was some minutes before the liquid seemed to lose its potency and stop eating through the surfaces it had daubed.

Trakis was hopeful he had managed to disconnect the internal sac of fluid from the ventral orifice through which it was projected, and seal it shut. He had no desire to test fate again by being anywhere near this creature when it was in a vengeful mood.

Nimmet was watching him, eyes slitted in that ridiculous expression of his. Could he possibly think he looked threatening with his face screwed up like that? Could he be so deluded? Trakis sighed inwardly, remembering the years of his young adulthood on Trabus, when graciousness and civility were the order of the day, when life moved in measured cadences like a well-structured symphony. All that had been lost in the Kazon uprising, of course, but Trakis held to the hope that his people would someday regain their lovely existence, unhindered by the barbarous Kazon, who with any good fortune would eventually kill each other off.

"Well?" said Nimmet, and Trakis wished he could come up with a more inventive opening question.

"I think I've provided a detailed report of the captive's anatomy and physiology, so far as I can tell. What more do you want?"

"I want to know what Maje Dut will want to know: Can this species help us to greatness?"

Trakis resisted a grimace at the inflated language. Nimmet spoke like an overheated orator, mouthing proclamations instead of simply communicating. It was, he ruminated, the mark of the ignorant and the unschooled, who hoped to convince others that they were more intellectually advanced than they really were.

"Exactly what is it that would help you to achieve this greatness?" he asked dryly.

"You know very well!" Nimmet all but shouted. He had low frustration tolerance, Trakis knew, as Nimmet took a breath and continued loudly, face turning a deep crimson in his indignation. "We must know if they can be used as weapons! We must know if they can be trained! We must know if they can communicate and if not what stimuli they will respond to! There are a wealth of questions that *must be answered!*"

Trakis waited for a moment until Nimmet's face had returned to its normal color. He had believed for a moment that he might have to administer to a cardiovascular attack, but Nimmet seemed to have regained control. Trakis proceeded calmly, speaking even more softly in contrast to Nimmet's overblown outburst.

"I'm sure you know I can't possibly provide those answers on the basis of a physical examination. And it's not likely this prisoner is going to cooperate long enough to allow me to investigate further." Trakis eyed the captive uneasily; his eyes were beginning to stay open for seconds at a time and he had begun to stir restlessly on the table.

"Narcotize him again. Do it until you have the information we need."

"I don't know if he'll survive another injection. The drug is a powerful one and he's already had more than I think is wise."

"No one cares if it's wise—we only care that we get answers."

Trakis looked down at the captive once more. Now his eyes were fully open, and he stared dully upward, huge compound eyes protected behind a transparent sclera. Trakis watched carefully for any indication that he was tensing his body—that had signaled the last attack—but he seemed dulled by the drug (and possibly by pain) and lay there limply. The physician felt a twinge of sympathy for what he was enduring, and he made no effort to prepare the narcotic.

Nimmet took a menacing step forward. "The Maje expects answers, Trabe. Need I remind you what will happen if he doesn't get them?"

Trakis knew that was an unveiled threat to his family, still at the outpost on Slngsnd. And it was not an empty threat, as all Trabe well knew. The Kazon enjoyed retribution against their former masters, and frequently used threats against vulnerable family members to insure cooperation from the scientists, physicians, and engineers that they needed so desperately.

Trakis turned to the equipment that lay on a tray nearby and began preparing the narcotic. As he worked, he could feel the captive's lensed eyes watching him.

Harry and Kes descended deeper and deeper, down the stone stairs, endless circular steps taking them to a depth Harry was finding it hard to imagine. The lower they went, the colder it became, until he could see his breath in the light of his wrist beacon. He had begun to doubt the wisdom of their exploration after a few minutes, but Kes led the way and seemed energized, drawn downward as though summoned by an unheard voice.

"Kes, I think we're getting a little far from the others. Maybe we should turn back." Harry's voice was hollow in the stairwell, and the condensation from his breath billowed into the darkness.

Kes turned to him and what he saw made him stop in his tracks.

She was transfixed. Her eyes shone with intensity and her brow furrowed slightly, as though she were concentrating on something with every ounce of her tiny frame. It made Harry uneasy to see Kes like this, for he realized she was in contact with something that was hidden to him.

"Don't you hear it?" she breathed, those frenzied eyes holding him fast, as though with a physical grasp. He couldn't look away.

"Hear what?"

"Clicking. Chittering."

Harry felt a chill envelop him. He heard nothing, only his own breath, which sounded ragged in the cold air.

"It's so odd. I've never heard anything like it. It can't be far from here."

And she started down the stairs again. Harry hesitated, then hit his commbadge. "Kim to Tuvok."

"Tuvok here."

"Sir, Kes and I have found a stairwell; we're following it to see where it leads. But maybe we're going too far afield."

"Continue your exploration, Ensign. It would be prudent to ascertain if there is another exit from this location."

"Aye, sir." Kim started down the stairs again. He saw Kes far below him, hurrying downward, pulled by whatever possessed her. Shivering, Harry stepped up his pace to catch up with her.

"It's very near. I feel as though I can reach out and touch it."

"Touch what?"

"I don't know."

Harry didn't particularly like the thought of reaching out and touching whatever it was Kes heard. This whole adventure had taken on an entirely different aspect, one that seemed even more immediately dire than the threat of the Kazon. Those enemies seemed far away now, and ineffectual; the clicking Kes heard had taken on a far more portentous aspect.

And then they were, at last, at the bottom of this interminable staircase, in the midst of a small chamber that had no apparent outlet.

Harry started instinctively searching for a symbol that might lead them to a portal, but Kes had no need. Without hesitation, she moved to their right and back under the stairs; against a section of the stone wall she laid her hand.

And the wall disappeared.

The effect was not unlike that of a transporter, Harry noted. Not magic, he reminded himself, nothing supernatural—just technology. He understood technology, he could cope with that. He moved after Kes into the space that had opened before them, determined to counter Kes' mesmerized state with the rational approach of a scientific investigator.

The chamber in which they now found themselves had one unique factor: it was illuminated, although Harry couldn't find just what that source was. But the room glowed—there was really no other word for it—with an incandescent glimmer that seemed to be green one moment, blue the next.

He looked for a fixture, a sconce, anything that might account for this ghostly luminescence. There was nothing, and he decided there must be photogenic particles in the air. A rational explanation.

Kes was turning slowly in the room, senses heightened, listening, reaching out with her mind. After a moment, she turned to him, a puzzled expression on her face. "I can't explain this, Harry. But—something is coming to life."

Uneasy, he turned back to the entrance through which they had entered the room. There was no sign of it; only a blank wall faced them now. And no matter where they placed their hands, no matter how they pressed, the surface remained solid and unyielding.

CHAPTER

14

A GRACEFUL SUMMER NIGHT'S BREEZE RUSTLED THE DROOPING branches of the weeping willow tree. On its gentle billows was borne the fragrance of Indiana: dusky herbs, heady floral scents, the fresh earthy smell of loam. As a little girl Kathryn had believed those aromas had healing powers; they could banish headaches and heartaches if you breathed them deeply enough.

And now, here she was, an adult of eighteen, still wanting to believe in the curative powers of those comforting scents, sprawling in her childhood hiding place and hoping to recapture some of the solace of those long-ago moments.

She felt dead inside. She was to leave tomorrow morning to report to Starfleet Academy, the first step in the fulfillment of her youthful dreams, but anticipation of the moment held no joy for her. She would go, because she was dutiful, and she would apply herself, because she was

MOSAIC

disciplined. But she couldn't imagine that there would be any satisfaction in any of it.

The crack of a twig made her jerk upright and peer through the darkness. Had she imagined it? Or was someone walking toward the tree through the corn rows? She squinted, trying to discern a human form among the tall stalks, which rustled in the breeze and cast dancing shadows on the moonlit ground.

She heard the sound again, and was sure of it; someone was coming toward her. She froze, motionless, not fearful because there was nothing to fear, but resentful of having her interlude broken. There was no one she wanted to talk with at this moment.

"Kath?" The voice emerged from the corn rows. "Are you there? I don't want to frighten you."

Kathryn exhaled. Hobbes Johnson. Maybe if she held very still, he wouldn't see her in the tree.

His dark figure emerged from the corn and looked upward. She couldn't tell whether he could see her or not.

"I don't want to intrude. I just thought I'd say goodbye, since you're off to school tomorrow." She was silent, hoping he'd leave. There was a moment's silence.

"Anyway," he continued, "I wish you the best. I hope we can stay friends." There was a moment of silence, then, "Well, so long. I know you'll do well."

And the figure turned and headed back toward the corn. Kathryn sat upright. "Hobbes—?"

He turned. "So you are there. I thought you might be. But if you'd rather be alone, I understand."

Suddenly she didn't want to be alone. She hopped off her branch and jumped down to the ground. "Please don't go," she said sincerely. "I'd love to talk."

She saw him smile in the moonlight and move back toward her. Hobbes wasn't nearly as vulky as he had been as a child, but he would never make anyone's heart beat

145

harder. He was still thin, though his teeth didn't protrude any longer and his skin had cleared up. His hair was still impossible, but then so was hers.

However, he still looked as though he simply didn't care what people thought of him. His hair was long, and somewhat unkempt; he kept running his fingers through it to keep it out of his eyes.

"I was thinking about you," he said, "and I remembered how I was feeling two years ago when I left for college. It was kind of scary. And while you don't strike me as someone who's easily frightened, I just thought I'd say good luck."

She felt an unaccustomed rush of gratitude. Hobbes wasn't handsome, and he wasn't exciting, but he was a good and decent person. She plopped down on the ground with her back against the tree and gestured for him to join her. "That's really nice, Hobbes. I guess I am feeling a little—" She hesitated. What was she feeling, exactly? Heartsick? Lonely? Scared? Depressed? She laughed slightly and shook her head.

"I'm feeling something, but darned if I can tell you what it is."

He smiled in return. "You've been through a lot this summer."

Her head jerked around to him. What did he mean? Was he talking about Cheb? About her father? About school? She didn't respond.

"Let me say this—the smartest move you ever made was to get rid of Cheb Packer. You deserve better than that, Kath."

She felt her cheeks burn. Was their breakup the stuff of discussion? She supposed so; it was a tight-knit community, and people genuinely cared about each other. The protracted on-again off-again romance had probably kindled all kinds of discourse.

"I could have handled it better." She tried to sound neutral, unemotional. "I could have stuck to it the first time I told him it wasn't working, instead of taking him back again and again."

"I know Cheb. He has a silver tongue. If he'd lived four hundred years ago he would've been a salesman."

Kathryn smiled. They'd studied about salesmen in school, about the time in Earth's history when people actually tried to talk people into acquiring things they didn't need, just to make money. It sounded so bizarre that she wouldn't have believed it if she hadn't studied the era and seen examples of the persuasive techniques such people used. Hobbes was right—Cheb would have been perfect in a calling like that.

"When do you go back to school?" Hobbes, she knew, was returning to Indiana University, one of the most prestigious non-Starfleet institutions in the country and one of the hardest to get into.

"In about a week. I'm finishing up an honors thesis I've been working on this summer."

"In what subject?" Kathryn realized that she'd known Hobbes since they were children, but had almost no idea of his interests, his studies, his hobbies. Did he still play tennis?

"Philosophy. That's my major field." He chuckled. "Probably not too thrilling to someone on the science track at Starfleet Academy."

"I've always enjoyed philosophy. It's just—not very active."

"Ah. Then you might enjoy reading Lat Nadeen, a twenty-second-century Bolian philosopher. Let's just say he's not one to sit in an ivory tower. I think you might be surprised by some of the things he advocates."

"Maybe I'll give it a try." An easy silence fell between them. Kathryn was surprised at how comfortable she felt with Hobbes. There were some positive aspects in being with a person in whom you had absolutely no romantic interest. They sat for a few moments, enjoying the late summer evening breeze.

"Did you know my dog died?" She hadn't intended even to mention this, but found the words on her lips nonetheless.

"No, I didn't. You had him for a long time, didn't you?"

Kathryn felt her throat tighten. It was still hard to talk about. "Eleven years. But I thought he'd live a lot longer."

"I lost my first dog when I was six. I'm not sure I'm over it yet." Kathryn found herself relieved to hear him say this. She thought she should be able to handle Bramble's death better than she had. After all, he had died peacefully and in no pain, after a long dog's life. But coming as it did in the middle of this tumultuous summer it had been almost unbearable for her.

"He was my best friend for years. He used to lick my tears when I cried." She stopped, feeling tears well even then. "I guess I'll just have to stop crying."

He reached out and gave her a little pat on the back— perfunctory, brotherly, an odd little gesture that made her feel awkward rather than comforted, though she appreciated his bumbling effort. Another silence ensued, and then Hobbes decided to change the subject.

"What does your father have to say about the Cardassian situation?" His question dissolved her sense of comfort instantly.

"He doesn't. He won't talk about it. I guess he must be under orders or something." She wondered if the bitterness in her voice came through.

That question was answered when Hobbes offered, "Sounds like it's a touchy subject."

Kathryn took a breath. She didn't mean to leak her feelings, and she certainly didn't want to talk about it. But something about the August evening, the fragrant breeze, and Hobbes Johnson's gentle presence overcame her inhibitions, and she found herself opening up.

"Whatever's going on with Cardassia has taken a toll on my family for years," she began. "My father was one of the first people Starfleet brought into it, and now it's taken over his life. He's never at home anymore, it's like his family doesn't exist. And they've got him in some top-secret classification so it can take days just to communicate with him." She paused, glancing over at Hobbes as though to gauge his reaction. He was watching her, listening, impassive.

"He was supposed to go with me tomorrow, get me checked into the dorm. We'd planned it all summer. Then I get a message that he's had to go to Vulcan for some conference. That's all—just a *message.*"

"Is your mother going with you?"

"She offered. But it's no huge thing. I can do it myself."

"Would you like me to go with you?"

Her head whipped around. She didn't know whether to laugh or not, didn't know if she felt grateful or humiliated. It was one thing to be taken to the Academy by her father, a Starfleet vice-admiral, and quite another to be accompanied by a civilian her own age who knew nothing about Starfleet.

"That's awfully nice of you, Hobbes. But it's not as though I'm a little girl. And there will be others going."

"Okay." As always, he seemed utterly unaffected by rejection. Was he? Or had he learned, through a lifetime of suffering it, how to cope? As she had so many times in her life, Kathryn felt sorry for him.

"Tell me about the university," she said by way of a gesture. "I've never even been there."

"You wouldn't like it. It's very traditional—they still have some of the original buildings, in a square around a

149

small woods. And most of the buildings they've put up in the last fifty years are in that same architectural style. It's not sleek and modern like Starfleet Academy."

She smiled, remembering their discussions of "traditionalism" when they were younger, when she had to play tennis and study ballet. "Do you still play tennis?" she queried.

"Sure do. Although not competitively. I'm on the swim team instead."

"You are?" Again, she was surprised. She didn't equate Hobbes with competitive athletics. She glanced at his thin frame and realized that though lean, he was actually well muscled.

"Free-style and butterfly. Indiana actually has a long history of excellence in swimming. Of course, now the women are the real stars, but we hold our own."

"I'll never make a team at the Academy. I wasted all those years playing tennis when I should have been developing skills in Parrises Squares."

"It wasn't a waste. You can play tennis all your life. That's not so with Parrises Squares."

"You *can* play tennis that long—but do you want to?"

"I do. It's still one of my favorite outlets."

"Really?"

They had entered into an easy banter, relaxed and genial. Without her even realizing it, Kathryn's anxieties were dissolving, floating away on the summer breeze along with the heady aromas of green growing things, which seemed to possess curative powers after all.

The weather in San Francisco was frequently cold and gloomy; Kathryn had come to terms with the trade-off from Indiana's climate: no freezing winters, but a lot of fog.

But today a warm sun bathed the city by the bay in a

golden glow, and she sat stretched out on a bench on Starfleet Academy's parklike grounds, enjoying the feel of the warmth on her skin.

And dreading the interview she was facing. Admiral Owen Paris had a reputation that was legendary, and while no one actually believed he ground up small children and sprinkled them on salads, it seemed a fair description of his demeanor.

Tough. Demanding. Unyielding. Those words might describe any of Starfleet's officers, but when used in conjunction with Admiral Paris, they always seemed to take on new meaning. The stories abounded: this was the man who demoted his aide, a highly respected full commander, for making a mistake on a padd entry. This was the man who flunked an entire class of cadets because one of them was late to class. This was the man who took cadets on wilderness training so punishing many dropped out of school rather than endure it.

Kathryn had, however, noted that no one who had ever undergone one of these atrocities had ever been heard from; the stories were all related as having happened to "a close friend," or "my friend's cousin." Secretly she wondered if this formidable reputation wasn't something Admiral Paris created for himself, a looming, mythic presence in Starfleet annals.

Even if that was true, she dreaded the interview. Admiral Paris was no longer on the active faculty of the Academy, having been transferred to Starfleet Command; it was bold of her even to approach him with her request. And if he did agree to be her advisor for her junior honors thesis, she would have to work twice as hard as anyone else, for Paris was that demanding. It was often considered unluckier to be one of his favorites than one of his discards; once the laser-flame of his attention fell on someone, that person's life was forever changed.

She looked up as a couple strolled by, laughing. The tall young cadet she knew from afar; his name was William Riker and she had spotted him during her first weeks at the Academy two years ago. He looked so much like Cheb Packer she had felt faint for a minute. The dark, tousled hair, the deep blue eyes—the resemblance was uncanny.

And so Kathryn vowed to keep her distance. She wanted that episode behind her, and didn't want even to be reminded of Cheb. Or risk getting emotionally involved with someone just because he *looked* like Cheb.

So she'd managed to get through two years in school without having met William Riker or had a class with him. Not that he would necessarily have taken notice of her— he seemed always to be attracted to women who were galvanizingly beautiful and supremely confident of their attractiveness. That, she realized glumly, was hardly her. In fact, she'd turned into something of a monk since coming to the Academy. The things that interested her weren't the parties or the dating; she was excited by her studies, by the new disciplines she'd been exposed to. Not only did they challenge and electrify, they didn't break your heart.

William Riker walked on by, laughing with a beautiful cadet, and Kathryn's mind turned back to Admiral Paris. What was the proper attitude to take with him? Deferential and submissive? Outgoing and assertive? Warm and likable?

She realized she couldn't begin to answer the question because she didn't know what she wanted: on the one hand, landing Admiral Paris for a junior honors thesis would be an incredible coup; on the other, it would provide an entire set of difficulties that would be obviated if she simply asked one of her major professors. The more she thought, the more she began to wonder why it had seemed like a good idea. Suddenly she felt faintly queasy.

Leaning over to get some blood to her head, she found herself looking into two dark eyes. A fat puppy had waddled over to her bench and was gazing at her expectantly, as though assuming she would provide for whatever needs it had. It was a golden retriever, still an off-white color that gave it the appearance of a round, fluffy snowball.

Kathryn looked around for its owner. No one was in sight except a couple of cadets walking in the opposite direction. She reached down and scratched the puppy's ears; he responded by rolling over on his back and extending all four pudgy paws into the air and wriggling in ecstasy. She stroked his silky stomach, which was almost distended with baby fat, and the pup wriggled even more.

Then he suddenly regained his footing and tried to put two paws on the bench, but he was still too short and he flopped on the ground. Eagerly he tried it again, seeming not to make any connection between his efforts and his failure.

Kathryn scooped him into her lap, stroking him and murmuring softly to him. "Where'd you come from, fella? Do you belong to anyone? What's your name?"

The pup snuggled in her lap and plopped his head down on her leg. As she scratched and caressed him, his eyes began to close, and in seconds, he was asleep.

If no one claimed him, she would keep him. Pets were forbidden in the dorm, of course, but as a junior she could live off-campus. She'd get an apartment for herself and the puppy, and she'd train him and brush him and comfort him. He'd never be unfed, or alone, or unhappy.

A profound peace settled over Kathryn. The warm sun, the soft presence of the puppy in her lap, the pastoral setting of the Academy's grounds—all combined to bring her to a condition of imperturbability that was almost nirvana-like. Her eyes closed, and she imagined she was back in the cornfields of Indiana, with Bramble on her tummy, sleeping in the sun.

"There you are, you naughty thing. I can't let you out of my sight, can I?"

Kathryn's eyes snapped open and she saw Commander Ruah Brackett heading toward her. The commander was a handsome woman in her thirties, a full professor in mathematics. Kathryn hoped to take her differential geometry course in her senior year; Brackett had a reputation as an inspired teacher.

Now she was reaching for the puppy, pulling him from Kathryn's lap and slipping a collar and leash around his plump neck. "He slipped right out of his collar, the little devil. I named him Chomel, which means 'peace,' but I suspect he has more of the devil in him."

Kathryn reached out for a final stroke of the puppy's satiny fur; an ineffable sadness came over her. "He's a beautiful pup. Where did you get him?" Maybe he has a sibling, she thought, maybe I could find his brother or sister.

"He adopted me. I was in Golden Gate Park one evening and he came out of the woods and sat down next to me. He couldn't have been more than five or six weeks old. I took him home and fed him, cleaned him up. He slept on my bed that night—and that's where he's still sleeping. I don't know what I'll do when he's fully grown."

Kathryn could see that Commander Brackett's eyes were shining as she told this story. She adored this puppy. Kathryn's eyes stung as she experienced her own sense of loss, and gratitude that the puppy had found such a loving friend.

It was after the commander had left, puppy in ungainly pursuit, that it occurred to Kathryn that perhaps she needed something to love.

* * *

Admiral Paris wasn't in his office when she arrived for her appointment. His aide, Lieutenant Commander Klenman, a dark-haired, gracious woman with a British accent, explained that he'd been called to an emergency meeting but he was expected in ten or fifteen minutes. Would she care to wait?

And so she sat in the admiral's office and studied the pictures on his walls and on his desk.

The walls were adorned with pictures of various groups of Starfleet personnel: Starfleet on Mars, on Vulcan, on Bole, on Risa. Meetings, conferences, commemorations—all showing at least one officer named Paris: Argonne Paris, James Paris, Caroline Paris, Bailey Paris, Mackenzie Paris. It was a display of some of the most revered names in Starfleet history, generations of brilliant, selfless officers who had dedicated their lives to the service of others.

The pictures on the desk were different. They were recent family pictures—a pretty, laughing woman Kathryn took to be Admiral Paris' wife, and several pictures of children of various ages. Kathryn determined there were three, a boy and two girls, who were depicted from their babyhood until what must be their present ages: the girls in their early teens, the boy—who had a particularly impish smile—around ten. They were all handsome, happy children, tow-headed and blue-eyed. If Admiral Owen Paris was an ogre, this laughing family seemed to flourish under his cruel ministrations.

She heard the whoosh of the door opening behind her and sprang to her feet.

"At ease, Cadet. After keeping you waiting for half an hour, I don't expect formalities."

She was looking into blue-gray eyes that were remarkably intense, that seemed to have the capacity to burrow into her brain and go probing around in there, discerning just what she was about. She took a breath and tried to shed the sensation.

Those disconcerting eyes were set in a genial face of regular features, with a straight, narrow nose and a puckish mouth that seemed to have to fight not to grin. Once-blond hair was now streaked with gray, all of it an unruly gnarl of waves and cowlicks.

The dreaded Admiral Paris reminded her of the cheerful farmers she had grown up with.

He waved idly at her. "Sit down, sit down. Let's get to it. I have the feeling you want me to rekindle my days as an Academy professor."

Kathryn was stunned. She had told no one about her plan. It was so unlikely that she didn't want to appear foolhardy. Could this man actually probe her mind? Was he a telepath? She felt her heart beating in her chest.

"It's remarkable you should say that, sir. I hadn't mentioned it to anyone, but I was hopeful that you would consent to being my advisor for a junior honors thesis."

The ever-present smile tugged at his mouth. "Junior honors thesis, eh? I might consider a senior thesis. Maybe you should wait until next year."

"Maybe you should wait until you hear what the thesis is about." The words were out of her mouth before she thought, and she realized they sounded impudent. But the admiral seemed amused, and he didn't fight the grin.

"Touché. Tell me, Cadet Janeway, what your thesis concerns."

"Massive compact halo objects."

The smile disappeared from his face, to be replaced by that first scrutinizing stare. Once again, Kathryn felt that he was scanning her brain. This time, he didn't seem to be getting results. "I see. And just what is it you would propose to offer about halo objects that provides new insight?" Halo objects, she knew, were a special interest of the admiral's; he had spent years trying to formulate a theory on the origins of these enigmatic and elusive space phenomena.

Kathryn leaned forward, feeling on surer ground now. "I've developed a new hypothesis concerning their origins. One that might revolutionize all the thinking that's gone into them so far."

"Very ambitious. Just what is this hypothesis?"

"With all due respect, sir—if you want to find out, you'll have to read my thesis. Which I can't write until I have an advisor."

He laughed out loud. "I like you, Cadet. Your reputation precedes you, you know. You're the young woman who reported finding a chordate in the caves of Mars. Stirred up a whole hornet's nest of scientific controversy."

Kathryn sighed inwardly. It was true that her claim— which she had considered carefully before making, since it would mean an admission of having gone cave-diving— had startled Starfleet's scientists. Well-equipped diving parties were immediately launched, but no fossil other than the one she had spotted had been found, and there was vast disagreement in the scientific community as to whether the find was in fact a chordate. Her admission had earned her a rebuke from her mother, but so far as she knew, her father was unaware of the escapade. He was too busy to care.

"I think we'll get along well," Admiral Paris continued. But then he leaned toward her over his desk and fastened her with those piercing eyes. "But I warn you—everything you've heard about me is true. I don't suffer slackers. You'll work harder for me than you've ever worked for anyone. You'll learn to live on four hours of sleep a night. And if you complain or whine or, God forbid, burst into tears, we're finished as of that moment. Are we clear on that?"

"Yes, sir."

He held her gaze, unblinking, for another full minute. She returned it firmly. Finally he leaned back, picked up one of the pictures from his desk. "What do you think of my family?"

"Very handsome, sir."

"Thank you. I'm proud of them. The girls are quite independent and have informed me in no uncertain terms that they don't intend to follow the family tradition and enter Starfleet. I respect that." There was a pause, then he continued. "But I'll admit I'm pleased that young Tom seems to have his heart set on the family career. I wouldn't push my children, but it would have taken something out of me if mine were the last generation of Starfleet officers."

"I understand, sir. I think my father feels very much the same."

Mention of her father seemed to sober the admiral. "I imagine you haven't seen much of your father lately. I ran into him on Deep Space Four a few weeks ago. He's working very hard on the Cardassian situation. I'm sorry to say it's not looking good."

"He doesn't talk about it. But I know he's worried." Kathryn didn't want to talk about her father; it made her feel uncomfortably vulnerable. She moved a bit in her chair, hoping Admiral Paris would pick up the cue and dismiss her.

But he seemed to want to talk. "Part of the problem is that we don't know much about the Cardassians. They've always been somewhat suspect, but of course we prefer to think they're people of their word. And they claim not to be interested in expanding their territory. But there've been some unexplained incidents near their borders that are a bit disconcerting."

"Yes, sir." What he wasn't saying was what no one wanted to say: the specter of war hung over the Federation.

It was a word everyone hoped had become obsolete, for there hadn't been armed conflict in the Federation for decades.

But in a distant part of space, a new enemy seemed to be stirring, and Starfleet's upper echelons were scrambling to try to avoid combat. Diplomatic endeavors were under way. But at the same time, Kathryn knew that strategic and tactical discussions were being held as well. She assumed her father was involved because of starship design, but she didn't know for certain. That was how far he had shut them out of his professional life.

Admiral Paris seemed to pick up on her reluctance to discuss the issue. He stood, offered her his hand, and dismissed her. "I believe your first step is to hand me a thesis proposal. I'll expect it on my desk by Monday morning at zero-eight-hundred. Understood?"

Kathryn felt the blood drain from her face. Hand in a thesis proposal in four days? Was he crazy? Even if she worked on nothing else she couldn't finish; and she had classes to attend and work for those courses and—

"Understood, sir," she said crisply. And she gave him her most confident look. For suddenly she was on firm ground. Do the impossible? Meet an outrageous deadline? Solve an insoluble problem? If anyone could do it, she could. She'd show him. She wasn't afraid of him, she wouldn't be bullied by him, and no matter what task he set for her, she'd do it—better and faster than he'd expected.

Hadn't she been doing that all her life?

When she returned to her dorm room, her roommate, a beautiful, patrician woman from Boston, Lettie Garrett, had an uneasy look on her face. Kathryn noticed it immediately, because Lettie never looked uncomfortable. She seemed to be one of those people who were born with poise and moved serenely through life without mishap, taking in stride any bumps one might suffer along the way. She had long dark hair pulled off her face in the simplest of hairstyles, and huge dark eyes ringed with long lashes. Kathryn suspected she'd dated every available man at the Academy at one time or another.

"Kathryn . . . what do you have planned this weekend?"

"This *weekend?* Staying up day and night to get a thesis proposal ready."

"Couldn't you take an hour or two off?"

"Lettie, what's going on?"

"I met someone I think you'd really like."

This was what Kathryn had suspected. Lettie couldn't understand her ascetic way of life and was forever trying to arrange dates for her. Kathryn had gone along with this several times, but nothing had ever seemed to work out; if a young man followed through and asked her out again, she began to feel pressed and rushed, and so retreated further into herself. There had been one young man—she couldn't even remember his name now—she had thought might be an interesting friend, but he had never called and after a day Kathryn had thought better of it and declined to call him.

"Lettie, it's sweet of you, but this isn't the time. I have to have a proposal on Admiral Paris' desk Monday morning."

Lettie's eyebrows lifted, a sight that gratified Kathryn. She'd pulled off something astonishing in getting Paris to work with her, and it was pleasurable to know that Lettie was impressed.

"I understand. But you have to eat. One hour, Saturday evening. A sandwich and a cup of coffee."

"I can have a sandwich and coffee right here at my desk. Which is what I'll be doing."

"You'll regret this for the rest of your life. He's handsome, charming, very intelligent—he's exactly the kind of man you'd be attracted to."

"That's what you said about that last one. The exobiologist? The one who wanted to practice his homework on me?"

"But he *was* handsome and charming and intelligent."

"I have to work. Absolutely, positively, irrevocably, inextricably *have* to work."

"I'll check with you around six on Saturday. Maybe you'll need the break. Maybe it will be the best thing you could do for yourself, and you'd come back refreshed and eager to sail in again."

Kathryn sighed. Lettie was as tenacious as a rat terrier. There was no point in fighting about it now; come Saturday she'd be deep into her work and would simply refuse to go. "Okay. Check with me then."

Lettie smiled, pleased. She had a generous heart, Kathryn knew, and truly wanted to help her friend expand her narrow horizons. She had no way of knowing that the world inside Kathryn's head was so rich and complete that she had little need of any other.

So no one could have been more surprised than Kathryn that she found herself walking with Lettie to a coffee bistro near campus on Saturday at eighteen hundred hours.

"Why am I doing this?" she asked Lettie. "How did I let you talk me into it? I'm not half done with my proposal; I have no business going anywhere."

"You'll thank me. You'll be down on your knees, bowing to me. This one is *special.*"

Kathryn sighed. She'd been persuaded only because she'd run into a wall with her proposal, and there actually was some validity to the idea of taking an hour—not one minute more—and getting some fresh air, a decent cup of Tarkalian coffee, and something in her stomach. She'd come back to her desk with renewed vigor, which she certainly needed; she'd had only two hours' sleep the night before and couldn't look forward to much more tonight.

They entered the coffee bistro, which was nearly empty. Kathryn wondered how it stayed in business; almost no one drank coffee anymore, and while this place served good food, most of the student crowd preferred the tea bars that had sprung up on just about every corner. But Kathryn loved coffee: loved the taste, loved the aroma, loved the mild "kick" it gave her. She was as disciplined about drinking coffee, however, as she was in the rest of her life; two cups a day, a formula she usually stretched to four by making a half-decaf blend.

Lettie was leading her to a corner table, where two cadets were sitting, backs to them. "There they are."

"Is that Howie? Your beau?"

"Yes, and his friend. The one you'll thank me for." They had reached the table and as they did so, both the young men got to their feet.

And Kathryn found herself looking right at William Riker.

She didn't even hear the introductions Lettie was making. Her mind swirled, trying to think of some way to get out of this. Say she was sick? That she'd forgotten she had to make a transmission to her mother? Nothing that made sense came to her, and she found herself sitting opposite the handsome young man with the dark hair and blue eyes. And he was talking to her.

"I'm sorry . . . what did you say?"

"Do you like to be called Kathryn? Or is there a familiar form you like?"

"Kathryn. Just Kathryn."

"I've always thought that was a beautiful name."

William Riker smiled, and if he was handsome before, he was gorgeous now. Just like Cheb.

Kathryn desperately felt the need to control the situation. She couldn't sit like this, addled, and let her feelings become engaged. She'd been caught off guard, momentarily stunned, and she was perfectly capable of regaining her equilibrium. She'd spend the requisite hour with this person and that would be the end of it.

"How about you? Is it William?"

"I'm usually called Wil."

"Then Wil it is."

"I'm surprised we've never met. We're in the same class; you'd think we'd have run into each other before this."

That's because I've gone out of my way to avoid you, thought Kathryn, but she simply smiled and said, "I've been on a science program. We've probably just been in different classes."

"I hear you landed the Scorcher for your junior thesis."

"Is that what he's called? I'd never heard that."

"He leaves only scorched earth in his wake. No prisoners."

"He's demanding, but I thought he was awfully nice. Very devoted to his family. Are you doing a junior thesis?"

"I'm focusing on exopaleontology. Someday I want my own ship, and I think a broad educational base with an emphasis on the evolution of galactic cultures is the best background I can have."

"Your own ship—as captain?"

"Right."

Kathryn was impressed. You didn't often hear people with those lofty goals expressing them so comfortably. She had no doubt that Wil Riker would get what he wanted.

"I've never had any interest in command. I'd like to be the science officer on an exploration into deep space— someplace no one's seen before. That would be thrilling."

He smiled easily at her. "Maybe we'll end up together. You as science officer on my ship."

There was nothing arrogant or self-involved about Wil Riker. He was low-key, comfortable, easy to talk to. Charming, as Lettie had said.

Dangerous.

Already, she'd been drawn into amiable conversation with him, her guard dropping in spite of herself. His blue eyes held her like lasers, and she realized she didn't *want* to look away. Her fingertips began to tingle.

Time to take control.

"My thesis is on massive compact halo objects. Are you familiar with them?" A long dissertation on her part about a dimly understood space phenomenon would put him to sleep. Hardly the subject for sparkling conversation and certain to dissuade any desire for him to see her again.

But, to her amazement, he was nodding. "A little. One of my science teachers at home in Alaska has done some study of them. She got me interested. What tack is your thesis taking?"

Kathryn was genuinely flustered now. Beyond his charm, beyond his good looks and courteous demeanor, he was also a serious student. She stared at him, wishing she could find warts on his nose, something, *anything* that would make him something other than the most attractive man she'd ever met. Because she wasn't going to get drawn into something as potentially painful as another love affair. There was too much to do, to learn, to accomplish, to waste emotional energy like that. Feeling panicky, she rose.

"I'm so sorry—I just remembered, I'm supposed to be at my terminal in twenty minutes to retrieve some research materials I've requested from the astrophysics laboratory." She was vaguely aware of the bewilderment in Wil's eyes, Lettie's shocked face, her friend Howie's surprise. She knew she was babbling, but kept at it, hoping to sound plausible.

"It's on gravitational lensing, and I can't risk losing the

transmission, it's a part of my proposal and I don't dare turn it in to the Scorcher"—a goofy smile toward Wil at this—"without that research. You understand. Well, so nice to meet you, and I wish you the best. I'm sure you'll get that ship. Goodbye. Howie, Lettie—thanks for everything. It's been delightful. Truly."

She was backing away as she went through this litany, smiling and nodding as though what she was doing was the most natural thing in the world. Only the three faces she was retreating from told her otherwise.

Kathryn's back was to the door of the dorm room; she was hunched over her terminal, doggedly inputting information. The doors opened and she heard Lettie enter.

"How could you? How could you have embarrassed everyone like that? I can't believe it—it's not even good *manners!"* Lettie was outraged. She marched over to Kathryn to continue berating her.

And saw that Kathryn's face was streaked with tears, eyes swollen from a long bout of crying. Lettie melted immediately. "Kathryn—what is it? Tell me, please. . . . I'm so sorry, I shouldn't have come in here like that. . . ."

"You had every right to," said Kathryn miserably. "I was awful. I know. But I couldn't stay there a minute longer."

"But why? What happened? Was he rude to you?"

"No, no, he's very sweet. Just like you said—charming, attractive, intelligent. He may be the most wonderful man I've ever met." And with that, Kathryn once more broke into tears.

She was never able to explain fully to Lettie the complexities of her despair—probably, she thought ruefully, because she didn't understand them herself—but Lettie finally claimed to understand her feelings, and promised never to rope her into a blind date again.

She also made Kathryn go to bed for three hours, at which time she woke feeling much better and stayed up the rest of that night, the following day, and all the following night.

And at eight hundred hours on Monday morning there was a padd waiting on Admiral Paris' desk containing her thesis proposal.

It was the beginning of a remarkable relationship.

CHAPTER

15

JAL SITTIK LISTENED AS MISKK SPAT OUT HIS ACCOUNT OF THE debacle in the fruit grove. One man dead, everyone else injured, some critically, from a horrific battle with reptiles that dropped from the trees. Miskk himself had nearly been killed, and would have been were it not for his prodigious strength, which allowed him to kill a serpent with his bare hands.

Sittik doubted this tale, but thought it unwise to challenge Miskk given the turn of events. It was he who had sent the men into the grove, and Miskk could easily make an issue of that, one which he would bring to Maje Dut. Sittik longed briefly for Miskk's own death in the coils of the reptiles, but accepted that fate had decreed he would live on to provide an ongoing obstacle to Sittik's quest for success. So be it— overcoming obstacles would only make him stronger.

"You acquitted yourself well, Miskk. It is unfortunate that Pelg did not survive, but his death will be spoken of as a sacrifice to the great victory we will achieve today. His name will be praised."

"Your great victory seems to elude you, Sittik. Have you even located the Federations yet?"

Sittik smiled. He'd been waiting for this. "Of course." He stomped his foot on the ground. "They're underground. Just beneath us."

There was a flicker of confusion in Miskk's face, and Sittik indulged himself in a small gloating laugh. He made a mental note to reward the man who had detected the Federation life signs beneath the surface, but saw no reason to acknowledge him to Miskk. "There are subterranean passageways—caves, perhaps—where they have taken refuge. We haven't yet found the opening, but it's just a matter of time."

"Why not simply blast an opening with weapons?"

"That's precisely what I intend to do, Miskk, if you'll stop prattling on about your mishap." Sittik strode away from him and toward the others, snapping orders at them, wishing even more strongly that Miskk had met his death—a slow one, preferably—within the snake-infested grove of trees.

Neelix had stayed with the injured at the main staging area of the underground structure. Greta Kale was feeling better and LeFevre fully recovered, though all of them remained somewhat shaken by their gauntlet through the reptiles.

Neelix thought briefly of the cake he'd made, still waiting on *Voyager* for Tuvok's delectation. The thought of the *nocha* confection was comforting to him somehow; at the least, thinking of it was better than thinking of those noxious snakes, and a lot better than thinking of the Kazon who were prowling above them, looking for a way down so they could slaughter everyone they found.

Captain Janeway, of course, would be looking for them, and undoubtedly effect their rescue. Eventually. Unless she had her hands full with the ship those Kazon soldiers came from—a distinct possibility, as Neelix saw it.

He made himself focus on the Grissibian cake, remembering the explosion of flavor as the *nocha* detonated on the tongue. Kes would love it.

He looked around, wishing she would come back. He knew not to appear overly protective of her—she hated that—but he couldn't help but be uncomfortable that she had so few compunctions about exploring this alien structure. There was no knowing *what* might be here. But Kes' curiosity always outweighed her fear, and nothing he could say or do would change that.

Suddenly a fierce explosion rumbled through the underground tunnels, and all of the crew instinctively drew phasers. Tuvok came running from a passageway, weapon drawn and tricorder scanning.

"They are firing from above. Trying to break through."

"That shouldn't take them long," Neelix replied, eyeing the ceiling of the structure with apprehension.

"We can't be certain of that. We're unfamiliar with the building material of this structure. It may be durable and quite resistant to weapons fire."

Another explosion rumbled, then another. Dust and dirt began to fall from the ceiling.

Tuvok hit his commbadge. "Tuvok to all personnel. Regroup in the main staging area at once."

Neelix took this as his cue to hit his own communicator. "Neelix to Kes. Did you hear that, sweeting?"

Only silence answered him. He hailed her again, then hailed Kim, with whom she had left. No one answered. He turned to Tuvok in some alarm.

"I wouldn't be concerned yet, Mr. Neelix. Ensign Kim

informed me that they were investigating a stairway they had found. They may simply be blocked from communication."

"But—where are they? And if they can't hear us, how will they know to come back? I don't like this at all."

"Please don't succumb to panic. We must all do our best to think clearly. Are the wounded able to travel?"

"Yes, everyone's basically all right. Where are we going to travel to?"

"I want to locate a position that is strategically advantageous, one from which we can defend ourselves most effectively."

The rest of the crew was beginning to collect in the chamber, and Tuvok gave them orders. Soon, they all began moving collectively down one of the passageways, and Neelix hoped desperately they were moving toward Kes and Harry.

Harry and Kes were exploring the chamber in which they now found themselves. Harry estimated it to be perhaps ten meters square, with neither windows nor doors, and its walls were of a material significantly different from that of the underground tunnels and rooms they had seen so far.

It looked metallic, of a blue-purple hue which was the same color as the ambient light in the room. Harry scanned the room and read that the walls were composed of a metal that was unknown to the Federation database. No surprise there. But unlike the corridors they had investigated, Harry found no indications of an organic component in these walls.

He glanced at Kes, who was looking around in puzzlement. "The clicking noise is gone," she said.

Harry was relieved that she was making rational statements; whatever trance had gripped her had seemingly released its hold. He continued to scan. "Now I'm reading energy signatures. There's technology of some kind at work here—" He stopped abruptly, for he had detected a more curious reading on his tricorder.

Life signs.

Faint, delicate, like the heartbeats of tiny birds. But unmistakable.

Where were they coming from? The room seemed to be empty except for the two of them. But he was most definitely reading the life signs of an alien species, throbbing gently.

They walked toward the wall. No seams were visible, no joints. The satiny surface was cool to the touch but not cold. They could find no mark, no pattern, nothing that gave them a clue as to their next step.

"We were led here, I'm sure of it," said Kes. "I felt— *drawn*—here. By the clicking sounds, and by a . . . a need to come. I couldn't resist it."

"I know. I saw you. Whatever it was must have tapped into your telepathic abilities, because it didn't affect me in the same way."

"It felt . . . urgent. Vital. I had to follow the sound wherever it took me because . . . because . . ." She trailed off in some confusion.

"Because why?"

"I'm not sure. I think I was going to say . . . because if I didn't come here—death would be victorious."

"What does that mean?"

"I don't know that it means anything. It's just what I was feeling."

"Do you feel that way now?"

"No. All the sensations are gone."

"Great. Now how the heck do we get out of here?" He hit his commbadge, but wasn't surprised when his hail

171

didn't raise anyone. He began scanning again, instinctively, looking for answers. He noticed that he'd begun to perspire, and hated to admit he was that apprehensive.

He began a tour of the room, scanning the walls closely. Maybe he could locate the source of the faint life signs. It was tedious work, and he wiped his brow several times before he completed his circumnavigation. When he had looped the room once, he came back to where Kes was standing, her fingers lightly grazing the shiny walls. Then she looked over at him in puzzlement.

"The wall feels warmer than before."

Harry realized Kes was perspiring, too. A few locks of her hair were damp. He reached out, touched the wall, and found that it was no longer cool. It wasn't what you'd call hot, but it had lost the satiny chill it had before. The tricorder confirmed it had risen several degrees in temperature.

Kes turned in the room, hands on her cheeks. "It's getting hotter," she said. And then they both noticed that the hue of the wall was changing, too. It had lost all hints of blue and was now a purple with decidedly red undertones.

"Mr. Paris, have you ever achieved orbit directly from warp?"

"No, ma'am, I can't say that I have."

"Well, this is your chance."

Tom Paris turned and glanced at the captain, though he knew she was serious. "Ma'am?"

"I want to get our people back. But in all likelihood, the Kazon are still monitoring the planet. I want to stay at warp speed until we're behind the limb, then go directly into orbit."

Janeway watched as Tom pondered this dangerous feat. She could almost hear his mind working, making the necessary calculations. A moment passed, and then he glanced up at her.

"Captain, begging your pardon, but have *you* ever accomplished this?"

"No, Lieutenant, but I've heard of its being done. Therefore it's a possibility."

"Yes, ma'am. What warp factor did you want to use?"

"The highest we can and still pull this off."

Tom turned again to his console, and ran his fingers over the touch-sensitive surface. Janeway knew he was entering parameters for one of the most difficult calculations he'd ever attempted to perform. The navigational computer, assisted by the multivariate computational skills of *Voyager*'s neural gel packs, would consider rates of acceleration and deceleration, the gravitational fields of the planet and its sun, the effect of the drag from the farthest reaches of the planet's upper atmosphere, and the performance efficiencies of the ship's warp nacelles. Tom was reviewing these numbers as they flashed across his screen.

But even the extraordinary power of *Voyager*'s computer system couldn't make the final choice among several viable trajectories; no computer could possibly take into account every subtle variable and contingency in such a complex calculation. Only the intuition of a gifted and experienced pilot could be trusted to make the final choice of heading and speed. And Janeway was banking on Tom's ability to do just that: to make a choice based on what *felt* right.

Finally, she saw him take a deep, quiet breath. "I think I can pull it off at warp four point two, Captain," he said, his voice betraying no hint of anxiety over the importance of this decision.

"Then do it."

"Aye, warp four point two. Engaging . . ." There was a slight hesitation as he took a careful breath; she sensed him stilling his mind, concentrating on the task. "Now."

Voyager leapt to warp. At this speed, the planet was only a few minutes away from the shell of gas and dust clouds surrounding the distant reaches of the star system. Getting there would be easy; the hard part would be bringing the ship into orbit a microsecond before *Voyager* slammed into the planet at over a hundred times the speed of light.

"Full power to inertial dampers," ordered Janeway crisply. She wanted to project an air of confidence about this maneuver.

"Twelve seconds to orbit," said Tom, his voice as calm as hers. His fingers tapped the console, programming a few last corrections before entering the automatic deceleration sequence. On the main viewscreen, the image of the planet grew at an alarming rate. Janeway made herself focus on it, trying to shut out doubt as to the outcome of this maneuver. If it didn't work, she thought, at least the end would be instantaneous.

Tom's voice didn't waver as he began to call out. "Dropping out of warp in five . . . four . . . three . . . two . . . one . . ."

The ship lurched violently, throwing everyone forward. Even at maximum power the inertial damping field couldn't completely compensate for the enormous change in acceleration. The ship listed slightly, and for one brief instant Janeway thought they had lost control and would hit the planet's atmosphere and incinerate from the friction.

But then *Voyager* eased into a gentle free fall a thousand kilometers above the surface. She looked down at Tom Paris, who was a little pale but smiling. He had every right to be pleased with himself.

"Good work, Mr. Paris," she said mildly.

He turned in his seat and looked up at her. His saucy confidence had returned in full. "Nothing to it," he grinned.

"See if you can find our people," Janeway began, but Chakotay was ahead of her, already manning his station, directing the sensors to scan for life signs of their crew.

"Captain, a Kazon ship has come into orbit on the opposite side of the planet."

"Then they'll find us in minutes. Any luck, Commander?"

"Negative. I see Kazon signs—about forty of them— but none of ours."

Janeway considered. That could mean Tuvok had found refuge in a place that was shielded from sensors.

It could also mean that the entire away team was dead.

But if that were true, why would Kazon forces stay on the surface? Why would the ship be monitoring the planet? She had to assume her people were alive, shielded, waiting for rescue.

"The Kazon ship is moving this way," intoned Paris.

They still couldn't risk a shoot-out with the Kazon; weapons arrays were dubious at best. They had no choice but to retreat again.

"Take us out of here the same way you got us here, Lieutenant. At warp."

"Aye, Captain." *Before this day is over I'm going to have this maneuver down pat,* thought Paris, as he rocketed *Voyager* from orbit.

Chakotay turned to her. "If Tuvok were here, he'd remind you that retreat is always an option. And that the soundest strategy protects the many at the expense of the few."

"But he's not here. And I'm not quitting until every option has been explored. Put on your thinking cap, Commander. We're going to figure out how to rescue our people."

Chakotay smiled, and Janeway returned it, reminded once more of how very glad she was to have him at her side.

CHAPTER

16

ENSIGN KATHRYN JANEWAY WATCHED AS EARTH RECEDED, and remembered that first flight years ago, when she and her father had taken the shuttle to Mars. She could still recall the visceral thrill she felt as the blue and white marble grew smaller and smaller and finally became just a dot of light in the blackness of space.

It was her first lesson, repeated here today, in the vastness of space, of Earth's relative unimportance in the heavens, and of man's place in the universe as just one species among many.

Her father had told her, when she was small, that a thousand years ago people believed that Earth was the center of the universe, that all other heavenly bodies revolved around it. When Copernicus suggested otherwise, and Galileo proved it, they weren't lauded for their discoveries; they were castigated. People then had raged at the truth rather than embrace it.

Kathryn had always found it comforting to feel part of a

vast family. First was the family of humankind, a planet of beings who were at one with each other, who had long ago stopped battling over imaginary lines in the ground, and who lived in peace and harmony.

But to consider oneself part of an even greater group—of the family of the galaxies and all their myriad species—was to feel a fortunate child, with billions of aunts, uncles, and cousins, to be alone nowhere in the universe. To Kathryn that was one of the wondrous privileges of life in a spacefaring age.

Now, sitting on the bridge of the starship *Icarus*, with Admiral Paris in command, setting off on an expedition into deep space in order to study massive compact halo objects, she thought she could know no greater happiness. She was actually the junior science officer on this mission, tapped by the admiral for his recently sanctioned Arias expedition just one year after she'd completed a doctoral degree in quantum cosmology. It was heady stuff for one so young to be chosen for such an important mission.

She sensed a presence near her station and realized Admiral Paris had moved closer to her, still staring at the viewscreen, where Earth was now a small dot, blue turning to white. "That's the last you'll see of home for at least a year, Ensign," he said. "I hope you won't be getting homesick on me."

She looked up at him, unsure whether he was kidding or not. She had learned that he had a wonderful, wry sense of humor, and enjoyed tweaking those he liked. But his style was so dry it often blurred the line between joke and truth.

"I'm not the homesick type, sir," she replied, preferring to play it safe by taking him seriously. But she wasn't surprised when his eyes twinkled and he grinned at her.

"Actually, Ensign, you're the *last* person I'd suspect of that particular malady."

He didn't explain himself further, and Kathryn found

herself wondering if the admiral thought a lack of suscepti-
bility to homesickness was a good thing or a bad one. And
then she wondered why it mattered so much what he
thought.

"I'd like to meet with the science team at eleven hundred
hours," continued the admiral. "I don't think you've met
everyone yet."

"No, sir. I'm looking forward to it." Actually, she was
fitfully anxious about that encounter. She was bound to be
the youngest and least experienced of the group, a fact of
which she was sure they were all aware. Would they accept
her? Would they respect her? Did they resent the admiral
bringing a raw ensign on such a far-ranging and scientifi-
cally significant expedition?

She would have to prove herself to them.

But as it happened, there was only one person with
whom that would prove to be necessary. When they
convened in the wardroom later that morning, Kathryn
sensed nothing but friendship and receptivity from most of
the people in the room as Admiral Paris introduced them.

"May I present Commander T'Por, whose expertise in
astrophysics is legendary." Kathryn looked into the solemn eyes of an elegant Vulcan woman of whom she'd
already heard a great deal. "Lieutenant Darren Ditillo, a
seasoned space traveler with proficiency in astrometric
analysis." A small, wiry man in his late thirties with
thinning hair and a ready smile shook her hand enthusias-
tically. "Ensign Sally Rhodes, only a few years out of the
Academy but already well respected in the field of con-
densed matter physics." The young woman was only a few
years older than she, and Kathryn was comforted to know
there was a friendly peer among the group.

They all seemed welcoming, and Kathryn began to relax.
But there was one other person in the group.

"And this is Lieutenant Justin Tighe, our engineering

liaison." Kathryn shook the hand of a lean, muscular man of about thirty with dark, tousled hair, whose grip was confident and whose eyes—deep, blue eyes—were challenging.

"Welcome aboard, Ensign," he said with a smile that was at once knowing and confrontational. Kathryn felt an unease that began at her fingertips and radiated up her arms and into her cheeks, which she realized were flushing. "Thank you, sir," she murmured, withdrew her hand and took her seat at the polished black table in the wardroom. She sat with her back to the wide window, outside which the ethereal streaks of warp stars illuminated the darkness of space. It was a sight that still mesmerized her, and she didn't want to be distracted during this meeting.

It meant, however, that she sat right next to Justin Tighe.

"I'm gratified to be leading this expedition," Admiral Paris began. "You all know that I've been intrigued by massive compact halo objects for a great many years. We are, of course, heading for the galactic rim, six hundred light-years beyond Deep Space Station Seven, where there's a suspected 'birthplace' of these enigmatic phenomena. I'd like to convene daily seminars for all of us to trade information and ideas so we'll be snapped in by the time we get there."

There was nothing remarkable in what Admiral Paris was saying, and Kathryn found herself uncomfortably aware of Lieutenant Tighe next to her. She kept her face turned away from him, toward the admiral at the head of the table, but his presence was palpable. She forced herself to shut him out, to focus entirely on the admiral, who was up on his feet now, pacing the room, pausing to stand by the window and stare out at the star streaks as he talked.

"There is, however, another aspect to this expedition. One which it was necessary to conceal from you until we had left Earth because of its top-secret nature."

He had everyone's rapt attention now. His voice was grave as he continued. "Ours is certainly a scientific endeavor, and we hope to return to Earth with a greater understanding of halo objects. If we accomplish nothing more than that, we will have expanded the field of galactic inquiry to a significant degree."

He turned to them, his kind eyes finding, and holding, a look with each of them in turn. "But that isn't the sole purpose for our venture. There is an additional, covert, mission to be accomplished during our journey." Paris paused here, as though thinking how best to introduce the subject he was leading to.

"First, I must remind you that this is a matter of the highest secrecy. Not everyone on the ship will be aware of it. It is essential that you speak of it to no one—not even among yourselves. I am telling you because, as the senior scientific staff, you might question some of the procedures we'll be choosing in the future. You will be curious as to some of the destinations we select. And it's essential that those questions not be asked. It may be that some decisions will interfere with your scientific explorations; it is imperative that you accept those disappointments."

Kathryn was staring at Admiral Paris, mind racing. What was going on? What could be of such magnitude that it was treated with this heavy cloak of secrecy? This was uncharacteristic of Starfleet—at least of the Starfleet she had experienced—and it made her uncomfortable.

"We are also an information-gathering mission," continued Paris. "We will be traveling near Cardassian space, at times quite close to their borders, and at those times we will be actively uploading intelligence about their troop movements, weapons depots, fleet size, and other data necessary to insure the defense of the Federation."

A long, solemn silence blanketed the room as he spoke those words. Kathryn found her heart pounding. The ship was on a *spy* mission. Her first venture into deep space wasn't an innocuous assignment to gather scientific data—it was an urgent military operation, crucial and dangerous.

Admiral Paris absorbed the stunned silence that greeted his announcement, and continued. "There are those on this ship who are part of an elite core of Starfleet's finest: a highly trained, disciplined group of Rangers who will also function as members of the scientific expedition. They will work among you without your knowing their identity. I am the only person on board who knows who they are."

He eyed them once more. "Now is the time for any questions. I will answer what I can. But after today, there will be no further mention of this matter. Are you clear on that?"

Several people nodded. Sally Rhodes raised a hand, as though she were back in school. Kathryn understood the feeling. "Sir," said Ensign Rhodes, "are we going to war with Cardassia?"

"I hope not. That's part of the purpose of missions like this—to prevent war. But I'm afraid that's more up to the Cardassians than to us."

Kathryn felt Justin Tighe stir next to her. "Sir," he asked—and he didn't sound quite so confident now—"do these . . . Rangers . . . know each other? Or are they all in the dark as much as we are?"

"They know each other. It's important that they be able to function as a unit, and they've been training toward that end for over a year. But I assure you they are also so grounded in scientific technique that you will be unable to single them out."

Commander T'Por fixed the admiral with her dark eyes. "It would be logical to assume that we will be in situations of danger. Am I correct?"

"Again, there's no way to predict that. But I would have to share your assumption." He paused, as though turning over a thought in his mind. "We don't know as much about the Cardassians as we'd like. They've kept their borders closed for decades. But what we're beginning to hear, unfortunately, isn't encouraging. They're mean ones. We believe they intend to expand their territory and they have no qualms about how they do it."

He stopped and looked down at the table for a moment. "Reports we've gotten about their treatment of some of our colonists they've captured aren't—pretty. They have some particularly advanced technology for producing pain, for example. It's been a great many years since we've encountered a culture which not only employs torture as a means of intimidation, but has elevated it to a near-religious status."

Kathryn felt queasy. She didn't like to think of people inflicting pain on each other; it was the most primitive kind of violation she could imagine. She knew her people's history was rife with equal cruelty, but it hadn't been practiced for hundreds of years. Now she was hearing that people like herself were being subjected to this most inhumane treatment.

"However," Admiral Paris continued, "there's no reason to believe we will encounter any Cardassians at all. Our surveillances will be technological in nature. The plan is to get the information we need without coming face-to-face with any of them."

He faced them, waiting for more questions. There were none—not, Kathryn suspected, because they didn't exist, but because everyone had been caught so off guard that they were still in a state of shock. "Any further questions?" queried the admiral, looking from one to the other. "If not, we'll proceed. But let me try to reassure you: If all goes as we hope, this will be the last time you'll be aware of our other mission. If it's successful, it will be carried out without disrupting our scientific inquiries and without noticeable interference in our day-to-day activities. It would be my profound hope that this will be the case."

He looked around the room one more time, then put the matter behind him and began giving short-term assignments. Admiral Paris was a mature and experienced officer; he clearly had the capacity to shed one subject completely and move on to the other.

But Kathryn didn't have that ability, though she determined at that moment to develop it. She was still so stunned by the admiral's revelation that she had no reaction at all when he assigned her to work with Justin Tighe in developing sensor-array modifications.

Like a panther, she thought. *Like a powerful, sinewy predator, sleek and assured.*

She was watching Justin Tighe move around the science lab, tapping commands into a padd, running his hand through his hair, occasionally staring off into space, then turning back to the padd.

What he didn't do was to include her in any of his musings. He asked no questions, requested no opinion, shared no thought of his own. He was a man working exclusively with himself.

She considered what to do. On the one hand, he was her superior officer; it was his right to proceed with their assignment in any manner he chose. But she resented being treated as a silent piece of the background; she was an official member of this team and she should not be frozen out.

It was always dangerous to confront a predator, she knew; but unless you did, you would never gain his respect.

"Lieutenant," she began mildly, "if I knew what kind of sensor modifications you were considering, I might be able to help out."

Tighe looked over at her as though he had forgotten she

was in the room. He blinked, coming out of some deep level of concentration. "What?" he said.

"I'd like to be able to contribute. But I can't unless you give me an idea of how you're proceeding."

He ran his hand through his hair in a manner that now demonstrated exasperation, rather than absentmindedness. "I appreciate your offer, Ensign, but it would frankly take more time to explain what I'm doing than it will just to do it myself. Once I've figured out a plan, I'll go over it with you."

And he returned to his pacing, his gazing, and his computing.

Kathryn felt her cheeks sting. The rebuff was so blunt, so total, that she felt physically misused. She forced her mind to clear and quiet. *Don't act without thinking*, she reminded herself, objectifying the anger she felt at the rude behavior of the man who was supposed to be her partner.

Justin Tighe was faced away from her, studiously tapping on the padd. She rose and circled so she faced him.

"Excuse me, sir." He looked up with mild irritation. "Permission to speak freely?"

He let out a breath of vexation and fastened his blue eyes on her. "Granted," he said dryly.

"We're going to be working together for the next year. Working closely together. I think it's important we establish some ground rules at the beginning." She paused and looked at him, trying to gauge the impact of her words. He revealed nothing, his features neutral, eyes icy.

"I realize I'm the most junior member of this team. But I *am* a member of the team. I think I can make a contribution—even if it's just as a backboard, someone to bounce ideas off. I don't care how I participate—but I insist that I do."

He didn't reply, just kept looking at her with those

otherworldly eyes. "I'm not willing to be shut out," she continued, "to be treated as though I'm less important to this mission than that padd you're using. I think you'll find that if you'll just let me in, I can help. At least give me a chance to prove that."

There was a very long silence then, with Tighe's eyes boring into hers, she holding his look steadily, willing herself not to blink, feeling her eyes grow dry in the effort.

And then he slumped, tossed the padd down on the table, and sprawled into a chair.

"Let me tell you about me, Ensign," he said, but there was a long pause before he did so, as though he were unaccustomed to self-revelation and unsure how to proceed. "I was born on Klatus Prime. Ever heard of it? I didn't think so. It's a small mining colony in Sector 22309. My family had been miners there for generations. It wasn't quite as easy a life as you have on Earth. When I was ten I decided I wasn't going to spend the rest of my life like my father and my grandfather." He glanced up at her as though to see her reaction to what he was saying. Kathryn tried to reveal nothing, just listened patiently.

"Twenty years later, I've managed to become a respected member of Starfleet. I had to earn every step of that journey. Nobody gave me anything, nobody made it easy for me." She heard no self-pity in his voice, no plea of victimization. He said what he did as neutrally as though he were reciting the table of elements.

He took a breath and leaned forward on the table, looking up at her. "I'm not easy to get along with. I know that. I wish it weren't so, but I don't know if there's anything I can do about it." He put his head down and ran both hands through his hair. "I'm not trying to shut you out, Ensign. I'm just . . . used to doing things on my own."

Kathryn moved to the table and sat opposite him.

"Thank you for being honest with me," she said. "It helps a lot. But try to understand: This mission is important to me. And my way of working is as valid to me as yours is to you. I'm willing to compromise, but I'll ask you to do the same."

There was a silence between them. Kathryn half expected him to go back to his padd, excluding her and enveloping himself in his work. Instead, the hint of a smile tugged at his lips, and to her dismay, she found her fingertips tingling—that old, familiar, treacherous sensation. No, she thought. No, no, no, no, no. Not again.

"You're a tough one, Ensign. I like that. Weak people annoy me. But—are you as tough as I am? I guess we'll have to wait and see."

And without further discussion, he swung the padd around and began to give her the notes on sensor resolution and sensitivity that he'd been assembling.

Her response was so deeply ingrained that it was barely conscious. Somewhere, deep inside, a voice was saying, "I'll show him. I'll win him over."

But far below that was another small, wounded voice with a cry that had never surfaced, one that Kathryn had never heard and yet had guided her through most of her life.

Six months later, she sat next to Admiral Paris in the two-person shuttle, and reflected on that initial encounter with Justin Tighe. She'd been proud of the way she'd handled the situation, and confident that the going from that point would be smooth.

Nothing could have been further from the truth. Lieutenant Tighe had proved to be an infuriating partner, a stern and demanding perfectionist, rigid in his work habits and intolerant of human error or frailty. There had been no change whatsoever in the way he treated her, which was essentially as a mobile tricorder, from the first day until now.

It was a relief to get away from him and accompany Admiral Paris on this short mission to one of the moons of Urtea II, where they had mounted a sensor array three months earlier. There should now be valuable records of the behavior of extragalactic neutron stars and nonbaryonic matter, two major components of the galaxy's distant halo.

"Hear much from your father?" ventured the admiral once they were underway.

"Actually not, sir. He sent me a subspace message a couple of months ago, but he couldn't really tell me what he was doing." *As usual,* thought Kathryn. "He looked tired. He must be working hard."

"I wouldn't doubt it." There was a silence between them, for talk of her father always raised the specter of Cardassia, and hence the questions that remained unanswered about their own mission—questions that couldn't even be posed.

To her relief, Kathryn had found that that other, covert, mission might as well not have existed. She was unaware of the ship's doing anything except surveying the galactic rim and amassing data on halo objects. If there was information gathering going on at the same time, she was gratefully ignorant of it.

"I got a communication from my son Tom the other day," continued Paris. A smile of what could only be called paternal pride played on his mouth. "He won the aeroshuttle derby at his school. Set a record for the course."

"You must be proud."

"I knew from the time he was a toddler that he'd be a pilot. I'd take him with me on routine flights, and I

187

remember from the time he was two he was fascinated by the controls. He'd sit and watch me work them and not move for hours. He was like a little adult, studying and learning. When he was five he asked if he could try the simulator."

Admiral Paris shook his head and smiled at the memory. "It was all I could do not to laugh. Put a five-year-old in a simulator? How could he possibly handle it? Well, I asked him a few questions and damned if he didn't know all the answers. So we went to the Academy one weekend and we fired up the beginning flight program on the simulator."

The admiral stared out the window as though to recapture that long-ago moment. "It was amazing. Here was this little mite of a thing handling that flight program as though he were an Academy cadet. The next day I brought some friends along and let them watch, because I knew no one would believe me if I told them a kid that age could handle a simulator." He chuckled briefly at the memory. "They said I must've programmed an autopilot sequence and just let Tom sit there and pretend. But of course they checked and saw that wasn't true."

"How old is he now, sir?"

"Fifteen. Already been accepted for admission to the Academy when he graduates." Kathryn thought she had never heard such naked pride in a parent before. She envied this young Tom Paris, who had a father that gloried so in his accomplishments. She doubted that her father ever regaled his cohorts with stories of her achievements.

"We're approaching the upper atmosphere of the moon, sir," she said, reading from her instruments. "Preparing landing sequence." Then she gasped as she saw something else on the sensors and heard the admiral grunt as he noticed the same thing.

"There's a ship behind the limb of the moon," she said

automatically, knowing he was well aware of it. He was already keying controls, swinging the shuttle in an arc to return to the *Icarus*. "I don't recognize the signature," she began, but he interrupted brusquely.

"That's a Cardassian ship, Ensign."

A cold knot formed in her stomach. This wasn't Cardassian territory. What was it doing here? "Should I alert the ship?"

"Maintain communications silence. It's possible they're unaware of the *Icarus*. I'd like to keep it that way."

Kathryn was aware that he was running a fairly complicated series of evasive maneuvers. What was he anticipating? She willed herself to remain calm, and focused on the sensors, which showed that a massive ship was rounding the limb of the moon. In seconds it would be within eyesight.

The shuttle was dancing in space, maneuvering gracefully but unpredictably, when the Cardassian ship appeared. It was huge, roughly arrow-shaped, with a variety of weapons systems prominently displayed along its hull. Kathryn felt her heart hammering, but her mind was focused and her hands on the controls were steady.

A deep violet tractoring beam suddenly emanated from the Cardassian ship, and Kathryn realized the admiral had been anticipating this; his maneuvers were an effort to keep them from locking on. He glanced over at her, and his grave eyes were worried. "This may get unpleasant for us, Ensign," he said. "Do your best, but don't be unnecessarily heroic." She didn't know what he meant.

For a few minutes he was able to avoid the tractor, but as they both knew, it was only a delaying tactic. Eventually the larger ship with its fat tractor beam would ensnare them—and that's exactly what happened, with a bone-jarring *snap* that tossed them around like toys. Kathryn's head bounced off the console; lights flared in her head, a brief but brilliant display that she barely registered before everything went black.

I did it, Daddy, she was saying, *I derived the distance formula.* She kept saying it over and over, but her father wouldn't look at her; he just kept his eyes straight ahead, not listening. She said it louder, trying to break through to him, yelling in her urgency to get him to turn and look at her. *I solved the problem, I know how to derive the distance formula! Daddy! Daddy! Daddy—*

The sound of her own groan pulled her to consciousness, and her father faded; she tried to get him back but the moment had slipped away. Now she was aware only of cold and dampness, and a dull pain in her head. She reached to touch it and encountered a thick crust of dried blood.

Where was she? She should be on board the *Icarus,* but what she felt beneath her was soggy earth. A holodeck program? She struggled to make sense of the situation.

She pulled herself to a sitting position and her head erupted in pain. She steeled herself, waiting for it to abate, and gradually began to assess her situation.

She could see nothing. Wherever she was, it was black as pitch. She reached out and patted the earth in front of her; it was dank and smelled of peat. She extended the range of her patting and quickly encountered a barrier of cold metal. Moving to her right, she followed the wall until it abutted with another at right angles; in this fashion she proceeded until she determined she was in an enclosure approximately a meter and a half square.

And less than that tall. She couldn't stand up, could barely sit upright without her head touching the ceiling. And she could only lie down curled into a ball; the pen wouldn't allow her to stretch out.

The damp ground had absorbed heat from her body, and

cold seemed to have penetrated into her bone marrow. Was she in danger of hypothermia? She began rubbing her legs and arms briskly, trying to warm them up.

What had happened? Her last memory was of being on the *Icarus*, working with a padd . . . Justin Tighe was there, cold and intimidating . . .

Wait. The shuttle . . . Admiral Paris . . . they were on their way to check a sensor array . . . and then . . .

A sudden sound, and an aperture opened in the darkness, flooding the enclosure with bright light that knifed into her eyes like ice picks. She covered them with her hands as a man's voice said, "Please, my dear, come out and join us."

Head down, eyes still shut, she crawled toward the light. She could feel warmth beyond the opening, a welcoming sensation that momentarily lifted her spirits. A strong arm took hers and helped her to her feet, but she couldn't stand; her legs buckled into the fetal position they'd held for so long. She thought of newborn animals, wobbly and unstable, trying to get to their feet. The strong arms held her firmly until her legs were steady, and then she looked up, still squinting in the harsh light, into the face of an alien.

He was of a species she'd never seen. He was quite tall and rather thin; his face and neck were corded with cartilage. It was an imposing presence, but the eyes that peered at her were kind. "I am Gul Camet," he said, and his voice was rich and pleasant. Kathryn began to relax somewhat.

"Please accept my apologies for the way you've been treated. I assumed my men had arranged quarters for you, and then I discovered you'd been treated like a common criminal. I assure you they will be reprimanded." The tall man inspected her head wound carefully. "This should be treated at once. Please, come with me."

Grateful, she followed him from the brightly lit court-yard of stone into which she had emerged from her box, down a corridor softly glowing with muted light, and into a somewhat grand chamber with low vaulted ceilings and ornate designs on the walls. A table and two chairs were its only furnishings.

Gul Camet pushed some controls on the table and gestured her to sit. "The physician will be here right away. How are you feeling?"

"I'm . . . not sure. Cold. My head hurts."

"You may have suffered a mild concussion. The physician will treat you. Do you remember how you were injured?"

Kathryn struggled to piece together the images in her memory. "I was in a shuttle . . . with the admiral . . ." Suddenly she remembered Admiral Paris and became alarmed. "Where is he? Where's the admiral?"

"Your companion? I'm afraid he was more seriously injured than you. He is in a hospital facility, but he should recover completely."

Kathryn was staring at him. She had remembered the final moments before the blackout. "You're Cardassian," she said softly.

"Yes," smiled Camet, "and you are human. Our species haven't had much interaction. I wish this one hadn't been so unpleasant for you. Why were you on one of our moons?"

Kathryn's head was clearing quickly. The Cardassian ship, the tractor beam, the admiral's final cryptic admonition—they were prisoners, no doubt about it, regardless of what this sleek and charming Gul had to say.

"I wasn't aware it was yours. In fact, I'm sure it's in Federation territory."

"*Was* in Federation territory. We have annexed it."

"I'm not sure I understand how you can annex what is not yours."

"It's quite simple. You take it." His eyes were not so kind now, she noted, and had become lidded, like a snake's. "Now, once more—what were you doing there?"

"My name is Kathryn Janeway. I'm a Starfleet ensign and a member of the United Federation of Planets."

Camet was waving off her words with a gesture of disdain and tedium. "Please, my dear, don't posture with me. If I choose, you will tell me what you were doing on our moon. You will tell me anything I ask, you will betray your mother, your father, your friends, and beg to betray others if I will just stop hurting you. That would be just before you went insane." He eyed her briefly to see how she responded to this statement. Kathryn did her best to be perfectly neutral.

"But I don't want to do that. You're quite young, quite lovely. And you seem intelligent. So I hope you'll see the wisdom of cooperation. After all, if you had a legitimate purpose on the moon, I have no quarrel with you. I understand that the Federation was unaware of our recent annexation."

Kathryn considered his statement. It sounded utterly reasonable—a tactic, she knew, of a skilled interrogator. On the other hand, she knew her heroic stand was, as he said, impossible to maintain, and she remembered the admiral's admonition as they were captured. Best to keep this Gul talking.

"We are on a scientific expedition, studying massive compact halo objects. We established a sensor array on that moon two months ago and we were returning to collect data."

"Ah. A mission of scientific endeavor."

"Exactly."

The door opened and another Cardassian man entered

with a satchel. Gul Camet instructed him to treat her injury, and the man began to clean the wound; his touch was gentle and experienced.

"In that case, Ensign Kathryn Janeway of the United Federation of Planets, why were there extremely sophisticated surveillance devices installed in that array?"

Kathryn wished that she knew nothing about the other mission of the *Icarus,* so that her innocence would be real, not feigned. "There weren't. You must be mistaking elements of our sensors."

"I most certainly am not. And it leads me to believe that this 'scientific' expedition of yours is really a military operation for gathering intelligence."

"Forgive me, Gul Camet, but your statement has a touch of paranoia to it."

He smiled, but it was without mirth. "You may be right. We are a society which has always distrusted outsiders. Unfortunately, that has always proven a necessity." He gestured toward the physician, who had finished cleaning and dressing her head injury. "Please show the ensign one of our implants."

The physician reached into his satchel and lifted out a round, flat device that was smaller than a communicator and constructed of what looked like a skinlike polymer. Gul Camet took it and held it out, inspecting it. "It's a remarkable device. Implanted anywhere in your body, it can receive commands from me which produce a level of pain which can only be called astonishing."

Kathryn slowed her breathing, trying not to show her fear. "How foolish," she said. "You must realize that one will say anything under torture. It's a ridiculous method of getting information."

"Of course it is. That is not the purpose of our techniques."

"What is the purpose?"

"Power. Control. The satisfaction of completely breaking the will of another being."

Kathryn felt an icy chill. She knew he was telling the truth, that once he began to inflict pain there would be no stopping it, there would be no confession, no outpouring of information that would make him stop. She was doomed.

"I regret that you have chosen to be so uncooperative. I would have preferred to treat you as our guest, with comfortable quarters and abundant food." He shrugged, a delicate gesture that bespoke genuine disappointment. "But as it is . . . ."

The door opened once more and two guards entered. Gul Camet nodded toward her and the guards approached her, took her by both arms, and jerked her roughly to her feet, hurrying her toward the door so quickly she was trotting to keep from stumbling.

Down the long corridor they ran, Kathryn struggling to keep her footing, but inevitably losing it and falling to her knees, at which point one of the guards kicked her savagely in the thigh, a sharp, painful blow that made her cry out involuntarily. She scrambled to her feet as quickly as she could and they resumed their headlong race, out of the corridor and into the stone courtyard she had exited a short time ago. The guards now flung her to the ground; she got to her hands and knees and tried to rise, when one of them ripped off the bandage the physician had just put on her head wound and then drove his fist viciously into the injury. It spurted blood which ran into her eye, blinding her on one side. Then she felt herself shoved toward the opening into the box, the pen, the cage, she had so recently exited.

When the door was slammed behind her, the dark and the quiet were a welcome haven from the guards' cruelty. But she knew that sanctuary would be fleeting.

* * *

She lay curled on the ground, freezing, knowing the cold earth was draining more of her body heat from her than was wise, but too tired to do otherwise. She had spent several hours on her hands and knees, then sitting, trying to let as little of her body come in contact with the ground as possible.

But the effort was too great, and she was exhausted. She had to get some sleep. Her head had finally stopped bleeding after she kept her palm on the wound for half an hour, and had crusted over once more. But it ached with a dull, throbbing pain. She tried to isolate the pain in her mind, wrap it up, toss it out, and she succeeded in reducing its impact. She felt a drowsiness come on her; if she could sleep for a while she could recoup some of her strength, and then she could concentrate on how to get out of this predicament.

Then the screaming started.

She bolted upright, cracking her head on the ceiling as she did so. Someone very close by was screaming horribly. She realized he must be in the stone courtyard just outside. The sound was ghastly, a throat-rending shriek of unendurable agony, and Kathryn instinctively shrank back against the far wall of the little cubicle, as though moving half a meter would get her away from the horrible sound.

She put her fingers in her ears and began to sing: the first tune that came, unbidden, to her lips was a lullaby her mother had sung to her when she was small. "*Kathryn klein, ging allein, in die weite welt hinein . . . hut und stock steht ihr gut, ist ganz wohlgemut . . . aber mutter weinet sehr, sie hat keine Kathryn mehr . . . Kathryn klein, ging allein, in die weite welt hinein . . .*"

The words, she remembered, were about a little girl who put on a hat and took a walking stick and set off into the wide world alone. Her mother was sad that she was going, but knew that her daughter had to make her own way.

Kathryn sang it loudly, then even more loudly, and was finally yelling it, over and over, trying to create a balm that would shut out the horrendous sounds of a man undergoing torture.

It was quite a while before it occurred to her that the screams she was listening to were those of Admiral Paris.

By that time she was somewhat numbed to the horror of what she was hearing. She had been able to disconnect her mind from the reality of the situation and objectify it; the shrieks took on a surreal quality that made listening to them a curious, hallucinatory experience that was, if not wholly tolerable, a bit less horrendous.

Were they trying to get information from him? Surely the admiral would realize that withholding it was empty heroism. No, Gul Camet had made it clear what he was after: the domination and destruction of the spirit. And Janeway had no doubt that he would achieve it—first with the admiral, and then with her.

How could she prepare for this ordeal? Were there any mental exercises that might help her endure it? Was quick capitulation the answer? She thought not—it would be distrusted. Gradually she realized that nothing could help her escape nightmarish cruelty, and with this inevitability, she felt her stomach clench with fear.

Now the screaming subsided, evolving into a series of low moans which weren't comforting, but which perhaps indicated that whoever was torturing the admiral had, for the moment, stopped. Did that mean they were coming for her? She drew great tortured gulps of air.

Suddenly she was aware of a tiny sound behind her. She shifted awkwardly in the cramped space and turned to see a small glowing dot appear in what was the back wall of the pen—a dot that traveled swiftly down from ceiling to floor.

Was this the beginning of some form of torture? Were

they going to bake her in this metal box? She drew more deep breaths, striving for calm, fighting fear, yet feeling utterly vulnerable in this dark, cramped space.

And then there was a ripping noise and she felt arms reach in and grab her, hauling her roughly through the back wall, now bent outward. She gasped and started to cry out involuntarily, but a gloved hand was clamped firmly over her mouth. She felt herself dragged along over rough terrain, the sudden intake of fresh cold air telling her she was now outside.

She tried to get her footing, but it was impossible; whoever had her in his firm grip was too strong, and too fast. Afraid of twisting an ankle if she kept trying, she finally relaxed and allowed herself to be dragged.

Then she was hauled upright and jammed up against what felt like a large tree. A faint glow of starlight provided some illumination, and Kathryn realized she was indeed outside, held in the grasp of a man dressed entirely in black, hand still pressing on her mouth.

Then his mouth came close to her ear, and a voice whispered to her—a voice that sounded strangely familiar: "Be quiet. Understand?"

She nodded, and the gloved hand came away from her mouth. She was aware of a lean, hard body pressed against hers, the mouth still near her ear.

"Wait here. Don't make any noise. Be ready to run when I get back."

And then she realized it was Justin Tighe. She nodded and he released her; she felt him moving away from her, was vaguely aware of other dark shapes moving with him, back in the direction from which they'd come.

And then she understood: these were the Rangers, the elite commando corps Admiral Paris had spoken of. Her partner, the intimidating Lieutenant Tighe, was one of them!

They had rescued her, and now they must be going back for the admiral.

That would be a far more dangerous feat, she realized, involving combat with the Cardassians, who would then be alerted to their escape and would marshal all their forces to capture them all. She began looking around her, trying to divine the plan, wanting to be ready for anything. She seemed to be in a dense woods that was damp and uncomfortably cold. Somewhere nearby she could hear water, a sound between a drip and a gurgle; she couldn't identify it.

Her eyes were adjusting to the darkness, and she could distinguish individual trees. She knew she could see well enough to run through these woods. And the sounds she now heard indicated she'd have to do just that.

Voices, calling out, yelling, the sound of phaser fire—the Rangers had engaged the Cardassians. Did that mean they had Admiral Paris? Or had they been attacked before they ever reached him?

She was disconcerted to realize that the sounds of the skirmish were moving *away* from her. What did that mean? Was she being abandoned? Did the Rangers have a transport site somewhere? Could she find it if she were left alone?

She struggled against panic. This was at least a situation in which she could function: she could take action, she could make choices, she could *do* something. As the sounds of the voices receded yet farther from her, she stepped away from the tree.

And was immediately slammed into by a man whose approach she had not heard at all.

"I told you to stay put," he hissed, grabbing at her arm and starting her in motion through the trees. "Now move!"

She broke into a run behind him; he wove his way through the trees, zigging and zagging in what seemed like a planned pattern. Her breath grew ragged; she realized fatigue, hunger, and thirst had all taken their toll on her. She ignored the burning of her lungs and kept running.

And suddenly stumbled onto a dark form on the ground and went sprawling. She realized it was Justin she had fallen over; he was curled on the ground clutching at his ankle. She crawled toward him and saw his face was grimacing in pain.

"My ankle . . ." he rasped. She realized he was lying just beyond a large root that poked up from the ground; he had caught his foot on it, and now it was twisted at a grotesquely unnatural angle: it was broken.

"Keep going," he ordered. "Transport site . . . thirty meters ahead . . . clearing . . ."

"Why can't they beam us from here?"

"Transgenic field . . . have to get to site . . . stop asking questions . . ."

Kathryn heard voices behind them, drawing nearer. The Cardassians were right behind them. There was another sound, too—an unearthly howling from several bestial throats.

"*Go,*" he said, in a tone that brooked no questioning. "Those are Toskanar dogs—they'll tear you to pieces."

But Kathryn had another idea. She had discovered the source of the water sound she had heard earlier—a marshy swamp a few meters away, surrounded by reedy growth. Grabbing one of Justin's arms, she dug her feet into the ground and began pulling him toward the marsh.

"Get out of here," he protested. "You have to make it to the transport site before they reach us."

"Stop giving me orders, Lieutenant. This time you'll have to listen to me."

He was lean, but well-muscled, and in her weakened condition she struggled to drag him. He helped as best he could by propelling himself with his other arm, and in this way they lurched the several meters toward the marsh. She pulled him into it behind her, then released him to snap off two of the reeds that grew along the bank.

"We're going under," she announced, giving him a hollow reed and then pulling him far enough into the mud that they could fully submerge. She could hear the voices of the Cardassians and the eerie wailing of the Toskanar dogs; they weren't far behind now.

She put the reed into her mouth and saw Justin do the same; she lay backward in the mud and forced herself under icy, brackish sludge.

She felt it seep over her face, slowly entombing her in a silty mask, covering ears, cheeks, mouth and eyes, and finally her nose. Thick and gritty, it was substantial enough that she worried for a moment that they wouldn't be able to submerge completely. But gradually she felt the chill muck encasing every part of her body; the thin reed was her only connection with the world above the marsh. She breathed slowly, trying not to think about the fact that the thick mud felt like concrete, hardening around her, gradually crushing her to death.

Her ears were filled with mud, but she could hear dimly the sounds of the Cardassian troopers and the howls of the Toskanars. The muffled sounds grew slightly louder, and that volume was maintained. Kathryn deduced that the group had stopped nearby. The dogs were clamoring loudly—had they found a scent? Wouldn't the marshy mud eliminate their human odor?

She sensed something moving against her side and immediately her heart hammered. Were the Cardassians probing the mud? If so, she and Justin would quickly be found. But then she felt fingers reaching for hers and knew it was Justin. He clasped her hand, squeezing it in comfort, and she responded gratefully. The chilling mud seemed a tiny bit warmer.

After what seemed an interminable time, the sounds of the troops and their animals moved on, but both of them knew it wouldn't be safe to surface for a while. They might have left someone behind. They might be coming back.

But another danger was becoming apparent: hypothermia. Kathryn was numb from cold and had lost feeling in her feet. Only the hand that Justin's held had any sensation. She conjured up images to help combat the chill: hot, humid Indiana summers . . . baking on a tennis court, sweating, running for the net . . . sun tingling the skin . . . splashing water on her face to cool off . . . putting a wet towel on her head to shelter her from the sun . . . she envisioned herself drifting through space, floating toward the sun, its golden heat drawing her closer and closer, warming her with fiery light, and not until she had dived into its molten depths was she even beginning to get warm . . .

Something was hauling her upward, out of the ooze. She scrambled to get her balance, eyes still covered with mud. She heard Justin's voice. "We have to go now."

She spat out the reed and dug at her face with mud-covered fingers, managed to scrape away enough to open her eyes slightly, peering at the woods through grit-encrusted eyelids.

"We might have bought ourselves enough time to get to the transport site."

"Can you walk?"

"No, but I can hop."

And he did, bounding through the woods on his good leg, gritting his teeth against the pain that seared through his broken ankle each time he landed.

After a few minutes, Kathryn saw a clearing, and knew they had reached the transport site.

But so had a Cardassian trooper. He stood in the clearing, holding a Toskanar on a chain. It was a powerful, sinewy animal that looked like a cross between a mountain lion and a bear, with muscular legs and a great, shaggy head. It was silent now, but straining on the chain, eager to get at them.

"Stay where you are," ordered the Cardassian. Kathryn surmised they were still within the transgenic field; unless they were completely into the clearing, they couldn't contact the *Icarus* to transport them. "Lie down on the ground with your arms above your heads."

Kathryn kneeled to comply, but Justin gestured toward his bad leg, still dangling off the ground. "My ankle is broken," he said.

"Lie down on the ground with your arms above your heads." Justin nodded and put one hand down on the ground as though to help himself to get off his feet, lost his balance and tumbled to his side—then came up with his phaser drawn, and fired.

Nothing happened. Kathryn stared at the weapon; it was covered with muck from the swamp and must have lost its charge. She looked up at the Cardassian, who was smiling at them through the darkness, and saw him unleash the huge dog. Instantly, it bounded across the clearing right toward her.

She saw it as though in slow motion: the beast opened its jaws, baring a double row of pointed teeth, frothy slaver falling from its tongue. Small, round eyes glittered like lasers in the darkness; it uttered a guttural growl of anticipation.

Suddenly Justin had thrown himself in its path, taking the impact of the animal's charge. Kathryn's hand snaked out for the thick tree limb she had spotted to her side; wielding it like a bat, she hammered at the animal until it unloosed Justin and started toward her. She gripped the branch and twisted to her left—and an old familiar power rippled through her. The target was a tennis ball. She eyed it carefully, timing the backhand, shoulders turned and pointed toward the target, back leg bent, ready to drive: and then she set her body in motion, hips uncoiling and pushing forward, arms swinging as the power of her legs drove them, the weapon on a flat plane level with the target, eyes never losing contact until—

The branch slammed into the face of the Toskanar with a sickening crunch; it didn't even yelp before toppling over, skull crushed.

The Cardassian was standing in shock, losing precious seconds in his astonishment at the dispatch of his vicious animal. Justin had crawled a few feet closer and was trying to get his phaser operative; without even thinking about it, Kathryn, bat still in hand, charged the Cardassian.

The rest happened quickly: the Cardassian regained his senses and grabbed for his weapon as Kathryn reached him and swung at it; it discharged against the tree branch she wielded, knocking it from her grasp in a violent surge of energy. She saw the weapon turn toward her when it suddenly seemed to explode in his hand, and she realized Justin had fired his phaser. The Cardassian toppled, dazed, and a fury rose in her; rage for what they'd done to the admiral, and to her, and to all their victims, and she swung her leg in a vicious kick against the Cardassian's temple and felt a surge of primal satisfaction as she felt cartilage and bone give beneath the blow. She swung to kick again, hearing Justin's voice behind her ordering the beam-out. Her leg dematerialized before it made contact again.

The rest of the Ranger team had successfully returned with Admiral Paris to the *Icarus;* he, along with Justin and Kathryn, were treated in sickbay. Justin's ankle was quickly healed, as were his cuts from the claws of the Toskanar dog, and both he and Kathryn were treated for hypothermia.

She listened as the doctor queried the admiral about the torture device that the Cardassians had implanted in his body, and a decision was made that the best way to remove it would be to use the medical transporter to beam it out. The implant was a highly sophisticated piece of technology that produced limitless levels of pain, but according to the doctor, no lasting physical injury.

Kathryn knew that psychological injury might be another matter. The admiral looked weak and ashen from the ordeal; he thanked the Ranger team and congratulated them on a mission perfectly accomplished, but there was a muted, subdued quality to him that suggested the extent of his trauma. When Kathryn joined him in his ready room at his request, she felt a swell of concern rise in her as she saw his eyes, once twinkling and merry, now dull, as though covered by a film of soap.

"Lieutenant Tighe tells me you acquitted yourself admirably during our recent adventure, Ensign."

"Thank you, sir. I have to say that the Rangers were the real heroes of the mission. Especially the lieutenant."

"I know you've had your problems with him."

Kathryn's head jerked up sharply. How had he known this? She'd made every effort to keep a smooth front to their relationship; she didn't want the admiral to think she lacked the ability to make a professional association work comfortably. The admiral smiled, but again, it was without his usual mirth.

"I pride myself in being able to see beneath the surface," he said, acknowledging her surprise. "And I know Justin well. He can be difficult. But he's a special young man and he's going to become very important to Starfleet."

For a moment, Kathryn had the distinct impression the admiral was trying to sell Justin to her, but she quickly dismissed that idea; he was simply a commanding officer proud of the heroes of his mission.

"I'd like you to know," the admiral continued, "that we were highly successful in obtaining intelligence about the Cardassians. In spite of their discovery of our technology on the Urtean moon. Starfleet Command plans to put commendations for everyone in our files."

"Thank you, sir. That's very gratifying."

A silence fell between them as Admiral Paris studied Kathryn solemnly. She felt herself growing uneasy under his gaze, but forced herself to remain quiet and calm.

"Ensign," he began, "I'd like to put an idea in your head. Not for you to act on right away, just to ponder for a while, turn it over, examine it with that remarkable intelligence of yours."

Kathryn was immediately curious. What could he be talking about? She strove for neutrality. "What's that, sir?"

"Your abilities in science are clear. And you'd be an asset as a science officer in any situation." He paused then, eyeing her with the newly flat, remote eyes. "But I'd like you to give some thought to command."

"Command?" Kathryn felt herself sounding vacuous, but his words had come as a surprise. She'd never considered a career track other than science.

"You're smart, you're tough, you think on your feet, and you don't panic under pressure. Those aren't the only qualities involved in command, but they're ones you can't do without. Just think about it. We can talk more about it if you like."

"Yes, sir. I'm flattered. I'll certainly think about it."

Kathryn hesitated, not sure if she should be broaching the next subject, but sensing that it might be better for the admiral to talk about it. "Begging your pardon, sir, but when the Cardassians were holding us—I mean, I could hear you screaming, and I know . . . it must have been terrible."

He looked at her with those filmed eyes. "It was," he said simply. "I could never have imagined."

"Did they—want anything? Information?"

He shook his head. "Not really. I told them everything I could think of, of course. There's no way to keep from offering them anything just to make them stop. But no, they were just interested in breaking me."

Admiral Paris stood and walked to the window, where warp stars streaked by in dazzling array. "I'm taking a risk telling you this, Ensign. But it might help you to understand some things."

He paused for a moment, then continued. "I underwent the Cardassians' torture for a little more than an hour. I'm not sure I'll ever be the same again." He turned to her and spoke softly, awe tinging his voice. "Lieutenant Tighe was taken by the Cardassians two years ago. They held him for three days, during which time he underwent constant torture. He managed to escape somehow and make his way back to our forces."

Another heavy pause. "How he has survived so well is amazing to me. How he had the courage to lead a rescue mission for us is astonishing. I just wanted you to know what an extraordinary gesture it was."

Kathryn felt a rush of emotions—amazement, wonder, respect, compassion—all of which quickly coalesced into a deeply felt gratitude. She looked up at Admiral Paris, and felt her eyes sting. "Thank you for telling me, sir. It makes a big difference."

He nodded curtly at her, seeming to withdraw into some protective isolation. "Dismissed" was all he said, and Kathryn exited quickly.

When she rang the chime outside Justin's quarters, her heart was hammering and her cheeks burning. Should she be doing this? She had no idea, but she was compelled by some inner need to go to him; there was something yawning between them that needed to be filled. She had to acknowledge the immensity of what he had done.

His voice through the closed door was dry. "Come in," he said, and the doors slid open. She stood there, not entering, wanting his permission before she would intrude. He looked up at her in some surprise. "Ensign Janeway. Please—come in."

She walked in, conscious of the fact she had never been in his quarters before. They had done all their work in the science lab or the wardroom—neutral territory. Her peripheral vision indicated a room devoid of individuality: a neat, spare space that could have been occupied by anyone. She had seen empty quarters with as much personal detail.

He was eyeing her with that cautious, wary look of his, an animal anticipating attack, poised and ready, blue eyes holding her look firmly.

She had absolutely no idea how to begin.

She didn't know exactly why she was there, or what she wanted to say. She didn't know whether to be direct or oblique, lighthearted or solemn. She only knew she had to make some kind of connection with him.

The moment elongated as she tried to find an approach, an opening sentence, anything to get her started. Suddenly he startled her by chuckling, a low, throaty sound she'd never heard from him before. She looked at him curiously.

"What?" she asked.

"Once my little sister had to ask my father if she could take an offworld trip with her school class. She knew he wouldn't approve, but she was determined to do it. I was with him when she came to ask. She stood there for about three minutes, not saying anything, all her emotions playing out on her face. My dad was perfectly content to let her squirm, and he just waited, not saying anything. Finally, when she opened her mouth to speak, he just said, 'You can go.'"

He looked at her, amused. "You looked a little like her just now."

Kathryn smiled and the tension was broken. She walked in and sat down. "I've been talking to Admiral Paris. I know what happened to you with the Cardassians. And I wanted you to know how grateful I am that you put yourself in danger to save us."

Justin shrugged, deflecting gratitude in a way that seemed to her reflexive. "It was my job."

"Admiral Paris seemed to think it was more than that." He was silent, and she felt uncomfortable again. She had to fill the void. "Did you ever think—about what would happen if the Cardassians took you again?"

"Of course."

"But you came anyway."

A long silence, some difficult inner decision on his part, a step considered and taken, and then he looked directly at her. "I just knew I wasn't going to let them hurt you," he said simply, and in that moment the chasm between them closed and she realized that what she had sensed between them, the wrongness, the awkwardness, was her futile resistance to the inevitable.

CHAPTER

17

HARRY AND KES SAT IN THE MIDDLE OF THE ROOM, WRINGING wet and gasping. The heat was now at a torturous level, and the walls were glowing a burnished red. They had exhausted themselves trying to find a way out, a control panel, some indication of technology—anything to stop this inexorable rise in temperature which now threatened to roast them to death.

To no avail. Degree by degree, the heat had increased, until the point where breathing itself was difficult. Kes looked flushed but unafraid; Harry admired her indomitable spirit but feared it wasn't going to survive this present calamity.

He slumped to the floor, trying to make his mind function and tell him what to do in this strange and dangerous situation. He tried to concentrate on all the survival skills he'd been taught at the Academy, first and foremost staying calm and not yielding to the situation, no matter how dire.

There was no evidence that the people who had built these underground catacombs were aggressors or that the capture of prisoners had any place in their society. It didn't stand to reason that this unusual chamber existed merely for the slow destruction of interlopers.

On the other hand, the universe didn't necessarily organize itself reasonably. People did strange things for strange reasons, and a slow, ritualistic death had had its place in many societies.

Harry's mind wandered in spite of himself. He dreamed idly of Libby, and of his parents; he dissociated from the present and seemed to drift through space and time. Hallucinatory images swirled in his brain . . . his first clarinet lesson . . . Libby dressed in white . . . the melodious tinkling of a wind chime in his father's garden . . . his mother's eyes shining at his graduation from the Academy . . .

All of those people undoubtedly thought he was dead. And in a few minutes, they would be right. He felt no particular regret at that moment. Death seemed merely a curious phenomenon rather than a dreaded event. What lay there? Were there answers to anything? The universe posed so many questions, and so few had been answered.

He reached over to Kes, who had also collapsed onto the floor. He took her hand and squeezed it and was comforted to feel a slight pressure in return. He was content to die like this, offering solace to, and receiving it from, a good friend, drifting through memories of those he loved; it would be a peaceful going.

He wasn't even aware of the cooling breeze for a few moments. His mind had taken him to the beach on a baking day, with gentle gusts from the ocean dancing over his skin. Presently he realized there *was* a breeze cooling him, and he opened his eyes; there, through sweat-encrusted eyelashes, he saw a figure looming above him, fanning him.

No, not fanning—not exactly. Moving something . . . Harry rubbed the moisture from his eyes and focused on the apparition before him.

It was humanoid, its head elongated and narrow. It was covered in dense layers of a hairy fur, and its eyes, dark and intense, were in the front, rather than at the sides, of its face.

And attached to its back were huge, plumed wings, which beat slowly, magnificently, stirring the air and cooling Harry's fevered skin.

Tuvok's entire team had reassembled, and he was leading them through the maze of corridors, away from the main staging area where they had first descended into the underground structure. Neelix' sense of unease was growing by the minute; they had found no sign of Kes or Harry, who were not responding to hails. The impact of weapons fire from above continued to jar them, and a fine dust had been loosened from walls and ceiling, smoking the air and coating them all in an irritating mist of particulates.

Neelix trotted alongside the tall Vulcan as he strode purposefully down the labyrinth, scanning carefully and mapping their route as they went. "Mr. Vulcan . . . isn't it true that the deeper we go, the more likely they'll be to trap us in the bowels of this maze?"

"We may be able to locate another way out. Ensign Kim reported finding a stairway. It is my intention to track his movements and locate that stairway."

Neelix' heart quickened—they were going to find Harry and Kes. But immediately some of the ramifications came flooding in on him.

"Even if we find them, it doesn't mean they've found a

way out of here. The Kazon could just wait us out. We have only a little food and water."

"We will have to face each eventuality as it presents itself. For now, this is the tactical strategy I have decided upon." Tuvok kept striding purposefully forward, checking his tricorder as he went.

Neelix settled into a a steady trot at his side, somewhat comforted by the Vulcan's calm demeanor. But his anxiety over Kes didn't abate. Her absence and her silence concerned him. Who knew what might lurk in the dark halls of this subterranean grotto? What unanticipated dangers might Kes and Harry have encountered? Neelix knew he wouldn't relax until he could see her sweet face again and hear her low, husky voice.

And then all their lights went out.

A murmured gasp arose from the group as they were plunged into total blackness. There was the sound of twenty wrist beacons clicking as the crew tried to get them started again, but to no avail.

Muffled explosions continued to rumble in the distance; the air was thick with grit; they were trapped in the dark. Neelix felt certain they were on the cusp of some monumental event, an occurrence of dire and overwhelming portent.

Jal Sittik picked at a hangnail which had turned bloody, trying to contain his anxiety. In spite of constant bombardment, the Federations had not appeared, and the men were beginning to cast irritated glances in his direction. He had struck a nonchalant pose and busied himself with his thumbnail, as though the outcome of the mission were so assured that he needn't give it another thought, and could concentrate instead on the nagging shard of nail.

But each time his eyes flicked upward, he saw more of

the men looking at him, doubt and aggravation etched on their faces. He decided to abandon the hangnail and began walking confidently toward them.

So far, the day was most definitely not turning out as he'd planned.

As the system's star had risen higher, the heat became more intense, and a cloud of insects had descended on them, buzzing annoyingly and inflicting nasty little bites on any patch of uncovered skin. The bites didn't hurt at first, but gradually turned into red blebs that burned like hot needles. No one's mood was helped by this. It was a time when a good leader reflected certitude and courage, so that his troops would persevere.

Sittik clapped one man soundly on the shoulder. "Tonight we'll feast together, my brother. I will pour hock ale for each of you, and carve the roast naggath myself." He smiled at the man, but was disconcerted to receive only a surly glare in return. He moved on.

"Teslin, my friend—when we tell Maje Dut what we've accomplished today, he will reward us with a showing of women." He leaned in to the man, conspiratorially. "I know you've had your eye on Kosla, who is under the protection of the Maje. Tonight—she will be yours." Teslin gave him a curt nod and kept firing into the ground.

Sittik moved through the ranks like this, sharing his vision of the celebration they would enjoy at the end of the day. It was vaguely troubling to him that they didn't respond with more enthusiasm, but he excused them for that because of the heat and the irritating insects.

He allowed himself to think briefly of Kosla, a ripe young woman who had caught the Maje's eye when she emerged into womanhood. Dark velvet eyes peered at the world from behind thick lashes; her hair when wound was thick and heavy, and he imagined it, unplaited, as long enough to cover her body. Her body. It was wondrous, plump as a nesting looci hen, always straining against her clothing as though longing to be free. He often thought that if he held one of her firm, supple arms and pinched the flesh between thumb and forefinger, it would burst with juices like fruit that had remained on the vine until it was thick and swollen.

These erotic visions had so completely invaded his imagination—and led him to decide that it would be he, not Teslin, who would spend the night with Kosla—that he didn't realize Miskk was standing in front of him, glowering.

"Yes, Miskk?" he asked pleasantly, still suffused with lingering images of Kosla. Only gradually did he realize the extent of Miskk's ire.

"How long do you expect us to continue this foolish tactic? Can't you see it's not working? Don't you have an alternate plan?" Anger had turned Miskk's forehead ridges a striated purple.

Outrage began to bubble in Sittik, as well, and he felt his blood course strongly through his veins. He could demonstrate purple ridges as well as Miskk. "Are you challenging me, Miskk? Shall we decide here and now who will lead this mission?" And before Miskk could answer, Sittik backhanded him viciously across the face with a fist shrouded in studded leather.

Miskk dropped like a stone, stunned and bleeding. Sittik kicked him in the ribs a few times but Miskk didn't move. Sittik reached down and removed his weapon, then turned to the men who had stopped, temporarily, in their efforts to flush out the Federations, and were now staring at him—in fear, Sittik noted ebulliently.

"That's what happens to those who oppose me. This one will be held in chains until his wrists rot." Sittik nodded at two of the men. "You two—take him to the shuttle and restrain him."

The two men moved warily toward Miskk, who was now sitting dully on the ground, holding the wound on his head, from which blood was streaming. The men pulled him to his feet and led him away. But as he passed Sittik, he gave him a final look, and in that look lay a hatred so powerful that Sittik was momentarily immobilized. He had not bested Miskk at all. Miskk was planning vengeance.

Captain Janeway stood by B'Elanna Torres' side, watching as the lieutenant scrolled through schematics of the weapons circuitry. Something was keeping the phaser arrays off-line, but so far the entire Engineering crew had been stumped by the problem. *Voyager* had been forced to return to the planetary nebula, the only part of space where they could buy some time in safety. The Kazon ship didn't seem to have pursued them into the murky gases this time, and Janeway hoped they'd be able to get the weapons repaired without having to evade the Kazon. The next time she emerged from the swirling gases of the nebula, she wanted to have the full power of *Voyager*'s arsenal at her command.

B'Elanna's face was smudged and her eyes were hollow. She hadn't slept since the Kazon attack, and every muscle in her body ached with tension, but she was determined to get them weapons again.

"It's something in the plasma distribution manifold," she told Janeway. "The EPS flow regulators are functioning perfectly, but when energy is released into the manifold, it isn't getting into the prefire chambers in the right sequence. If we try to use the phasers, we could end up with a backfire explosion."

"Have you tried recalibrating the magnetic conduits and switching gates?"

"Several times. And I've run a diagnostic on the command processor, just to make sure the glitch isn't in the computer. Now we're remachining the nadion injectors, in case there's an undetected burr in the valving assembly."

B'Elanna looked over at Janeway. "I'm going to get to the bottom of this, Captain," she promised.

"I know you will. Keep me posted."

B'Elanna turned again to the schematics, and Janeway headed again for the bridge. Her shoulders ached with tension, and she kneaded first the right, then the left, trying to unloose the tightly knotted muscles. When the weapons were ready, she had to be at her best.

CHAPTER

18

"WOULD YOU CARE FOR ANOTHER BROWNIE, LIEUTENANT?" Gretchen Janeway smiled at her guest as she held the plate in front of him. Kathryn smiled as she saw Justin hold up a fending hand against the platter of rich desserts. He'd already had two, in addition to several helpings of corn stew and tomato salad.

"Thank you, ma'am, but I won't be able to eat for several days as it is. I must say, I don't think I've ever tasted a meal like that."

"Mother cooks from scratch, Justin. We almost never had replicated food when we were growing up." This from Phoebe, now twenty-three and still in school, studying fine arts, painting, and generally enjoying life. She was a beautiful young woman, with a mass of dark, curly hair and her father's clear, gray eyes, and a personality that might have come from an alien planet. From this family of steadfast, responsible workers had emerged a free spirit, an irrepressibly buoyant individual who blew through life like a whirlwind, radiating energy and enthusiasm.

Edward Janeway sat at the head of the table, listening to the banter with amusement. Kathryn was ecstatic that he was here; he had actually canceled an important conference in order to meet the man he suspected would become his son-in-law.

"The girls didn't particularly appreciate it at the time," he offered. "Everyone they knew had replicated food, and they found their mother's cooking distasteful."

"Not all of it," said Kathryn. "I *always* liked the brownies." She turned to her mother. "Is there any coffee made?"

"You drink too much coffee," said her mother gently.

"It's my only vice," Kathryn retorted, rising. "Would anyone else like some?" No one did, and Kathryn went into the kitchen to pour herself a cup. As she did, a warm presence lifted itself from the floor and rubbed against her legs. It was Blanca, Phoebe's dog, a fluffy Samoyed mix, belly noticeably swollen with pregnancy.

Kathryn leaned down and took the gentle face in her hands, nuzzling Blanca's cheek. "You shouldn't be banished to the kitchen, girl," she murmured. "Come out and be with us." She poured herself coffee and held the door open for the fluffy white dog.

"Hello, mamma," squealed Phoebe, spreading her hands wide to welcome the dog to her. Blanca waddled obediently toward her and laid her chin on Phoebe's knee. Phoebe scratched her head as she prattled on. "She's due in three weeks. The vet says there are four pups, two male, two female. I want to give you and Justin one as a wedding present. You'll have your pick of the litter."

"Phoebe, how sweet. I'd love to have one of Blanca's babies." Kathryn was genuinely pleased. She had been trying to develop a closeness with Phoebe that had eluded them when they were younger and seemed to be in constant conflict. The offer of a puppy was interpreted by Kathryn to be a welcoming gesture on Phoebe's part.

She turned to Justin. "What do you think? Male or female?" But she saw hesitancy on Justin's face, and suddenly felt something unpleasant flutter in her stomach.

"I guess . . . either one. But how do you imagine we can have a dog, with both of us spending so much time in space?"

"I can take care of it when you're both gone," answered Phoebe practically.

"Maybe Justin should get the chance to decide whether he even wants a dog," suggested Gretchen amiably, and Kathryn realized it had never even occurred to her to ask. She'd assumed that everyone liked dogs. But she realized that Justin was looking uncomfortable and a bit embarrassed.

"I've never had a pet," he acknowledged. "When I was growing up, it was all we could do to feed the family. Giving food to an animal was unheard of. I've just . . . never gotten used to the idea of living with a . . . a furry creature."

Phoebe was staring at him as though he were mad, an uncomfortable silence fell on the group, and Kathryn jumped in to appease. "It's my fault, I should have asked you. I just didn't think . . ."

"Who would have imagined anyone could fall in love with Kathryn and not like dogs?" queried Phoebe, clearly irritated. "Never mind, I'll give you a pair of candlesticks or something."

Edward rose and gestured to Justin. "Would you come into my study for a few moments, Lieutenant? I've got some schematics for a test vessel I'd like you to look at."

"Yes, sir." Justin rose, face somewhat flushed, and

followed Edward out of the room, looking neither at Phoebe nor Kathryn. When they had gone, Kathryn turned on Phoebe.

"How could you do that? Embarrass him in front of everyone? Phoebe, that's so rude."

"How can you think about marrying someone who doesn't like dogs? Maybe you've learned something important tonight, and you have me to thank."

Kathryn was furious. Why had she thought Phoebe had changed? She was as stubborn and self-involved as ever. "Maybe someday you'll grow up, Phoebe, and learn that in a relationship, the other person's needs are at least as important as yours."

"If I have to have a relationship like that, I just won't have one. I won't change who I am just to accommodate someone else."

"Girls," interjected Gretchen, "please don't blow this out of proportion. You can settle your argument doing the dishes. Just like when you were little."

And she left the room. Kathryn turned back to Phoebe, unable to quell the anger she felt. "I want you to apologize to him for the way you behaved."

"I certainly won't. You're making an issue out of nothing."

For a brief second, Kathryn realized that might be so, but a fierce protectiveness of Justin had risen in her, and she couldn't stop herself. What did Phoebe know of him? How he'd grown up, how he'd lived, how he'd made something of himself single-handedly? "What right do you have to judge him—over a dog, for heaven's sake? He's an extraordinary man, and he's going to be your brother-in-law."

Phoebe dug her heels in, unwilling to back down, and Kathryn realized they were locked in an ageless pattern, one they'd played out a thousand times or more. Would it always be this way between them? Why was Phoebe so stubborn, so willful? Couldn't she ever yield a point?

"I'll do the dishes, Phoebe. I'd really rather do them alone."

"Fine. I'm taking Blanca and going back to school."

"All right."

"All right."

And Phoebe was gone, leaving Kathryn shaking and angry, but not sorry she'd stood up for her husband-to-be.

"You have to say something to her. You're the only one she'll ever listen to, and she has to realize how rude she was."

She was with her father in his study after Justin had left, the study where she had spent some of the most golden moments of her childhood. Memories of those times flooded over Kathryn now, producing both joy and pain: she wished for a moment she were a tiny girl again, back in that shadowed past when she knew Daddy loved her, before the Cardassians caused so much trouble and made him spend all his time dealing with them.

It was urgent that he support her now, that he take her side and reprimand Phoebe, who was so clearly in the wrong. But it didn't seem to be working that way. Her father listened carefully, neutrally, to her, but didn't quite see things the way she wanted. "Phoebe has a capricious personality and often says things that sound worse than she intends them. You mustn't let yourself get drawn into unnecessary turmoil because of it."

"How can you say that? The way she behaved—it was awful. Cruel."

"I was with Justin for almost an hour after that. He didn't seem particularly upset."

"You don't know him. He'd never let anyone know he

was upset. He handles things without inflicting them on others—which is more than can be said of Phoebe."

Edward ran his hand through his hair (hair that was thinning, Kathryn noted, and flecked with gray; when had that happened?) and took a breath. "I don't want to take sides on this, Kathryn. You and Phoebe have to work out your relationship. You're both adults now and I can't reprimand her as though she were a little girl. This is your issue, not mine."

Kathryn stared at him. She felt betrayed, bereft. Old pain bubbled up in her. "You're taking her side, just like always. She's your pet, she has been since she was born. And because you let her get away with everything, she's turned into a thoughtless, ill-mannered brat."

"Kathryn, I want to drop this. I'm sorry you're so aggravated, but I think it will look a lot different in the morning." He reached for the schematics on his desk. "Let's move on to pleasanter subjects. I've spent a very worthwhile hour with Justin, going over these plans, and I'm quite taken with him. He's smart, sensible—and he's tough." His eyes flickered with humor in an attempt to bring levity to the situation. "He'll need that, to be married to you."

But his words pierced her like a stiletto plunging to the bone. Is that what he thought of her? Someone so difficult that a mate required strength in order to endure her? She heard her voice quaver a little as she tried to answer. "He's a very special man, Dad. He's hard to get to know, but once you do, you'll see how remarkable he is."

She realized her father was staring at her with concern, then felt stinging in her eyes. Tears were overflowing the lids, and she swiped at them in embarrassment. "Kathryn—what is it?"

She started to make an excuse, but when she took a

breath, it became a gulp of air that triggered a huge sob. And then she broke down, weeping, racked by long, shuddering wails, covering her face with her hands, crouching over in her anguish, tears coating her face.

Her father, stricken, rushed to her and pulled her into his arms. He patted her back and whispered, "There, there," over and over, a helpless mantra against this unexpected and frightening demonstration as Kathryn disgorged years of loss and pain: the birthdays, the graduations he'd missed; the months-long absences; his departure from her life—each of those wounds poured from her in an expiation of mucus.

Presently, the sobs abated to an occasional gurgling shudder, and gradually she regained control, able to breathe only through her mouth, eyes swollen and nose stopped. By then, they were sitting on his couch, her head on his chest, where his shirtfront was now wet with her tears, his arms still holding her firmly. He was stroking her hair and making soothing sounds.

It felt as good as being four years old again.

When every gasp, every shudder, every sob had spent itself, she pulled herself away and went to his desk to get a tissue. Where the aquarium had once sat was a Starfleet console; she realized she didn't remember when the lion-fish had been replaced.

Wiping her face, she returned to the couch. "I'm so sorry, Dad. I guess I've been under some stress."

He looked gravely at her, putting his fingers under her chin and tilting her head up. "What is it, Goldenbird?" he asked gently. "What is it, really?"

She struggled with the decision. She'd never complained to him, never let him see her weakness. It was important that he regard her as *beyond* weakness, someone who wouldn't be a burden to him, or make demands on him, someone strong enough to—

To ignore.

She looked up at him now through scratchy and swollen eyes. "Oh, Daddy, I just want you to be proud of me."

He looked at her in abject puzzlement. "Kathryn, I am proud of you. There aren't words to tell you how much. Ask anyone I work with—I'm afraid I drive them crazy talking about my daughter."

"You do?"

"I've told my colleagues about every honor, every accolade, every commendation you ever received. And there were a potful of them. I'm a terrible braggart about my Kathryn."

"Admiral Paris talks about his son all the time. I wanted you to feel that proud of me."

Her father threw back his head in a snorting laugh. "Are you kidding? Owen talks about Tom from time to time—but he isn't in the same league of gloating fathers as I am."

Then he turned to her and rubbed her cheek softly. "How could you think I wasn't proud of you? How could you imagine it?"

"You never told me," she said simply, and saw his face crumple. He rose abruptly, moving away from her, fists clenching and unclenching in distress. He stood like that for a horrible moment, then turned back to her.

"War takes many tolls, Kathryn. I'm all too aware of the massive ones—slaughter, torture, misery, starvation . . ." He moved to sit next to her again. "Those things you can't ignore. I guess I didn't pay attention to some of the others. I was asked to help prevent war from befalling the entire Federation, and I never hesitated. I'm still trying."

He looked solemnly at her, his gray eyes burrowing into her, those kind, loving eyes, urging her to listen, to believe him, to accept his absolute sincerity. "You and Phoebe, and your mother, paid the price. I simply wasn't there when you were growing up. I knew your mother had enough love to give you, and I thought—I hoped—that would be enough. But I swear to you, I thought of you every day, every hour, missing you so much it was like a physical pain.

"And it seemed as if you were flourishing. You excelled at everything. We were more worried about Phoebe—she lacked direction, she wasn't motivated. I was relieved when she found she loved painting, because it gave some focus to her life. But you—you were never a concern."

Kathryn couldn't ever remember her father talking to her like that, talking about personal things. She felt as though she had been unburdened of a huge tumor, one that had melted into the million tears that had flowed out of her body, leaving her weightless. She snuggled into her father's arms again, and they sat for another hour, talking about her childhood, about Phoebe, about Justin, and about whether she should take Admiral Paris' advice and switch her career track to command.

Her father was strongly in favor of the idea because "the best of the best should be in command—and that's you, Goldenbird."

Kathryn made popcorn and hot chocolate, and they ate bowl after bowl, washing it down with the velvety sweet liquid.

And later that night, after they'd gone to bed, she woke, and with the house dark and quiet, her mother and father sound asleep, she crept downstairs to the study and curled up in the kneehole of his desk, where she sat contentedly until the sun rose.

A month later, she, Justin, and her father were seated in the prototype ship *Terra Nova* as it entered the Tau Ceti system. It was an impressive vessel, small and lean, highly maneuverable—and heavily armed.

It was Starfleet's necessary response to the mounting threat of war with Cardassia.

Edward Janeway had been working on its design and construction at the Utopia Planitia shipyard for two and a half years, had test-flown it himself on numerous occasions, and was now overseeing its first long-range flight—a three-day journey to the Tau Ceti system, where it would undergo a series of experimental flights conducted in a variety of spatial environments. Lieutenant Justin Tighe was the pilot.

They had spent the previous night at Mittern Station, enjoying a festive meal with Admiral Finnegan, whom Kathryn had first met years ago on Mars Colony. His red hair was now mostly gray, but his sense of humor was as keen as ever, and they had lingered over coffee, laughing and telling stories.

Even Justin, not the most social of people, had relaxed and enjoyed himself, and told a funny story about growing up on a mining colony. She couldn't remember his ever having been able to laugh about his childhood, and to her it was proof that he was truly becoming comfortable with them. Her heart had warmed as she saw her father and Admiral Finnegan's response to him: they liked him and respected him—but most important of all, they enjoyed him.

"On final approach to the Tau Ceti system, sir," she heard Justin say, jarring her out of her reverie.

"Stand by to execute the warp thrusters maneuver," replied her father.

The *Terra Nova* was designed to function in a variety of battle conditions. One of the innovations of the ship was warp thrusters, which provided quick bursts of speed without engaging full warp engines, allowing the ship to maneuver quickly out of dangerous circumstances, change position, and return to the fray from an unexpected direction. Computer simulations had originally indicated intractable stresses to the hull from the maneuver, but Admiral Janeway had eventually solved this and a host of other design problems.

They spent an hour testing the new thrusters, which functioned perfectly. Kathryn enjoyed watching Justin at the controls, which he handled like an artist, seeming to become at one with the ship as he worked it through the complicated commands. Her love for him swelled in her like a living thing, enveloping her in a warmth of a sort she'd never known before. She had the giddy and irrational thought that she didn't deserve this much happiness.

"Solar winds are kicking up, Lieutenant," her father said. "Let's give the port thrusters one more burst and then call it a day."

"Aye, sir. It's been a good first run."

What happened then occurred so quickly that, years later, she couldn't pinpoint exactly what the sequence of events was. All she could recall was that one moment she heard her father say "Wind shear—" and the next she was falling through space, slowly, drifting, vaguely aware of strange chilly breezes but not bothered by them. She felt as though she were in a hammock, swaying gently, floating toward the surface like a scrap of paper tossed on the winds but settling inevitably lower and lower.

There was no sense of disaster, or even mishap. She felt mildly curious as to these puzzling circumstances, but not alarmed by them. The downward drift was so soothing that she almost wanted it to go on indefinitely.

She sailed that way for a long time.

Then she heard a rush of air and her body absorbed a massive impact; pain screamed through her bones and she thought they must all be broken. She lay stunned for a period of time she couldn't determine, waiting for the pain to subside, waiting for her vision to clear—

—she couldn't see. That fact finally registered in her mind. Only darkness surrounded her, a black, agony-filled universe that began and ended with her body, racking her, obliterating her efforts to quell the suffering. She tried, without success, to use her pain-reduction techniques, then finally resigned herself to the hurt.

Time passed. She had no clear idea of how long, and knew she might have been passing in and out of consciousness. Eventually the pain ebbed and she began to feel tranquil again; a narcotizing effect seemed to have pervaded her brain—a natural secretion of endorphins, she thought instinctively—and she felt consciousness begin to slip away.

Something was in her mouth. And her nose. She couldn't breathe, she was suffocating, that was why she was drifting off . . . strange, that she could acknowledge that she was dying, recognize the cause, and yet be unable—even unwilling—to do anything about it.

She coughed. Felt a sudden intake of cold substance, and then choked, gasping, sucking air but ingesting instead whatever that cold substance was, wishing she could return to the cocoon of unconsciousness once more. Dying, she realized, wasn't frightening; living was infinitely more difficult.

Without conscious will, she lifted her head. A realization invaded her mind: she had been lying facedown in a snowbank. White crystals clung to her face, and to her eyelashes, obscuring her vision. She dug at her eyes, brushing away snow and bits of ice, and suddenly she could see again.

Parts of a small space ship were strewn around a vast, ice-ridden landscape; everything was white for as far as she could see, and the horizon blended almost indistinguishably into a pale gray sky, making her feel as if she were inside a vast white sphere. Snowy cliffs rose abruptly from the ground several kilometers beyond her, and grotesque white shapes on the ground, like abstract ice sculptures, testified to the irregularity of the terrain.

She sat up and involuntarily cried out; bones were broken for certain. She moved gingerly, trying to get her bearings, and realized she was sitting on the rear empennage of the ship. A drogue system must have deployed, slowing her plunge to the surface, but even so if she hadn't landed in a soft snowbank she would never have survived.

She had no idea what had brought her to this snowy wilderness. She could remember nothing that led up to her present existence, pain-racked and cold, on an unknown ice planet. How had she gotten here? What ship was now scattered in wreckage all around her? Were there other people here, too?

Other people. A vague alarm rose in her, but she couldn't identify it. Was she with others? If not, why would she have been flying alone? She wasn't a particularly accomplished pilot, it didn't seem likely that she'd be on a solo mission.

But what was the mission, then? And if there were others, who were they? And where were they?

Dizziness engulfed her and she lowered her head, trying to keep blood flowing to her brain. A vast confusion began to overtake her, and she couldn't think what she should do next. Lie down again, perhaps. It had felt so much better to be lying prone, in the pillow of snow and darkness, than to stare, bewildered, into this milky landscape.

She started to put her head back onto the snow when another feature of the terrain caught her eye. An iceberg. A huge shard of jagged ice, jutting from . . . from . . . the ground? No, icebergs didn't form on land. There must be water there.

Maybe it wasn't an iceberg. Maybe it was just another of the strange icy formations that dotted the surroundings . . . but no, no, it was definitely an iceberg. She was sure of that, but unclear *why* she was sure.

She became intrigued, then obsessed, with this question. How did she know with such certitude that she was looking at an iceberg?

She pondered what she knew about icebergs. They were floating masses of ice, broken from the end of a glacier or a polar ice sheet. They drifted according to the direction of sea current. They most assuredly required a huge body of water to support them. Ergo, there must be water here.

Isolated bits of iceberg-information came climbing upward from memory like salmon. Only one-ninth of the mass of ice is seen above water. The *Titanic* was destroyed after impact with an iceberg. Many bergs are tilted, as the result of wave-cutting and melting that disturb their equilibrium.

She glanced up at her berg, and saw it tilted at an angle. It was rapidly fulfilling the requirements of being what she was so sure it was. Nonetheless, it was increasingly important to her that she be absolutely, positively, unequivocally sure that she was looking at an iceberg.

She forced herself to her feet, shuddering with the pain that knifed through her with each movement, standing shakily, light-headed. The horizon swam and undulated like silk billowing in the wind, and she knew she was about to faint; but this strange desperation to verify her observation superseded everything. *Was this an iceberg?*

Gradually the world stopped fluctuating and she forced her eyes to focus on the area around the—the object she was trying to verify.

And, indeed, there was water surrounding it. It protruded from a dark, glassy pool, which seemed to lap and roil around it in unusual agitation. Another strange thing: the pool was small. There was no sea here, no ocean, just the ring of agitated black water that bubbled around the tall shard of ice.

Then, could the object in fact be an iceberg? Was it possible to designate it as such in the absence of an ocean? And if not, how should it be designated? She felt her mind move into a frenzied Socratic dialogue, feeding on itself and becoming ever more urgent.

She must determine if there was, in fact, no ocean. Empirical evidence. Prove it for certain, one way or another.

She took a step and very nearly collapsed. Something was broken—leg, ankle . . . something—but it couldn't be allowed to stop her. She would use the pain, turn it to her own ends, create from it a focusing lens that forced her to concentrate on her quest. With each agonizing step, her mind would fixate more intently on the task at hand, narrowing the beam of determination until it was an unstoppable laser point.

And so, in that cruel way, she made her way forward.

Several truths began to reveal themselves. The first validated her single-minded undertaking: there was a body of water present—probably a vast body of water—that was frozen over. The iceberg (yes, now definitely deserving that definition) jutted from its depths, but she could see surrounding it other holes in the ice sheet, holes and cracks, long, ragged gashes through which the dark liquid below was seeping, as though a giant had plunged a massive pick through the ice, over and over, cracking it open in an orgy of destruction, and the more she looked the more holes she saw, larger holes, huge holes, holes that were smoking as though the water were boiling from below, over some unseen flame.

The second truth was that her mind wasn't working properly. More than her body had been injured; she must have sustained a concussion. What was this mad determination to prove an iceberg was an iceberg? She was losing rationality. She had to begin functioning, to treat her wounds and get shelter; she'd be dead from hypothermia before long if she simply stood and stared at her iceberg.

She tried to reason through this strange conundrum in which she found herself. Something had broken through the ice sheet. That's why the water was turbulent, why the ice was so mutilated. Parts of the ship she'd been on must have rained down on a vulnerable section of the frozen sea and ripped it apart, superheated from flaming entry into the atmosphere, steaming the water into a huge, heaving cauldron.

Parts of the ship she'd been on. What ship was it? She looked around her at the scattered debris; only one section, the empennage she'd been sitting on, was intact. She noted a console that still flickered, partially functional, but the rest of the rubble that was strewn about was in pieces smaller than a meter square.

Where was the main cabin?

Who was the pilot?

What was the last thing she remembered before standing alone in this vast, ice-shrouded wilderness in front of a steaming vat of black water?

Suddenly she wondered if the lionfish was in that water, parboiled now, flesh flaking off the bone, sightless eyes running like jelly.

And then the third truth, like a hideous specter that looms in a nightmare, stood dancing before her, monstrous and obscene.

Her father. Her husband-to-be. They were in the cabin of the ship.

They were now entombed beneath that ravaged sheet of ice.

Her mind instantly became lucid and crystalline. She knew with awful clarity what she must do next. She lifted her broken leg and began to stamp it on the ground beneath her, gently at first, then harder and harder, because only the excruciating pain that she was inflicting on herself stood any chance of offsetting the third truth. Brutal physical torture could demand her full mind and keep it from acknowledging the third truth; and in that way, she kept the specter dancing in front of her, at a distance, unable to overwhelm her, until the pain obliterated her consciousness.

As she sank to the ice, just before blacking out, she realized that her iceberg was gone. It had melted from the heat of the smoking water, disappearing forever to join Justin and her father in their dark and lonely grave.

CHAPTER

19

TRAKIS THE PHYSICIAN STARED CALMLY INTO THE EYES OF MAJE Dut. He felt strangely composed, considering what would seem to be the seriousness of his situation. Maje Dut was not known to be magnanimous toward those who had failed him. But Trakis knew that the Maje was also somewhat deficient in intellect (like most Kazon, in his opinion), and he felt confident he could weather this latest mishap.

The Maje, it was true, was furious, his forehead ridges dark and his eyes red-rimmed. He gestured toward the prisoner, lying motionless on the examination table. "You've accomplished nothing. We know no more than we did before you began your inept examination. And now you've butchered him."

"It's you who's butchered him. You insisted that he be continually narcotized. I warned your minion that the drug might kill him, and now you see I was right."

At least, thought Trakis, the prisoner hadn't suffered. He simply proceeded from oblivion to death—and what, after all, was the difference?—without even being aware of it. Of course, he had no idea if the being had anything approaching awareness, anyway. The Kazon's foolish insistence on narcotizing him had precluded any of the sophisticated testing that might have allowed Trakis to ascertain if the species was sentient. All he had was a catalogue of anatomical and physiological data—not particularly helpful for the Maje's purposes, he suspected.

"Careful, Trabe. That tongue could be pulled from your head if it's not kept in check." The Maje glowered at him for a moment, but Trakis merely held the look with an even stare.

Maje Dut circled the examination table, gazing at the body of the prisoner. "It was a miracle that we found any of these beings. We have no access to another. This was our one opportunity to study the species." He glanced back at Trakis. "It would seem your usefulness is at an end, physician."

The implication was clear, but Trakis wasn't cowed. "You're wrong about that, Maje. I can perform a necropsy. I'm likely to discover a great deal more from this specimen dead than I was able to alive."

Maje Dut's eyes flickered with renewed interest. "Such as?"

"Brain structure. Neural architecture. Synaptic integration. I can probably determine just how the Krett were able to control them."

The Maje's arm snaked out and grabbed Trakis by the throat, holding him firmly. "You'd better do just that, Trabe. And quickly. Once the Federations are dispatched we must act quickly."

"If you want me to do this with any efficiency, then keep the Control out of here."

"Nimmet? He hasn't been empowered to harm you."

"His presence is harmful. He's a nattering fool who

constantly interrupts my thought processes with inane comments or superfluous commands. I could complete this project much faster without him."

Maje Dut stared at him for a moment, and Trakis knew he was weighing the request. Trakis smiled ingenuously and spread his palms. "After all, Maje—where could I go?"

Dut finally nodded curtly. "Very well. But I want hourly reports from you. And I expect those reports to be substantive."

Trakis inclined his head in acquiescence. "I think you will be most surprised, Maje."

Dut swept out and Trakis turned back to the carcass on the table. The eyes, in death, were as dark and unfathomable as they had been in life. "I'm sorry, friend," Trakis murmured. "I would rather not have harmed you. But perhaps we can still be of use to each other."

And after invoking a brief blessing for the dead, Trakis began to lay open the creature's brain.

Never had Neelix been so grateful for Tuvok's unflappable bearing. It was possible that panic might have overcome the group under other leadership, but Tuvok simply proceeded as though this enigmatic situation were a routine mission, easily accomplished. His superior Vulcan eyesight had quickly adapted to the darkness, and he was able to read the faint markings of his tricorder.

"Take the hand of the person in front of and behind you. Each of you, with the exception of myself in front, and Ensign LeFevre in back, should be joined with two others."

There was a hasty shuffling in the dark as the crew members followed his order. "All set, sir," came LeFevre's voice from several meters down the corridor.

"Very well." Tuvok's rich voice rang through the passageways. "Mr. Neelix, you're directly behind me. We will proceed."

Neelix put one hand in Tuvok's; the other was held by Greta Kale. Almost subliminally, he registered that Tuvok's voice had sounded different as he called out the last command, but he couldn't put his finger on just what had changed.

Tuvok kept up a fairly steady accounting of his plan and the route they were following—largely, Neelix suspected, to function as a calming presence for the group. "I am reading signs of Kes and Ensign Kim's progress through this passageway," he intoned. "We are most assuredly following the path they charted."

Tuvok's voice definitely sounded different. There was no question about it. Closer. More—muffled. What had caused this change? Neelix spoke out himself, curious if his voice would sound similar. "Are you reading any signs of Kes and Harry themselves, or just their trail?"

He sounded strange to himself. His voice seemed to be absorbed into the air and hang there, as though he were inside a thick cocoon.

"At this point, I am only detecting their trail. I have yet to detect any life signs." As Tuvok spoke, Neelix pinpointed what had changed: the Vulcan's voice didn't echo. The bare stone walls of this underground structure had heretofore bounced the sound of their voices in several directions, resonating hollowly through the passageways. Now sound wasn't reflecting. It was being absorbed.

"We will be turning to port," announced Tuvok, but he did so before Neelix had registered the order, and his shoulder grazed the stone corner.

But it didn't feel like stone anymore. It had yielded to his grazing touch.

He didn't want to alarm Ensign Kale by dropping her hand, so he maneuvered close to the wall, then raised the hand that clenched Kale's so that he could feel the surface.

It was sticky. Gelatinous, like a thickly textured Yasti

pudding. Neelix recoiled at the feel, and instinctively scrubbed his knuckles—and Kale's—on his trousers. "Mr. Vulcan," he said, with his voice sounding in his ears as though he were underwater, "I believe something is happening to the walls."

Tuvok halted immediately. "Feel them," Neelix implored. "It's almost as though—they're melting."

Neelix dropped his hand and could sense the Vulcan, in the inky darkness, reaching out to touch the wall. Then he saw the faint glow of the tricorder as Tuvok scanned.

"The wall does in fact seem to be metamorphosing," the Vulcan intoned. "Further, the organic readings in the material have increased significantly."

"What does that mean?" asked Neelix, decidedly apprehensive about this turn of events. Stone that changed texture and exhibited organic signs was not stone that he cared to have surrounding him thirty meters underground.

"I cannot be certain. I would suggest, however, that it would be advantageous for us to increase our pace. Join hands and follow."

They did so, and Neelix felt himself begin to perspire. Was it nervousness, or was it, as he suspected, because the air was becoming warmer? And is that why the walls were beginning to melt? And if the former was true, how hot would it get and would the walls melt completely? And if they did, what would happen then?

Burdened by questions, Neelix was grateful when Tuvok discovered a stairway—undoubtedly the one Kes and Harry had reported—and they started downward. It would be taking them closer to Kes, and with any luck, away from the disquieting presence of the melting walls.

Harry watched in stupefaction as Kes seemed to have a one-sided conversation with the winged humanoid, though so far as Harry could tell the creature wasn't talking.

"Time for what?" she asked, and then, after a short pause, "I don't understand. I don't know anything about it's being—time."

Then she lapsed into silence. "Kes?" ventured Harry somewhat timidly, and was rewarded by her silencing hand held toward him. She frowned slightly, as though focusing on something difficult to understand, then began looking around the room.

This behavior continued for some minutes, as Harry looked from one to the other. And then, abruptly—at least as far as Harry was concerned—the winged being shimmered out of existence. He turned to Kes. "Was that a hologram?"

She nodded. "I think he was a program that was created to leave a message—telepathically—but it was a confusing one. He kept talking about it's being *time* for something to happen. It may have been some kind of regeneration ritual, because he kept talking about a reawakening."

Harry noted that the temperature had dropped a bit; while still hot, it wasn't as overwhelming as it had been a few minutes ago. "We may have triggered a program to start up by coming in here. Maybe they rigged the room to produce the messenger when someone enters."

"Well, he wasn't much of a messenger. After listening to him, I still don't understand what's happened, or what's going to happen, if anything."

"I think it's getting cooler," observed Harry, moving again toward the wall through which they had entered, and scanning once more. "And look at this—something's going on, all right. I'm reading energy signatures that weren't here before." He circled the room, taking readings as he went, and Kes did the same.

"Some kind of technology has been activated," she noted. "Can you tell what it is, Harry?"

"I'm afraid not," he admitted. "It's organometallic, but

in a state of flux. Not registering in the Federation database, of course." He pondered the whole strange situation briefly. The chamber was now cooling rapidly, and was almost comfortable again. Was that significant? "You say the messenger communicated telepathically. Could you tell anything about him? Did he seem belligerent, or warlike?"

"Not at all. He was focused. Composed. If he's any indication of the whole species, I don't think there's any hostile intent here."

Harry was vaguely comforted by this assessment, though still apprehensive about a situation over which they seemed to have no control whatsoever. He determined to concentrate his efforts on getting them out of this mysterious chamber, and he walked purposefully toward the wall through which they had entered.

What he found there was as surprising as anything that had happened.

At the end of the room was a closed door, and beyond that, another room—a room she must get into, because it had to be cleaned. She moved toward the door, but stopped when she heard Admiral Paris' voice behind her. "Wait, Kathryn, I need you here." She turned to face him but when she did, no one was there. When she turned back to the door, it was gone . . . how could she get into the room . . . ?

Janeway's head snapped up and she realized she had drifted off while sitting on the bridge. No one seemed to have noticed; Chakotay wasn't in his chair, having gone to oversee the ongoing repair efforts in Engineering, and the rest of the bridge crew was quietly busy. Still, it bothered her that she had lost momentary control, and she vowed to toughen herself mentally so it wouldn't happen again.

For she certainly had no wish to revisit the house of many rooms, or to renew her efforts to go through the closed door.

CHAPTER

20

AT THE END OF THE ROOM WAS A CLOSED DOOR, AND BEYOND that, another room—a room she must get into, because it had to be cleaned. She moved toward the door, but stopped when she heard Admiral Paris' voice behind her. "Wait, Kathryn, I need you here." She turned to face him, but when she did, no one was there.

Kathryn's eyes opened at that point and she stared dully at the ceiling of her childhood bedroom. The dream had become so commonplace she no longer woke with her heart pounding, as she had when she first began having it, and even the vague sense of misgiving that pervaded her when she woke had begun to abate. The dream was losing its ability to make her feel, which was of course exactly what she wanted.

She rolled over and prepared to go to sleep again when there was an irritating chime at her door. She ignored it, burying her head in pillows and pulling a blanket high around her neck.

She was annoyed when she heard the door open anyway, and realized someone was crossing the room toward her bed. Her mother. Her mother made these visitations several times a day, sometimes bringing hot soup or tea, sometimes just sitting with her for a few moments, rubbing a shoulder gently. These were comfortable intrusions, demanding nothing of her except a few mumbled words of thanks.

This time, though, she felt the pillows wrenched from her head and the blanket flung back. Startled, she sat up and stared into the eyes of her sister Phoebe.

"You've spent enough time in bed, Kathryn. Time to get up and start living again."

Mild aggravation was the most potent emotion Kathryn could summon. Her sister was a buzzing mosquito, easily swatted aside. "Go away," she muttered, reaching again for the blanket.

But Phoebe threw it off the bed and tossed the pillows to the other side of the room. "I'm not leaving until you're up and showered and dressed. Then we'll have lunch and maybe play some tennis."

Kathryn gazed up at Phoebe, too tired to get into an argument. "Have to sleep," she mumbled, and lay down without benefit of either pillows or blanket and closed her eyes. Then she felt strong hands grip her shoulders and pull her upright.

"You've slept enough. Get up, Kathryn—don't make me take drastic measures."

The mosquito was becoming more of a nuisance. Kathryn felt a surge of something beyond irritation, and her eyes opened again. "Get out, Phoebe. I don't want you here."

"Too bad. You're stuck with me. Are you getting up or do I need to do something extreme?"

"Just leave."

There was a brief silence and then Phoebe turned and left the room; Kathryn closed her eyes once more, drifting into soothing oblivion.

The next thing she knew, a gallon of icy water cascaded down on top of her, drenching her and soaking the bed. She leapt up with a yelp, pulling sodden hair from her face. "Are you crazy? What are you doing?"

"Making sure that bed is too uncomfortable to sleep in. Now get up and take a shower."

Genuine anger began to rise in Kathryn. She stood up, shivering from the frigid ice bath, and glared at her sister. Phoebe glared right back. "Does Mom know you're doing this?"

"She certainly does. She encouraged it."

"And what, exactly, is it you hope to accomplish?"

"Today I'll be happy if you get up and get dressed. You don't go back to bed until it's night. Tomorrow you'll get up by seven and we'll play tennis or hike in the woods. In three weeks you report for duty."

Kathryn felt a dull headache begin to throb. "I don't have to report for a long time. Months."

"It's been months. You're back in three weeks."

Kathryn tried to absorb what Phoebe was saying, but the effort required concentration and she quickly abandoned it. Phoebe was simply wrong.

But now she was tugging on Kathryn's arm, pulling her toward the bathroom. "There's soap, and shampoo and towels. I'll have lunch ready when you get out."

Kathryn didn't have the strength to argue; bargaining seemed the easier way out. "If I get dressed and have lunch, will you leave me alone?"

"Not until we've gone outside and done something physical."

"Fine. *Then* will you leave me alone?"

"Until tomorrow."

Kathryn sighed and moved into the bathroom, unable to argue further. She'd deal with tomorrow when it came. If it came.

The sunlight was so intense it felt like a thousand tiny needles in Kathryn's eyes. She tried to shield them from the light, but it was relentless.

"I have to go back and get a hat," she complained, but Phoebe kept marching. "You'll adjust," she said tersely, not looking back. Kathryn couldn't find the strength to insist, and so followed behind.

They were walking on the frozen ground of the barren cornfields. In six months the new corn would be as high as your eye, but today on this cold January day, the ground was hard and clumpy; Kathryn kept stumbling on frozen clods of earth.

"How much farther?" she asked, lurching again as her foot slipped into a rut.

"Until you're physically tired."

"I am. I promise."

"I'll know when you really are."

Kathryn subsided once more. Just get through this, she thought. Stumble through the cornfields until Phoebe was convinced she was breathing hard, and then she could go back to bed. She settled into a sullen silence, concentrating on not twisting her ankle on the unfriendly earth.

She had managed to eat some of the vegetable bouillon her sister had made her, and gulped down several cups of coffee—Phoebe did make the best coffee in the family, no doubt about it—which she actually enjoyed. Now they were on this mindless trek, walking nowhere for no reason, just waiting for her to get tired. The more she thought about it, the less sense it made. Finally, she stopped short.

"That's it, Phoebe," she said firmly. "I'm not your prisoner. I don't have to go any farther if I don't want to. I'm going home."

Phoebe circled around in front of her, clear gray eyes holding hers steadily, cheeks flushed a patch of pink from the cold. "No, you aren't," she retorted. "You don't seem to understand. I'm not going to let you sleep your life away. You've indulged yourself long enough."

Indignation leapt up in Kathryn, a righteous ire that was as close to real feeling as she'd had in months. "Indulged? Excuse me, Phoebe, if I'm not snapping back from this according to your time schedule, but I wasn't aware I had to live up to your expectations. Is it asking too much that you maybe have a modicum of sympathy?"

But Phoebe showed no such thing. She glared at her sister, chin tilted, carried by her own tide of righteousness. "You've had nothing but sympathy from everybody. Good grief, Kathryn—it was an awful thing that happened. But you're not grieving, you're wallowing in grief. It's consuming you, and we're not going to let that happen."

Kathryn started to retort, but Phoebe took another breath and kept going. "Do you think you're the only one in pain? Of course it was worse for you, you lost two people—but I lost Daddy, too. And Mom lost her husband. She can't do her own mourning because she's so worried about you."

Phoebe looked at her, waiting for a response, but Kathryn had none. She felt suddenly naked in this bright winter sun, stripped of defense. She began to shiver.

"We've given you time, we've waited on you, we've done everything we can to help you get through this. But you're sinking deeper and deeper—I didn't know it was possible to sleep as much as you do. That's not good for you, and it certainly isn't good for Mom and me, who love you and care about you. So I'm not taking it any longer. You're going to get up, you're going to face life, and if it hurts for a while it's just going to have to hurt. That's the only way you're going to get better."

A vision of the closed door flashed in Kathryn's mind, and she started to tell Phoebe that she'd never get better until that door was opened, but then she realized she didn't even know what that meant. Her sister's words crawled around on her for a moment while Kathryn tried to reject their truth, but eventually she couldn't resist them, and she felt her mind absorbing them all.

Phoebe was right. She couldn't go on like this. Daddy and Justin weren't coming back no matter what she did, so she'd better get on with life.

But could she? In her bed, eyes closed, pain receded. Standing out here, in the cold winter air, she felt misery begin to rise in her, erupting in the pit of her stomach and then snaking out to envelop the rest of her body. She felt queasy. She had to lie down, get warm again. Close her eyes.

She felt Phoebe's strong grip on her arms. "I'm here for you, Kathryn," her sister's voice promised. "You might get mad at me because I'm going to push you. But I promise I'll stick with you."

Eyes squeezed shut, reeling in the cold sunlight, stomach raw and nauseated, Kathryn reached out and clutched Phoebe's hand, holding as tightly as she could to safe anchor.

Four nights later, a fierce winter storm came sweeping across the plains. The sky had turned leaden in midafternoon, and the temperature dropped precipitously. Snow began falling as Kathryn, her mother, and her sister were eating dinner, and they gazed through the broad windows of the dining room onto a blizzard of white.

Kathryn had stayed out of bed during the daylight hours all four days, going to the bedroom only to sleep. Except that now, irony of ironies, she couldn't sleep, but lay awake in silent agony, trying not to think of Justin and her father lying in the dark frigid waters, flesh now devoured by water creatures, white bones settled in the silty residue of the alien sea.

But of course she couldn't *not* think about them. She found it was easier to envision them dead than to raise the specter of their manner of death. Had they died immediately upon impact? Or were they conscious, sucked under with the fuselage of the ship to drown in icy, brackish water? Or did they lie, injured and in pain, in an air pocket of the ship, dying slowly of shock and hypothermia?

Better to think of glistening skeletons, quiescent and inert.

Daytime brought a hollow-eyed fatigue, which Phoebe steadfastly ignored. They ate breakfast, lunch, and dinner, exercised, and visited The Meadows, their old school. Kathryn dutifully fulfilled each of these requirements, growing more ragged and exhausted with each hour, dreading impending nightfall and her futile battle with memories.

She didn't want to tell Phoebe that her plan wasn't working, because she could tell it meant a lot to her mother that she was making this effort. Her mother had never shown her anything except love and generosity, and she wasn't going to be a cause of concern for her. In a few weeks she'd report for duty at Starfleet Headquarters, and she would request a science post on a faraway station; once there, she could sleep when she liked.

At dinner, her mother and Phoebe made delicate small talk, and Kathryn forced herself to join in; the relief in her mother's eyes was reward enough for the effort. But then she felt herself staring out at the blizzard and thinking that she could go out and start walking . . . just as she had walked home from the tennis match so long ago . . . and be swallowed up.

A serenity descended on her as she pondered this, and her mother's voice became mellifluous, a soothing euphony which lulled and pacified. She smiled at Phoebe, and tried not to notice the responsive joy in her sister's eyes.

"Maybe I'll take a walk," she offered when dinner was over. Her mother turned to her, startled, protesting, "It's a blizzard out there—" but Phoebe interjected quickly. "It's a great idea. Nothing so bracing as a walk in the snow. I'll come with you."

Kathryn smiled at her again. "We've hardly been apart for the last few days. Isn't it time I ventured out on my own?"

Phoebe shrugged. "If you say so. But I wouldn't stay out too long. And take one of the palm beacons."

And in another five minutes, Kathryn was out of the house, bundled like a polar bear, head down against the driving wind. It was a mean storm, the snow icy and granular, assaulting her face like sand. She plowed forward, wanting to find her willow tree, but already losing bearings in what was a virtual whiteout.

She walked for some time like that, soon giving up thoughts of finding the tree, content to march forward in whatever direction her feet took her. The swirling snow obscured everything, and soon she felt she was walking on a vast, dead planet.

Dead planet. Planet of the dead. Snow planet. The unbidden visions leapt to her mind with a quickness and ferocity that took her breath away. She felt an unreasonable anger beginning to form: she had come out here to achieve oblivion, not to have her wounds laid open again. She picked up her pace, as though she could outrun the unwelcome thoughts.

She proceeded at that brisk pace for some minutes, head down, not knowing or caring in what direction she walked. Finally, she stopped, breathing deeply, and watched her breath crystallize in the air in front of her. She turned slowly in a circle, staring into a void of snow-whirled blackness. If she lay down, the snow would form a blanket for her, gradually piling up like goose down, enfolding her in gentle sanctuary and shielding her from visions of icebergs and hungry fish.

It was easy. She could bend her knees and sink to earth. It would be so natural it hardly required a decision.

And yet she remained upright. She was losing body heat, she realized. If she wasn't going to lie down, she should keep moving. And suddenly there was a decision to be made and the ease went out of everything.

It was at that point that she heard the noise. The first time, she discounted it, thinking it was a variant of the wind. But the second time, she knew it had an entirely different quality, a plaintive whine tinged with desperation.

She hadn't yet snapped on her wrist beacon, but did so now, throwing the beam in a circle as she tried to determine where the sound was coming from, but the beam scarcely penetrated the snow cloud. She began moving in the general direction of the soft whine, straining to hear it more clearly.

From the corner of her eye, she saw something moving on the ground, and she turned to throw the beam of light on it.

At first, it seemed to be a short, light brown snake, but it didn't move like a snake; it was actually hobbling on stubby legs. It took a moment for her to register that it was a hairless puppy, no more than a few weeks old, trying to scrabble along the snowy ground on legs that were too weak to lift its pitifully thin body off the ground. The pup was mewling forlornly, a miserable bundle of cold and hunger. It found her boot and promptly collapsed on top of it, as though realizing it had found safe harbor.

Kathryn scooped it up, feeling the frail bones through the puppy's skin. It had lost a lot of body heat, and had clearly given its last measure of effort to make the trek to her boot.

She tucked it inside her parka and felt the little thing's tiny heart beating wildly. For a moment she was afraid it was going to die under her coat, its life's last energy spent on the journey to haven. But gradually it calmed, and she even thought she felt it growing warmer.

She had to get home. The puppy needed food, and warmth, and medical attention. If it had the grit to survive this long in such wretched conditions, she wasn't going to let it die on her watch.

She turned in the still swirling whiteout, trying to get her bearings. She had no idea how long she'd walked, or in what direction. Making the wrong choice could take her deep into frozen fields of farmland, kilometers from her house.

But purpose honed her instincts. Without quite understanding how, she knew where home was. She set off, walking briskly, unerring, determined to save the fragile life of the tiny being she held to her bosom.

"Petunia, heel! Heel, Petunia!" Kathryn used her most authoritative tone of voice, but the four-month-old pup paid no attention. Now a healthy, silky bundle of fur—and from appearances a generic black retriever—Petunia had become a sassy, irrepressible being with unlimited energy, insatiable curiosity, and endless tenacity.

Of course, it was that very life spirit that had helped Kathryn to heal. For days she had nursed the starved, dehydrated puppy back to health, and in doing so, found a reason to connect again with the world. She had reported for duty at Starfleet Headquarters and announced her intention to pursue command; Admiral Paris arranged for a postgraduate training program, which allowed her to remain on Earth for six months before being assigned to a space mission.

Six months, she figured, would be enough time to properly train Petunia and introduce her to Phoebe's household of animals. But Petunia had other ideas. She seemed to enjoy puppyhood too much to start behaving like a well-trained adult dog. She greatly enjoyed chewing Kathryn's shoes (so much more tasty than dog toys), climbing on the living-room furniture (so much more comfy than her bed), and playing a cunning game of hide-and-seek with the padds on Kathryn's desk (so much more satisfying than fetch).

Kathryn knew it had been a trying experience for her mother, but she also knew her mother was so glad to have her back among them that she would have welcomed a dozen Petunias.

Kathryn had brought the dog to the Botanical Park, a sylvan setting of lush flora that was, on this May evening, abundant with spring blooms. Dogwood and magnolia vied for attention with spectacular blossoms, and lilacs cast their heady fragrance on the warm breeze. They'd been coming here in the evenings for several weeks now; she found the lovely setting comforting. The pain of losing Justin and her father seemed as intense as ever, yet she knew it was beginning to recede because some things— Petunia, this flowered park—had the power to soothe her and even invoke a sense of well-being, if only for a short time.

"Petunia, come. Petunia—good girl, that's the way. Now, heel." They were working without a leash, and it wasn't going well. Petunia was enjoying the new freedom from the choke chain and had no wish to confine herself to the restrictive boundaries Kathryn was trying to impose. She found the acacia bushes fascinating, and enjoyed the feel of damp earth on her paws, and what could be more fun than a headlong romp through a maze of flowering plants?

Kathryn sighed, knowing she had to get the upper hand here. If she didn't remain consistent, and firm, a headstrong pup like Petunia could mature into a dog that was out of control. "Petunia, *heel.*" Her voice took on an additional timbre of authority that she hoped communicated itself to canine ears.

Petunia fell into line at her left side, keeping pace with her, nose sniffing the scented air curiously, eyes drawn from rustling bush to hovering moth and back again.

It was the fireflies that were her undoing. A flock of the flickering insects suddenly surrounded them, and Petunia was fascinated. All thought of heeling instantly vaporized, as Petunia broke and began leaping in the air, trying to turn herself into a firefly.

"Petunia, come!" snapped Kathryn, to no avail. Petunia was gone, a leaping dervish, bounding and twisting in the warm evening air. She crested a small embankment and was instantly out of sight. Kathryn went plowing after her, but it was as though the pup had blinked out of existence. She willed herself not to panic; Petunia was immature and overactive, but she also knew who filled the dog dish each evening. She'd be back.

Kathryn sank onto a park bench, one of several dotted throughout the gardens, and nodded to some passersby. It was a communal place that people frequented throughout the day, and Kathryn realized she was beginning to enjoy the feeling of connection with other people. She must be on the mend.

Now she wrestled with a decision that must be made:

whether or not to accept a command post on a deep space mission that would depart for the Beta Quadrant in three months. It would be a way to ascend the command ladder rapidly, but it meant being away from Earth, from her mother, and Phoebe, and Petunia, for two years. In the last months, she'd made a nest here, she felt secure with her family and her childhood home; the night devils were at bay.

And, of course, that was precisely the reason she believed she had to go. Haven is comforting, but it can be an insidious trap. Her bed had been a refuge for months, and she realized now it had actually been a prison. If she was truly going to heal, she had to put herself out there, hiding from nothing, embracing the journey she had chosen for herself.

A silky black head appeared over the embankment, and Kathryn smiled. Petunia had, in fact, come back.

But what was hanging out of her mouth? Kathryn rose, dismayed, to see that Petunia held a half-eaten sandwich in her mouth, gently, as though she were retrieving a duck. Proudly, tail wagging, eyes shining, the pup dropped the sandwich at Kathryn's feet and looked up at her as though expecting praise.

"Oh, Petunia—what have you done? Whose is this?" She looked toward the embankment, fearing the sudden roaring appearance of an outraged picnicker.

What she saw was the figure of a man, somewhat shaggy and rumpled, climbing toward her over the embankment, shoulder pack dangling at his side, hair tousled and a bit unkempt. And so familiar . . .

She stared, trying to distinguish the face in the gathering gloom. Finally, it wasn't the face, but the loping gait that told her she was right.

"Hobbes?" she breathed, and the man stopped in his tracks, staring at her.

"Kath—is that you? I don't believe it." And he was running toward her, swooping her into an old-friends hug, laughing as he saw his doggy-licked sandwich lying at Kathryn's feet. "It was my fault," he assured her. "I broke off part of my sandwich and fed it to your pup. When she snatched the rest I knew I had only myself to blame."

He backed off from her and stared for a moment, his grave brown eyes absorbing her intently. "You look terrific," he announced. "But you look like you've lost a lot of weight."

Kathryn nodded. Eating was something she still had to force herself to do. But she felt no need to comment; Hobbes' observation had been just that, not a value judgment.

"I heard about your dad . . . and your friend. I'm so sorry."

Those words of commiseration from someone she'd known almost all her life had a potency she was unprepared for. She felt tears—tears? she hadn't shed tears yet over the tragedy—flood her eyes, and she blinked them back desperately. "Thank you. Oh, Hobbes, it's so good to see you."

He took her hand and they sat on the bench while Petunia gleefully ate the rest of the sandwich. "What are you doing now?" Kathryn asked, eager to reestablish the comfortable relationship they had managed to achieve.

"I'm part of a philosophical symposium that's based in South America. It's great, Kath—a bunch of us just sit and think about all the unanswered questions, and talk about them, and argue, and distribute papers about our arguments. I've never had so much fun."

"You're part of the Questor Group?"

He nodded, and Kathryn looked at him with deepened respect. This was an august body of philosophers who incorporated the most innovative aspects of science and technology into their formulations. The entire Federation waited for the distribution of their papers, for they were always challenging, stimulating, and provocative. Imagine: Hobbes Johnson—vulky Hobbes Johnson—part of that exalted company.

"Hobbes, that's wonderful. I can't imagine anything better suited for you. But you must be the youngest person there."

He laughed, throwing back his mop of unruly hair. "That part is right. But I've met some people in Curitiba, and there's a tennis club I spend a lot of time at."

"You still play?"

"As much as possible. How about you?"

"Phoebe's gotten me out on the courts lately. But I'm set to do a two-year deep-space mission, so I don't imagine I'll be honing my tennis game for a while."

"We'll have to play before you leave."

"I'd like that." She paused, looking fondly at him. "You know, I used to hate tennis. But somehow I keep coming back to it. There's a—satisfaction—to it that I couldn't appreciate as a child."

They sat like that, talking easily, for an hour, while Petunia, for once, lay quietly at their feet, belly full of cheese sandwich, dreaming happy puppy dreams. They talked about their childhood, and their lives since they'd lost track of each other, and eventually Kathryn found herself talking about the awful accident on the ice planet: about the snowy plain, and the dark alien sea, and the iceberg—particularly the iceberg—all the images that were seared in her mind as though with a fiery brand. Hobbes put his arm around her shoulder and she felt a warm strength flow from him to her; a bit of burden seemed to ease.

They made plans to play tennis on the next day, and finally stood to rise, Kathryn snapping on Petunia's leash so there wouldn't be another runaway attempt on the walk home. Suddenly awkward, Kathryn extended her hand to Hobbes. "I'm so glad we found each other again, Hobbes."

He took her hand and smiled, comfortable always. "Me, too. But you should know—hardly anybody calls me Hobbes anymore. That's actually my middle name, and I decided to switch to my first name." He chuckled slightly at himself. "Maybe if I'd done that when I was younger, I'd have avoided some unnecessary ribbing about my name."

"I think it's a wonderful name. But I'll call you anything you like. What's your first name?"

"Mark. Mark Hobbes William Johnson—all of that is on my birth record. My folks, for whatever reason, chose 'Hobbes' from those myriad choices, but I like the simplicity of Mark. I think it suits me these days. I'm pretty much a simple guy."

"Then Mark it is." And she smiled at him.

CHAPTER
21

HARRY AND KES STARED AS TUVOK, NEELIX, AND THE REST OF the bedraggled away team poured through the space which used to be the chamber wall. It had shimmered away before their eyes, as it had when they themselves entered, and now their comrades were streaming in, all looking harried and shaken.

"Sir, I'm not sure it's wise for you to come in here—the opening might disappear. Maybe we should all take this opportunity to leave," suggested Harry as Neelix headed for Kes.

Tuvok looked uncharacteristically perturbed. "I think not, Ensign," he intoned. "We can only hope this chamber is some kind of sanctuary."

"Have the Kazon found us?"

"No. But it appears we have awakened another nemesis."

At that point LeFevre, the last of the group, plunged through the opening and stumbled to the ground, his face and arms a mass of scratches and lacerations. "They're right behind us," he stammered, and the group turned in apprehension to the opening, only to see it shimmer closed once more. They were all contained within the doorless chamber.

"Sir, what do you mean, 'awakened'?" Kes, after a warm embrace from Neelix, came forward.

"I cannot think what else to call it. As we moved through the passageways, the walls began to metamorphose, revealing the presence of alien beings who had been somehow embedded within."

Harry and Kes exchanged a look. "The reawakening," she breathed, and as if in response, the hologram of the winged humanoid glimmered into view. There was a collective murmur from the members of the away team, who had not seen this apparition before, and Tuvok instinctively reached for his phaser, but Harry gestured for him to withdraw it. Kes moved directly in front of the creature, concentrating on receiving his telepathic message.

There was a hushed silence as she stood looking up at the magnificent hologram, whose great wings, as before, beat gently, stirring the close air of the chamber. Finally, the hologram disappeared once more.

"Apparently the hologram is triggered when someone enters the chamber. It happened when we came in, too," said Harry, turning to Kes. "Was the message the same this time?"

She nodded. "He said he assumes the time has come, he's gratified for the help of whoever has come into the chamber, and hopes that some of his kind is left to witness the reawakening of the Tokath."

"I detected energy readings emanating from this chamber," added Harry. "It's possible that when we entered, we triggered a mechanism which set some kind of program in

motion. It got really hot in here about half an hour ago—
that might have been evidence of the metamorphosis you
mentioned."

"It was as if the walls were melting," said Neelix, in
support of this theory.

"The Tokath," said Tuvok solemnly. "That must be the
name of the alien species contained within the walls."

"In some kind of stasis?" wondered Harry.

"It would appear so. But for what reason, and in what
way, and by whom—those are unanswered questions."

"You said they were a nemesis. What made you call
them that?" asked Kes.

Greta Kale answered, indicating the torn sleeves of her
uniform. "They were grabbing at us, clawing us as they
began to emerge from the walls. If they hadn't still been
stuck in that gelatinous mess, they could've ripped us
apart."

"There was one more thing the hologram said." Kes
looked around the group, as though uncertain whether to
purvey this part of the message. "It said that if there were
none of their kind to watch over the Tokath, then whoever
had come into the chamber should stay here. It would be
the only place that was safe."

And hearing that portentous statement, the group surveyed the now crowded room with apprehensive eyes.

When the ground began to fall, Jal Sittik felt a momentary consternation. Were the Federations mounting some
kind of offensive? Had they formulated a plan to take him
by surprise? But the anxiety quickly changed to a premoni-
tion of triumph: the Federations had simply been flushed
from their lair by the incessant pounding from his weapons. Now it was just a matter of picking them off as they
emerged.

"Stand ready!" he called to his men, who were already

poised, weapons lifted, anticipating the battle. The ground, he realized, was sinking in a circular pattern, in four triangular wedges that eventually formed ramps, up which, Sittik presumed, the Federations would rush in their desperate and headlong dash for freedom.

The four wedges settled onto the floor of the underground cavern, and Sittik tensed, waiting for the war whoop he presumed would announce the charge of the doomed Federations.

But there was only silence. Puffs of dust rose from the wedges of earth and suffused the stifling air of the planet. Sittik was aware once more of the annoying insects, who had suddenly swarmed around them again, nipping and stinging in a frenzy. Did they sense the impending battle? Were they trying to become part of it? Sittik had a sense that all the forces of nature were joining him in this epic encounter.

Where then, were the Federations? Did they think he was so stupid that he would have his men venture down into what could only be a trap? He shook his head in disbelief, savoring the quiver of the ornaments in his hair.

"Come out, Federations," he bellowed confidently. "If you surrender your death will be swift and painless." He listened carefully, but there was no answering call, and he began to grow impatient. His moment of glory was being postponed by these stubborn foes. He nodded toward his men to fire into the pit, and the air was laced with the sound of their weapons.

After a few minutes, he gave the signal to cease. Dust now rose in heavy clouds from the pit, and Sittik waved the acrid mist from his face, peering downward to see what effect the weapons burst had had.

He thought he detected, through the dust, a bit of movement at the bottom of the pit. It had worked! They were coming forth to assure his triumph. Tonight he would sit at the Maje's right hand . . . would watch Kosla parade before him, hoping for his notice . . . would feel the supple curves of her flesh beneath his lips.

Now there was definitely a figure coming from the pit. Rising from it. Rising?

Confusion clawed at Sittik's mind. There was something perplexing about the situation. Granted, it was difficult to see clearly through the cloud of dust raised by their weapons, but the figure he saw didn't seem to be climbing the ramps—as he would have thought the Federations must—but was rather ascending through the air. Had they developed a new technology which allowed them to fly like insects? He had never heard any intelligence which suggested the interlopers had such an ability.

And yet, here they were (for there were now more of them visible in the dust cloud), most definitely rising from the pit, closer and closer, a growing band of them hovering, inspecting the assembled Kazon troops in silent assessment.

It was not the Federations.

The beings that hovered before them were huge brown parasectoids nearly half a meter long, with fierce-looking mandibles and an elongated snout that contained a large, powerful jaw with sharp, wicked teeth. Their underbellies were a mottled green, and they were coated in a coagulated substance that dripped from them like thick jelly.

He realized they must be the Tokath, but was unsure as to the significance of their appearance. Had the Federations found these beings and made use of them as an advance unit? Were they intended as a diversion, allowing the Federations to escape? Or was this Miskk's doing, his vengeance? Sittik didn't know the answers to these questions, but he was certain their departure from the pit did not bode well. And as if they read his mind, the creatures began a disturbing sound, somewhere between a click and a squeal. He made an automatic response.

"Fire," he ordered his men, and they immediately unleashed their weapons on the creatures.

Under the withering barrage, the creatures began to emit a high-pitched shriek that assaulted the eardrums like a knife point. As they tumbled back into the pit, dead or mortally wounded, a wretched odor began to emanate from them, fouling the air even further.

But to Sittik's dismay, more and more of them began to appear, rising from the dust-occluded pit which was now becoming a graveyard, chittering in that unnerving wail that chilled his blood and rent his ears. Where were they all coming from? How could there be so many?

The Kazon soldiers kept up a relentless fusillade, but no matter how many of the hard-shelled bodies tumbled, dying, into the pit, even more took their place, pulsing upward on the thick clouds of dust and smoke. Sittik found himself coughing uncontrollably as his lungs tried to reject the thick particulates they were being forced to ingest.

The Tokath were coursing upward, spilling out of the pit now, too many for even the weapons of his men to dispatch. He stared in amazement as they kept coming, dozens of them, wings pulsing, pushing them beyond the bounds of the depression in the ground.

Something wet hit his face and he daubed at it, then screamed as it began eating into the skin of his cheek and his hand. Frantically, he pawed at the awful substance, which was quickly making a paste of his skin; the more he tried to wipe it off, the deeper he gouged it in. He sank to his knees, desperate with pain, trying to make a poultice of dirt, smearing it into the wound but quickly realizing nothing helped.

Another glob of the stuff hit him in the forehead, and the process was begun again. Around him, he was vaguely aware of his men in the same circumstances, and he realized that these hideous creatures were emitting the noxious liquid, spraying it from their underbellies, reducing his proud squad to a wailing, helpless mass, squirming on the ground and begging the gods to put an end to their misery.

That prayer, at least, would be answered, though not quickly. Sittik looked up to see one of the creatures flying at him, awful mandibles extended, then felt them drill into his abdomen and clutch his intestines. The agony redoubled as the creature tore his entrails from his body, then seized them in its powerful jaws and began eating them.

A blood-red cloud descended over Sittik's vision; in it Kosla briefly danced as he realized he would not be spending the night with her, or with anyone ever again, and yet it didn't matter because oblivion was all he craved now and it couldn't come quickly enough.

Trakis the physician worked the console quickly, nervous that someone might enter unexpectedly and discover him. He wasn't entirely familiar with the communications technology on the Kazon ship—in their ineptitude, the Vistik had cobbled together two separate systems that weren't completely compatible, probably because they were incapable of repairing either one. He was working through the circuitry carefully, trying to find a frequency upon which he could piggyback a message, but the process was tedious and frustrating.

The body of the captive lay on the examination table, dissected now as a result of his necropsy. Trakis had found nothing remarkable during the procedure; in spite of the Kazon belief that these creatures might be harnessed in some way to act as a fighting force, the physician could find no evidence that the Tokath possessed a large enough brain to be intelligent. As he suspected, they functioned purely on instinct—and as such, were an unruly and potentially dangerous ally. It would be like trying to train a pack of feral dogs.

Trakis finally found a frequency that looked promising, a low-energy subspace band almost indistinguishable from the ship's warp-core emissions, and he began a carefully modulated series of hails. It would require some luck, to be sure, but his chances of getting off this ship alive had just risen dramatically.

"Captain, we're being hailed." Rollins looked down at her in some puzzlement, and Janeway turned to him.

"By whom?"

"I'm not sure. It's coming from the Kazon ship, but the message is being piggybacked on a very low frequency subspace carrier wave. I don't know why the Kazon would go to that trouble."

"On screen." She looked up and saw a staticky image fill the screen; she couldn't see the figure well and couldn't understand him because of a noisy interference.

"Attempting to clear the transmission," said Rollins, and within seconds the sound had cleared significantly though the image had improved only slightly.

". . . attempting to contact the Federations on their ship. Is anyone receiving this message? I am Trakis, a Trabe physician taken prisoner by the Kazon. Repeat, I am attempting to contact the Federations—"

"This is Captain Janeway of *Voyager*. We are receiving you."

The figure on the screen seemed to slump in relief. "Captain . . . I'm glad to hear from you. I'm asking for asylum—the Vistik have no further use for me and I suspect they'll terminate me soon. Can you use your technology which transports individuals to bring me onto your ship?"

Janeway's mind raced, assessing risk factors. "Our transporters only function within a distance of forty thousand kilometers. We'd have to put ourselves in weapons range of the Kazon—and at the moment our phaser arrays are off-line. What's more, we'd have to drop shields to bring you on board."

The figure leaned toward the screen. She still couldn't see him well through the interference, but she recognized the desperate tone in his voice. "I have information which will be of value to you—the reason the Kazon are so interested in this planet, and why they are trying to destroy you."

"Dr. Trakis, you don't have to be valuable to us in order for us to assist you. If we can help, we will."

"Thank you, Captain. I am in a small laboratory on the starboard side of the ship, near the ventral airlocks."

"Remain at your station until you hear from us."

Trakis acknowledged, and the transmission ceased. Janeway pondered the implications of this conversation. It could be a Kazon trick, of course. That was probably the more likely explanation. And yet, there was something genuine in the fear Trakis had projected, and it was true that a Trabe was never safe at the hands of the Kazon.

She was intrigued by his promise of information. Did he know something that would help her retrieve her crew? It was a tantalizing prospect. But before she could reflect further, she was interrupted.

"Engineering to the bridge."

"Janeway here."

"Captain, we've got the phasers back."

"Good work, B'Elanna. What was it?"

"A microfracture in the PDM crystal. So small it was virtually undetectable—we had to infer it from the prefire chamber response. But we're back on-line now."

Janeway's mind raced. Now they could face the Kazon as equals—even superiors. They must act quickly, while the Kazon still thought they were disadvantaged. She turned to Chakotay.

"Battle stations, Commander. Rollins, divert all auxiliary power to the shields. Mr. Paris, take us out of the nebula and in range of the Kazon ship."

The sleek ship hove to and began to move out of the nebula. Janeway felt her pulse quicken as she anticipated the encounter with the Kazon, hopeful they might be willing to talk once they realized *Voyager* was back at full strength.

"Mister Rollins, prepare to hail the Kazon ship as soon as we've cleared the nebula and are within range."

"Aye, Captain. I've got them on sensors now. Hailing on all channels."

A minute passed, then another. Finally Rollins stated the obvious: "They're not answering, Captain." Then Chakotay reacted to something on the center console. "They're powering weapons."

"Ready evasive maneuver chi-eight, Mr. Paris. We're going to have to pull a few tricks to get that Trabe doctor off the ship."

But before she could indicate what those tricks might be, the ship was rocked violently by a huge weapons blast. But this time *Voyager* was ready, and though they were knocked around, no serious damage was done.

"Return fire, Rollins. Target their weapons arrays and propulsion systems."

"Aye, Captain, firing."

Beams of phaser fire leapt across space toward the Kazon ship, but hit only a glancing blow; the Kazon pilot was also flying evasive maneuvers. Fire was returned, and the two ships kept this barrage up for several minutes, *Voyager* all the while working its way closer to the Kazon vessel.

"Captain, the shields are starting to degrade. The closer we get to their ship, the more impact their weapons have," observed Chakotay.

"I know. We just have to hold out a few minutes more. Mr. Paris, I want you to take us directly *underneath* the Kazon ship. It's going to be a little tougher for it to fire at us in that position. Just snuggle up to its belly like a baby kitten trying to nurse."

Tom Paris smiled at the image and entered the commands. Janeway saw the underbelly of the Kazon ship looming ahead of them, trying to buck and roll away from them, but Tom's skillful piloting kept *Voyager* all but glued to them.

"Mr. Rollins, when I give the order, drop shields and simultaneously initiate transport of the Trabe life sign near the starboard ventral airlocks."

"I'm locked on, Captain," replied Rollins smoothly.

"Do it," snapped Janeway, and at the same moment the shields dropped, a huge blast from the Kazon hit *Voyager*'s dorsal plane. The hull buckled, causing instant depressurization until the automatic forcefield activated, but in that moment havoc was wreaked. Conduits exploded and consoles threw sparks. Emergency circuits frantically rerouted power to critical systems—but the transport had already been initiated.

Trakis had been pacing nervously in the laboratory, jarred by the weapons blasts from the Federation ship, and wondering if the female captain would be able to bring him aboard. How that would be possible in the midst of a pitched battle he had no idea, and he had begun to resign himself to staying with the Kazon. As he was trying to figure out how to survive the day, Nimmet entered, a smug smile playing on his face. Trakis turned to face him, an uneasy feeling in the pit of his stomach.

"Did you think you could outwit us, Trabe?" rasped Nimmet, eyes slitted in that ridiculous guise. "Did you think we were so foolish we wouldn't pick up your transmission to the Federations?"

"What are you talking about, Nimmet? Have you misread the sensing indicators again?"

"Don't bother with this pretense. I know you contacted their ship." Nimmet paused, as though for dramatic effect, and then spoke in a hoarse, affected whisper. "And I have been granted the privilege of ending your pitiful life."

A huge impact blasted the ship and Nimmet momentarily lost his balance. Trakis took advantage of the mishap to put the examination table, still holding the carcass of the dissected creature, between him and Nimmet. But Nimmet was soon on his feet and brandishing an ugly-looking knife as he advanced on Trakis.

"I haven't yet made my report to Maje Dut about the necropsy I performed," Trakis began urgently. "He'll be most unhappy if you remove the opportunity for him to gain insight into the creature."

"It was Maje Dut who sent me here," replied Nimmet easily. "He no longer has faith in your abilities. You've proven traitorous, so who is to say your information would have any merit?" Nimmet shrugged and moved closer, wielding the vicious knife with intimidating familiarity.

"Nimmet, my friend, listen to me—"

"I am not your friend, Trabe. You have treated me like a servant since you came on board. Do you think I don't recognize your condescension? It will be a pleasure to see your life's blood draining away."

Nimmet leapt for him and in one sweeping motion

Trakis grabbed the lifeless shell of the dead creature and presented its green underbelly toward Nimmet's slashing blow. The knife laced through the belly and, as Trakis had hoped, directly into the parasectoid's poison sac. Nimmet jerked the knife out and then began to scream, clawing at his hand as the toxic fluid began eating into it.

Trakis caught one glimpse of Nimmet's fevered eyes, which fastened on his in a mixture of pain and rage, and then the entire room began shimmering before his eyes. He blacked out momentarily and then, miraculously, he was standing on a small stage in a room he had never seen before, staring at a uniformed Federation. His head swam dizzyingly as the man approached him, took his arm, and said, "The captain wants to see you on the bridge."

They swept out of the room, entered a conveyer of some kind, and minutes later Trakis stumbled onto a bridge that appeared to be in chaos. A malodorous coolant gas was venting from a conduit; an alarm was sounding continuously, and in one corner a wounded crewman was being tended to. The ship continued to reverberate as it was pounded by Kazon weapons, and Trakis wondered briefly if he would be any better off on this ship than he had with the Kazon. His mouth was dry and his legs trembling, but he didn't know if that was a result of the strange, disembodied journey he'd made from the Kazon ship to this one, his near-death at the hands of Nimmet, or of his quite natural reluctance to die on an alien ship surrounded by strangers.

A small, trim woman approached him, and he realized this must be the fabled captain of the Federation ship.

"It's not as bad as it looks," she reassured him. "Our shields are holding."

He circled immediately to her, his mission clear. He had to convince her to depart immediately. "There's no need for you to endure this, Captain. If you leave this area of space, the Kazon won't pursue you."

"I can't leave. I have crew who are trapped on the planet."

"The Kazon will never let you get near the surface. They think you want the Tokath, and they'll keep you away at all costs."

"The Tokath?" Janeway began, but then the ship took a terrific jolt and everyone, including Trakis, went tumbling. Trakis cracked his elbow painfully on a nearby console, and he yelped, rubbing it to reduce the lancing pain that now consumed his arm.

"I can explain everything—but it would be easier if we were in circumstances where we could remain upright. Please—all you have to do is leave, and we'll all be safe."

Suddenly, to Trakis' amazement, the woman captain grabbed his jacket and steered him firmly into one of two chairs at the center of the bridge. She leaned in close to him; her eyes were a penetrating blue-gray, and her voice had a timbre that resonated like a cymbal. "I told you I'm not leaving my crew. Now you tell me what you know about all this, so I can figure out what to do." She turned to the others. "Mr. Paris, continue evasive maneuvers. Rollins, fire at your discretion." Then she turned back to Trakis, who was frankly more unnerved by her than by the Kazon attack.

"Most people thought it was apocryphal," he began urgently, for he believed that the faster he could tell his story, the faster they could get away from this ominous planet and the pounding of the Kazon. "But it's true—the Tokath are real. I've examined one myself, and it's everything the myth suggests."

Another hit rattled them and Trakis looked around in some desperation; the bridge was venting more coolant gas and several consoles had exploded. He turned back to the captain, whose eyes had never left him, and the tempo of his recitative increased. "The Tokath are what we call a parasectoid species, hard-shelled creatures lacking intelligence—but which are vicious and deadly. They'd adapted to survive in almost any habitat—air, water, even space. They were an almost ideal defense force, and they kept this planet safe from all invaders for centuries."

A series of hits knocked them about again and the captain glanced over at one of her crew. "Shields at eighty-seven percent, Captain, and holding. I'm betting they'll get tired of this before we do," he said, and Trakis marveled at his buoyant confidence. He realized that the attitude on this combat bridge was different from any he'd ever witnessed. The Kazon were veritable wild men when in combat, shouting loudly in what Trakis felt was an effort to shore up their courage; the Trabe were usually nervously desperate, the result of years of running from the Kazon. Never had he seen behavior in battle that was so composed, so professional.

The woman turned back to him, and there was no doubt he was to continue, and quickly. "The planet was also inhabited by a humanoid species, the Krett, who possessed the power of flight—a wise, gentle people who communicated telepathically, and who had a genuine affection for their unusual protectors. That's why they went to such extraordinary lengths to save them."

She looked at him questioningly.

"A massive plasma eruption burst from the star's equatorial zone thousands of years ago. It created an electrical disturbance in the planet's atmosphere which would eventually kill almost every living thing on the planet—which is the only one in the system that supports life. The Krett were technologically advanced, and had spaceships. They could evacuate, but there was no way to take millions of the Tokath with them. So they transformed the Tokath habitat into hibernation chambers, put them into stasis, and departed—hoping one day to return to their world." He shook his head sadly. "But they learned what a hostile part of space they occupied. Without the protection of the Tokath, they were set upon at every turn. Like us, they were decimated."

The woman looked at him intently. "What does all this have to do with us? Why are the Kazon attacking *Voyager?*"

"They're fixated with the idea of finding the Tokath and resuscitating them, turning them into a personal fighting force, and thereby dominating the sector. They believe you have the same thing in mind, and they're determined to stop you."

"How did the Kazon learn all this? How did they know where to look for these creatures?"

"The Kazon-Vistik stumbled on the truth during one of their nasty little raids on unprotected outposts. They discovered a small Krett colony which had endured over the centuries—with a few of the Tokath, which they had taken with them, still extant. The Krett, hoping to gain sympathy and be spared, told them the tale of their ancient diaspora, and of their belief that the Tokath might still live. In return, the Kazon slaughtered them all and took the remaining Tokath with them for examination. And managed to kill all of them but one."

Trakis paused with genuine sorrow. He still regretted his actions on the Kazon ship, and the fact that he, a physician, had caused the creature's death. And all for nothing, all to feed the Kazon obsession. He had to convince this icy captain that the only recourse they had, the only way to prevent more killing, was to retreat. He clutched the arm of the chair as a series of muffled explosions thudded in the distance, and beseeched her once more. "I can lead you to

273

a Trabe planet. You'll be welcome there, to repair your ship and take on stores. Leave the Kazon to their wild dreams; my experience has been that they're so inept they'll never succeed."

"If the Maje would only answer my hails, I could explain to him that we have no interest in the Tokath. All I want is to get my crew back."

Trakis stifled a rise of irritation; this woman showed little understanding of the Kazon. As though Maje Dut would listen reasonably to her statement, accept it at face value, pause in his assault long enough for her to retrieve her crew, and then send them on their way with a wave and a smile. This obstinate insistence on saving part of her crew—perhaps at the expense of all the others, and the ship as well—was evidence of weakness. In some things, the Trabe and the Kazon agreed: women simply weren't suited for positions of leadership. They were too idealistic, too sentimental, too emotional.

He sighed and began to think of another means of helping her see the error of her ways when two of the crew spoke at once—the pilot and the man standing behind her right side. "Captain, I'm reading something—" "We've got activity from the planet's surface—"

The captain moved immediately to the pilot's console. "What is it, Mr. Paris?" she asked crisply. The blond young man was working his controls rapidly. "Something rising from the planet—a convoy of ships . . . no . . ." He looked up at her, puzzled, and Trakis took the opportunity to move closer to them.

The man from the rear station called out now. "Captain, I have organic readings. There's a mass of life signs—millions of them—ascending through the ionosphere."

"On screen," said the captain, and Trakis looked up at what was revealed there. At the same time, he realized that they were no longer taking hits from weapons; apparently the Kazon were as curious about what was happening as the crew of this ship.

And when the screen before them revealed a view of the planet below, he understood fully. What he saw there made his legs suddenly lose stability and his stomach sour.

A brown miasma, vast and inexorable, was rising into space from the surface of the planet. Trakis rubbed a damp palm on his pants and turned to the captain, who was staring in puzzlement at the screen.

"Captain," he said, trying to keep his voice from quavering, "those are the Tokath."

CHAPTER

22

"A REVIEW BOARD IS STANDARD PROCEDURE, KATHRYN. ALL captains go through the process after their first mission, and frequently after that. Don't worry about it." Admiral Paris' blue-gray eyes crinkled as he smiled at her.

Kathryn sat opposite him in his office—the very office she'd waited in when she first met him over ten years ago. Now, she'd just returned from a six-month mission into the Beta Quadrant; she'd collected some valuable scientific data on microsecond pulsars, and she was annoyed that her trip home—where Mark was waiting—was being delayed for a routine and, in her mind, wholly unnecessary procedure.

"I'm not worried about it—that's the point. There's nothing to worry about; the mission was a complete success, nothing was amiss, and I don't see why everyone's time has to be wasted with this superfluous review."

"You're proving to be an excellent captain. I'm more proud of you than I can say. But you may need to pay some attention to one of the finer details of command: an abiding patience for Starfleet rules and regulations. You'll have to set the standard on your ships, Kathryn. It won't do to have a captain who plays fast and loose with the rules."

She drew a deep breath. He was right, of course. She was just so eager to see Mark, and Phoebe, and her mother. But two days more wasn't the end of the world, and she'd have a full month to spend with them before catching another assignment. "You're right, sir. Thanks for the reminder."

He started to reply but suddenly the door to his office opened and his aide, the dignified Mrs. Klenman, now a full captain, walked in, her face reflecting alarm. "Excuse me, Admiral," she said quickly, "but I think you should get over to the Academy right away."

Kathryn saw Admiral Paris's face go ashen. His son Tom was now a senior at the Academy. "What is it? Is something wrong?"

"There's been an accident. Commander Lewis wouldn't give me any details—but I know he was concerned."

Kathryn saw the naked fear that only a parent can know take its hold on Admiral Paris. He glanced at his console, considering sending a transmission to the Academy, but then shook that off, preferring to go in person. "Let the commander know I'm on my way."

"Sir, do you want me to come with you?" Kathryn felt she should at least offer support.

"No. Thank you. I'll see you at the review board tomorrow." And he was gone, fear propelling him. Kathryn had the sudden insight that she was glad she had no children, and wasn't hostage to the powerful concerns of parenthood; it was more vulnerability than she felt she could tolerate. She turned to Commander Klenman.

"Will you let me know what's happened? I'll be at the Officers' Quarters tonight."

"Of course, Captain." Klenman was clearly worried, too. She'd spent more than ten years with Admiral Paris, and was devoted to him and his family. Kathryn left the office with a heavy heart.

The news that evening was tragic, but it was to spare the Paris family for now. Tom had been leading a fighter squadron in maneuvers; one of the cadets had made a miscalculation, which led to an error, which led to an accident, and three of the vessels collided, killing the pilots. Tom had risked his ship to prevent the mishap, but to no avail.

Admiral Paris was pale and grave the next day when she entered the conference room where the review was to be held. She went immediately to him. "I'm so sorry about the accident, sir," she said. "It must have been hard on Tom."

Paris nodded. "It's always difficult to lose people under your command—I'm afraid you'll find that out eventually—but it's one of the risks. Tom did his best, but sometimes these things happen. He'll have to work through it, but in the long run it will toughen him."

Kathryn nodded and then turned to stand at attention as two other admirals entered. She was pleased to see that one was Admiral Finnegan, whom she'd met so long ago on her first trip to Mars, and with whom she'd had dinner the night before her father and Justin were killed.

"Good to see you, Captain Janeway," said Finnegan. "Of course you know Admiral Paris, and this is Admiral Necheyev."

Kathryn nodded to a trim, blond woman with sharp features and piercing eyes. The woman exuded authority without effort, a fact Kathryn found herself admiring; she wondered if she projected that same easy confidence, and feared she didn't. On this, her first command, she'd often felt she had to work at being authoritative.

"We're just waiting for the tactical officer," continued Finnegan. He was going over some last-minute figures." This remark puzzled Kathryn. Last-minute figures? Regarding tactical operations? Why would there be any issue with that part of the mission?

As her mind raced with these questions, the door opened and a man walked in. He was a dark Vulcan, and didn't appear to be a young person; yet he held the rank of ensign. Admiral Finnegan turned to him genially. "Captain Janeway, may I present Ensign Tuvok."

Kathryn extended her hand and felt it taken firmly by the Vulcan. His eyes were dark, and seemed to Kathryn to be opaque: they were not a window to his soul so much as a barrier to it. He was erect and formal, his voice a deep and fulsome baritone. "Captain," he acknowledged simply, then set a stack of padds on the table.

Admiral Finnegan called the review to order, made a few complimentary remarks about Kathryn, then turned to Tuvok. "The bulk of the review involves Mr. Tuvok's area of expertise, so I'll turn the proceedings over to him." Kathryn was puzzled—what was going on here?

Tuvok began to speak, and in a few minutes her cheeks were flaming and her heart thudding in her chest: she was furious. She worked to control her temper as the Vulcan's rich voice droned on and on. ". . . and tactical logs indicate that there were no test firings, no battle drills, and only two weapons reviews during the mission. All told, there are exactly forty-three violations of tactical procedures, ranging from the minor to those I would consider significant."

With that pronouncement he set down his last padd and folded his hands in front of him, solemnly regarding her. A deep hush had fallen on the room, and Kathryn realized she was going to have to defend herself. Admiral Finnegan turned to her, and though his voice was quiet, it held no hint of pliability. "You may feel free to answer the charges, Captain."

Kathryn took a moment to compose herself, then stood. "Sir, I was raised in the traditions of Starfleet. I learned the precepts of this organization at an early age; I admire and honor them." She paused, looking from one to the other, but studiously ignoring Tuvok the Vulcan.

"It has always been clear to me that Starfleet is first and foremost an institution which is dedicated to exploration and investigation. Its primary responsibilities are the acquisition of knowledge, the seeking out of new worlds, and the establishment of cordial relations with other species.

"Those tasks represent the mandate we have created—a mandate which is both positive and powerful." She looked directly at Admiral Finnegan. "This is not, strictly speaking, a military organization. It functions as such only when there is a need for self-defense. The military aspects of Starfleet—its command structure and nomenclature, for example—are in place primarily as a framework within which its members can function according to clearly established guidelines."

Now she turned directly to Tuvok, looked him square in those shielded eyes of his, and drilled into him. "Tactical functions, weapons checks, battle drills—those are activities I consider low-priority. As long as I am assured that we are at the ready in case of attack, I see no need to spend large amounts of time drilling the crew in the mechanics of war. I am satisfied that the weapons systems and the crew were ready for any eventuality, and as such, that I fulfilled the tactical requirements adequately."

She and the Vulcan held a look for a long, quiet beat, and then she turned to Admiral Finnegan. His face was devoid of expression. He turned to Tuvok. "Any comment, Ensign?" he asked mildly.

Now Tuvok stood, but Kathryn didn't sit back down. They faced each other at opposite ends of a table, like combatants squaring off in a gladiatorial ring. Kathryn's heart was still hammering, but Tuvok was utterly composed. He might as well have been ordering dinner. She'd never understood Vulcans, never comprehended their icy reserve, never really trusted the capacities of those who eschewed emotion. Her humiliating tennis defeat years ago at the hands of Shalarik suddenly enveloped her, reopening old wounds. She was gripped with the determination that she mustn't fail this time; this Vulcan could not best her.

"The captain's idealism is admirable, of course," he intoned. "However, that very structure of which she speaks is an absolutely essential component of a smoothly functioning organization. Regulations do not exist in a vacuum; they are in place for specific and legitimate purposes. Starfleet Command has set the rules and I am certain they did not do so frivolously. We must assume that regulations are established for the most definitive of reasons."

And now it was his turn to look Kathryn in the eye. "If it is left to the individual to decide which rules are to be followed, and on what schedule, then the rules cease to have meaning. The only possible result is anarchy. The smooth functioning that Captain Janeway speaks of so eloquently does not come spontaneously; it comes at a cost and that cost must be paid."

Kathryn felt the eyes of the three admirals on her. "Anything else, Captain?" queried Finnegan. She took a breath and, still staring at Tuvok, rebutted. "By its nature, the captaincy of a ship on a deep-space mission requires flexible discretionary powers. A captain must be able to confront unexpected circumstances and have enough leeway to respond appropriately. Slavish adherence to rules can undermine the very individuality that has made the finest of Starfleet officers so outstanding. Again—if the safety of the ship and crew is not compromised, surely I have the latitude to apportion time as I see fit."

There was a long silence which neither Kathryn nor Tuvok tried to fill. Admiral Finnegan sat back in his chair. "If neither of you has anything more, you're excused while we confer. Please wait in the corridor."

Kathryn and Tuvok nodded, then turned to exit. She could feel her adrenaline pumping, fueled by anger and determination. They took seats on opposite sides of the corridor; Kathryn felt a lock of hair fall across her eye and she jerked it back. Damn her hair! She had to find a style that wouldn't betray her, something that was neat, and professional.

The irrationality of worrying about her hair at a time like this suddenly struck her, and she heard herself chuckle aloud. Tuvok looked up at her. "Captain?" he queried politely.

"Nothing," she retorted. She wasn't about to tell this arrogant Vulcan about her problems with her hair. She was sure he would find it utterly capricious that the subject would enter her mind at this moment.

But apparently he didn't need her help in commenting on the human condition. "It is intriguing to me," he intoned, "that humans so often use that term to indicate its exact opposite."

"I beg your pardon?"

"At the very moment when there is clearly 'something' of some import affecting the individual, he or she will say that 'nothing' is bothering them. I am curious as to why that would be."

Irritation was added to the other emotions Kathryn was experiencing. "It's a way of protecting our privacy. I don't necessarily want to share my innermost thoughts just because someone wants to know what they are." Her voice sounded harsh, even to herself.

But Tuvok merely reflected on her statement, then finally nodded. "I see. Thank you, Captain. That does clarify the matter." His manner was mild and thoughtful, and Kathryn thought she had never encountered anyone so annoying.

The door opened and Admiral Paris stood there, beckoning to them. "You can come in now," he said. They returned to their seats, not making eye contact as Admiral Finnegan spoke.

"You are both eloquent and persuasive speakers," he began. "We all thought we'd enjoy hearing you engaged in formal debate." He smiled slightly at the prospect and the other admirals followed suit. "However, our purpose today is not to assess debating skills." He turned to Kathryn. "Captain, you completed your first mission in fine style, and I'm entering a commendation from Admiral Paris into your record; he feels the pulsar data you compiled is of extreme value."

"Thank you, sir."

"You show all the potential to become an able captain, indeed. However, Mr. Tuvok here is quite right in his insistence that tactical regulations not be ignored because of your interpretation of Starfleet's charter. From now on, you're to stick to the rules."

"Yes, sir." Kathryn was stung by the rebuke, but swallowed her feelings.

"However, we had a thought which might serve everyone's best interests. We've been looking for a suitable post for Ensign Tuvok, who is eager to return to deep space. We've decided to assign him to your ship to serve as tactical officer on your next mission."

Kathryn couldn't believe what she was hearing. This imperious, condescending man on her bridge? This stickler for rules on her senior staff? What could Admiral Finnegan be thinking?

"We think you might balance each other well." He looked at Kathryn and his merry eyes crinkled at the edges. "And you'd be sure your tactical drills would never go undone." He paused, then looked at them both. "Well? What do you think?"

"I would be honored to accept such a post," said Tuvok immediately.

Kathryn felt Finnegan's gaze shift to her. "I'd like some time to think it over, sir," she replied.

The admiral nodded genially. "Take all the time you'd like, Captain. But realize—this decision has been made."

The three admirals gazed implacably at her and she felt the blood rise to her face. "I see. Yes, sir. Thank you, sir. May we be excused now?"

Finnegan nodded, and she turned on her heel and walked out of the room, back erect. They could force this annoying officer on her, but they couldn't make her like him, or treat him with anything other than the disdain with which he treated her. With any luck, after this one mission everyone would realize the pairing was a dreadful mistake and Tuvok would be sent off to serve on a ship that was commanded by a Vulcan—someone who would believe his imperiousness to be an asset. Because she certainly never would.

CHAPTER

23

ALL THE BRIDGE CREW STARED IN ASTONISHMENT AT THE viewscreen, watching as the brown cloud rose from the planet, all but obscuring it from view. It was densely thick, a solid mass of undulating matter that spread relentlessly from the planet's surface, through the atmosphere, and into space, toward the two ships now poised in anticipation, their own conflict forgotten for the moment.

"Captain," whispered Trakis, voice hoarse with anxiety, "you must go. Now. Quickly. They'll overwhelm the ship. They emit a caustic substance which will gradually neutralize your shields and then eat through your hull. They'll be inside the ship in an hour and they'll kill everything that moves."

As she watched the approach of the brown sludge, Janeway was tempted to agree. There was something almost unbearably ominous about this vast aggregate. Her ship was in peril.

But so was her away team. She turned to Trakis, who had

gone pale at the approach of the Tokath. "Is there a way to repel them?"

"I don't know of any. They're relentless—it's impossible to destroy them all. You might kill thousands, but they just keep coming."

Janeway watched as the umber cloud rose higher and higher, gaining definition now, a roiling mass of organic matter in which one could begin to distinguish discrete forms. They vaguely reminded Janeway of beetles, one of the most abundant life-forms on Earth, except that they were much larger and, of course, had apparently adapted to survive in space.

The scientist in her had a curious fascination about these beings, but her command instincts told her they posed a greater threat to *Voyager* than the most technologically advanced starship.

"Captain, you can outrun them—they can't travel at warp. It's the only way to survive," said Trakis, who was still pallid and shaken. Janeway turned on him.

"Dr. Trakis, you have some value on the bridge because you know something about these creatures. But if you don't stop trying to persuade me to leave, I'll have you escorted to quarters. Because I'm not going anywhere. I intend to use the distraction of the Tokath to get past the Kazon and down to my crew on the planet." She was pleased to see Trakis go an even paler shade at this. "Do we understand each other?"

He nodded, and she continued. "Is conventional weaponry effective against them?"

"Yes. But there are simply too many of them. When your weapons arrays are drained of energy, they'll still be coming."

"I have no wish to slaughter creatures who are only acting on instinct." Janeway turned and addressed Rollins.

"Voyager may have a few tricks that ships in the Delta Quadrant lack. Rollins, prepare a polaron emission. Maybe that will make us less attractive to them."

But sudden activity on the viewscreen caught their attention, and Janeway heard an audible gasp from the Trabe physician. Tom Paris turned to her.

"Captain, the Kazon ship is attacking them."

And so they were. Weapons fire burst from the ship and plunged into the mass of writhing brown bodies. Hundreds of them incinerated instantly, but within seconds it was as though nothing had happened: the powerful surge of creatures continued unabated. The Kazon ship unleashed a ruinous fire, and Tokath by the thousands disintegrated before their eyes.

But more kept coming. The crew of *Voyager* watched in stunned silence as the Kazon kept up its unending volley, lacerating wave after wave of the beetle-like creatures with absolutely no appreciable effect. The brown mass rose steadily through space, coming closer and closer to the two ships.

"Maybe they'll focus their attention on the Kazon, since they're the ones attacking," ventured Paris, and Janeway acknowledged that she was thinking the same thing. Trakis emitted a short, derisive laugh but apparently thought better of speaking his thoughts aloud, and subsided into anxious silence.

The Tokath validated Paris and Janeway. As soon as the Kazon began attacking them, the swarm careened toward their ship, concentrating its advance on the aggressor. That was all Janeway needed to act.

"Mr. Rollins, is that polaron emission ready?"

"Yes, ma'am."

"Begin releasing it. Mr. Paris, prepare to descend to the planet's surface and land. Let's take it nice and easy."

"Aye, Captain. Blue alert."

The alarm sounded for the rarely used blue alert, and an azure wash permeated the bridge.

"I've plotted a descent course," said Paris. "I'll try to bring us down within two kilometers of the away team's landing site."

"All decks report Condition Blue," announced Chakotay.

Paris's hands danced over controls. "Atmospheric controls at standby. Landing mechanisms on-line. Inertial dampers at maximum."

Gently, the ship descended. The Tokath, streaming toward the Kazon ship, seemed to ignore *Voyager* and focus on the Kazon, who were still butchering them by the thousands.

"So far, so good," murmured Paris. "Thanks to the Kazon, we might just pull this off."

Janeway glanced over at Trakis, and noted that he seemed no more encouraged by this maneuver than he had been earlier. He was watching the viewscreen intently, perspiration moistening his brow, which was furrowed in anticipation of dire consequences.

Slowly they sank, as though through a pit of dark tar, eddies of mottled bodies swirling around them, streaming past, sliding off their shields as if they were oiled. It reminded Janeway of her diving days, descending through a dense school of fish, silvered bodies gliding effortlessly around her. It was always a pacifying feeling, and she tried to re-create that sense of calm now.

"Altitude one thousand kilometers, Captain," said Paris. "Nine hundred seventy kilometers and still dropping."

Chakotay spoke from her side. "I'm reading our shuttles on the surface—and a Kazon shuttle. But no Kazon life signs."

"What about our people?"

"No signs, Captain."

"Acknowledged."

And still they descended, through the ionosphere and into the mesosphere, and still the Tokath streamed upward. How many could there be? wondered Janeway. And would they all have left the surface by the time *Voyager* was ready to land? That would be key to rescuing her people. It was disconcerting to hear that Chakotay couldn't detect life signs even as they drew nearer the surface, but she had to count on Tuvok's having found shelter. She was convinced that success was just minutes away.

The first contraindication to that assumption was a seemingly insignificant one. Rollins's voice was calm as he noted, "I'm reading a minor disruption to the shields, aft port ventral."

"Nature of the disruption?"

"Unknown. If it's the Tokath, they aren't doing much damage."

"Increase the level of the polaron emission."

"Aye. Now at maximum."

They descended silently for a minute more, and then Rollins spoke again, this time more urgently. "Captain, I'm reading further disruption to the shields. This time more widespread."

"The Tokath?"

"I think so—I'm reading life signs penetrating the shields. Aft port ventral is beginning to degrade."

"Ready a positron charge. Maybe we can shake them loose."

"Ready, Captain."

The viewscreen showed an amber flash, and a momentary reaction from the swarm of bodies that surrounded them. They recoiled briefly but then resumed their swarm. Hundreds of mottled green underbellies coated the shields, spewing black venom that would eventually eat its way through to the hull. She could sense Trakis next to her, breathing deeply, seeing his demise before him.

"It's over, Captain," he rasped. "Once they attach, they don't let go. We're all dead."

Paris glanced up at her, as though waiting for orders. But what orders could she give? If what Trakis said was true, it didn't matter if they retreated or not.

On the other hand, if they no longer perceived *Voyager* as a threat to the planet, there was the possibility they would lose interest.

"Captain, the shields are degrading pretty rapidly," said Chakotay. "Down to sixty-three percent and falling."

Janeway acted. "Mr. Paris, abort landing sequence. Set a course away from the planet."

"Aye, Captain. Standing down blue alert."

Now they reversed course, and swam with the Tokath, rising swiftly through the mesosphere and ionosphere, and soon breaking orbital velocity. They had a brief glimpse of the Kazon ship—or rather, the shape of the Kazon ship— covered with the writhing hard-shelled bodies of the Tokath. It reminded Janeway of a visit to Georgia she'd made as a child, where she saw an entire forest covered in a vine called kudzu. She could see only the shapes of trees underneath the all-encompassing vine, which had blan- keted every surface in its path.

The Kazon ship was no longer firing weapons, and was listing randomly, apparently powerless. *Voyager* streamed past it, and finally broke free of the swarm of Tokath, which was clustered between the planet and the Kazon ship. They watched intently to see if any of the creatures followed them. After a few moments, Paris ventured, "It doesn't look like any more are coming after us, Captain."

"But the ones on our shields aren't letting go," added Chakotay. "Shields now down to forty-seven percent."

"Reroute power from the weapons and propulsions systems to reinforce the shields."

"Yes, ma'am," responded Rollins crisply. But in a few moments Chakotay reported that the move hadn't helped much. "Shields still degrading. Now at forty-one percent . . . thirty-eight . . ."

"Captain, at this rate they'll penetrate the hull in another eight minutes."

Janeway's mind raced. What could she use to pry these sticky creatures off her shields? They were stuck there like wood ticks, and soon they'd be working on the hull.

Wood ticks . . . the image resonated in her mind. Getting rid of wood ticks . . .

She put a hand on Paris's shoulder. "Lieutenant, set a course for the primary star of this system. We're going to burn those things off our shields."

Paris grinned and immediately went into action. Trakis looked over at her, and she thought she detected a faint smile from him, as well. "You're remarkably courageous, Captain," he conceded. "I admire that in you—even if it accomplishes nothing."

"We'll see," Janeway snapped, tired of this Trabe physician and his negativity. But then the viewscreen began to emanate a golden glow, and all eyes moved toward it.

The fiery disk of the yellow star loomed ahead of them, somewhat obscured by the bodies of the Tokath, growing larger as *Voyager* approached. "Distance fifty thousand kilometers," announced Paris.

"Hull temperature rising, now at two thousand degrees Celsius. Radiation levels at twenty rads per minute," chimed in Rollins.

Chakotay moved next to Janeway. "Shields are down to twenty-six percent. We won't be able to get much closer."

"Maybe we won't have to. It's hotter for them than it is for us."

The ship raced still closer to the star, and Janeway realized they could feel a temperature difference already. Their degraded shields just weren't protecting them from the massive heat generated by the star—and yet the Tokath showed no signs of distress, no indication that they were going to let loose of their death hold on the ship.

"Hull temperature at twelve thousand degrees and climbing. Radiation at forty rads per minute."

"Distance, ten thousand kilometers."

"Hold us here, Mr. Paris," said Janeway. It was definitely getting hot on the bridge. She could feel the closeness of the air, the perspiration dampening her face, and she saw the others becoming flushed.

"What's the temperature in the cabin?" she asked, and Rollins, voice a bit breathy, answered, "Fifty-five degrees C."

"How can they survive the heat? Why aren't they dropping off?" Chakotay asked, frustrated.

"They've adapted to so many environments we have to assume extreme heat must be one of them," suggested Trakis. "But there has to be a limit as to how long they can withstand temperatures of this level."

"Shields now at nineteen percent and dropping."

Minutes passed as the bridge crew became more and more debilitated, and the Tokath maintained their tenacious hold on the ship. Officers were slumped in their chairs, mopping dripping foreheads, gasping for air. Janeway realized they couldn't go much longer like this, and she turned to Chakotay.

"Can we implement the metaphasic shielding program?" she asked.

"I'm not sure. We've routed so much power to the shields we don't have much to support the metaphasic program."

"Get it from somewhere. We have to get closer to that star."

"Aye, Captain," he replied, and began working a console. "Borrowing some from the impulse reactors . . . environmental . . . transporters . . . let's give it a try. Establishing metaphasic program—now."

Almost immediately, there was relief from the heat. The metaphasic shielding program, an innovation implemented just before *Voyager* was commissioned, had been developed on the former flagship of Starfleet, the *U.S.S. Enterprise*-D. It had been added to the defensive systems of certain classes of starship, and was supposed to provide enough protection from heat and radiation that a ship could actually enter a star's inner corona. Because it was a new technology, there hadn't been the opportunity to accumulate much data on its reliability. But it was the only hope Janeway had now of providing enough protection to take her ship closer to the fiery star.

"Mr. Paris, move us closer. Thrusters only."

"Aye," said Paris, and they watched as the solar disc grew larger still.

"I can't guarantee how long we'll be able to keep the metaphasic program stable," Chakotay warned. "It's draining our power reserves pretty rapidly."

"The Tokath can't survive this much longer," replied Janeway. "They'll have to let go and get away from the star, or be incinerated."

"Hull temperature at fourteen thousand degrees. Radiation levels at seventy rads per minute."

"Distance from the star, twelve hundred kilometers."

And still the creatures clung to the shields. Janeway stared at the viewscreen, amazed at their tenacity, and willing them to admit defeat and let go. Minutes passed, silence broken only by Rollins's sonorous announcements:

"Hull temperature fifteen thousand degrees. Radiation at seventy-five rads per minute."

Now, even with the metaphasic program in place, the temperature again began to rise inside the ship. Janeway felt herself growing light-headed. She knew that the stress of the last eight hours was taking its toll, and she took several deep breaths to get oxygen to her brain.

In her mind's eye, the image of the closed door suddenly appeared, and she shook her head to clear it. Why was that bothersome illusion cropping up now? A wave of anxiety flooded her, and she felt a moment's panic that she was losing control. But gradually the apprehension faded, and she refocused her attention to the viewscreen.

"Captain, the metaphasic shielding is losing integrity," Chakotay reported. Janeway turned to him. Without that added buffer, they couldn't survive this close to the star. "Can you stabilize it?"

"I'm trying—but without power reserves it's not going to be easy."

"Hull temperature seventeen thousand degrees. Radiation levels at ninety rads. Cabin temperature sixty-two degrees."

Janeway wiped perspiration from her forehead. A decision was being forced on her: they had to move away from the star. A wave of frustration swept over her as she looked back at the viewscreen.

The Tokath were beginning to drop off.

They all noticed it simultaneously. "It's working!" crowed Paris. Rollins chimed in with his sensor readings: "Life signs are disappearing from the shields, Captain."

One by one, the brown and green bodies fell away from their field of vision, revealing the flaming disk of the star more fully. The temperature on the bridge was now almost unbearable.

"Metaphasic shielding is failing, Captain," said Chakotay tersely. "We have to move away from that star."

"Just a minute more—Rollins, tell me when the shields are clear of the Tokath."

"We're there, Captain. No life signs showing on the shields."

"The metaphasic program is collapsing—"

"Lieutenant, get us out of here."

Paris worked, and *Voyager* veered away from the star. Janeway moved to her chair and sank gratefully into it, listening to damage reports as they filtered in.

"Shield integrity barely holding at thirteen percent—"

"Damage to the aft port ventral—"

"Hull buckling on deck fourteen—"

"Initiating repairs to propulsion systems—"

"Sickbay reports twelve crewmen suffering from radiation sickness—"

The well-trained crew was already springing into action, doing whatever was necessary to restore *Voyager* to operating condition. Soon repairs would be completed and they could—

—what? Be on their way? Abandon their comrades on the planet and hope they'd find a way to survive? Continue the journey home without the great and good friend Tuvok? Tuvok, whom she'd initially disliked so fiercely but had grown to love as a brother . . .

. . . and sweet Kes . . . and dear Neelix . . . Greta Kale . . . Nate LeFevre . . . over twenty people in all that they'd never see again . . .

She realized Chakotay was seated next to her, addressing her. She turned to him.

". . . though the Kazon don't appear to be a danger anymore, we can't risk another attack by the Tokath. We wouldn't survive another trip into the star."

"What are you suggesting, Commander?"

Chakotay hesitated, knowing the seriousness of his recommendation. "I don't see any way we can return to the planet, Captain."

She looked away from him, instinctively wanting to deny his statement. Quickly she reviewed the options as she understood them, and quickly she realized there weren't any more. She might have found a way to defeat the Kazon, but that other, unexpected nemesis—an ancient, brilliantly evolved life-form—was apparently invincible.

She looked back at Chakotay, whose wise, patient eyes held hers, reflecting concern and empathy, and nodded once. It was over. She'd fought with every bit of her skill and ingenuity, and she'd lost.

The defeat was palpable. A chill passed through her and she became light-headed again. Images of her crew, trapped on the planet—perhaps under attack from the Tokath?—swirled in her mind. She began to feel disconnected from the present, from what was happening directly in front of her. The bridge began to spin.

She felt as though she were encased in her own warp bubble; time seemed to freeze, the voices of the crew faded, and the bridge washed out into a pastiche of pale color—an abstract impression of sound and motion.

She was moving toward the closed door, hand outstretched, determined to open it this time. No impediments, no obstacles—nothing would keep her from finding out what was behind that barrier. It must be cleaned out. Her heart pounded as she reached out, and an overwhelming sense of urgency cascaded through her. The door opened at her touch, surprisingly easily, after all. She took a breath and stepped through, ready to greet the clutter and mess she was sure lay there.

She was freezing. All around her was a white wilderness, bleak and unremitting, a milky landscape of snow and ice. She'd been here before, of course. She had crashed here with her father and Justin, who'd lost their lives beneath a cold, dark sea. She'd almost died, as well, her body temperature dangerously low before a rescue ship had picked up the automatic distress signal and beamed her aboard.

Why was she back here? Why did the closed door lead here? It was not a place she wanted to revisit. She tried to bring her focus back to the bridge, back to the here and now, but something refused to let her go. Images of the death planet lasered her mind with cruel clarity.

She'd been buried in a snowbank . . . and then she looked up . . . stood, painfully . . . and saw an iceberg.

The iceberg. She'd stared at it for the longest time, confused, trying to decide if it were an iceberg. Why had that seemed so crucial? Why had there been doubt?

Now, in her memory, she was facing away from the iceberg, and she began to doubt that it was actually there. She had to turn and make sure it was—but she was frightened. Terrified, in fact. She was equally compelled to turn, and not to turn.

A dreadful minute passed as she was pulled on this rack, agonizing, paralyzed. On the one hand, what did it matter if she turned and looked at the iceberg? It would be there—and if it weren't, what did it matter? This was a memory, nothing more.

But it was a memory she'd kept behind a closed door for a long, long time. What did that mean? Why was the iceberg so potent an image? What gave it that power?

The only way to incapacitate it was to turn and look at it. Demystify it. Turn, Kathryn, turn . . .

Slowly, slowly, a millimeter at a time, she forced herself, in her mind's eye, to turn and look at the iceberg. The turn seemed to take forever, during which time she began to realize something would be vastly different when she completed the turn.

And so it was no great surprise when she looked into the middle of the dark sea—the frozen sea which had been cruelly penetrated by a flaming object from the heavens—and saw no iceberg.

She saw the shape of an iceberg. An object jutting from the sea which might have resembled an iceberg if it were made of ice, if it had in fact broken from a glacier and floated, shards sticking out, through the alien sea.

But of course no icebergs floated in the alien sea because it was frozen over, except for the dark gash which had been rent in it by the plummeting spaceship.

It was that ship whose fuselage now projected from the watery bed, nose up, violated and broken, looming out of the water like a huge and formidable iceberg. It was that ship in whose cabin she could clearly see her father and Justin, dazed and bloody, but alive.

She had immediately gone into action. Of course, she would—she was accustomed to pressure, to emergencies, to disasters. They were simply challenges, and Kathryn Janeway had always risen to the challenge. She had figured out how to multiply elevens and derive the distance formula, she had become a good tennis player and she'd saved Hobbes Johnson from drowning, she'd convinced Admiral Paris to mentor her and she'd saved Justin from death once before, at the hands of the Cardassians. She would not fail to save the two people she loved most in life.

A console was flickering in the section of the cabin in which she'd ridden to the surface. There was still power, something was working. She flew to the controls and began entering commands; to her relief, they responded. She might be able to transport her father and Justin from the shell of the ship's cabin.

She focused intently on the console, quickly realizing she'd have to cobble together several circuits in order to have enough power for a site-to-site transport. To transport two people she'd need eight hundred megawatts. Their patterns would already be encoded within the ship's systems, of course, standard practice for the crew of any vessel.

She glanced over her shoulder to take a visual sighting of their positions, and made a mind-numbing discovery: the ship's fuselage was sinking. It was almost a meter lower in the sea than when she'd begun working, though the two men in the cockpit were still safely above the yawning pit of black water.

She turned back, working quickly. Two emergency microfusion generators were still on-line. They could be routed to the primary energizing coils. She brought the targeting scanners on-line and initiated a coordinates lock. This process would verify that the transporter system was functioning within operational standards, something she couldn't be sure of because of all the damage.

The scanners refused to lock on to the two figures in the ship's cockpit. Quickly checking the system, Kathryn understood why: the annular confinement beam was too unstable to hold two bodies in the spatial matrix within which the dematerialization process occurred. She had enough power to transport only one person. Not two. One.

Fear clutched at her. Though the air was bone-chilling, she didn't notice the cold. Adrenaline coursed through her body, her heart hammered, and her head pounded with every heartbeat. She looked back at the sinking ship, its two occupants slumped over their seats, but moving slightly, still alive. Justin, her fiancé, whom she loved and adored, and with whom she would spend the rest of her life. And her father, beloved Daddy, who had challenged and inspired her and made her what she was.

How could she choose that one would live and the other die? Flash visions of life with Justin—knowing she had sacrificed her father to allow him to live—flooded her mind. How could she be happy with Justin after paying that price?

Life without Justin, knowing she had sacrificed him to save her father, was equally intolerable. How could fate have presented her with this bitter dilemma?

She took a deep breath of the frigid air, trying to clear her mind and rise to this challenge. She would thumb her nose at fate. She wouldn't yield to this situation, but create the situation she wanted. She would transport both of them, somehow. There had to be a way.

She turned to the console, mind racing with every fact and figure she could remember about this experimental ship. The phaser banks were recharged through a neodyne capacitor circuit. If the capacitors retained enough residual charge, she might be able to bring the annular confinement beam up to eight hundred megawatts—the minimum she'd need to transport both men. But the only way to find out was to tap into the capacitors. She'd have to try to engage the beam and see if it gained enough power.

Rerouting through the phaser couplings, she drew a deep breath and activated the transporter circuit. She needed that eight hundred megawatts only long enough to make one transport. Just five seconds, to dematerialize her father and Justin, transfer their molecular patterns to the storage buffer, and rematerialize them. It had to be possible.

Little by little, the beam gained power. It was working! Just seconds more, and she'd have them both safely on land, next to her. The emergency medical kit was in her section of the cabin; she could stabilize their injuries and keep them warm until a rescue ship found them. They were being tracked on Starfleet scanners and it shouldn't be too long before help arrived.

The annular confinement beam power inched upward in maddening slow increments . . . five hundred eighty megawatts . . . six hundred ninety . . . seven hundred forty . . . Valuable seconds ticked by as Kathryn concentrated with all her intensity on the readings, willing them to reach the needed number. Seven hundred seventy-five . . . seven hundred ninety . . . and then finally, the beam power registered eight hundred megawatts. She could transport them both. Quickly, she initiated automatic pattern lock, bypassing the diagnostic process in order to save precious milliseconds, manually activated the annular confinement beam, and whirled to meet them.

The ship's fuselage had disappeared, sunk beneath the inky waters of the alien sea. And her father and Justin were not materializing next to her. She turned and reentered the commands; surely she could pull them from beneath the water's surface. But though she went through the process time after time, endlessly, with every combination and permutation of commands, there was no response.

She had lost them both.

She stood, numbed, staring at the black pool of water, churning from the upheaval it had endured. It was a long time before she became aware of the pain in her broken leg, and when she did, she began to stamp that tortured leg repeatedly on the ground, trying to create an agony that would surmount the one she wasn't sure she could live with.

When that proved impossible, she'd simply found a way to bury that pain so deeply that she could go on. For over a decade, as she rose through the ranks of Starfleet, as her love for Mark deepened, as she became a captain and her friendship with the remarkable Tuvok flourished, as she took command of *Voyager* and was swept into their phenomenal adventure in the Delta Quadrant—for all that time, the bitter truth of her failure had lain enclosed in her memory, sealed like a plague bacillus which, if it were unleashed, might destroy her.

How then, to save herself now? The vile truth, bubbling

up like acid, could never be banished again; it would eat at her every minute of every day, fouling her mind and corroding her spirit.

No. No, that simply couldn't happen. Too many people depended on her, too many needed her strength, her indomitability. She mustn't fail them.

The memory must be neutralized. This wasn't a conscious thought so much as a fully formed intuition that sprang from her mind like Athena from Zeus. There was only one way to strip it of its awful dominion: use it. After all, the locked door was open now, and the room could be swept clean. Bright light and fresh air could blow through it, chasing darkness and cobwebs. The dream, she was sure, would never come again. And so there must be a way to turn its pain to power.

She was on her feet without realizing it, moving toward the conn, where Paris was still working to move them away from the star—how long had it been? It seemed a lifetime had passed since she'd moved into the mists of memory, but she became aware that only seconds had gone by; the crew was still engaged in assessing damage and assigning repair crews.

"All stop, Mr. Paris," she said, and Tom's tousled head swung around to her in surprise.

"Captain?"

"We're not leaving the away team. We're going to go back and get them."

Now Chakotay was approaching, brow furrowed in puzzlement and concern. "Do you have a plan, Captain?" he queried.

Janeway stared at him. No, no plan, just flinty determination. But sheer grit wouldn't solve their problem, wouldn't get them past the fiercely protective Tokath. How was that possible?

She felt every eye on her as the crew waited, trustingly, sure their captain had come up with an idea. Her mind seemed to flutter, agitated, starting to panic. She'd made an announcement that was foolhardy, made it with sheer bravado. Now she must back it up—but how?

Suddenly she was four years old again, sitting in her father's study, trying to figure out the elevens. She had closed her eyes then and focused, visualizing the situation, and the answer had presented itself to her. The answer was always there, it just had to be accessed. She closed her eyes now and visualized the Tokath, reviewing what she knew about them. She imagined them as they must have been long ago, fierce protectors of a gentle people, sealing the planet from intruders and allowing them all to live in peace.

Until the dreadful accident. She saw in her mind's eye the sun's unexpected eruption—undoubtedly a continuation of the shedding of matter from its atmosphere, the very process which created the nebula in which they had taken refuge—and the havoc it created in the planet's atmosphere. She envisioned the consternation in the population and their desperate plan to save the Tokath, the fierce creatures which had kept them safe from harm for so long. . . .

Her eyes opened and she saw the bridge crew watching her, patiently, trustingly. And as though their confidence were a vast wellspring of positive energy, feeding and nurturing her, the plan came to her.

"Dr. Trakis, the environmental disaster that drove the Tokath into hibernation—it happened as this star was shedding its outer atmosphere?"

The Trabe looked at her curiously. "That's my understanding. A massive eruption near the star's equator sent a dense cloud of plasma directly at the planet, ionizing its atmosphere."

Janeway turned to Chakotay. "We can cause an eruption like that. Re-create the event that sent the Tokath into hibernation."

She could see Chakotay take the idea and work it over in his mind. "Our energy systems are pretty much depleted. I'm not sure how we'd be able to create such a massive eruption."

"A narrow nadion beam, focused on an instability in the star's photosphere, might initiate a chain reaction."

"I wouldn't want to be anywhere in the neighborhood of an explosion like that."

"We won't be. We'll go to warp as soon as the instability goes critical."

"What about the away team? Will they be in any danger?"

"If we time the eruption with the rotation rate of the star, we should be able to create a plasma ejection that grazes the planet's outer atmosphere, but doesn't ionize it. That should be enough to scare the Tokath back into hibernation."

He grinned at her. It was a desperate, seat-of-the-pants plan, full of jeopardy with no guarantee of success, and she knew Chakotay was aware of that. And loved it anyway. "What are we waiting for?" he quipped.

And so they set to the task, making the critical calculations necessary to time this bold maneuver. Chakotay scanned his console intently, then reported, "I'm noting a gravitational instability in the photosphere."

"Rollins, target the nadion beam to those coordinates."

"Targeting." And the deep blue nadion beam sprang from the ship and knifed into the burning gases of the yellow star. Janeway imagined the process, as the nadions collided with the particles of the sun: hydrogen, helium, lithium, beryllium. Each tiny collision would produce more collisions, which would in turn create still more, fusing atoms and generating heat energy—a quickly spreading chain reaction that would gather immense power in a matter of seconds, further disturbing the gravitational instability until it must release the massive energy buildup.

"Three hundred megajoules per cubic meter and rising, Captain," said Rollins tersely. "Four hundred ten . . . four ninety . . . five hundred thirty . . . six hundred—it's going critical."

"Go to warp, Mr. Paris."

Tom worked the controls swiftly and the ship leapt into warp just ahead of the monumental nuclear explosion. When they were at a safe distance, they put the distant star on screen at highest magnification.

It was an awesome sight. The force of the chain reaction exceeded by many times the energy of a warp-core explosion. Arcs of plasma hundreds of thousands of kilometers long projected from the corona in a promethean display of power, as though a giant were flinging huge fireballs through the heavens.

Not one word was spoken on the bridge as the eruptions continued. When, finally, they began to subside, Janeway turned to Rollins. "Do sensors detect any life signs around the planet?"

"Going to extreme long-range sensors . . . I'm reading life signs . . . and Captain—it looks like they're in retreat."

"What are the atmospheric conditions on the planet?"

"There's a lot of high-altitude turbulence. Radiation levels are rising."

"Chakotay, will our shields protect us if we move in to investigate?"

"We won't be able to call on the metaphasic program, but I think we can channel enough energy to the main shields to be safe."

"Then let's do it. Mr. Paris, move us in, slowly, toward the planet. Be ready to get out fast."

"Yes, ma'am."

And the sleek ship turned to and headed back toward the system, Janeway keeping careful watch over radiation levels, until they could put the planet on high magnification and get an image on the viewscreen.

What they saw brought the first hope, the first semblance of joy they'd had in hours. A stream of brown, shelled bodies was flowing toward the surface of the planet. The Tokath were going home.

As *Voyager* moved closer, the crew saw the Kazon ship, listing oddly, its hull riddled with cavities where the creatures had eaten through and descended into the ship. What happened then was best left to the imagination, but the pocked ship was undoubtedly now an orbiting graveyard.

The Tokath were flooding toward the surface, the dark miasma retracing its path of the last hour. Janeway's gamble that they retained a memory of the disastrous conditions that had prevailed so long ago—but would seem like a recent event to them because they'd been in stasis—had apparently been validated.

Their retreat, however, was just a first step in the ultimate goal: rescuing the away team. And as yet, Janeway had no clue as to their whereabouts or their condition. The nagging thought that they could have suffered the same fate as the Kazon was one she kept to one side of her mind. She'd come this far and she wasn't about to let quibbling doubts stop her now.

Many of Tuvok's team had fallen into an exhausted slumber, the events of the last nine hours having taken a heavy toll. Tuvok and Kim, however, were determined to analyze and master the technology that was operative in this strange chamber, and to gain control over the entrance. They couldn't simply stay cooped up in this room forever; somehow, they had to find a way out of the underground labyrinth and make contact with *Voyager.*

But so far, their efforts had been futile. Harry had tried every approach to alien technology he'd ever studied and quite a few that he invented there on the spot. And finally, he decided to try the one thing his scientific mind had rejected. "Sir," he said to Tuvok, "it's possible the technology is telepathically controlled. Maybe you could try accessing the program that's controlling this chamber."

Tuvok's eyebrow lifted slightly, but he immediately put his fingers on the panel they believed to contain the controls, and brought his formidable Vulcan telepathic powers to bear on them. But after several minutes, he removed his hands and turned to Harry. "I am unable to make a telepathic connection," he stated.

Harry moved immediately toward Kes, nestled in Neelix's arms, and roused her from a drowsy slumber. "What is it, Harry?"

He repeated what he'd said to Tuvok, and Kes listened intently. "I'm not sure how to do that," she replied.

"Neither am I. But you seemed to have some kind of intuitive connection to whatever was happening here—you were drawn toward this room for no clear reason, you heard things . . ."

She looked up at him, eyes troubled. "You're right. And I certainly heard the message the humanoid left. But I don't know about accessing a program—that's pretty specific. I wouldn't know how to start."

"Maybe you could focus on the humanoid projection. It could be more of an interactive program than it first appeared—you might be able to get him to reappear. At least it's a beginning."

She nodded, and went to the panel that seemed to

contain the controls. Harry saw her close her eyes and concentrate, frowning slightly with the effort. Minutes passed as Harry and Tuvok watched and waited, accompanied by the sonorous breathing of the sleeping crew.

Occasionally, a flicker of something would seem to cross Kes' face, and the two men would become alert, watching for some indication that she was achieving success, but each time her features relaxed again into her pose of concentration.

Finally, she opened her eyes and shook her head. "It's no use. I've tried every technique I know. When I wasn't trying, I seemed to get all these sensations, but I can't get them back now."

No sooner had those words left her lips than the holographic humanoid shimmered back into view, wings beating gently as before. Startled, Kes turned to him and refocused her concentration. Harry and Tuvok watched as she stood silently for a moment, listening, and then the hologram disappeared once more. Kes turned to them.

"We have to leave," she said. "I don't exactly understand what's happening, but apparently the reawakening isn't supposed to happen now."

"What does that mean?" wondered Harry, but Kes simply shook her head.

"The message isn't exactly forthcoming with explanations. But we're invited back in the future—whenever the reawakening does occur."

"No, thanks," said Harry immediately, but at that moment something else drew their attention.

The door had reappeared in the wall, open and beckoning. Tuvok moved toward it, phaser drawn, hand held up to warn the others to stay back. He approached the door and lifted his wrist beacon, pressed the control, and saw the beam penetrate the darkness of the stairwell outside.

He saw nothing. He took a few cautious steps into the

stairwell and played the light up the stairs. Still, nothing. He looked back at the crew. "Follow me. Keep your weapons at the ready and stay tightly grouped."

And in this fashion they proceeded back up the stairs, scanning constantly, mounting step after step, forgetting how far they had originally descended and marveling that they seemed to climb upward forever. The air in the stairwell was pleasantly cool and fresh, a relief after the stuffy confines of the chamber.

Eventually they reached the level of the corridors, and Tuvok began leading them according to the path markers stored in his tricorder, winding this way and that, retracing the path they had taken while searching for Harry and Kes.

They'd been walking like that for ten minutes when Tuvok heard a distant noise. He held his hand for silence, then ordered, "Shut off your beacons."

Thirty lights snapped out, leaving them once more encased in the blackest darkness. And like that they waited in apprehension as a faint but ominous whirring sound drew closer and closer. Harry felt his breathing deepen and his hands grow clammy: What was that sound? Some new and horrible menace to threaten their lives? It was an awful sensation to stand perfectly still in a darkness so complete not one glimmer of light penetrated it, not one feature of the person immediately ahead visible, and to listen to the approaching sound of an unknown threat.

He could hear the breathing of the entire team, frozen in their places, tensing, ready for anything. The sound grew louder and louder, until he knew whatever it was must be almost upon them.

The next sensation any of them had was of waves of pulsing air brushing by them, soft flutterings as something swept past on either side of them, whirring loudly, but paying no attention whatsoever to the crew which stood, rooted, in their path. Streams of beings skimmed around them, hundreds, thousands, tens of thousands, an endless current swarming through the labyrinthine passageways of this underground sanctuary.

The crew stood like that, immobilized, for the strangest half hour any of them had ever spent, uncertain as to what exactly was happening, surmising that they were being skirted like water around a rock by the Tokath—the same creatures who had attacked when they emerged from the walls—and wondering if it was only a matter of time before one or more of the beings decided to renew the assault and turn this section of the corridor into blood-soaked carnage.

But the Tokath seemed uninterested in the humanoids who stood in their habitat. They continued their headlong rush down the passageway as the crew demonstrated its remarkable self-discipline by standing absolutely still, silent and unflinching.

Eventually, the headlong flight came to an end, and the last of the whirring creatures swam around them. Only then did Tuvok cautiously turn on his beacon and begin to lead his team out of the maze, watching in amazement as the creatures settled themselves into the gelatinous walls like eggs encased in aspic, then seeing the gelatin begin to coalesce, and harden, until by the time they reached the original staging area the walls were as hard and stonelike as they had formerly appeared.

The ramps that led to the surface were down, and a dim light filtered in, revealing a carpet of dead Tokath. A quick scan revealed no Kazon life signs above, and Tuvok led the group, running now, toward the surface and out of the dank underground which had been their prison for so many hours. Neelix turned to Tuvok. "You've done an excellent job, Mr. Vulcan. And there's a little token of my appreciation waiting for you on *Voyager* right now." And

Neelix could almost taste the *nocha* cake at that moment.

When they emerged, dusk had fallen, signaling an end to this extraordinary day. The growing darkness muted only slightly a horrible scene: there were dead Kazon everywhere, mutilated and eviscerated. Flies and insects had already begun the inevitable process of gleaning them, and the dreadful stench of death filled the air. But the crew barely had time to react before they began, one by one, to dematerialize.

When Chakotay and Rollins reported simultaneously that they had detected the crew's life signs on the surface, Janeway immediately ordered them transported to the ship. She didn't want to take any more chances, didn't want to take the time for them to launch the shuttles and ascend to *Voyager;* both crew and shuttles could be beamed aboard easily enough. And when the transporter chief reported that all hands were safely on board, Janeway felt a moment of giddy relief. The crisis was over.

"Mr. Paris, resume course for the Alpha Quadrant," she said, and noted that her voice sounded hollow in her ears. She rose, heading for the Turbolift to meet the away team in sickbay, when she noticed everyone on the bridge was staring at her. Uncertain, she stopped, looking from one crewman to the other.

Chakotay's dark eyes peered at her intently, and for a brief moment she wondered if she appeared ill. Were they concerned about her? Was she showing the strain and fatigue this ordeal had produced?

But they were thinking something very different. Chakotay rose to his feet, lifted his hands and began, softly and slowly, to clap them. She found herself puzzled by this action, then looked toward Tom Paris as he followed the lead, stood, and began to applaud. Then the entire bridge crew joined in, honoring her in the age-old fashion, signaling their respect, admiration, and gratitude for the captain who had once again brought them all through danger and into safe harbor.

As she realized what they were doing, her eyes began to sting. She deserved no applause for simply being what she was. All she had done was to carve one more pattern in the mosaic of her identity, that constantly unfolding design which had been growing, square by square, since she was a baby, and which was becoming more intricate with each passing year. The design was not of her own choosing; it was etched by the circumstances of life, which she could not control, and by her relationships with others. Her mosaic was multi-hued, many-textured, and infinitely complex. Swirled in its design were the people she had loved and those she had disliked, events that traumatized and those that pacified, experiences that had challenged her limits and those that had rewarded her unconquerable spirit. The mosaic would continue to grow, its unfolding an infinite mystery, blending sorrow and ecstasy, dappling the pathway of her life with sunlight and shadow until, in the final moment, the design was complete.

With the applause of the bridge officers still ringing in her ears, Kathryn Janeway went to welcome back the crew whose lives she had saved.